THE

ALLIANCE

Also by Shannon Stoker

The Collection
The Registry

THE
ALLIANCE

A REGISTRY NOVEL

SHANNON STOKER

WILLIAM MORROW
An Imprint of HarperCollinsPublishers

For the Wapole family, past, present, and future

THE ALLIANCE. Copyright © 2014 by Shannon Stoker. All rights reserved. Printed in the United States of America. No part of this book may be used or reproduced in any manner whatsoever without written permission except in the case of brief quotations embodied in critical articles and reviews. For information address HarperCollins Publishers, 195 Broadway, New York, NY 10007.

HarperCollins books may be purchased for educational, business, or sales promotional use. For information please e-mail the Special Markets Department at SPsales@harpercollins.com.

FIRST EDITION

Library of Congress Cataloging-in-Publication Data

Stoker, Shannon.
  The alliance : a Registry novel / Shannon Stoker. -- First edition.
    pages cm
  ISBN 978-0-06-227176-1 (paperback)
  I. Title.
  PS3619.T6453A55 2014
  813'.6--dc23

                                           2014009610

14 15 16 17 18   OV/RRD   10 9 8 7 6 5 4 3 2 1

Acknowledgments

A huge thank-you to my agent, Paula Munier; I think I would have dropped dead several times during this experience if I didn't have you by my side. An equally giant thank-you to my editor, Amanda Bergeron; words cannot express how talented you are, and I am in awe of you every day.

Thank you to the wonderful people at HarperCollins, including Camille Collins, Molly Birckhead, Lauren Cook, Alaina Waagner, and everyone else who helped me along the way. I am honored to have worked with you on this crazy project. Thank you to Mumtaz Mustafa and Martin Sobey for your hard work on the beautiful covers of this series.

I have to make sure my parents, Laura and Rod, know how much I appreciate everything they have done for me. None of this would have been possible without your support. Also, thank you to my husband, Andrew "Andy" Stoker; you are my rock. I know my dog can't read, but I have to thank Nucky since none of this would have ever happened if it weren't for him. I have to thank my brother, Frank, who has always been a huge influence on my life. A giant round of applause has to go to the Wapole family. I love that we are such a large bunch that if I named you all it could fill an entire book.

A million thank-yous to my friends. Shout-outs to Dalmy Bolivar, Katie Drum, Laura Alms, Erin Reid, Rachel Marsden, Nina Draganowski, and Megan "Jean" Long; thank you so much for being a part of this journey. I would be remiss to forget John Schaeffer and Jason Drum, who never minded when we had a girls' night and chose to join us in the celebrations every once in a while.

Also thank you to my "superfans" Meredith Stange, Elsa and Gary Miller, Josh Austin, and Dustin Inboden. A big thanks goes to the Gail Borden Public Library and all its wonderful staff.

Finally, thank you to all the readers out there! I hope you had as much fun reading this series as I did writing it. Happy reading.

Chapter 1

Our enemy has been defeated and I am eager to return home. It has been three months since I have heard from Wallace and I hope he still wants to marry me when I arrive. I know he was scared about his fiancée heading to war, but once he sees my face I am certain all the old feelings will come flooding back.

—The diary of Megan Jean

Lightning crashed and Mia slid along the floor of the boat, clawing at the floorboards, hoping to stop herself from slamming into the opposite side of the hull. Her efforts did little good and she braced for impact. Pain exploded through her right arm, but immediately the ship straightened itself out again and Mia landed on her left side with a thud.

They had told her to stay down here for her safety, but she wasn't doing a very good job of protecting herself from the effects of the storm. Another boom sounded from above and Mia couldn't take her feelings of helplessness any longer.

She forced herself off the ground and headed toward the small set of stairs that led up to the deck. The boat continued to wobble, but she made her way to the railing and gripped it tight. Filled with resolve, Mia did the only thing she'd been instructed not to: she climbed the stairs and reached for the handle, determined to offer her help in saving the ship and the rest of the crew from the storm.

Little effort was needed to open the door. The wind pulled it and it started to drag Mia out of the cabin. She saw a wave crash against the deck and water rush at her feet. Not that the excess water would make much of a difference; the rain was coming down fast and Mia's face felt like it was being pelted with pebbles instead of drops.

She saw several people trying to reinforce tarps over the center of the deck. Mia forced the door closed behind her and went toward them. She recognized Andrew. He was bent over, holding the tarp in place. She leaned down next to him.

"I want to help," she yelled over the roaring storm.

He moved his head toward her and even in the dark she could recognize the anger on his face.

"What are you doing out here?" he yelled. "Go back under."

He pointed toward the door Mia had just come through. She shook her head.

"I can help," she said.

She reached down and grabbed the tarp from his hand. Another loud clap of thunder went off and Mia looked up just in time to see a wall of water ready to drop onto the deck. She raised her hands to protect her head and felt Andrew grab a hold of her wrist. The water hit and Mia fell back onto the wood. It felt like she was underwater and her body was being dragged away. Andrew tightened his grip and Mia was certain they were going overboard with the wave as it pulled back.

Suddenly they stopped moving. She wasn't sure which direction was up but if Andrew let go Mia thought she'd never see the surface again. The water rushed away and Mia felt its pull on her weaken. She opened her eyes and gasped for air. The boat was upright again and Mia was dangling off the side, hanging from Andrew's arms.

Mia tried to keep her grip on Andrew's forearm, but he completely let go of her. Her skin was too wet, she was sliding down. She raised her eyes and tried to get Andrew to give her his free hand. She continued to grab at Andrew with her other hand, but he didn't return her gesture. He looked down at her. His face wasn't the bundle of nerves she expected. Instead his brown eyes held a vacant stare. In her confusion Mia let herself slip down. Her arms flailed in the air, but it was no use. She braced herself for the impact of the ice-cold water.

The cold water never came. Mia's eyes flashed open as she sucked in a large breath. She started to cough since her inhalation of air came as too much of a shock to her system. Mia felt a hand patting her back, trying to help her with the coughs. She turned, expecting to see Andrew, but instead Zack was behind her, handing over a bottle of water.

"Where's Andrew?" Mia asked.

She appreciated Zack's presence. The tall, blond man had proved himself a worthy ally during Mia's time with Affinity. She remembered when she first arrived in Guatemala at one of Affinity's bases. It had looked so quaint and rustic, but appearances were deceiving and Mia quickly realized the group had an arsenal of electronics and people behind it. Before becoming acquainted with Affinity Mia never would have thought stopping the Registry possible, but that was the group's core mission. Mia was proud to call herself a member and work toward that very goal.

She looked out the window at the small airstrip. She was three hours from Affinity's base but knew she would soon be farther than that when she arrived in France.

"He's loading the plane," Zack said. "I convinced him to let you sleep some more."

"I can't believe I fell asleep," Mia said.

The group had left the Affinity base at three A.M. They'd traveled south to the nearest airport, about three hours away. Even though that had interrupted Mia's normal sleep schedule she'd thought her nerves were too rattled to rest.

"I was hoping we'd have some time to talk before we left," Zack said.

Mia nodded. Zack had been born and raised in Affinity, while Mia had only been a member for a few weeks. Her time with the rebel group had been spent preparing for this mission, the only mission that mattered to Mia: infiltrating America and stopping the Registry and mandatory service.

Chapter **2**

The positive spirit of the troops has faded since none of them have received orders to return to America. I am sympathetic to their frustrations since my editor refuses to respond to any of my mailings, either electronic or print, or send me an itinerary of my travels home. This is the last time I agree to cover a war story. I am leaving this wasteland tomorrow and paying my own way. I'd better be reimbursed by the magazine when I arrive.

—The journal of Isaac Ryland

The day was growing tedious. The backward teachings of Ian, the current grand commander, were too boring for Grant to focus on.

"So that is why we are funding an expedition into the wastelands," Ian said.

"Because another country asked for money for a stupid project, we feel the need to hand it over?"

Grant made sure to speak in a low voice.

"What?" Ian asked.

"Because another country asked for money for a superior project, we must step in and take it over?" Grant asked. "The project, not the country."

"Right," Ian said. "Well, I think it's important American soldiers accompany these scientists. If Africa or South America becomes inhabitable I don't want another country to colonize it first."

"They're nuclear wastelands," Grant said. "The Great War destroyed any possibility of life there."

"I always forget how well-informed you are," Ian said. "Either way, some scientists think the lands may be clear again, or at least safe enough to test. If the Great War taught the world one thing it was the dangers of superior weaponry."

"You disagree with nuclear warfare?" Grant asked.

"I think it's important we remember that if there are no people left alive then there are no countries to rule," Ian said.

Even with Grant's desire to learn about all types of weapons, he had been unable to discover much on the nuclear front. Once he was in charge that would change. Grant didn't care if the rest of the world survived. He would bring back that weaponry.

"So you would create an American colony there? Expand our lands?"

"Precisely," Ian said.

"Wouldn't that make the people harder to control? Risk an uprising?"

Ian frowned.

"From what we know the radiation will still be too strong anyway," Ian said. "At least if we're part of the expedition we will know firsthand the condition. And it never hurts to have good international public relations. The Australians will see this as a sign of goodwill on our part and hush any crazy notions of human rights campaigns."

Ian stopped walking. They were in front of the secret room that housed the master lists, in a bombproof bunker that was impossible to take out. The server that held the data for the Registry as well as the service records. It was the only one in existence, updated manually by Ian every few weeks. The code to enter the room was one of the only key pieces of information Grant had yet to learn from the grand commander.

"This is the final project I have for the day," Ian said.

Grant tried to look as Ian punched in the code. He couldn't see what digits were entered. It was the tightest security available and beyond cracking.

"Sir," Grant said, "why not use an iris or fingerprint scan?"

"What, and give someone the idea to chop off my hand or pluck out my eye?" Ian asked, an eyebrow raised.

Grant had to admire the man's astuteness. It was true that had that been an option Ian would have been long since disposed of. The metal door opened up and Grant followed Ian into the small room. Ian pulled out a card and slid it into the master Registry server. A few lights started to blink and the information was updated.

"There is much more cutting-edge technology available," Grant said.

"But I know how to use these well," Ian said. "And they require little to no maintenance, and there is absolutely no way to reach them remotely. Every time the public databases are uploaded, I manually transfer the information to those servers. When you're grand commander, don't underestimate your enemies. They may be closer than you think."

Ian was correct about that too. Grant doubted he would change out the hardware in this room. Only the code for the door would be switched. Grant would create another hidden master list though. Ian had expressed his fear that having more copies to protect would lead to more disasters to avert, but Grant thought this server too valuable to have only one in existence. Ian finished his business and the two men returned to the hallway, and the hidden room vanished into the wall again.

"Three weeks until the wedding," Ian said. "I hope you're not getting nerves."

"Nothing to worry about," Grant said. "Your daughter will make a dutiful wife."

"Unlike your first choice," Ian said.

Grant tried hard to keep a straight face. Amelia may have escaped, but Grant knew she was returning and he would have his revenge.

"I'm not speaking about the bride or ceremony," Ian said. "There will be many important guests. Dignitaries from all over the world are coming to meet you."

"I'm still not comfortable with allowing foreign nationals within our borders," Grant said.

Normally he kept his disagreement with Ian's ideas quiet, but when the man had told him outside influences were coming in he couldn't hide his objections.

"And I explained we are only allowing absolute allies inside," Ian said. "Representatives from nine countries. This way it will be covered by all the international news outlets and your transition to grand commander will be well respected."

"It's still dangerous," Grant said.

"Nonsense," Ian said. "They're all arriving with detailed itineraries and will be escorted by our top agents. None of them will do anything to harm our way of life. All of them jumped at my offer. Keeping the world happy keeps trouble away from our doors. How to conduct foreign policy is one of the most important and most difficult lessons to learn."

They reached the exit of the Mission, the capitol building of America.

"Have a safe drive home," Ian said.

"I'll see you next week," Grant said.

He shook the man's hand and walked out toward his sports car. The hour-long drive home was Grant's favorite part of his day. He thought back to Ian's snarky comment. Amelia was disrespectful, and worse, she wasn't satisfied with merely avoiding his grasp. Grant was aware she'd taken up with a rebel group and was planning on reentering the country. Carter Rowe had made sure Grant had that knowledge.

"We're all coming back," Carter said. "Including Mia."

"When should I expect you?"

"That wasn't part of the deal," Carter said. "Now let me talk to my father."

"The deal has changed," Grant said. "I want to know everything your little club is up to."

"Five weeks," Carter said. "We'll be there in five weeks."

"That's cutting it close to dear old Dad's deadline," Grant said.

"We'll be there," Carter said. "Then you make the trade. Mia for my father."

"And you can continue to call every day to check in with him."

"I won't be able to," Carter said. "It's getting too dangerous. We need to stop communication. They're starting to suspect something."

"So you're sacrificing the opportunity to speak with your father?"

"If it means staying alive, then yes," Carter said. "If they think I'm a rat and in bed with you this whole journey will get called off. Five weeks and she'll be on your doorstep."

"With a pretty bow wrapped around her?"

Carter made a disgusted noise and Grant couldn't help but laugh in response.

"Remember," Grant said. "You're on speakerphone."

He walked into Rod's makeshift hospital room and held the phone up so Carter could check in with his father.

That phone call had been two weeks ago. But there were too many coincidences. The end of Carter's phone calls and foreign nationals on their way to Grant's wedding meant two things: Mia's return would be sooner than next month, and Grant would be ready.

Chapter 3

My commander has abandoned his post. Half of my convoy is heading into Europe, while the other half is going to make its way back to the States. Even though there is no word from Wallace, I have decided to join the group headed home.

—The diary of Megan Jean

"You are the most important part of the plan," Zack said. "Proving to the American people that you are alive will rally their spirits and force them to question what their leaders tell them."

Grant, the man who'd purchased Mia through the Registry and paraded around as if he were her husband, had made it well known that she had been killed during a kidnapping attempt. There'd been no kidnapper. Mia had run, and she was alive and well. Grant had been busy since Mia's escape though. He was regarded as a national hero and likely successor to America's supreme leader.

Mia pictured his face. He'd chased her and her companions across the country. Mia remembered the feel of his gun pressed against her temple, the look of glee on his face when he thought he had stopped her, but Mia's friends had managed to save her, even if it was at the expense of their own lives. Mia grimaced at the memory.

"That being said, I'm the one in charge," Zack said.

This was an uncharacteristic comment from Zack. The man was normally a team player and very open to others' suggestions.

"Okay . . ."

"I mean it," Zack said. "This is a dangerous mission. You're brave to have volunteered yourself."

"Stop with the compliments," Mia said. "What are you trying to say?"

Zack let out a sigh.

"Mia, you have lots of strengths, but you're no good to us if you're dead," Zack said. "You need to listen to every instruction you are given and above all keep yourself alive. We are all expendable, except for you. If we enter a situation where anyone, including myself, Carter, or Andrew, will be injured, you need to step away. I won't allow you to assist."

"I didn't agree to help so I could sit in the background and do nothing," Mia said. "One of the reasons I want to stop the Registry is so women no longer have to blindly listen to everything men say. I've played a big part in planning this attack."

"This isn't about gender and you know it. If everything goes smoothly there won't be any action for you to step into," Zack said. "But in order to make sure it stays that way I need you to listen to me."

"I'm a member of External Tactics," Mia said. "In case you've forgotten, that's the division of Affinity that handles strategies for stopping America."

Zack's face went hard. Mia knew she'd crossed a line by trying to pull rank.

"We're leaving Affinity," Zack said. "The divisions don't matter for the time being. I am in charge and you will do as I say, or else you will risk hurting those around you."

Mia reached into her pocket and pulled out the queen, the chess piece Riley, her onetime mentor, had left for her. Mia realized that in this situation, *she* was the queen. The most deadly piece, which should never be sacrificed.

"I understand," Mia said. "But I want to know what's going on. Don't keep me in the dark."

Before Zack could respond the door to the van opened. Andrew stood outside, and Mia felt her concerns start to dissipate. Andrew would be with her; he would never let Zack push her to the side.

"The plane is loaded," Andrew said.

Mia slid out of the van and she didn't turn around to see Zack step out.

"What's going on?" Andrew asked. "Neither of you look very happy."

"Zack and I have a new understanding," Mia said.

She looked to Zack and he nodded his head. Mia took that as a guarantee of his word and started walking toward their newest mode of transportation.

Mia increased her speed. She saw the big metal plane they would be boarding, along with Carter and the other two Affinity members who were accompanying them on this mission.

The rest of the members who had driven them to the drop point were loading the few belongings the group was bringing. Mia wished they were bringing more firepower, but if they were caught sneaking weapons into America it would mean instant death for all of them.

Chapter 4

There are no flights scheduled for America. Nobody has any information from inside my country. I am starting to think something is seriously wrong. I feel terrible for thinking Wallace deserted me. Now I just hope he is alive.

—The diary of Megan Jean

There were no windows in the aircraft. Mia had never been in an airplane before; she thought about her time in the helicopter and told herself that was worse. As the group sat on the hard, cold floor, Mia thought back to the pictures of airplanes she had seen when she was little.

"I always imagined seats," Mia said.

"What?" Andrew asked.

"Sorry," Mia said. "I was thinking out loud."

"This isn't a commercial airplane," Zack said.

He stood up from his spot on the floor and went to one of the crates. Zack popped open the lid and took out a piece of fruit.

"This is a shipping airplane," he said.

Mia remembered going over every detail of the trip, but she had never asked any questions about what type of plane they were flying in.

"Why didn't you tell us it was this sort of plane?" Mia asked.

Zack shrugged. Mia looked at Andrew.

"Did you know?" she asked.

His brown eyes shifted before settling back in on Mia.

"No idea," Andrew said. "Does it matter?"

"What happens when we land?" Mia asked.

"France has a large number of American bases," Zack said. "We hope to get off the plane without running into an American soldier."

"Why would we run into an American?" Mia asked.

"Part of their strong military presence," Zack said. "There are usually a small number of American soldiers at all foreign ports. France is a large ally, so it wouldn't surprise me if America had complete control over their airports. They usually justify it by saying that they're looking for deserters."

"And what if we do?" Mia asked.

"You will stay hidden," Zack said, "until we make sure everything is clear."

Mia looked at the rest of the group. She didn't know Bryan or Jesse well. They had been born in Affinity, like Zack. Jesse had a head of curly black hair and Bryan kept his red hair short. The two weren't paying attention to Mia's questions. She saw Carter sitting against a wall. His eyes were closed. If he was listening in on the conversation he didn't care much. Mia frowned; he hadn't shown much interest in anything the past few weeks. Finally Mia looked to Andrew.

"The entire time exiting the plane was glossed over," Mia said. "I was more worried about the flight than getting off."

"You'll be fine," Andrew said.

He draped his arm over Mia's shoulder.

"I won't let anything bad happen to you," he said.

Mia looked away. Normally she loved being so close to Andrew, but his words sent a chill down her spine. Mia didn't want protection, she wanted to help. A sinking feeling set in that there was a lot she wasn't aware of.

Chapter 5

We landed at an abandoned airport. All forms of communication are down. The small group I am traveling with decided not to part ways. We are taking a break before finding a car and traveling toward Washington, DC.

—The journal of Isaac Ryland

The plane bumped up and down as it landed on the runway. Everyone was holding on to pieces of cargo, but as they started to taxi Andrew loosened his grip. Mia was next to him; she'd spent the flight quieter than normal. Andrew wasn't much for conversation and didn't want to answer any more questions. He hoped her silence meant things would go smoothly. Carter came up and tapped him on the shoulder. They walked toward the back of the plane as the door started to lower. One of the towers of boxes held their belongings. Bryan and Jesse joined them as they unloaded the aircraft.

Andrew was starting to resent this lifestyle. He had spent his whole life preparing to fight for America in the armed services, then after he got caught up in Mia's escape that future had vanished. Everything else he'd worked out was a fake life. First it was forced participation in a militia, then working as a trainer in Affinity, which at one point had seemed like a viable option, but now if anyone asked, he was a shipper. This was not a real life and

Andrew was growing weary. He wanted a stable future, and he wanted that future with Mia.

"Do you have your docking papers?"

Andrew's head sprang up. His mouth hung open. Even in the darkness he recognized the uniform. This was an American soldier, armed with a large weapon. He had known this could happen, but he still felt the hairs on the back of his neck rise. If this man figured out Andrew was a deserter, it meant he would be killed immediately.

"Do you speak English?"

Andrew looked at Carter.

"Sorry, they don't," Zack said.

He walked up behind Andrew and Carter and handed the man some papers. He glanced at them but then went back to staring at Andrew and Carter.

"You're traveling from Stahl?"

"Yes, sir," Zack said.

"Are you American?"

"Yes, sir," Zack said.

Zack reached in his pocket and handed over his identification, phonies Affinity had created back in Guatemala.

"What brings you across the sea?"

"Money," Zack said. "I can make more of it here. Then return home and buy the prettiest bride I can afford."

"What branch did you serve in?"

"Army," Zack said. "I fought in the Slavic wars."

"I did too," he said. "Who did you fight under?"

"I was in the third battalion," Zack said.

"That's not very specific," he said.

"Most of my unit didn't survive," Zack said. "It's not a topic I enjoy discussing."

The officer raised an eyebrow but didn't push the issue.

"I'm on my third round of reenlisting. Did you get out after one?"

"Yes, sir," Zack said.

"Pity," he said. "Can I board your plane?"

"Absolutely," Zack said.

Andrew didn't understand why this man wanted to come aboard. This was not a scenario they had practiced; if he spotted Mia the whole thing could blow up in their faces. The soldier did not attempt to walk inside yet.

"Is your whole crew from Stahl?"

"No, sir," Zack said. "Jesse and Bryan are American veterans as well."

Jesse and Bryan stepped forward with their fake papers.

"Are you two expatriates or making money overseas as well?"

"Money," they both replied.

The man smiled and nodded before turning back. Andrew felt some relief, but it vanished when he stopped in front of Carter.

"The people of Stahl tend to have dark hair and eyes," he said. "You don't seem to fit the profile."

"He doesn't know what you're saying," Zack said.

"Then I'll say it in Italian," he said. "The official language of Stahl."

There was a cruel smile on his face. Andrew doubted the man spoke Italian, but he might know a few phrases from his time in service. Andrew knew Carter didn't speak any.

"Based on the age and the features, you look an awful lot like an American youth. I think this plane may be sneaking an unserved male out of the country. Which all of you know is treason. If any of you step forward and admit this fact, your life will be spared," the officer said.

Andrew clenched his fists. This was the time to take the man out. He hadn't told anyone they were here yet. It would be simple to knock him out and shoot him with his own gun.

"That's preposterous," Zack said.

"*¿Habla español?*" Carter said.

The man's attention was diverted back to Carter.

"We sailed from Stahl," Zack said. "But this young man is from Nalley. After the two countries finished their war he was orphaned. If you can speak Spanish I'm sure he'd love to talk your ear off. None of us can understand a word he says."

The officer's face seemed to relax. The odds of an unserved American knowing a second language were slim to none. The boys were left uneducated, to fend for themselves. Carter's being raised by his father came in handy here. The officer turned around to face Zack.

"What is your purpose in France?"

"Restock and relax," Zack said. "Perhaps show the young men a brothel or two."

"Don't spend all your money," the officer said. "Not if you want a decent bride."

He stepped back and Andrew felt the breath rush out of his lungs. He hadn't realized he'd been holding it in for so long.

"Get back to work," Zack said. He clapped his hands and everyone continued unloading the plane. Andrew went toward the hull, knowing Mia was not going to enjoy the next part of their trip.

Chapter 6

As soon as the boat we commissioned hits the shores of America I am going straight home to look for Wallace. I no longer care about obeying my orders since there aren't any.

—The diary of Megan Jean

Anger and rage filled Mia. She was so unsure whom to direct it at. Maybe Affinity, who had made it out like Mia was a valuable part of the mission, or Zack, whose idea this was, or Andrew, who had convinced her to go along with Zack's method of transporting her. She decided all of them deserved her ire. The vehicle they were in stopped moving. The sound of the wind had died down and Mia could hear again. She wished she could see where they were, but hiding in a burlap bag did not afford her that luxury.

"Your rooms are ready," an unfamiliar voice said. "You will wash up and change, then be at Madame Martineau's in the morning."

Mia found the man's accent enchanting. His voice was light and it was almost as if he sang his words. Mia wondered if she was going to get smuggled into the hotel still inside this sack. Whoever was there to let her out would feel her rage. She felt a hand grab the bag.

"No," the man said. "Leave the cargo."

Mia cringed. She was being referred to as property.

"This cargo stays with me," Andrew said.

This situation could not get more degrading.

"It is nonnegotiable," the man said. "Madame Martineau expects the cargo for dinner."

Mia wasn't sure if that meant their next host wanted to eat with Mia or thought she was getting a special food delivery.

"Everything will be fine," Zack said.

The hand on Mia's bag let go.

"Don't be scared," Andrew said in a whisper. "I'll see you first thing in the morning."

Truthfully, Mia wasn't scared. She was annoyed. Everyone piled out of whatever type of vehicle they were in and Mia was alone. She heard the driver walk around to his door and they took off. More than anything Mia wanted to climb out of the bag and feel the wind blow across her face, but since Andrew had explained the situation with the army officer she knew it was a dumb idea. Instead she let out a sigh and stayed in the sack, feeling as useful as a piece of fruit.

The vehicle started to slow down. Mia heard her driver open the car door and walk around toward the back.

"You're still in there?" he asked. "I thought you would have crawled out by now."

Mia took that as her cue and burst her hands through the tiny opening. The man laughed and Mia took a big gulp of fresh air.

"I suppose it was best you stayed cautious," he said. "But a woman traveling alone or at all won't bring much suspicion in this country. Come, I'll help you down."

Mia was in the bed of a truck, but it was low to the ground and had wooden sides. Not like the big ones she'd seen in America or the military vehicles Affinity possessed. Since she'd learned how to drive, cars held a new fascination for Mia. She stood up and walked to the man, who helped her down.

They were in the back of a beautiful house. Mia looked around the gardens, which were gigantic. She saw a wall bordering the property and sculptures and fountains placed around the area.

"What is this place?"

"This is the garage," he said. "Employee quarters as well."

"Am I posing as a servant?"

He let out a laugh.

"I'll walk you to the main house," he said. "Madame Martineau is eager to make your acquaintance."

"Who is she?"

"The prime minister of France," he said. "This is the estate of whoever holds that title."

Mia looked around at all the splendor. The buildings looked time-less. She and her escort walked along a path surrounded by beautiful flowers. In the distance she saw the home that must have belonged to the prime minister. It was a giant stone house and matched every other aspect of the property in its beauty. Mia had never thought a place so grand existed.

"What is your name?" Mia asked.

"Albin Fabre," he said. "I am one of Madame Martineau's advis-ers. How was your journey?"

There were so many words to describe Mia's trip—"awful," "con-fusing," "boring," "agitating"—but Mia didn't want to respond with any of those choices.

"Fine, thank you," she said.

"You are a very brave woman," he said.

Mia looked up at him and he smiled back at her, nodding his head.

"I'm sure Madame Martineau will want to tell you most of the details about the next leg, but rest assured we all support you here."

While Mia was eager to learn what her future held, her main con-cern at this point was that she had a hand in it, or at least some control. They approached the large house and a person walked out to greet them.

It was an older woman; she had short blond hair and wore a fitted dress that showed off her toned arms. She held them open and walked toward Mia, giving her a kiss on each cheek.

"Welcome to France," she said. "My name is Florence Martineau. Please, call me Flo."

Two other women standing behind her came forward and each kissed Mia on her cheeks. Flo wrapped her arm around Mia's shoulders and guided her up the steps.

"I am certain you are filled with questions," she said. "And exhausted from your travels. But I will give you the choice; what is the first thing you would like to do here?"

"Shower," Mia said. "I smell."

Both of her companions let out a laugh.

"Yes," Albin said. "They hid her in a sack used for seafood."

"Ick," Flo said. "*Fille de poisson.*"

Flo and Albin laughed again. Mia looked wide eyed around the entry room. The entire house looked like it was made of gold and the ceiling was decorated with one of the most elaborate paintings she'd ever seen.

"Albin will show you to your room and get you set up," Flo said. "Are you hungry?"

"Yes," Mia said.

"Would you like food brought to you or do you want to dine with me?"

The idea of sitting alone again was too much for Mia. It was as if Flo could read her mind since she didn't wait for Mia to respond.

"We will give you an hour to freshen up," she said. "I will see you after that."

She bowed her head and went into the giant house.

"I think you will love your accommodations," Albin said. "Please follow me."

"I'm only here a week, right?" Mia said. "Then back to America?"

"Shhh," Albin said. "Don't speak of those things so openly. Not everyone present is familiar with the plans. You can speak openly with me in private; I will be accompanying Madame Martineau as her escort."

Mia nodded and realized her mistake in getting too comfortable too soon. She kept her mouth shut the rest of the time they walked through the great house. Albin stopped in front of a door and opened it up.

The room was pale blue, with a large bed and a dresser set. The ceiling was painted in a similar manner to the entrance. There were painted children seated among clouds with rings over their heads. It was breathtaking. Albin walked to the far side of the room and opened a door.

"Here is the bathroom," he said. "There is clothing in the closet and everything you should need."

"Should I wait for you to come get me?" Mia asked.

"You don't have to," Albin said. "The whole house and grounds are open to you. But finding the dining room may be tricky. I'll come just to show you where it is."

"Thank you," Mia said.

Albin nodded and left the room. Mia was used to entering foreign lands. But this one seemed far different from the others. She didn't know what a prime minister was, or how Flo fit into the grand scheme, but Mia knew that things were about to change.

Chapter 7

*There are no cars on the road with drivers. We have passed
several empty vehicles. None of my group will say what we are
all thinking. The war overseas is over, but the apocalypse took
place stateside.*

—*The journal of Isaac Ryland*

"You didn't say anything about separating from Mia," Andrew said.

"Look," Zack said. "Once we got into France, Affinity wasn't in
charge anymore. We're lucky the prime minister shares an interest in
our cause. She agreed to take all of us over the border and we need
to respect her decisions."

"You've spent the past few weeks telling me over and over again
how Mia needs protection, how everything is done if she gets hurt.
Do you have any idea how hard it was for me to convince her to stay
out of the way? I knew she was bored out of her mind, wanting to
help, but I listened to you. Then we just hand her off like she's nothing."

"You did a great job," Zack said. "The prime minister is looking
after her tonight. Nothing bad will happen to her."

"Affinity must be so pleased with themselves," Andrew said, "that
they stumbled upon this great weapon. A girl who can symbolize
everything that's wrong with the Registry."

"There's no way you're serious," Carter said.

"Excuse me?" Andrew said.

"Mia's not a symbol of what's wrong with the Registry," Carter said. "She's just a girl. One that too many people have deemed important. But if you take away Grant's interest in her, then she's nothing. A spoiled brat who whines all the time and thinks she's special."

Andrew's protective instincts rose.

"I seem to remember when you thought she was pretty special," Andrew said. "But then she decided I was the one she wanted and now you're bitter."

"Cool it, guys," Zack said.

The group of five was in a midsize open room with two double beds. Carter didn't make an effort to stand up from the one he was currently sitting on. Andrew's words had no effect on him.

"What is going on with you?" Andrew asked. "Why are you even here if you hate Mia so much now?"

"I don't hate her," Carter said.

"Then what is it?" Andrew asked.

Zack lost interest in Andrew and Carter and walked over toward Jesse and Bryan.

"Nothing," Carter said. "I should keep my mouth shut."

"I can read you," Andrew said. "You need to tell me what's going on."

Carter's face went blank. He lowered his voice before speaking.

"My dad is alive," Carter said.

Andrew felt the blood rush out of his face. He admired Roderick Rowe but had seen him fall out of a helicopter to his death. He shook off the feelings of hope Carter had; there was no way his father had survived. Andrew made sure he answered in a hushed tone.

"I know it's hard to admit," Andrew said. "But he's dead. You need to move on."

"No," Carter said. "He's alive."

"Let's stop the insults," Zack yelled from the other side of the room.

"Don't tell anyone," Carter said. "Especially Mia."

There were so many questions Andrew wanted to ask, like how Carter could be holding on to such an insane belief, but Zack walked back over before the conversation could continue.

"Mia is in capable hands and you three will be reunited in the morning. Can we focus on tomorrow? Tell me our cover again."

"We're servants," Andrew said.

"They don't have servants here," Zack said. "This is a much more modern country. We're employees."

"Sorry," Andrew said. "We're escorts of the prime minister. New bodyguards assigned to escort her overseas."

"What does that mean?" Zack asked.

"It means for the next week we need to play the part," Carter said. "We can't let on that we're up to anything or that we're acquainted with Mia, who's posing as a member of her entourage."

"What are we doing for the next week then?" Andrew asked. "Just following them everywhere?"

Zack walked over to the wall of the small hotel room and pulled out a bag from his luggage. He took out his computer and sat on the bed. "Part of the time," he said. "The rest we need to spend going over our plans for once we arrive in America."

"You mean once we get to the capital," Andrew said.

Zack gave him a look.

"Our contact will meet us outside the city," Zack said. "There we wait for Rex to come with Mia's file. Hopefully by then someone will have cracked the password to enter the secret room and we'll destroy the master servers."

"What if the password isn't cracked?" Carter asked. "I mean, it's not on a system. The only place it's stored is the grand commander's head."

"Then Florence Martineau will gift the grand commander with this," Zack said.

He held out a small pin of the American flag.

"It holds a tiny camera," he said. "We'll watch every move he makes and once he decides to punch in the code we'll get a front-row view."

"That's if he wears it," Carter said.

"He will," Zack said. "It's made from the finest diamonds in the world."

Zack put the pin away.

"Next Mia goes live on every television set in the country. She proves that she is Grant's first wife, that she's not dead, and shatters lots of Americans' faith in the system. Then they find out the system doesn't exist anymore and will see her as a symbol of hope and freedom. Things they never dreamed possible."

"This whole thing is too rushed," Andrew said. "We needed more time to plan."

"We need to act while we can," Zack said. "If Grant actually becomes grand commander the people of America will be even farther out of reach. Besides, this is the first time in years foreigners have been invited inside American borders. We couldn't ask for a better cover."

"What happens next?" Andrew asked. "For us?"

"We escape again," Zack said. "Make our way back to Affinity and wait for further instructions. Crossing the border will likely be easy. America will be in disarray. Without the records people can't be forced to behave a certain way anymore."

"So we're going to create chaos and then abandon the people?" Andrew asked.

"The chaos will die down," Zack said. "And a new America will be born. One where all are treated equally."

"How?" Carter asked. "Will the rest of the international community that has done nothing to help for the past hundred years step in?"

"Affinity will step in," Zack said. "When the time is right."

Andrew's job kept changing. From soldier, to shipper, to body-guard. He had too much on his plate to help Carter with his crazy delusions. But one of his tasks was constant: keep Mia safe. And right now he felt like he was failing. He hoped wherever she was, she was staying out of trouble.

Chapter 8

I gave every cent I had to the ship captain. He didn't bother getting off his boat to inspect the shores. None of my fellow travelers have any money to pay their way home. Never in a million years did I think I'd resort to this, but I am hoping to hitch a ride from a stranger.

—*The diary of Megan Jean*

Mia lay on her bed. She stared at the ceiling, studying the children's faces. They were painted in a way that made it impossible to tell whether they were happy or sad. The shower had felt amazing. Mia was so dirty and was happy to wash away the scum of the sea. She chose a pair of black pants and a red ruffled shirt, unsure what the dress code for dinner would be. There was a knock at her door and Mia sat up on her elbows. She was surprised when Flo walked in.

"I'm sorry," she said. "Did you decide you would rather sleep than eat?"

"Oh no," Mia said.

She stood up.

"I was admiring the painting. I've never seen one like it before."

"This is one of my favorite rooms in the estate," Flo said. "The angels watch over you while you sleep."

"These are angels?"

"Yes," Flo said. "You see their wings and the halos over their heads?"

"I've never heard of an angel before."

"They're religious icons of the old world," Flo said. "Mankind has been fighting for as long as they've been breathing. Many wars were over religion."

"I don't know much history," Mia said.

"You're about to become part of it," Flo said. "Once your mission is successful you will be remembered as the girl who stopped injustice in the western world."

Mia was unsure how to respond.

"I know Albin warned you about speaking of these things," Flo said, "but I want you to feel free to express yourself when you are on my property. We kept your name as Jeanette, but changed your last name to Freeman. My employees believe you are the wife of an American diplomat stationed in France."

"Are there American women over here?"

"Not many," Flo said. "If they are here they live as free people. We have fine relations with America, but I will not deport any women back to them."

"Then won't your employees find it strange that I'm here?"

"Not at all," Flo said. "You're going to act as my guide on my American trip. A country I have never been to before. Once we land, your story will change though."

"How?" Mia asked.

"The Americans will believe you are French," Flo said. "A trusted young student eager to show the world America is not as bad as it seems. Don't worry, I have plans to train you for the part, and there will be a few opportunities over here for you to test out your new skills."

"How did you get invited in?"

"I am the leader of this country," Flo said. "The grand commander, as your people call it. I was voted into my position though."

"A woman in the highest spot in her country is invited to one where the women are treated as property?"

Flo let out a light laugh. "I know it is strange," she said. "But I have kept all American bases open since my appointment, and have quieted down many campaigns calling for France to step in and stop the Registry."

"Why?"

"I say it is not France's fight and we should leave the American people to govern themselves," Flo said.

"Then why help Affinity?"

"Because what I say in public and how I behave in private are two different things," Flo said. "The people of France are starting to despise me."

"How come?"

"My lack of interest in helping America," Flo said. "They see my trip as a sign of favorability toward the American way of life. They call me names and think I don't care about human rights, but if I had been more vocal about my opposition then I wouldn't have this opportunity."

"Doesn't it bother you that all those people saying hurtful things about you are wrong?" Mia asked.

"My dear, I learned a long time ago that the world is bigger than myself," Flo said. "I know who I am and what I stand for. That is good enough for me."

Mia was overcome by Flo's self-confidence. She wished she felt the same way about her own self.

"Let's get something to eat," Flo said. "Then I can fill you in on the plans for our journey."

Mia's stomach let out a low growl and she nodded. There were so many questions filling her head, but more than anything she wanted to know how Flo achieved such a sense of peace about herself.

The chocolate mousse was the best dessert Mia had ever tasted. She had to avoid the temptation to pick her dish up and lick it clean. The dining room was smaller than Mia expected, but it was more elegant than she could have imagined. They were seated at a fine mahogany table and a giant chandelier hung from the ceiling. Conversing with Flo was simple and easy. She stuck to light topics like the weather and her favorite parts of France. Mia was too nervous to approach the subject looming over her head and was thrilled when Flo took the lead.

"We land next week in the Southeast," Flo said. "From there our group will be escorted across the country. We take a week-long tour and we will visit some major cities and see some of the sights your homeland has to offer. Then we will end in the North-west, right outside your country's capital, and close to the home of your former intended."

"Grant lives in the Northeast though," Mia said.

"He lied," Flo said. "His home is very close to the capital."

"But I swear he said Northeast," Mia said, "and I thought I read that somewhere to . . ."

"A man of his wealth has lots of homes," Flo said. "But I can tell you for certain, the house he currently resides in is in the Northwest."

Mia could think of hundreds of reasons for Grant to lie about his home territory and none of them were pleasant. She accepted Flo's word and moved on with her main concerns.

"Won't it draw suspicion?" Mia asked. "I mean, you're a woman. Women aren't even allowed to travel without a man in public."

"There will be plenty of men traveling with us," Flo said. "I've been instructed not to reveal my station. The American people won't know that I am the important one. I'll seem like a wife traveling with her husband."

"Are you married?" Mia asked.

"No," Flo said.

In America unmarried women Flo's age were in retirement camps around the country, if they were left alive at all. A woman without a husband was afforded little respect and few rights.

"I know it is hard for you to imagine," Flo said. "A single woman running a country. If it makes it any easier I have a long-term partner and he is quite proud of me."

"Partner?" Mia asked.

She had only heard that term used to describe two men married to each other. The image of Frank and Alex, her onetime saviors, came to mind and Mia smiled.

"We have been together for twenty years," Flo said.

Mia thought about Andrew. She wondered how he would feel if this were their situation. He'd spent the last several weeks being so overprotective. As if he'd forgotten Mia was capable of taking care of herself at all.

"Do you have any children?" Mia asked.

"No," Flo said. "I have two nieces I love like daughters, around your age. They're both away at university."

"They're students?" Mia asked.

"One is studying medicine, the other dance," Flo said. "They couldn't be more different and I couldn't be more proud of them."

"I've never studied anything," Mia said.

"No woman in your country has," Flo said.

She glanced around the dining room and leaned forward to whisper.

"Maybe you will change all of that soon."

It was obvious Flo thought Mia had a big part to play. But she didn't feel that way.

"I'm just a prop," Mia said.

"What do you mean?"

"I'm starting to realize I don't have much say in what's going on," Mia said. "Affinity doesn't want my contribution. They want my face. I understand why, but I can't stop feeling helpless."

"Well as long as you are in my care I am in charge, not Affinity," Flo said. "And as far as I am concerned you are much more than a beautiful face."

Mia smiled.

"It has been a long few weeks for you, I am sure," Flo said. "How about starting tomorrow you tell me your entire story and we will make sure your life is in your own hands."

"I would like that," Mia said.

Her mind still hung on a comment Flo had made earlier.

"You said you know who you are and what you stand for," Mia said. "Can I ask how you figured that all out?"

Flo nodded her head.

"We can discuss that tomorrow," she said. "I have a feeling we are going to get along quite well."

A yawn forced its way to Mia's mouth and she nodded her head in agreement. Flo stood up and Mia did the same. She was more than excited to spend the next few weeks at Flo's side.

Chapter 9

In a strange turn of events, I committed a felony. No telephones were in working condition and I had few other options. I stole a car parked at the shipyard and am driving toward Wallace.

—The diary of Megan Jean

Mia had slept surprisingly well. She did not miss her cramped cabin at Affinity. She appreciated the absence of Carter and Andrew. Mia went to her closet. She chose a pair of purple shorts and a white long-sleeved T-shirt. The material was soft on her skin. She pulled her long blond extensions up in a ponytail and went into the hall.

Flo had not given her directions on the day's events before she went to sleep. Then Mia remembered Albin's advice. She was not a prisoner here but a guest. So she decided to take a walk down to the dining room. She didn't notice another soul in the giant house as she walked through the halls. When she entered the room, Albin and Flo were eating. They stood when she entered.

"Good morning, Mia," Flo said. "How did you sleep?"

"Well," Mia said. "Thank you."

"I would have sent someone, but I thought you might need some extra rest. I am pleased you felt comfortable enough to come down here. We were just discussing today's activities. Please, have a seat."

Mia took one of the open chairs. Flo passed her an egg dish and

Mia scooped some onto her plate. She took a bite and was not surprised that it was just as delicious as the dinner from the night before.

"Your friends are arriving today," Flo said. "They will be staying in the employee houses though."

"You must act like you don't know who they are," Albin said.

"Why?" Mia asked.

"Because they have been hired as extra protection for Madame Martineau's overseas trip, and you are her equal."

"That doesn't mean you have to ignore them," Flo said. "But you shouldn't treat them like you have survived a great deal together."

After having spent the last few weeks in such close quarters with Andrew and Carter, Mia was fine with having some space, but being near Andrew would be difficult. Mia was having a hard time not grabbing on to him every second she could.

"We leave in six days," Flo said. "That means there is little time to teach you how to behave."

"What do you mean?"

"The people here think you're an American guiding me," Flo said. "But once we arrive in America the people there will think you are a Frenchwoman accompanying me on my trip."

"They'll know I'm not as soon as I open my mouth," Mia said. "Your accents are so different from mine."

"You will learn how to imitate ours," Flo said.

"What else will I have to learn?"

"How to stay under the radar," Albin said.

Flo gave Albin a dirty look.

"Along with my bodyguards American agents will also accompany us," Flo said. "We don't want any of these men to think you stand out from the rest of my group. So you will learn how to behave as one of us."

"How is your behavior different from mine?"

"We see ourselves as equals to men," Flo said. "I am certain you do as well, but you must not show the slightest bit of fear. They will prey on it. There are also a few customs; we greet everyone with light kisses, and I know that is not the American way. It will be more in the way you carry yourself. Mia, you are a strong woman, and that must be reflected on the outside as well as in."

Mia nodded her head, but in reality she wasn't feeling very strong lately. She felt more like a puppet and less like a contributing member of a team.

"Once you're done eating, take a walk with me," Flo said. "I want to hear everything about your journey this far, and maybe I can answer some questions you have."

That was all the incentive Mia needed to eat quickly. This woman radiated power and Mia wanted to know how she'd gotten that way.

Chapter 10

I sat in my stolen car outside my apartment complex and mustered up the courage to make my way inside. I am not sure if my pause was out of fear that Wallace wouldn't be there or fear that he would.

—The diary of Megan Jean

As Mia predicted, the lawns were even more beautiful in the light of day. She and Flo walked along the path toward the employees' house and Mia divulged her entire life story.

"You have lived a more extraordinary life than most in your few years on this earth," Flo said. "And you had no idea that enrolling in the Registry was a bad thing until your sister showed you."

"And she lost her life because of it," Mia said. "Her husband wrote and said she became ill, but I know he killed her."

"Your parents must have been so upset," Flo said.

"They weren't at all," Mia said. "All they cared about was money. And me and my sisters' marriages brought them plenty of that."

"You shouldn't bear ill will toward them," Flo said.

"They deserve it," Mia said. "I told my mother I didn't want to get married and she slapped me."

"In her way," Flo said, "I am certain she was trying to protect you.

She didn't think you had any choice but to be a bride. She didn't want to send you off into that life without you realizing that. It wasn't her fault, she is just part of the injustice in the world."

"I don't see it that way," Mia said.

"Does hanging on to your anger help you at all?"

"It gives me some motivation," Mia said.

"You should not focus on the past," Flo said. "If it weren't for her actions maybe you wouldn't have run away."

"So you think she wanted me to run?"

"I don't pretend to know answers like that," Flo said. "Yesterday you asked me how I became so self-assured, and letting go of unnecessary anger led to my happiness."

"How do you tell what is necessary anger?" Mia asked.

"Does it benefit you to stay angry? Will it help with your personal development?"

"I don't even know what personal development is," Mia said.

"Of course you do, Mia," Flo said. "What kind of person do you want to become?"

The question was so powerful it almost knocked Mia down.

"I want to have control of my own life," Mia said.

"My question runs deeper than that," Flo said.

"I don't know," Mia said. "I guess I never really thought about it before."

"Well, start," Flo said. "Ask yourself questions you've always been too afraid to answer. Once you confront your issues you can really start living and appreciating everything around you."

Again Mia was at a loss for words. She thought Flo was a little off base. Of course Mia should be angry with her parents. Whatever Mia was feeling on the inside didn't seem to have much relation to her actions. The world was what it was and Mia merely felt part of it. They stopped walking. Mia didn't realize they'd arrived at the employees' house.

"I thought you'd like to greet your friends," Flo said. "Let's go inside."

Flo held open the door and Mia entered. There was a set of stairs that Flo walked past. They were in a main room, with several couches and a television set. Mia was happy to see Carter sitting on the couch along with Bryan and Jesse. Everyone rose, but their eyes were on Florence.

"Madame Martineau," Zack said.

Mia spun around to see him and Andrew walking down the steps. Andrew took two long strides toward Mia and wrapped his arms around her. Mia returned his hug.

"I'm so glad you're all right," Andrew said. "I was worried."

"Why?" Mia asked.

Andrew didn't respond at first.

"Because we were apart," he said after a moment. "I always worry about you when you're not with me."

Mia knew he meant the words to comfort her, but she didn't appreciate his tone. It was as if Andrew had forgotten all of Mia's accomplishments. The way that she rescued him when the militia held him hostage, or how she was successful in figuring out what the militia wanted in order to get them to leave Affinity alone. She dropped her arms and backed away from him.

"I was fine," Mia said. "I can take care of myself."

"That doesn't mean you have to," Andrew said.

Their attention was diverted back to the rest of the group.

"I wanted to welcome all of you to France," Florence said.

All of the men stared at Flo with blank faces.

"Two of you should come with us," Flo said. "Start following us around the grounds. That way your presence will be known to my other employees. Fake papers have been drawn up for you. Once we land in America you are all playing the role of men in the American armed services handpicked to accompany me. Memorize your parts, because I fear you will be questioned."

"I'll go," Andrew said.

"No," Mia said. "Bryan and Jesse. I know them the least. It will be easier for me to ignore them."

Andrew looked hurt, but Mia didn't care at the moment. The idea that he would be watching her every move like she was a child was too much right now, and she didn't think she could handle the temptation to speak with him. The two men stood up and walked over to them.

"I'll see you soon," Mia said.

She leaned in and gave Andrew a kiss on the cheek before walking back toward the door. Mia wasn't sure if Flo was ready to leave, but she didn't care at the moment. What kind of person did Mia want to become? Right now, a self-sufficient one.

Chapter 11

I regret not staying in the parking lot, I regret not staying over-seas. I opened the door to my apartment and was greeted with a horrid stench. My deepest fears were realized. Wallace lay on the floor, unmoving and long bereft of life.

—The diary of Megan Jean

Jesse and Bryan didn't say anything to Mia as they sat outside and waited for Flo. Mia felt a pang of guilt for wanting to avoid Andrew, but she didn't appreciate his demeanor toward her as of late. She didn't know much about the two Affinity members. They'd spent two weeks preparing for this journey but never got to know each other. Mia had spent most of that time with a trainer, honing her hand-to-hand combat skills. She had wanted to work on the strategy of their mission, but Zack insisted she be fully capable of defending herself. At the time Mia thought he was right, but now she realized those skills would never come into play and Affinity was trying to keep Mia distracted.

"Well that was awkward," Flo said. "I thought Andrew was your . . . man?"

"He is," Mia said.

"Trouble in paradise?"

"Excuse me?" Mia asked.

"I find it so strange that you're unfamiliar with clichés," Flo said. "Is there a problem with your relationship?"

"Not exactly," Mia said. "He's starting to make me feel like I'm not capable of taking care of myself."

"Well, is that a problem with him or a problem with you?"

Mia raised an eyebrow.

"Let's keep walking," Flo said. "You're meeting with an accent coach this afternoon."

"What will he teach me?"

"*She* will teach you how to sound French," Flo said. "It won't be very exciting."

"I like learning new things," Mia said.

"Tell me, Mia, have you ever thought about the spiritual side of things?"

"Like ghosts?"

Flo let out a loud cough mixed with laughter.

"Not exactly," she said.

"I don't understand," Mia said.

"You're very sensitive," Flo said. "You harbor anger; you get angry with your boyfriend because of the way you feel about yourself, and I mean no offense. Yesterday you mentioned wanting to know how I came to trust myself. I know that I alone am in charge of my own destiny."

"Isn't that a contradiction?" Mia asked. "If destiny is predetermined, how can you be in charge?"

Flo flashed a warm smile. "Those are two separate schools of thought," she said. "Do you think things are predetermined? You could never have ended up anywhere but here?"

Nobody had ever asked Mia anything remotely similar to this. She wanted to prove to Flo that she was capable of answering tough questions. Rather than responding with an "I don't know," Mia thought carefully.

"No," Mia said. "I think I could have ended up a number of places."

"And was it your series of decisions that led you to this point?"

"No. If I hadn't forced Andrew to help me I never would have left America. If I hadn't learned from Riley I never would have rescued Andrew and Carter. Other people have assisted me."

Flo nodded her head.

"You're a giver," she said. "You give lots of credit to those around you, instead of allowing yourself to receive some."

"Without Corinna's pushing I never would have run in the first place. I owe all of this to my sister," Mia said. "She's the one who should be here, not me."

"Aha," Flo said. "Do you think that has anything to do with your motivation?"

"No," Mia said. "I can't help her. She's dead."

"But you can help all the women in America in her place," Flo said. "Set them free as your sister did you."

"Stopping the Registry and mandatory service just seems like the right thing."

"Always look deeper," Flo said. "That is how you can harness your energy."

"How do I do that?"

"Never stop asking questions."

When Mia was learning how to form strategies with Riley she had asked questions nonstop. Her mentor had scolded Mia for asking too many.

"I ask questions all the time."

"To other people," Flo said. "Ask them to yourself."

Mia went silent. Flo stopped walking and turned to face Mia. She reached out and grabbed hold of both her hands.

"We can't change other people," Flo said. "We can only educate them and give them the option to change themselves."

"Are you talking about Andrew?"

"I'm speaking about every soul who walks this earth."

Flo squeezed Mia's hands.

"I have some official business to attend to," Flo said. "But one last piece of advice. If you're angry with someone, clear and open communication is the best way to get over your fear."

"I'm angry, not afraid."

"Anger is only a form fear takes," Flo said. "And there's no shame in being afraid. Particularly for a person like you with a challenging road behind and ahead."

Flo released Mia's hands and leaned in, giving her a kiss on each cheek. Mia watched as she reached into her pocket and pulled out a small box. At first Mia thought she was getting a present, but instead Flo turned to walk away.

"What is that?" Mia asked.

"A gift," Flo said. "For your grand commander. I am sending it ahead. It should arrive in a day or two and will hopefully help with your cause."

This was the exact sort of information Mia wanted to know—how the small gift would help—but Flo had given her so much to think about that she didn't have the urge to ask. There was nothing this woman would keep from Mia, and if that small gift was meant to stop the injustices in America, that was all Mia needed to know.

"Enjoy your lessons," Flo said. "I'll see you at dinner."

"Good-bye," Mia said.

Flo walked off. Bryan and Jesse followed her. Mia debated walking back to the employees' house and speaking with Andrew and Carter about their recent behavior. Open and clear communication. Instead she decided to focus on Flo's other advice. Mia needed to ask herself some hard questions and not be afraid of the answers.

Chapter 12

I thought I saw the worst carnage of my life covering the war stories; I now see the error of my thoughts. We have yet to encounter a single living soul. Every area of DC is filled with corpses. The soldiers I traveled with are cleaning up the dead, but I am of little use to them. Whatever happened here is equal to, if not worse than, the terrors of war.

—The journal of Isaac Ryland

Confrontation was never something that Grant avoided. However, between trying to placate Ian until he officially passed down the grand commander title and dealing with Roderick Rowe's questioning of his situation, Grant was forced into avoidance.

He walked through one of the secret passageways he had built to the east wing of his mansion. He had once thought the large area would house all his servants, but next to none of them desired to live on his property. Once he was grand commander that would change. Grant planned to follow Ian's lead and take many women as private wives. Technically they were government property and since Grant would be the American government they would become his property. He even planned on stationing some servicemen in his home in order to keep everyone in line. It would be a nice lifestyle lift. One a man of his wealth and stature deserved.

He made it farther into the east wing and started to realize why Dr. Schaffer had summoned him. Roderick's yelling echoed through the halls. Ever since the man had been severely injured during Amelia's escape he'd lost his memories of the time leading up to the attempt, completely forgetting the fact that he had been aiding a young woman in escaping the country. Thus far Grant had successfully convinced the man he had been in a car accident outside the capital and Grant was caring for him out of generosity. That story was wearing thin.

"Where is my son? Why won't you let me go? I need my phone," Roderick yelled.

Grant took a breath before entering the room. Roderick was trying to pull himself out of his bed, but the double leg casts would make it impossible to stand. Dr. Schaffer was cowering away from the irate gentleman.

"What's the problem?" Grant asked.

Rod took a few breaths and stared at Grant. The past few weeks had seemed like a standoff. Rod didn't appear to want to reveal what he knew any more than Grant wished to disclose his secrets. It looked like the boiling point had come. Rod narrowed his eyes and pressed his lips together.

"Where is my son?"

"Carter said to expect his arrival early next month," Grant said. "But between us I expect him sooner."

Rod did not respond or break eye contact.

"Dr. Schaffer," Grant said, "you appear a bit rattled; why don't you take a break?"

The doctor nodded his head and left the two men alone. Grant closed the door and pulled up a chair. He smoothed out his yellow and brown striped shorts and matching yellow polo before crossing his legs. He would hate to see his outfit wrinkled.

"Tell me the truth," Rod said.

"You first." Grant was quick to respond and let a wicked grin cross his face.

He liked to unnerve his prey and right now Roderick Rowe seemed on the verge of breaking down.

"I'm not the one holding you hostage," Rod said.

"I suppose not," Grant said. "Tell me, did all of your memory return to you or just part of it?"

"The last thing I remember is playing cards at a neighborhood game," Rod said. "Next thing I know I wake up here, a thousand miles from home with one of the wealthiest men in the country taking care of me."

"I highly doubt that."

"You're being modest?"

"Oh no," Grant said. "I am one of the wealthiest men in the world. What I meant was, I highly doubt that is all you remember."

Rod snorted and looked away.

"If you tell me the truth I will gladly answer all of your questions."

The man turned his eyes back toward Grant.

"I was giving assistance to your wife," Rod said. "Helping her escape the country and the terrible life that she would have had with you. I'm assuming she was successful in her escape."

"Momentarily," Grant said. "Please, go on."

"That's all."

"Fair enough," Grant said. "Ask away."

"Where is my son?"

"He claims he is working with a rebel group in Guatemala."

Rod smiled and looked relieved. "Then you lost," he said.

"Aren't you curious why you're still alive? If I am the big loser here?"

Rod's look of relief vanished.

"I made a deal with your son. In exchange for Amelia he will get you," Grant said. "So don't worry. The two of you will reunite shortly."

"He would never do that."

"Why not? Carter loves you. It makes me sick actually, but in this instance it is a bonus for me."

"Can't you just let her be?"

"No," Grant said. "She is a loose end and I want her tied up."

Rod looked disgusted. Grant uncrossed his legs and leaned forward.

"Please, let me ask you a question," Grant said. "What made Mia so special? You knew who I was, what resources I had at my disposal. Why did you think you could all get away?"

"You," Roderick said. "Your interest in her makes her special."

"So you admit that? It isn't because she is a lovely person?"

Rod looked taken aback. As if he was trying to form an answer to cover his misstep.

"Well, now we can end this charade," Grant said. "If you're thinking about killing yourself, don't bother. I am a man of my word and once Amelia is returned to me, Carter will get your dead body. It won't change anything. The deal is done."

"You are the worst person to ever live. You will be dead by—"

"Sorry," Grant interrupted. "I don't care what you have to say on that matter. Now please, let Dr. Schaffer keep looking after you. You're helpless at the moment, and causing a huge fuss won't do anyone any good."

Grant stood up. Rod continued to hurl insults but Grant tuned him out. At least one of the people annoying him was taken care of. He left the room and closed the door, making sure to flip the dead bolt on the outside. Not that it mattered; a man with two broken legs wasn't capable of escape. Now if only dealing with the Ian problem could be as simple.

Chapter 13

I combed the rest of our apartment complex; all I can find is dead bodies. I tried my best to bury the dead, but I need answers.

—*The diary of Megan Jean*

As Mia forced herself to use the muscles in the back of her throat she felt like she was literally spitting out the words.

"Hmmmm," Vivien said. "Maybe you should try to stay silent as often as possible on this voyage."

Mia frowned at her accent coach. A knock on the door broke up her lesson and she welcomed the intrusion. Flo walked inside the room. Mia caught a glimpse of Andrew and Zack standing behind her.

"How are the lessons going today?"

"Not well," Mia said, trying her hardest to sound French.

"That doesn't sound so bad," Flo said.

"*Bonjour, je m'appelle Mia.*"

"*Très bon,*" Flo replied.

"The happy house hits her heart," Mia said, elongating the words and dragging out the H sound.

"Very good again," Flo said.

"If only every word in the English language started with H," Vivien said.

"Well hopefully you won't have to speak much," Flo said. "I was wondering if you wanted to come with me this afternoon?"

"Yes," Mia said.

She didn't care where Flo was going, but after spending the last four days working on French customs Mia welcomed any change.

"Excellent," Flo said.

She turned and walked into the hallway.

"Thank you," Mia said to Vivien.

Vivien nodded her head and waved Mia off. Mia kept her back straight and followed Flo, hoping Vivien realized she was taking the lessons seriously. She tried her hardest to look like a confident diplomat.

Neither Andrew nor Zack acknowledged Mia. Andrew was born for this type of position. He had always excelled at hiding his emotions. Mia wasn't sure this was the best situation for him. He had come so far since leaving her parents' farm. After being tortured by the militia he had started to open up about his problems. Now he was training himself to hide them again. She shook her head, telling herself Andrew was strong enough to not slip backward.

The town car stopped. Mia looked through the tinted glass at an ordinary building on a busy street. Flo did not move to open the door.

"I'm surprised you don't travel with more people," Mia said. "You're so important. What if someone wished you harm?"

"On official business I have quite the entourage," Flo said. "But this is a personal matter."

She put away whatever handheld device she was using and opened the door. Zack and Andrew were already standing on the sidewalk, having traveled in a separate car. Both drivers waited with the vehicles. Flo kept her head down and went straight into the building. The signs were written in French and Mia still had no idea where they were headed or what they were doing.

A woman came out and greeted them. She wore a white pantsuit almost identical to Flo's purple one. Mia's shoulders were bare in her yellow polka-dot sundress and she immediately regretted not changing. The two women kissed on the cheeks.

"Jeanette," Flo said. She was referring to Mia by her fake name. "This is a very good friend of mine, Madame Dulac. Jeanette is going to accompany me on my American trip; she is the wife of an American diplomat."

"*Bonjour,* Jeanette," Madame Dulac said.

She wasted no time giving Mia a light hug and a kiss on each cheek. Mia didn't have to respond because Madame Dulac returned her attentions to Flo. The two women spoke in French and Mia couldn't comprehend a word they were saying. The group started walking and Mia followed.

Madame Dulac pushed open a set of doors and they entered a giant open room. There were children screaming and running around. They were doing a variety of activities. Some were playing with balls, others sitting in a circle clapping their hands. The ages and genders varied. All of them were smiling and their energy was infectious. One young girl stood up and pointed toward them.

"Florence," she called.

As if on command the room went silent. All of the faces turned toward them and the whole group came running. Florence was almost tackled as she was met with hugs from the children.

Madame Dulac spoke in French and the kids started to back away.

"Good afternoon, children," Flo said. "We have a special guest with us today, so why not demonstrate your English skills for her. This is my good friend Jeanette."

"Hello, Jeanette," the children said.

"Can I show you my new painting?" one of the children asked Florence.

"No, come see mine," another said.

"I want to show you the new trick I learned," yet another said.

Soon they were all vying for Flo's attention.

"I promise my afternoon is yours," Flo said. "Let us start with the artwork."

There was a cheer and Flo was dragged off by a group of children. Mia remained still, unsure of whether or not to follow as Andrew and Zack had. Madame Dulac walked up to Mia and stood next to her.

"As you can see our children's homes are quite different from those of your country," she said. Her voice was cold.

"What is this place?" Mia asked.

"You throw your boys out and your government raises them as savages," Madame Dulac said. "In France we cherish our youth. Even those who don't have parents."

"Where are their parents?"

"Some have died, others didn't want their children," Madame Dulac said. "Others are not fit to raise them. We take in these little ones and help them."

Mia didn't know how much to let Madame Dulac know. This woman seemed to believe Mia supported the American way of raising boys. Flo had not instructed Mia to let her believe otherwise. There was a tug on the bottom of Mia's dress. She turned to see a small girl smiling through her missing teeth.

"You speak English?"

Mia nodded.

"I know a song," she said.

Mia bent down to the girl's height.

"I would love to hear it," Mia said.

The girl cleared her throat and, in a voice that could not yet appreciate the concept of pitch, started to sing.

"Head, shoulders, knees and toes, knees and toes," she sang.

Mia smiled as the girl touched her corresponding body parts. She continued singing, finally ending with her tongue sticking out. Mia let out a laugh and clapped her hands in approval before the young lady ran off to join her friends.

"We will make sure she grows up educated," Madame Dulac said. "That she will care about herself more than finding and pleasing a man."

"What makes you think that's all I care about?" Mia asked.

"Isn't that all American females care about?" Madame Dulac asked. "I suppose it's not your fault. You're only a by-product of the system you were raised in."

Mia wanted to laugh at that comment. This woman had no clue what Mia had been through and her presumption was preposterous. "Trust me when I say I care about more than my husband," Mia said.

"Like what?" Madame Dulac asked. "Please, enlighten me."

Mia cared about stopping the Registry and the injustice in America, but she couldn't share that with this woman. She struggled to think of another answer, but that was all her life had been. First caring about landing a husband, then caring about escaping her husband, and now rescuing the women back home. Madame Dulac made a smug face.

"That's what I thought."

She turned and walked away, leaving Mia stunned. Flo came back into the main room, followed by Andrew and Zack. Mia cared about Andrew an awful lot, but even that wouldn't have been a good enough answer for Madame Dulac, or for Mia. It had taken coming here for Mia to realize it, but at this point in her life she didn't have a clue what type of person she was.

Chapter 14

I packed what supplies I could find and am leaving to find other survivors, hopefully some with more information.

—*The diary of Megan Jean*

The group had returned from the orphanage hours ago, but Madame Dulac's question and Mia's lack of an answer still plagued her. She barely touched her dinner. Now as she walked along the grounds with Flo she didn't find herself any more alert.

"Mia?"

"What?" Mia looked up at Flo, who wore a mischievous grin.

"You haven't said a word all evening," Flo said. "Are you lost in your head?"

"Sorry," Mia said. "I suppose I'm just nervous."

"Only two more nights until we fly out," Flo said. "Don't worry. You'll do fine. What did you think of the children?"

"Wonderful," Mia said. "I didn't realize other countries had problems with parents not taking care of their kids."

"The whole world has problems," Flo said. "It's how the people manage them that shows their character."

"What kind of person do you think I am?" Mia asked. "I know that we just met, but lately I'm not sure who I am anymore."

"I think you are brave and intelligent," Flo said. "I think you put others before yourself and are scared to upset people. But what I think shouldn't matter. The only opinion that should is the one you have of yourself. What kind of person do you think you are?"

Mia sighed and shook her head.

"Have you been questioning yourself lately?" Flo asked.

"I feel like I'm not my own person," Mia said. "I have these specific goals. If we are successful and the Registry is stopped, what then? I feel like a symbol, not a person."

"You will find a way," Flo said. "Trust in yourself. Are you still upset with Andrew?"

"No," Mia said.

"Have you spoken to him?"

Mia shook her head.

"Go see him tonight," Flo said. "Sometimes seeing ourselves reflected in another's eyes helps."

"Won't that draw attention?" Mia asked.

"We can go now," Flo said. "People will think we are reviewing our security detail for the trip."

Flo switched directions before Mia could object. She didn't know why she wanted to anyway. Maybe Flo was right and seeing Andrew would do Mia some good.

They arrived at the employee housing and as Flo had promised she walked off with Zack. Jesse and Bryan weren't around and Mia was left with Carter and Andrew.

"How's learning to act French?" Carter asked.

"Interesting," Mia said. "How's being a bodyguard?"

"Boring," Carter said.

He stood up from the couch and started to leave.

"Where are you going?" Mia asked.

"To leave you two alone," Carter said.

Mia wanted to tell him to stay, but she did want alone time with Andrew. She took his spot next to Andrew.

"How are you?" Mia asked.

"Nervous," Andrew said.

"Did you memorize your cover story?"

Andrew relaxed on the couch and turned toward Mia. He lifted his hand and started to twirl a lock of her fake hair.

"I'm nervous for you," Andrew said. "There's a lot riding on this."

"For some reason I'm not that scared," Mia said. "Flo is very smart and she's in charge."

Mia lifted one of her legs and tucked it under herself. She placed a hand on the couch between her and Andrew. He lifted his free hand and set it on top of hers.

"We can still call this off," Andrew said. "France is a safe country. The two of us can live here together."

"You know that's not an option," Mia said.

"I had to say it anyway."

Mia thought about the type of person she wanted to become and Flo's suggestion about open and honest communication.

"Why wouldn't you let me help out on the trip over here?" Mia said. "Or at least include me in the planning?"

"We've been over this," Andrew said.

"I have helped a lot," Mia said. "I was just as important to you when we stopped the militia from raiding Affinity and you didn't object. I saw the look in your eyes. You know more about this mission than I do."

"It was Zack's call," Andrew said.

"So you're back to following orders?"

Andrew pulled his hand away and Mia grabbed it back, pressing it between both her palms.

"That's not fair," Andrew said.

"I didn't like being treated that way," Mia said. "Promise you won't keep me in the dark?"

"I can't," Andrew said. "This is what you wanted. If anything bad happens to you the plan falls apart."

"What about you?"

"I'm expendable," Andrew said.

"No," Mia said. "If anything happens to me, would you fall apart?"

Andrew looked Mia straight in the eyes. He let out a light laugh and his eyes went warm. He opened his mouth to answer but then shut his lips and shook his head. That look was all Mia needed to know his answer was yes. She reached up and grabbed his chin, pulling his face down toward hers, and planted a light kiss on his lips.

"You're not expendable to me," Mia said. "And you can't protect me from everything. Especially if your protection gets in the way of me living my life."

Andrew brought his hand down on Mia's back and started rubbing up and down.

"I want to though," Andrew said.

"That's not your call," Mia said.

"I promise," Andrew said. "I won't keep you in the dark."

Mia leaned her head against Andrew's shoulder and he wrapped his arm around her. She closed her eyes. Flo was right. Talking about this and letting go of her anger did make Mia feel much better.

Chapter 15

We have spent days reviewing every document we can get our hands on. Whatever caused this disaster was man-made. For the first time in a long while I am grateful I don't have a family.
—The journal of Isaac Ryland

The grand commander's desk was made of fine wood and he sat in a chair that was much taller than him. Grant sat across from Ian and tried his best to focus on the old man's words, but his mind kept wandering toward the not-so-distant future, when Grant would finally occupy that seat.

"Gifts are already coming in from our foreign counterparts," Ian said.

He pulled his shirt forward, so Grant got a clear view of the jewel-encrusted American flag pin. The red and gold gems looked over-the-top and garish.

"What country sent this?" Grant asked, trying his hardest not to let his true opinion shine through.

"France," Ian said.

Grant was curious why Ian was receiving gifts when Grant was the one who was getting married, but not enough to ask. Grant saw little need for presents; he could afford anything he wished to purchase, and that included feminine jewelry. He smiled, thinking of how Ian was decorating himself like a woman, convincing Grant more and more of the old man's incompetence.

"Tell me," Ian said. "What do you know of the world's history?"

"Life before the Great War or after?"

"I'm afraid I may have phrased the question wrong," Ian said. "It is important you are polite and respectful to our international guests. I want to ensure you are aware of their cultures."

"The only ideals that matter are American ones," Grant said.

As soon as he spoke he regretted his choice of words. This would only result in Ian handing out more lessons.

"Of course," Grant said, "I am aware of the ever-shifting global climate."

"Indulge me," Ian said. "Speak about Ireland."

"Ireland is a series of islands in the Atlantic Ocean," Grant said. "It has grown significantly in size, taking over what was once referred to as Scandinavia as soon as the Great War was over. About thirty years ago the former United Kingdom came under its control as well. Ireland was one of the few countries that stayed out of the Great War and was met with little resistance when it acquired its new lands since its neighbors were broke and beaten from the battles."

"Hmmm," Ian said.

Grant thought the man would be impressed by his knowledge. He wasn't finished yet.

"Some people would say it is the second-strongest country next to America, since it has a strong economy, but its armed forces are nothing next to ours. Our international relations with the Irish are weak at best. They detest our way of life. I believe it is safe to say their leaders will not be invited to the festivities."

Ian took a breath before responding.

"They are not on our guest list," Ian said. "I must say I am a little alarmed that a private citizen like yourself has access to such knowledge."

"I previously confessed to you, sir, that I have been known to stroll the international Internet from time to time."

"I suppose I should take some comfort that you are aware of what is happening in the world yet stay loyal to American principles. If others have also found a way to step outside our guards maybe they feel the same."

"I am confident there are no others," Grant said.

Ian gave a half smile and nodded his head. Grant was not the average American. He was special in many ways, including his technological advances.

"You are wrong about Ireland though," Ian said.

Grant tried his best to look interested and not annoyed, making sure he raised his eyebrows in the least condescending way possible.

"The countries didn't put up little resistance," Ian said. "They put up no resistance, opting instead to welcome the shield of the Irish flag. We don't want that to happen again."

"If countries think they can go to Ireland for aid over America it would not benefit the country?"

"It is necessary to avoid an attack on America at all costs," Ian said. "Remember that. Keep many men stationed overseas, and give aid to foreign countries that are worthy."

"That is a fine idea, sir."

Ian again nodded his head, happy with Grant's answers. He switched the subject back to the gifts and Grant started fantasizing again. Only a few more weeks, then the official announcement would be made and Grant would no longer have to repeat Ian's sentiments. Once he was grand commander Grant would squash any Irish threat by sending the men stationed in Europe into that country. He would give the go-ahead to destroy anything and everyone, sending a message to the whole world that America would always reign supreme.

Chapter 16

*My heart is still racing. I came across my first group of sur-
vivors. Fellow soldiers who also returned to this catastrophe.
They were nice at first, but one attacked me. I shot him and ran.
I have never taken a life on American soil before, but I fear this
won't be my last.*

—The diary of Megan Jean

"I sip a full glass of water," Mia said.

She repeated the phrase, making sure to draw out her vowels.
Tomorrow was the day they left for America and Mia worried her
French accent wasn't going to fool anyone at this point. A knock on
Mia's door came and she saw Albin enter the room.

"How are you doing?" he asked.

Mia cleared her throat and tried her best to speak with the
accent, opting to respond with one of the few French phrases she
had picked up.

"*Je suis bien,*" she said.

"One last opportunity to see France this afternoon," Albin said. "I
will escort you to Madame Martineau."

Mia hadn't expected another trip out but thought anything sounded
better than pacing around in her room obsessing over tomorrow.

"Please try to speak like a Frenchwoman," Albin said. "You must exude confidence and sophistication. This is the final test of your skills."

Mia nodded her head. She picked up the white cardigan that was on her bed and pulled it over the nude tank top she wore. Mia glanced in the mirror at her tight black pants and wondered if she should change. She didn't want to ask, since she'd decided to get used to speaking as little as possible.

The car dropped Mia and Albin off at a storefront. Mia looked through a large glass window and spotted Flo. She didn't bother looking at the rest of her surroundings and instead made a beeline to her mentor. Mia was quick to greet Flo with a kiss on each cheek and the woman smiled warmly at Mia. Albin was greeted in the same manner and Mia looked around the building. There were black chairs spaced out, each in front of a vanity. Different beauty products lined the counters. Before Mia could ask where they were Andrew and Zack appeared from the back, with two strangers also dressed in black, though their outfits were less intimidating.

"The area is secure, madame," Zack said.

Mia looked around the empty building. They were the only ones inside. She caught a glimpse of the street through the window, which was now guarded by at least five men.

"Hiring American bodyguards now?" one of the strangers asked. She was a young woman who did not look impressed.

"They're on loan," Flo said. "For my trip overseas."

The woman scowled. Mia knew she needed to ignore the two men. Andrew was playing the role of a stranger. Mia thought not acknowledging his presence would be the most difficult part of today and wished any other guard had come.

"America has done good things for our country," Flo said. "We don't have to agree with their way of life but we must respect them. Angelique, this is Jeanette; she will be accompanying me on my travels."

Mia walked toward the woman, expecting a greeting with the typical cheek kiss, but Angelique made no effort to move forward.

"*Approuvez-vous la politique américaine?*" Angelique asked.

"Please," Flo said. "English only, I don't want my new guards to think I am speaking about them."

Angelique rolled her eyes.

"I said: and do you agree with American politics as well?"

Every part of Mia wanted to scream about her hatred for the Registry, her firsthand knowledge of the horrors America was capable of, but she knew that was not an option. Besides, today was a test of Mia's accent, not of her values. If she could fool an actual French person into thinking she was from France, then convincing other Americans should be a breeze.

"I agree with Madame Martineau," Mia said.

Angelique rolled her eyes and walked off. The man standing behind her came forward and kissed Flo, then Mia. He was much friendlier.

"My name is Valentin," he said. "Pleased to meet you, Jeanette. Don't mind Angelique, she fancies herself an activist."

"Valentin and Angelique are two of the best beauticians in all of the world," Flo said. "I thought it would be nice to freshen up for our trip."

Mia touched her long hair. The last time she'd had a makeover it was done with little consent. The women had glued fake hair to her head.

"Yes," Valentin said. "I will start with removing those extensions; they look cheap."

"That is not very kind," Flo said.

"I may be kind in certain areas," Valentin said. "But not when it comes to beauty, and you, Jeanette, are as gorgeous as they come. Please tell me what you would like and I will try my best to keep my opinions to myself."

"Actually I was hoping Angelique would work with Jeanette," Flo said.

Out of all the hairdressers in France, Flo had picked the one who hated Americans the most and was sending Mia straight into her clutches. Valentin nodded and held his arm out, signaling to Angelique, who was standing behind a chair. Flo wore a large smile on her face and nodded her head. Mia threw her shoulders back and tried her hardest to walk with confidence and sophistication.

Mia didn't say a word as she took a seat in Angelique's chair. The woman was mumbling in French and Mia was glad she couldn't understand the words.

Angelique spoke louder, switching to English. "Valentin was right," she said. "These are cheap extensions. Did you get them in this city?"

Mia shook her head. Angelique let out a sigh.

"Well, what do you want? I am not a mind reader."

Trying her hardest, Mia mustered up the best accent she could.

"Whatever you think looks best," she said.

Mia looked at Angelique in the mirror; the woman was frowning and examining Mia's head. Mia felt a moment's relief that her accent didn't draw suspicion.

"I'm going to try my best to remove these and then we will see what we have to work with," Angelique said.

Mia nodded and the woman left her to get whatever supplies she needed. Mia kept her eyes glued to the mirror and was thrilled to see Flo leaving her chair and approaching her. Mia turned to see the older woman, who was quick to speak in a low whisper.

"Small steps," Flo said. "Trust me, you're fine. Remember your lessons."

She reached up and squeezed Mia's hand before returning to Valentin. Angelique returned with a basket of oils whose labels were in French. She pulled up Mia's real hair and started rubbing liquids on her scalp in a less-than-friendly manner.

"I don't know how you stand her company," Angelique said. "She ran promising fair treatment of everyone, yet continues to offer support to America. She is a hypocrite and I cannot wait until the next election when she is voted out of office. Then maybe someone with actual morals will replace her."

"She is a good woman," Mia said.

"And I know her guards can hear me," Angelique said. "And I don't care. This is the free world. They cannot stifle my opinions."

Mia let out a small yelp as Angelique tugged on her hair.

"In my eyes if you support her you are just as bad as her," Angelique said. "Do you have any children?"

Mia shook her head.

"Keep still," Angelique said, grabbing the sides of Mia's face.

"No," Mia said.

"If you did would you throw them away like garbage or sell them to a complete stranger?"

Mia was all too familiar with the system Angelique was describing.

"No," Mia said.

"Then why are you going with her?"

Every bit of Mia wanted to scream at this rude woman, to tell her that Mia was going back to put a stop to the very system she was describing, but doing so would jeopardize the mission. Defending herself to a stranger was not worth that compromise.

"I trust her," Mia said.

"Blind faith is no way to live," Angelique said.

Mia let out another cry and the extra hair came out from her head in Angelique's hands. Mia felt the back of her head, expecting to see blood on her fingers, but instead there was oil.

"Come with me," Angelique said.

She didn't wait for Mia before walking toward the back of the shop. Mia followed her toward a chair with its back to a sink.

"I have to wash your hair now," Angelique said. "You must look perfect for the Americans."

She wore a smug smile and Mia felt her frustration grow. Mia took a seat and leaned back. The water was too hot, but Mia didn't complain. She was glad the noise from the sink blocked out whatever Angelique had to say.

This woman could not have been more wrong about Flo or Mia. It wasn't fair for her to judge them so harshly. Mia wanted to stand up for herself, to let the world know what her intentions were. Then she wondered what would happen if she did. Sneaking into America would no longer be a possibility. Ending the Registry would be off the table, and that was much more important than the opinion of another.

Like the water washing away the oils from Mia's scalp, some things became clear to her now. If she were a symbol to the world of what was wrong in her home country she wouldn't have to deal with this persecution. But Mia wanted more than that. She was ready to have a real place in the upcoming rebellion. That was much more valuable than anyone's opinion of her.

Mia let her eyes close. She understood one of Flo's lessons. Caring about other people's opinions did not matter because Mia knew what she represented to herself, and that was enough for her.

Chapter 17

I've given up driving at night and am avoiding all main roads. My last contact with my poor Wallace was four weeks ago now. If that marks the start of the downfall of America, nature is starting to reclaim what we took from her. It is hard to find a building with running water or electricity. I am happy the winter months haven't set in.

—The diary of Megan Jean

Everyone was making last-minute preparations for the trip tomorrow and Mia was left alone for dinner. She took in the beauty of the dining room once more before heading up to her room. Mia hoped sleep would come easily that night but was doubtful.

She stood in front of her bathroom mirror and examined her new hairstyle. It was just her real hair this time. Mia was surprised it had grown in this much, since she'd only chopped it off less than three months ago. At the front it came just to her chin but angled backward, with lots of volume at the crown. A style Mia was certain she would be unable to replicate every day but for the time being looked effortless.

Staring in the mirror had once been Mia's favorite way to pass the time, but the reflection looking at her now was not that of a vain, naïve little girl obsessed with landing a husband. Mia wasn't sure who she was yet, but after this afternoon she knew she was well on her way to figuring it out.

A knock on her bedroom door broke Mia's concentration. She went to answer and was thrilled to see Flo on the other side. The woman's blond hair looked more prominent now, but that was the only noticeable change.

"You did fabulous today," Flo said. "May I come in?"

"Please," Mia said.

The prime minister walked in and sat down on Mia's bed.

"I'm surprised nobody commented on my accent," Mia said. "It wasn't flawless."

"I may have told them my guest suffered from a speech impediment and not to make note of it," Flo said.

Mia laughed a little at Flo's ingenuity.

"I have to say I think it is good enough to fool an American," Flo said. "And everyone traveling with us tomorrow knows of our plans."

"When I first arrived you said I would be part of those plans," Mia said.

"And you will," Flo said. "Right now there isn't much to discuss. We land in America and we will be escorted across the country to the capital. Then I will attend your husband's wedding while the group breaks into the Mission and destroys the Registry. Then you will be broadcast on television and share your story with the world, complete with proof that you are who you say you are."

"It doesn't sound like I have much of an active role," Mia said.

"You have complete discretion over whatever words you choose, dear," Flo said. "And what you say is the most critical part of all of this. Never underestimate the power of words. In the event we are unable to wipe out the Registry your words might still spark a rebellion. You are a leader, Mia."

Warmth made its way through Mia. "I will be sure to let everyone know your role," Mia said. "I promise."

"That is for you to decide," Flo said. "Don't think it necessary. I did not sign up for this for the glory. I only want to help people."

"Isn't it hard to listen to people like Angelique all the time?"

"You did well with her today," Flo said.

"It was like there was something growing inside me," Mia said. "All her anger only fueled my resolution and I stopped caring, only for a moment, what she thought, because I knew the truth. That was enough for me."

"You're starting to answer those questions we've talked about," Flo said.

"I suppose so," Mia said.

"Beauty may fade, intellect dulls, but your spirit, that will live on forever," Flo said.

Mia reached out and wrapped her arms around Flo. The woman returned her embrace.

"Try not to worry," Flo said. "I know that you are facing the world right now and at such a young age it must be even more difficult. Never forget who you have at your side."

Flo released Mia and stood up. Mia did the same, not wanting the woman to leave.

"Wait," Mia said.

Flo paused.

"Thank you," Mia said. "For your kindness and your inspiration."

"Repay me by passing it on to the world," Flo said.

Flo walked to the door, stopping once she reached the handle.

"I thought you might want some company tonight," Flo said.

She pulled open the door and standing behind it were Andrew and Carter, both dressed in black attire.

"I will see the three of you in the morning," Flo said.

The two boys walked into the room and Flo shut the door behind her. Mia couldn't stop the smile from coming onto her face and ran toward Andrew, throwing her arms around his neck. He wrapped his around her back and lifted her up in the air. When he set her down she pulled away, locking eyes with him as he leaned down and gave her a light kiss.

"I knew I shouldn't have come," Carter said.

Mia pushed off of Andrew and went for her friend. She didn't give Carter a chance to back away and pulled him in for an equally powerful hug.

"I bet mine doesn't end with a kiss though," he said.

Mia ignored his comment and squeezed harder before releasing him.

"You know tomorrow might be it," Carter said. "There's a chance we'll land and RAG agents will be waiting to arrest us."

"Don't think that way," Mia said.

"I'm serious," Carter said. "It could be our last night on earth."

"Every night could be our last night," Andrew said.

Mia frowned. She looked at the two men. They had been through so much together. She did not think tomorrow was the end, but if it was she couldn't think of two people she would rather spend her last night with.

Chapter 18

A fire broke out and we were forced to leave DC. Our group is traveling in a caravan to Washington State, to the general's home city. A radio broadcast has been set up, urging other survivors to meet us there.

—The journal of Isaac Ryland

The plane ride was a new experience for Andrew. The sensation of flight was so different when there were windows to view the skies. He sat in the back with the other bodyguards, while Mia and Madame Martineau were closer to the front. Albin sat in the middle, as if trapped between two stations. He was posing as Madame Martineau's escort for the event.

"I've never been in a plane before," Carter said.

"We flew out here," Zack said.

"It wasn't like this," Carter responded.

"You were in a helicopter once," Andrew said.

"That didn't end so well," Carter said.

Andrew had been too busy this past week to notice Carter's moods, and apparently Carter had been too busy to remember that he was mad about something. Andrew had even forgotten about Carter's insane proclamation that his dad was still alive. Last night Carter had been in good spirits and Andrew hoped that would continue. It made things easier.

Things were good between Andrew and Mia too. After he'd promised not to keep her in the dark any longer she seemed more at ease around him. It was hard not to sit next to her now, but in the event the pilot or one of his staff walked around the positions needed to look legit.

"Is there any word from Affinity?" Andrew asked. "Is the grand commander wearing the camera pin?"

"He's wearing it," Zack said. "But he hasn't gone to the server yet, so no password. We're confident he will. There are still more than two weeks."

Two weeks. It wasn't that much time but it felt like an eternity. Andrew closed his eyes. In two weeks the whole world could change. He didn't care about that as much as he cared about his personal world changing. Mia would have more time for them. They could be a couple, out in the open. As soon as the Registry was destroyed the group would retreat back to Affinity headquarters in Central America. Andrew knew there would be more missions, but Mia wouldn't be as crucial a part. The two of them could start their lives together.

"Then what?" Carter asked.

"Who knows?" Zack asked. "Peace, hopefully."

Andrew scoffed. Peace was more of an idea than a plausible reality.

"You find that hard to believe?" Zack asked.

Andrew did not want to explain his theories on the world. He hadn't meant to make his disapproval audible.

"Everything is random," Andrew said. "I wouldn't be here if Mia hadn't tricked me into helping her in the first place. You wouldn't be here if Mia hadn't stumbled upon your website."

"We have more control than you think," Zack said.

"What's that supposed to mean?"

"Mia is important," Zack said. "Too important to leave to chance."

Carter unbuckled his seat belt. Andrew thought he looked ill.

"I'm going to the bathroom," Carter said.

Carter walked away before Andrew or Zack could comment.

"That kid has to get over Mia picking you over him," Zack said.

Andrew didn't care about that at the moment. And he didn't think that was what was bothering Carter.

"Answer the question," he said. "How was it not by chance Mia contacted Affinity?"

Zack fidgeted in his seat. Andrew glared at the man, not ready to let him off the hook.

"I shouldn't have said anything," Zack said.

"Well you did, so finish your thought," Andrew replied.

"Any person Mia tried to reach out to would have led to us," Zack said. "She clicked on a link for a vacation, but that computer was wired for Affinity's interception."

Everything was staged. Andrew had been lied to. Mia had been lied to. It didn't make sense.

"How could you do that?"

"We have lots of contacts inside America, including Roderick Rowe. We were the ones who found out Mia was in Saint Louis. We instructed him to pick her up."

"Does Carter know?"

"No," Zack said. "It's for the best that you keep this between the two of us."

"Did you know about the militia?" Andrew asked.

He felt his rage starting to bubble. His fists clenched and he wanted to knock Zack in the side of the head. The man finally returned Andrew's gaze.

"I promise you we did not," Zack said. "As far as Affinity was aware all three of you died with Roderick Rowe before crossing the border. We were shocked when you arrived."

"Why didn't you tell us the truth then?"

"Look, we don't have time for this. Everything is going according to plan. I need you to keep it that way. If you let Mia know, or Carter know, it could ruin everything we've been working toward."

"They deserve the truth."

"And you can tell them," Zack said. "Once we're all safely back in Affinity. We had our reasons for keeping you in the dark. But if you tell Mia about this it will only upset her. There's a lot riding on her shoulders. Do you want to cause her any more worry?"

Andrew looked toward the front of the plane. He could see Mia talking with Madame Martineau. He heard her laugh. She was finding some comfort and Andrew wouldn't be the one to take it away. He thought of the promise he'd made to Mia: no more secrets. He told himself keeping this from her wasn't a secret. He was only delaying the truth, not lying.

Carter sat back down and buckled his seat belt. Andrew could feel Zack's eyes on him, waiting for confirmation. Andrew looked down at his own clenched fist; the knuckles had turned white. He forced his palm open and let his hand relax. He wasn't that person anymore. Andrew wasn't a fighter. He was a protector. Keeping this secret from Mia was necessary at the moment. He looked toward Zack and gave him a slow nod, which the blond man returned.

Andrew's attention remained on Mia the rest of the flight. He promised himself that as soon as the Registry was destroyed he would get all the answers he needed and tell Mia everything.

Chapter 19

I made a new friend. Another woman, who lost her whole family. She says this was caused by a vaccination the government mandated that everyone receive. I asked her why she is still alive and she is unsure why she was so lucky. Knowing the reason for America's fate does not comfort me.

—The diary of Megan Jean

The plane touched down and Mia felt the numbness disappear from her fingers. The reality was setting in: Mia was back in the most dangerous place in the world for her. She gave Flo a nervous smile, but the woman was busy looking at her phone. Mia watched as she powered the device down. Flo unbuckled her seat belt, even though the plane was still moving, and went to a safe seat at the front of the aircraft. Mia watched as she typed in a combination and dropped her phone inside. Next she pulled out two bags.

"Follow me," Flo said. "You will want to hear this."

Zack, Andrew, Carter, Jesse, and Bryan were sitting in the back of the plane. All of them were dressed in black suits and all of their faces remained blank. Flo handed one of the bags to Zack, who pulled out a smaller bag with his name on it. From inside the smaller bag he pulled out some paperwork and a cellular phone.

"Preapproved American cellular phones," Flo said. "Each of you take one. All of the other numbers are programmed inside already so you can contact each other. I managed to find someone willing to install them all with GPS too, so you can locate each other if you highlight the contact and hold down the number seven. I know you have all studied your identities carefully. Inside you will find your travel visas and proof-of-service cards. From here on out we need to exercise the utmost caution. No unnecessary speaking of our plans. Good luck."

Flo started back for her seat. Mia smiled at Andrew, but he glanced away, looking at his phone. Mia was hurt a little; she knew why he was getting into character already, but she would have appreciated one more stolen glance. She let out a sigh and followed Flo to the front of the plane. The two women sat back down and buckled their safety belts. Albin joined them in a third seat, ready to play the part of Flo's escort.

"Before I forget," Flo said. "Here."

She handed Mia a small black phone.

"This one is special," Flo said. "There are some extra numbers stored in there and it has international capabilities in case something arises and you need to flee. I also didn't want the GPS enabled for your phone. If anything happens you can find the rest of the group, but they cannot find you."

"Isn't that dangerous?"

"You have good instincts," Flo said. "I trust that if we are separated you will use your judgment in locating the rest of the group. On the other hand, if one of us is caught I don't want our phones to let the enemy locate you."

Mia nodded her head. She dropped the small black phone into her purse and caught a glimpse of her travel documentation. Flo doubted it would be requested, but Mia had it at her disposal nonetheless. The plane came to a stop and Mia smoothed out her pastel purple pantsuit. She picked up her wide-brimmed white sun hat and placed it on her head. Flo told her it made her look exotic and elegant, drawing attention away from her face, but Mia was not convinced.

The flight attendant came out of the cockpit and Mia caught a glimpse of the pilot putting on his coat before the door slammed shut.

"Prime Minister Martineau, I trust you had a safe flight?" the fligh attendant asked.

Mia studied his French accent, hoping to pick up on any last details before she needed to switch over.

"I did," Flo said. "Thank you."

"Our travel visas do not permit our presence in America," he said. "As previously arranged we will continue on to Canada and retrieve you at the airport closest to the American capital in fifteen days. Anything you choose to leave on the plane will be safeguarded until your return."

"Thank you," Flo said.

"The same courtesy is extended to your guests," he said.

Flo stood up again and kissed the attendant on each cheek. Mia appreciated how Flo treated everyone around her with dignity and respect. Even though she was the prime minister of a country, she held nobody above herself.

The men came up from the back of the plane. Zack and Jesse walked in front of the women, ready to greet whoever was on the other side of the plane's door. Mia heard the airlock go off and sunshine fell inside the aircraft. A man in a black suit walked aboard. A RAG agent. Recovery of Abducted Girls workers did much more than simply look for runaways. Mia knew they would be her escorts, but the last time she'd met with one he had died by her hand, and the image of smashing his skull in with a rock came flooding back.

"Welcome to America," he said.

He tried to walk around Zack, but the blond man blocked his move.

"I am in charge of the prime minister's security," Zack said.

"Oh yes. All of our guests are escorted by American soldiers," the agent said. "Do you and your men have papers? I hope you don't mind my verification of your identities."

"Not at all," Zack said.

He turned around and the group of men handed him their passports.

"I have Florence Martineau, Albin Fabre, and Jonathan Jolivett on my passenger list. Does that correspond with your party?"

"It's Jeanette Jolivett," Zack said.

Mia didn't dare look over at the agent. She could feel his eyes on her; he was not expecting a second female on his passenger list.

"We were told Jonathan," he said. "You're escorting a young woman as well?"

"We do our job as instructed," Zack said. "And I am sure you do the same. Does that include hassling the prime minister's escorts?"

Mia glanced out of the corner of her eye at Zack and the agent. The agent was about the same size as Zack, with brown hair. The two were in a standoff, and Mia hoped Zack would win out.

"Then I don't suppose her verification is necessary," he said. "Please stay on the plane for a few minutes while I check you and your men."

Mia knew Affinity had placed all the names in the government's online database. Still, she was nervous the hack had been caught and the names booted out. The whole plane remained silent. Flo placed a hand on Mia's arm.

"Don't look nervous," she said. "This was expected. We don't want to give them a reason to suspect anything."

"I am nervous though," Mia said. "This is a stupid idea."

"All the good ideas are," Albin said.

Mia told herself to breathe. The man returned and handed Zack the stack of passports.

"Welcome back to America, Captain Mishler," the RAG agent

said. "You may call me Agent Barker. I hope you take no offense at our screening."

"None at all," Zack said. "In fact I find it commendable."

"Please," Agent Barker said, "exit the plane."

Zack nodded and the agent led the way. Zack and Jesse followed, then Flo, Albin, and Mia. Carter, Andrew, and Bryan took up the rear. They walked down steps and Mia saw their luggage being loaded into two black SUVs on the runway. The air was thick with humidity; Mia had never been to the Southeast Area before and she felt a little homesick for her Midwestern weather for the first time since she'd left.

"You and your party must ride with me in the first car," Agent Barker said to Flo. "Your security detail will follow in the second."

"No," Zack said.

"I must brief the prime minister on the rules," Agent Barker said.

"Captain, I am certain our hosts will not let harm come our way," Flo said. "Please, these are your countrymen, after all."

Zack could not come up with a rationale for objecting and the security detail moved to the second SUV. Agent Barker opened the door and Mia climbed inside. The seats were not set up as she expected. Instead of both rows facing forward, there was one facing backward, so the passengers could speak to one another face-to-face. Flo took a seat next to her while Albin sat across from them with Agent Barker. Whoever the driver was, he did not turn around and wasted no time taking off.

"I am sure you are exhausted from your travels," Agent Barker said.

"Yes," Flo said. "We are all eager to reach the hotel."

The agent didn't hide his eye roll. Mia was certain he would continue to make his attitude toward women well known.

"There is a very strict schedule we must stick to," Agent Barker said. "We are five hours away from your lodging for the evening."

"Five hours after that flight?" Albin asked.

The agent ignored his question. Mia looked to Flo, who did not seem fazed by Agent Barker's lack of respect.

"I am certain you memorized the instruction packet sent to your country but I must review some of our country's concerns."

"Please do," Flo said.

Agent Barker shook his head a little and wet his lips before continuing. "No American citizen is to know you are here or your station. Mr. Fabre must appear to be the important party. You are to be seen as his wife, and Ms. Jolivett your daughter. Do you understand?"

"Absolutely," Flo said.

"The grand commander has a detailed itinerary for you. Since your country is to our east and we did not want your plane flying over our land you were forced to land across the country from your final destination. The capital is in the Northwest Area, over three thousand miles away. Tonight you will stay in your hotel room, where dinner will be provided. Tomorrow we leave for the capital. Along the way there are a number of places you have been granted access to visit. The whole trip is scheduled to take seven days. Once we arrive in the capital all of your time will be scheduled and the rules do not change. Tomorrow you will see a facility used to house young men."

"One of your orphanages?" Flo asked.

"We don't use that term," Agent Barker said. " 'Home for young men' is more appropriate. Grand Commander hopes you will be satisfied with everything you see in America and report the results of your trip to other global leaders."

"I believe I will," Flo said.

The car went quiet. The agent leaned back and raised a corner of his lips.

"How could your country elect a woman?" Agent Barker asked.

"Excuse me?" Flo said.

"I am a professional," he said. "But you are not my equal, and it is disgusting that I must treat you with any respect."

"Is this the sort of behavior your grand commander wishes me to report?" Flo asked, unruffled.

"I . . . apologize," Agent Barker said.

"Well, you have already broken your façade of respect for me, so let's take a moment and get it out of the way," Flo said. "Please use this car ride to discuss any of your concerns."

"Why did you bring a teenage girl with you?" Agent Barker asked.

"Jeanette?" Flo asked. "She is a friend's daughter studying human rights at university. I thought this trip would give her a unique perspective. Show her that all the awful things her professors say about Americans' treatment of young women simply aren't true. Though, I could have made a poor choice here."

"You don't belong in school," Agent Barker said. "You should be married by now, taking care of your husband."

Mia didn't acknowledge the agent. She kept her eyes glued to the window.

"It is rude to ignore someone speaking to you," he said.

"On this I have to agree with the young agent," Flo said.

Mia closed her eyes and moved her head toward the man, then popped open her eyelids; she didn't dare break away from his gaze. His eyes left her face and went up and down her body.

"If you were American you would go for a pretty penny in the Registry," he said. "It's a shame really. Your life would be much less complicated."

Rage was building inside Mia. Her life was complicated because of the Registry and this man was blind to that. She didn't know if she could keep her French accent and hold her voice at a normal volume, so she pressed her lips shut.

"Quiet," he said. "You really would have made an excellent wife here."

"That is quite enough, Agent Barker," Flo said.

The agent had a smug look on his face and Mia went back to avoiding his eyes. She looked out the window, hoping that the time would fly by but knowing the ride would drag on.

The car came to a stop. The driver exited and the side door opened.

"Wait here," Agent Barker said. "I'll come back with your room keys."

He exited the vehicle and Mia let the air out of her lungs. She wanted to voice her frustration but the trio kept quiet, knowing every area they were in was likely bugged.

"Well, that went as expected," Flo said.

Albin let out a yawn.

"The time change affected me more than I thought it would," he said. "I think we will all feel a little better after some sleep."

Even in the air-conditioned vehicle Mia could feel sweat forming on her forehead. She tried to focus on her breathing and felt her body cool down. This mission was bigger than her ideals or the idiot agent's outlook on women. Agent Barker's views didn't matter. In only a few short weeks the Registry would no longer exist and he would have to deal with a new way of life.

Chapter 20

We arrived to see that about one thousand survivors had picked up our message and traveled to our destination. Almost all of them are soldiers and they are celebrating new faces. Something is wrong though; the men outnumber the women at least ten to one, if not more. The general seems confident more will come, but it seems to me the only people who survived this poisoning are people who were not present.

—The journal of Isaac Ryland

The Mission was becoming a second home to Grant. He didn't appreciate being summoned at Ian's beck and call but was getting used to the building. He knocked on the door to Ian's office and let himself inside. He couldn't wait until this room belonged to him. Ian was behind his desk and waved Grant over. The old man was on the phone.

"Splendid," he said. "Please keep me up to date on their travels."

Grant sat down and smoothed out his striped shorts. They were black and white with small red lines. He wore a light red sweater to match. Grant leaned back in the chair and brought his foot up to his knee. He noticed a scuff in his black penny loafers and tried to rub it out.

"Did you look into the backstory?" Ian asked. "Remember,

these people are our allies. I don't think it's anything to worry about as long as everything checks out all right. Some information may get lost in translation."

The scuff was coming out and Grant was glad to have a way to hide his interest in Ian's conversation. He wondered what problem the grand commander was overlooking now.

"Thank you," Ian said. "Good-bye."

He set the phone down and wasted no time engaging Grant in conversation.

"Our international guests are starting to arrive."

"Is there a problem?"

"No," Ian said. "A typo on one of the forms. Three of the nine countries have arrived. They will be here by the end of the week."

"Could I take a look at who is coming?" Grant asked. "I would like to memorize their information."

"You only have to worry about the countries' leaders," Ian said, "not their escorts."

"I want to use everything at my disposal to charm them," Grant said.

This was the third time he had made this request. Grant was pleased when Ian opened his desk drawer and pulled out a flash drive.

"Since you've asked so nicely," Ian said. "Is your home coming along?"

"Everything will be perfect for the wedding," Grant said.

"Tamara is excited," Ian said. "It's all she'll speak of."

"Is that why you called me down here today?"

"Of course not," Ian said. "I scheduled another taping of *The Greg Finnegan Show*. You haven't been in public for almost two weeks. He is going to interview you about the wedding."

Grant smiled through his teeth. He hated Greg Finnegan and his television show. It was the most watched program in all of America and the people regarded Finnegan as their nightly source for the most important news. The man was a flake though, and Grant wished he could limit their interaction.

"You could have phoned to tell me that," Grant said.

"The last time I did that you had an excuse why you couldn't come down," Ian said. "This way you're already here. Besides, the taping will take place in the Mission. The people will become comfortable seeing you here. Trust me when I say this may appear minor, but we want the transition as smooth as possible."

"Instead of worrying about our citizens," Grant said, "I was hoping you could tell me more about the position itself. What do I have left to learn?"

"Everything else you will learn over the next few years," Ian said, "watching me."

"What about the security codes?" Grant asked. "I think I've earned your trust."

"I am the only one who knows those," Ian said.

He raised a white eyebrow at Grant.

Grant smiled politely and nodded. "My concern is about an accident though," he said. "What if you meet an untimely death? What would happen then?"

"I have thought about that before," Ian said. "I hope you would create a copy of the information the public uses before a group of renegades have the chance to hack those. You would have the authority to create a new master list and I hope you would act quickly."

"But those are vulnerable to attack," Grant said.

"Nothing will happen to me," Ian said.

Outside of Grant's wanting control he could see that Ian's belief that he was infallible was a mistake. There was no use trying to talk sense into the man. Grant changed the subject.

"I see you are still wearing the American pin our French guests sent you," Grant said.

"I do like it," Ian said.

Grant let the smile linger on his lips, but he could not draw his eyes away from the pin. It represented everything Ian was doing wrong: accepting gifts from outsiders, caring too much about keeping the status quo instead of making America a better, stronger country. As soon as Grant had those codes he would rip that pin off of Ian's shirt and shove it down his throat.

Chapter 21

We received a radio message, urging people to head to Washington State. I keep thinking of my run-in with the other traveling party, but my new friend is insistent we join the new civilization emerging on the coast.

—The diary of Megan Jean

The sun flooded Mia's hotel room and she was happy to get out of bed. Whatever sleep had come to her the previous night had been minimal, and at least now she had an excuse to start getting ready for the day's activities.

She had become so obsessed with speaking in a French accent that even her internal monologue was producing one. Still, she hoped Agent Barker would have fewer questions today.

Mia showered and tried her best to style her hair. She found it strange the short hair took longer to get presentable than her long hair did. Once she was finished she dressed in a pair of orange wide-legged pants and a white short-sleeved blouse. She plopped her wide-brimmed hat on her head just as a knock on her door came. In the hall were Albin, Flo, and Agent Barker. Mia forced a smile before joining them in the hall, pulling her small suitcase behind her.

"Did you sleep well?" Albin asked.

"I miss France," Mia said.

She meant it too. The hotel room wasn't a single percent as exquisite as Flo's home. It was a tiny space with a small, uncomfortable mattress, but Mia knew that wasn't the reason for her lack of sleep.

"Well, maybe you shouldn't have come," Agent Barker said.

Flo turned around to defend Mia, but the agent was already starting down the hall.

"Where is the security?" Mia asked.

"They're waiting outside," Flo said. Under her breath she added, "It seems Agent Barker had them sleep as far away from us as possible."

"Why?" Mia whispered back.

"To prove he is in control," Albin said.

"We have a strict schedule," Agent Barker said. "Please keep up."

The trio broke off their conversation and followed the agent down the hall. They stayed on the first floor of the empty hotel and nobody noticed their presence. When the group went outside the two black SUVs were waiting. Agent Barker opened the door to one and climbed inside. The driver grabbed Mia's bag and loaded it into the rear.

"Where is our security?" Flo asked him.

The driver did not respond.

"Sir," Albin said. "Please answer the question."

"They are in the second car," he said. "Already loaded up."

Mia took note of the fact that the driver responded to Albin with ease yet ignored Flo altogether. She was more used to this behavior than the prime minister but had a feeling it wasn't affecting Flo in the slightest. Mia wished she had the older woman's self-control.

The three entered the SUV. Flo sat next to Agent Barker and Albin sat across from him, giving Mia the seat farthest from the man. She was grateful for that distance.

"We have an eight-and-a-half-hour drive," Agent Barker said. "Then we'll stop and tour a youth home. After that we'll drive four more hours and rest for the night. All your meals are scheduled."

"We didn't get breakfast," Flo said.

Agent Barker kept his eyes glued to Albin.

"There are pastries for you and your guests in the side compartment," he said.

Albin smiled and leaned over, coming back with a white box. He offered Flo the first choice, then Mia. She shook her head. There was no way her stomach could hold food. Albin shrugged and picked out a frosted treat before putting the box on the seat.

"They should be serving you," Agent Barker said.

"Can we keep it civil?" Flo said. "If you have such a problem with our ways maybe you can switch places with a member of my security? They have been much more agreeable."

Barker didn't look at Flo. Instead he tapped twice on the partition and the driver took off. Mia gazed out the tinted window. She didn't want to stop at the orphanage. More than anything else Mia wished this trip were over with.

"You look so familiar," Agent Barker said.

"I am in many pictures with the prime minister," Albin said.

"Not you," Barker said. "Jeanette."

Mia turned to face him.

"Where do I know you from?"

Her heart jumped in her throat. The man was examining her face and Mia tried her best not to tremble. The government might have destroyed all photographs of her, but if Agent Barker had been active during her escape there was no doubt her face had crossed his desk on many occasions.

"Jeanette used to model," Flo said. "Mainly cologne."

Barker laughed. "Cologne is for men," he said.

"Sorry for the translation issue," Albin said. "She means perfume."

"I bet you could sell a lot of things to men," Agent Barker said.

The car went silent.

"I value my mind more than my appearance," Mia said.

"That's a shame," Agent Barker replied.

He appeared content with the explanation and reached for the box of pastries.

"Tell me, are you married?" Albin asked.

"No," Agent Barker said. "I want to wait, maybe another ten years. My wife will be beautiful. Perfect."

"Then maybe you should stop speaking of things you have such little knowledge of," Albin said.

Agent Barker leaned back in his seat. He did not have a response and Mia was grateful. She went back to staring out the window, certain the agent's eyes were still fixed upon her. Mia closed her own, hoping sleep would come and take her away from the ill feeling that she would never make it across the country alive.

Chapter 22

I always prided myself on being an educated man, but now it appears a weakness. Brawn is more favored than brains in our new society and I am forced to keep my mouth shut as we work to build it.

—*The journal of Isaac Ryland*

The images on the flash drive were projected onto Grant's wall. He could use his hand to rifle through them and pull up the file that went with the corresponding face. There were nine countries invited, yet photographs were available of only the supreme leaders of the land. In total twenty-three guests were making their way to his country, and that did not include their American soldier escorts. Some groups had one or two, while others had as many as six or seven.

Grant had pulled all of their names and every one checked out. There were no girls around Mia's age on any of the manifests. Several of the groups reported bringing young men into the country with them and Grant wondered if Mia was back to posing as a male.

It had taken a few hours, but Grant had finally used the information to find the names of the RAG agents in charge of the foreign visitors. Six teams were already in the country. It made Grant's skin crawl to think America was being invaded like this. He picked up his phone and dialed the next number on his list of agents.

"Agent Fuller," the man said as he picked up the phone.

"Special Agent Fuller," Grant said. "This is Grant Marsden. I'm calling to check on the status of our guests."

There was silence for a moment on the other end.

"Is this a joke?" the agent asked.

"No," Grant said. "Please tell me, how are our foreign visitors?"

"Sir," Agent Fuller said. "It is an honor to hear from you; I'm one of your biggest supporters."

"Thank you," Grant said. Each of the four phone calls prior to this one had gone similarly. With each number he dialed, Grant's patience was spread thinner.

"Were there any problems or issues with our guests?" Grant asked.

He had his computer screen up with the information Ian had supplied. A photograph of the supreme leader of each country, along with the names and dates of birth of their civilian escorts, then information on the American soldiers escorting the parties.

"Problems? No, sir, none at all," the agent said.

"I know you are eager to please," Grant said. "But I want to hear all the details. Is everyone on the itinerary accounted for?"

"President Mannhouse's flight landed safely," Agent Fuller said. "He brought along his son Bradley. They appear content. No issues to report."

"No females in the group?"

"None, sir," Agent Fuller said.

Grant let out a sigh; another wasted phone call.

"I would love to take this time to tell you how inspiring I find your story. Everyone is expecting Grand Commander to announce you as his replacement and I think the country couldn't be left to better hands."

"Thank you for your time," Grant said.

"The way that you have overcome so much with your wife's pass-ing and how you have dedicated your life to bettering our armed services are an inspiration. I would love to—"

Grant hung up the phone. He didn't care about his celebrity status. There were too many coincidences going on at the moment and Grant was certain Mia was on her way into the country. The last name on his list to call was an Agent Barker. Grant pulled up the picture of the French leader and rolled his eyes as he saw the woman's picture on his screen. Her itinerary listed two male companions. Grant dialed Agent Barker's phone number.

"Agent Barker," the man said.

"Hello. This is Grant Marsden. I am phoning to check on the status of our international guests."

"This is . . . *the* Grant Marsden?"

"Yes," Grant said. "Now, how are my guests doing?"

"Sir," Agent Barker said, "this is truly a privilege to hear from you. I—"

"Thank you for your words," Grant said, interrupting. "But my time is limited. How is your trip?"

"Yes, sir, of course. We're stopped at a gas station right now," the agent said. "Refueling for the rest of the trek. We are an hour away from visiting the youth home."

"I don't care about your itinerary," Grant said. "I want to know about the visitors. Were there any issues?"

"None other than the ones I've already reported," Agent Barker said.

"Please," Grant said, "give me those details."

Grant sat up in his chair. He felt his heart skip a beat with excite-ment.

"The young man listed on the guest list was in fact a young woman," Agent Barker said.

"Can you take a photograph of this woman and send it to me?" Grant asked.

"We don't have that type of technology," Agent Barker said.

Grant rolled his eyes in frustration over the technology ban. "Describe her," Grant said.

"Shorter dark blond hair," Agent Barker said. "Blue eyes, average height, quiet."

"Is she very pretty?" Grant asked.

The agent didn't respond at first.

"I've been annoyed at having to escort a female leader," Agent Barker said. "But if I think about it, I would say she is stunning."

"Do you have a GPS locator?" Grant asked.

"I haven't seen one of those since my time in service," Agent Barker said.

"Do you know your exact location?" Grant asked.

"I can give you the location of the youth home we're visiting and the hotel we're staying at tonight," Agent Barker said.

"You're in the Southwest Area?" Grant asked.

He pulled up the itinerary of this group on his computer screen. It was at least a five-hour flight away.

"Yes," Agent Barker said. "Should I be concerned?"

"Not at all," Grant said.

The last thing Grant wanted was for Mia's presence to become public knowledge.

"One last question," Grant asked. "The soldiers escorting the group; I see there are five listed. Is one of them young, tall, and lean, with dark hair and eyes?"

"Yes," Agent Barker said. "I haven't had a lot of conversation with the escorts."

Mia and Andrew were together, traveling with the French. Grant slammed his fist down on his desk. He wasn't sure if it was in triumph at finding them or in aggravation over their attempt to infiltrate America.

"Sir," Agent Barker said, "does this affect our schedule?"

Grant did not want Mia to know he was onto them. He also technically had no authority over this RAG agent and didn't want Barker calling his superiors and notifying them. This had to be taken care of personally.

"No," Grant said. "Proceed as normal."

Grant hung up the phone. He jumped up from his desk and ran out of his office. He spotted his butler, Brandon, in the hallway.

"Make the arrangements for my plane," Grant said. "I want to land as close as possible to the Hotel Austin in the Southwest Area."

"Yes, sir," Brandon said.

Grant appreciated that he didn't ask many questions. Grant went toward the front door and paused by the mirror hanging in the hall. He was wearing a navy blue cashmere sweater with navy and green checked pants. It would have to do; Grant didn't have the time to change. Tonight he would meet an unsuspecting Amelia Morrissey in her hotel room and safely dispose of her forever.

Chapter 23

I have convinced my friend to avoid joining the group for the past two months, but she has announced she is going with or without me. I do not want to stay out here alone but am uneasy about whatever this new regime has to offer.

—The diary of Megan Jean

The car came to a stop and Mia's eyes flipped open. She did not feel any more rested.

"I need to secure the perimeter," Agent Barker said. "I'm sure your security team will want to join me. Please remain in the vehicle."

He exited the SUV without waiting for a response. Mia rubbed her eyes, hoping to wake up more.

"Where are we?" she asked.

"The youth home," Flo said.

Under normal circumstances, Mia would have been curious to see these places, but with the task of destroying the Registry looming over her head she was focusing hard on calming her nerves. Spending time around people she didn't know was not helping her situation.

"Why couldn't we have flown to the capital in an American plane after we landed?" Mia asked.

"Because then I wouldn't get the chance to complete my good-will mission," Flo said. "I need to report back all my findings to my government and you wouldn't get this firsthand knowledge that is necessary for your education."

Mia's attention was diverted when she saw Andrew and Carter walk past the tinted windows. She leaned closer to the door and watched as they circled the building. Mia had expected a big city, or at least a city after all, but the youth home was just a long building surrounded by dirt and loose gravel.

"I pictured these being closer to civilization," Mia said.

"We've been driving on dirt roads for over an hour," Albin said. "I am surprised you slept."

"I didn't sleep much last night," Mia said. "How long was I asleep for?"

Albin checked his watch.

"Almost nine hours," he said.

This information woke Mia up even more. At first she didn't believe Albin. There was no way the car would have lasted that long without stopping. These were American vehicles and required fuel.

"How did the car last that long without stopping for gas?" Mia asked.

"We did stop," Flo said. "Twice. We are bordering the Midwest area now and not a lot of stations are along the way so there are gas cans in the back. This is our last stop, so I would make sure you use the restrooms while we are here."

Mia wondered where they were. She closed her eyes and tried to picture the American territories. She wasn't that skilled with geography and wished she could get her hands on an actual map.

"It will be quick," Flo said. "Then we will continue on our way."

Flo's statement broke Mia's concentration. Her attention returned to the building. Andrew had spoken a little about his time in an orphanage and none of it sounded pleasant. The French children were taken care of and Mia thought the American boys would prove a sharp contrast. She did not want to try to keep calm while viewing children in deplorable states.

"Think of this as a learning experience," Flo said. "You should always want to help those less fortunate than you, and who is in more need of care than abandoned children?"

Pangs of guilt worked their way toward Mia's heart. Her face warmed as she looked into Flo's eyes. This was the type of person she wanted to become. Selfless, but self-aware at the same time.

"That's odd," Albin said.

Mia's attention shifted outside the window. Andrew's group was nearing the building, but behind them were seven additional RAG agents, plus the two who had been driving the SUVs, bringing their total to fifteen. Flo's security was outnumbered two to one.

"Why are there so many of them now?" Mia asked.

"They want to make sure they stay in control," Flo said. "We must have picked up an additional SUV."

"Why all this protection?" Mia lowered her voice and continued. "Do you think they suspect something?"

Flo raised her finger to her lips, urging Mia to stay quiet. Mia felt bad for her slipup, but she wanted to know the answer.

"Both of you stop," Flo said. "I am sure this is standard procedure."

Mia watched as the group walked away from the car. She assumed every one of them was armed and wondered if Zack and Andrew had the same protection.

"Did they take away our guards' weapons?" Mia asked.

"Not that I'm aware of," Flo said. "They won't disarm their own countrymen."

If the RAG agents' numbers were only meant to intimidate it was working. Mia hoped her men would keep their cool. She spotted Agent Barker heading back toward the car and turned away from the window; hoping to appear uninterested, she stared at her nails. He pulled open the car door.

"Everything looks good," Agent Barker said. "We're ready for you."

Mia tried to focus her thoughts on the young men she was about to meet. With any luck their lives would soon be changed forever. Mia needed to focus on that and ignore whatever dreadful conditions she was about to encounter.

Chapter 24

Our new society is coming along. We are up to almost five thousand members and more come every day. Everyone except for me is the same age and from a military background. I've brought this fact up to the general, who continues to focus on the now and not the future.

—The journal of Isaac Ryland

The RAG agents wore sunglasses. Andrew was sure their suits were made of lower-quality material, but outside of that minor detail he fit right in with them.

"So are you still in the middle of your service?" one of them asked. Andrew nodded.

"I figured," he said. "You have the look of someone with a lot left to lose still. Once your time is over you'll start to relax. My name is Quillian; I just got out last year. France is a sweet station. I bet you don't see a whole lot of violence though."

"How did you get the RAG position?" Andrew asked. He'd always heard the RAG agents were the best of the best.

Agent Quillian raised his eyebrows a few times in a row. "I saved my commander's life," he said. "An armed civilian in Canada tried to shoot him. I spotted the man in time and took him out. A single shot through the forehead. I have awesome aim. So once I was done my commander pulled some strings for me."

"You were stationed in Canada?" Andrew asked. Canada was America's closest ally; he didn't think many troops were stationed there.

"For a year," he said. "Real far north. Apparently people get a little forgetful about who their friends are when they're surrounded by cold all the time."

"Agent Quillian," another RAG agent said. "Please keep conversation to a minimum."

The young RAG agent stopped talking to Andrew and went back toward his unit.

"Hey," Carter said. "I still need to talk to you . . . alone."

Another RAG agent walked by and Andrew watched the man walk toward the building.

"We're not alone now," Andrew said.

"It's about my dad," Carter said. "We need to make a plan."

Andrew looked at Carter. The blond man's jaw was clenched. His eyes burned into Andrew. Andrew didn't have time to explain to Carter that his father was dead.

"Later," Andrew said. "Come on, we have to get moving."

Carter sped up, not waiting for Andrew. The two had always had a contentious relationship, most likely spurred on by the fact that they both were interested in Mia at one point. Andrew guessed he did consider Carter a friend though. He was curious why Carter was so certain Rod was alive. Zack stopped at the door to the orphanage. The rest of the crew lined up next to him, waiting for Mia and Florence to exit their vehicle.

When Andrew was a youth in one of these homes he didn't have any friends. During his time on the fighting circuit nobody had bothered to get to know one another. There was a good chance that you would end up in the ring on opposite sides and you would have to end up killing your opponent. The experience had made him so hard he had never socialized with the other boys when he ended up at Mia's father's farm. Andrew wasn't sure he knew how to be someone's friend.

"Where are all the boys?" Carter asked.

Zack gave him a stern look.

"Soldier, I'm surprised to hear you speak so freely," Agent Barker said. "Your command unit seems to have a lot of relaxed regulations."

"This is a private mission," Zack said. "Private Logan knows better than to speak out of turn, but he does have a point."

Neither Carter nor Zack had ever had to live in one of these units. Andrew's had been in an urban environment, but he did remember there were always boys running around. He figured being in the middle of nowhere would make them more inclined to make noise.

"The prime minister's tour is limited to facilities only," Agent Barker said. "The young men who live here have been sent away for the day."

Andrew was pleased to hear that. During his stay he had been lucky if he showered once a week. It was the same for everyone staying in the overcrowded structure. This would be easier to get through if he didn't have to see poor, dirty children. He gulped and came to a realization: he was nervous.

The roof leaked water onto Andrew's bed, waking him up. As soon as the rain stopped he could climb outside and patch the holes. He was almost thirteen, about to get discharged into the real world and more than capable of balancing outside. He deserved to spend his final days there in a bed that wasn't constantly wet.

Andrew sat up. The rest of his classmates were sleeping. He heard one of the other boys snoring across the room. Andrew was glad his bed was far enough away from the noise. He rose and walked to the open staircase that led to the floor below. He needed water. Maybe once he was done with his drink he would sleep with the cup positioned in his hands to catch most of the rain.

The orphanage had five floors. The basement housed the babies and the female workers owned by the government who were responsible for their care. The second floor had the classrooms and the kitchen. The third was for the children aged four to seven. The fourth was the communal bathrooms for the entire facility and the health ward, which was always at capacity. The top held Andrew's group, ages eight to thirteen. Their age range was much larger because not all of the seven-year-olds would see age eight and some who did opted to run away instead.

Andrew walked into the bathroom. The fluorescent lights were on round the clock here. The long wall had eight showerheads sticking out for the three hundred boys who resided here. They only blasted cold water. Andrew ignored them and went to the sinks. He turned the handle and waited for the brown water to turn clear before grabbing a cup off the ledge and filling it up.

"Could I have some?"

The voice made the hair on the back of Andrew's neck stand up. He spun around to see a younger boy, definitely one from the four-to-seven age range. His hair was shaved off and there were big black bags under his eyes.

"Please?"

Andrew handed the cup down to him and the kid gulped down the rest of the water.

"We had a lice breakout," he said. "In the clinic. That's why my head is shaved."

On instinct Andrew backed away from the child. He had managed to avoid a stay in the clinic his entire life and did not plan on visiting during his final year.

"Could you get some more for me?" The boy held the now-empty cup out to Andrew.

Andrew responded by sliding down the sink away from the child, never breaking eye contact.

"I'm so thirsty," he said.

Then the young boy started coughing. That was a sign for Andrew that it was time to leave. He started running toward the exit.

"Wait," the boy said. "Don't leave me."

Andrew didn't respond. Instead he ran up the stairs and straight toward his bed. The leak didn't seem so bad now. He hoped whatever that kid had hadn't been passed on to him.

Whoever the boy from Andrew's past was, he never saw him again. Andrew was ashamed of his twelve-year-old self's behavior. He should have helped that kid, not run away from him. But a part of Andrew knew his behavior was acceptable. If that kid had been contagious Andrew could have caught his disease. Still, Andrew shook his head, knowing that whatever the kid had, it was brought on by their terrible living situation.

That was seven years ago. He knew whatever was on the inside of this orphanage wouldn't be much different from the environment he was raised in. Andrew could deal with seeing the inside of the dirty building, especially if he didn't have to see the children who were forced to live there.

Chapter 25

We arrived today in the new city. My friend is filled with relief, but I am apprehensive. We gave an inventory of our skills, but the way the men are looking at us, I have a feeling what we are capable of does not matter to them.

—The diary of Megan Jean

The men formed a gauntlet and Mia kept her chin up as she walked through them, trying her hardest to fake the self-confidence Flo possessed. Agent Barker opened the door to the building and Mia hustled inside. She prepared for the worst, but once she entered her jaw dropped open.

Mia was standing in a large blue room. There were matching brown couches set up with a television set hanging from the wall. On the opposite side were a few tables and some bookshelves, filled with board games as well as books. The room had a very warm feeling. Any comfort Mia felt quickly vanished when Agent Barker walked in front of her. She heard the footsteps of the other RAG agents walking behind her, but none of them entered the space.

"Surprised?" Agent Barker asked.

"This is a nice space," Albin said. He started walking toward the tables in the back, touching the couches as he moved.

"We are not the barbaric society your people make us out to be," Agent Barker said.

"Impressive," Flo said. "But let us see the rest of the facility. Where is our guide?"

"You're looking at him," Agent Barker said. "I am more than familiar with the layout of this place. About once or twice a month I come and entertain the boys. They love me here."

Something was missing. Mia could tell. She closed her eyes and envisioned the youth home in France. There were drawings all over the walls and scuff marks on the floor from children's shoes. This place looked untouched.

"How many people live here?" Mia asked.

"This is one of our larger accommodations," Agent Barker said. "One hundred children, six teachers, and two principals."

"Principals?" Albin asked.

"The teachers are all unwed women," Agent Barker said. "The principals are the men in charge of their care. Every youth home has at least one teacher per twenty-five students. Follow me and we can continue our tour."

Agent Barker pushed open a swinging door toward the back of the room. Albin followed, trailed by Flo and then Mia. She heard footsteps behind her but didn't look to see if it was her boys or more RAG agents. She assumed a mix of the two.

The next room was a decent-size kitchen. There was a large island with stools surrounding it and pots and pans hanging from the ceiling. An industrial-size fridge and freezer were against the walls along with a large stove and double oven. Cooking had once been Mia's main passion and this was one of the finest kitchens she had ever come across. Agent Barker opened the fridge and walked inside.

Mia glanced at Flo and Albin. Both wore casual expressions of approval. Mia continued to look around the room and saw three of the men were accompanying them. She only recognized one, Andrew. He was looking upward at the ceiling and she noticed his heavy breathing. Mia felt her heart jump. She could read Andrew too well and he was trying his hardest to keep whatever he was feeling bottled up. He wouldn't look at her and Mia didn't want to draw any attention to him. She wanted to tell him it was okay and to focus on the future, not the sham of the orphanage Agent Barker was presenting. The man stepped out of the cooler with his hands full of food.

"I wanted to give you an example of how the young men eat," he said. "As you can see we offer a wide variety of fruits and vegetables. I am certain you noticed but the climate around here can't support farming. We have fresh food delivered to them twice a week."

He tossed an apple at Mia. Her reflexes were on edge and she caught it with ease.

"Take a bite," he said.

Mia didn't want to play his game, but she forced herself to focus on what really mattered: getting through this and on to the next phase. She hoped Andrew was thinking the same way. Mia bit into the fruit. The flavors exploded in her mouth and Agent Barker's smug smile returned to his face.

"Let's visit the sleeping quarters," he said.

He walked out of the kitchen with Flo and Albin following. Mia wanted to wait for Andrew, do anything she could to give him some reassurance, but it wasn't worth blowing their cover. Instead, she continued out of the kitchen and back into the main room. Agent Barker walked to the other side and opened a closed door. The group walked down a hallway. He stopped and entered another room on his left.

"I don't want to spend a lot of time here," he said. "This is one of our four bathrooms. All of them are identical. Each boy has a personal cabinet to hold his belongings. Then there are five shower stalls and ten toilets."

Mia stuck her head in the room. It was a pale green color and the lighting was warm. She glanced at the giant vanity that spread across the long wall that included four sinks. The bathroom looked like it was meant for girls more than boys.

When she pulled out of the room she used the opportunity to glance at Andrew. He was staring straight ahead. Mia didn't think he was looking at anything. The brown orbs of his eyes looked empty, like his mind was taking him somewhere else. She felt a hand on her arm and whipped her head forward. Flo was lightly touching her.

"You will have much to talk about with your friends," Flo said. "Once we are back in France of course."

Mia nodded. She hoped Flo was the only one who had noticed her checking up on Andrew. Agent Barker shut the door and continued down the hall. He passed many other rooms, opting not to open them up. He stopped at the last door on his left and swung it open. Albin led the way and the group walked inside.

There were three bunk beds taking up the wall space with three matching chests of drawers. An open closet took up the rest of the wall. Mia noticed dress pants, shirts, and ties hanging.

"Six boys to a room," he said. "As you can see there is plenty of space for them. Only dress clothes allowed in the closets."

"Why do they need dress clothes?" Mia asked.

"We have some formal events," Agent Barker said. "Our young men are quite cultured."

"Is this your newest home?" Albin asked.

"Not at all," Agent Barker said. "The youth homes across the country are all similar. Men, wouldn't you agree?"

The two unknown RAG agents nodded their heads. Andrew remained motionless.

"I know you're American," Agent Barker said to Andrew. "You weren't feeding our foreign friends lies about your living situation, were you?"

Mia watched Andrew. She wanted to will him to speak. He had to know they all knew this was a façade.

"This is identical to my experience as a youth," Andrew said.

Mia turned back toward Agent Barker. The man continued to smile at Andrew. Mia was sure Andrew wasn't about to break eye contact with him.

"May I use the restroom before we leave?" Mia asked.

"Of course," Agent Barker said. He slowly broke eye contact with Andrew and looked toward Albin. "I think you have seen enough to get the idea. We have a lot of driving ahead of us. Agent Quillian will wait outside the restroom for you."

Agent Barker led the group back out of the room. When they passed the bathroom Mia went inside. She made a break for the sink first and poured cold water on her face. She breathed heavily and looked in the mirror. Mia was relieved and proud Andrew had managed to keep his cool for the most part. Only a few more days and they would arrive at the capital and be finished with the charade. She was certain the group could hang on until then.

Chapter 26

A fight broke out last night. I thought our settlement would burn to the ground. Several men lost their lives. It was over what I have been mentioning nonstop, the fact that there are so few women compared to so many men.

—The journal of Isaac Ryland

The muscles in Andrew's neck were tight. He tried his best to tilt his head toward the left to stretch them out, but it wasn't working. *These people are lying.* The idea was overpowering. He tried his hardest to focus on anything else—his aches, the weather, even the paint colors—but nothing was working. He found it even more offensive that the RAG agents weren't doing a good job with their charade.

He wondered what this building's real purpose was, or at least tried to make himself wonder, but his mind kept going back to the simple fact that they were lying. To compare the place Andrew had lived to this palace was unfair and cruel. They headed back into the main area.

"I must admit, we are pleasantly surprised," Albin said.

Andrew felt his rage boil again. Did the Frenchman actually buy this setup?

"Indeed," Florence said. "It is a shame we couldn't meet any young men though."

"Your presence would distract them too much . . ."

Andrew tuned Agent Barker out. He watched the man's lips move but didn't try to hear whatever words he was saying. Everyone around him was a liar. Zack lied about Affinity, America was lying about how they treated their boys, and now the French were buying into it. Andrew had sacrificed eighteen years of his life for the American ideals. Work hard, train for service, do your time, then buy a wife. He had wasted so much time believing that he couldn't take it anymore.

"Liars," Andrew said.

It slipped out so fast Andrew wasn't sure the room had even heard him. But they had. Everyone in front of him turned their head slowly toward him. Andrew was certain everyone behind him was watching as well. He didn't care about them either at this point. He deserved some honesty.

"Excuse me?" Agent Barker said.

"I think the private is overtired," Zack said.

Andrew clenched his jaw shut. He did not want to make another mistake. The agent did not look away from Andrew. Their eyes were glued to each other. The agent tilted his head to the side.

"Who are you?" he asked. "I knew the moment I saw your crew something wasn't right."

"We are from unit five-zero-sev—" Zack started to say.

"I wasn't talking to you," Agent Barker said. "There is something wrong with all of you. Taking an extra woman, not on the manifest, into the country. Guards too young to deserve this type of position. Questions have been raised about your group already. Some very important people are interested in you."

"Why would anyone be interested in us?" Flo asked.

"Keep your mouth shut," Agent Barker said. "The only one I am interested in hearing speak is this man."

Andrew saw the sweat beading on his forehead. Their eyes stayed connected. With that one small slipup Agent Barker now thought Andrew was the weak link in the group. He had to prove him wrong.

"*Answer me,*" Barker yelled. "Who are you?"

Andrew's eyes darted toward Zack.

"*Look at me,*" Barker said.

With a quick motion the agent reached to his side and unholstered his weapon. He pointed it directly between Andrew's eyes. Andrew remained still, with his arms at his sides. This wasn't his first time staring down the barrel of a gun.

"Who is the liar?" Barker asked. "Aside from you and the girl."

Andrew's eyes widened when he mentioned Mia. Something or someone had tipped the agent off. Andrew knew he should repeat his cover story, but something had unhinged Agent Barker. There was no way to walk away from this situation without giving the best explanation possible.

"I could answer your question better if you told me who the interested party is," Andrew said.

"Agent McMahon," Agent Barker said without looking away from Andrew.

Out of his peripheral vision Andrew saw a man step forward from the line of RAG agents.

"Go bring back the girl and Agent Quillian."

The man took a step forward and Andrew heard the sound of a gun being pulled and cocked. Andrew didn't break eye contact with Agent Barker, but he saw Jesse pull his gun and point it at the agent walking away. Andrew heard the sound of more people pulling their weapons. Flo huddled near Albin, since they were unarmed.

"I demand you stop this right now," Flo said. "All of you. What is going on?"

"Tell me," Barker said. He looked right at Andrew.

Andrew remained still.

"Why is Grant Marsden interested in you?"

The name made the hairs on the back of Andrew's neck stand up. It felt as if the entire world had slipped away and it was just him and Agent Barker in the room. Adrenaline took over as he swiftly lifted his arm and punched Agent Barker in the neck. A gunshot rang out and Andrew felt a bullet whiz past his ear.

As quickly as the world had faded away, it faded back in. Andrew dropped to the floor on his back. Zack, Jesse, and Bryan had their guns drawn and were shooting at the other RAG agents. There was a loud scream but Andrew didn't look to see who it was coming from. Instead he kept his weapon in the air and fired at the standing RAG agents. One, two, three. They were all on the floor with shots to the head.

Andrew took a second to glance back at the Affinity team. Bryan was on the floor. Zack was leaning against the wall, gripping his shoulder. Andrew went back to the line of RAG agents. The way they were standing made it easy to fire. Four, five, six, seven. They all hit the floor. His eyes went back to his team. Jesse was on the floor now and Zack crouched down next to him. Andrew went back to the remaining agents. There was one left. Andrew fired. Eight. He fell to the floor.

The room was filled with a high-pitched echo. Andrew looked around; nobody was standing. He pushed himself up from the floor. Zack was still next to Jesse. He was screaming, but Andrew couldn't hear him. Then, as if the world had come back to a normal speed, his screaming was too audible.

"*What did you do?*" Zack yelled.

Reality came crashing back in and Andrew dropped his gun. Bodies covered the floor. One man was making a gurgling noise in the corner. Mia. Where was Mia? Andrew spun around and looked toward the hallway. Standing there was the last RAG agent with his arm around Mia and his free hand pointing a gun at her head. Andrew immediately felt regret for his actions.

Chapter 27

We were given a home. I noticed all our neighbors are women and our area is fenced in. They say it is for our protection, but it feels like a cage to me.

—*The diary of Megan Jean*

There was so much blood. Once Mia heard the firing she knew people were dying. The RAG agent had burst through the door and gripped her arm. She didn't say a word to him. The noises died down in less than a minute and he dragged her into the hall. She was already too filled with worry to care when he pointed his gun at her. As soon as they reached the main room and Mia spotted Andrew standing up without a mark on him she felt a strange sense of calm. He was alive. Then her situation came crashing back on her before she could focus on the rest of her friends.

"Drop your weapons," the RAG agent said.

Mia watched as Andrew raised his hands. He didn't even have a gun. Zack was on the ground and started to stand; his gun hit the floor with a boom. Mia scanned the black-suited bodies and didn't see Carter. Whatever peace she'd felt vanished as her eyes continued their scan. Flo was lying on the floor. She wasn't moving. Mia tried to dart forward and felt the RAG agent pull her back.

"Where do you think you're going?" he asked.

Mia's focus shifted to his gun, which was now pointed at her forehead. She didn't have time for this. Flo needed her help. The RAG agent's eyes shifted back toward Andrew and Zack. He released Mia from his grip but didn't move the gun.

"Answer the man's question," the RAG agent said. "What did you do?"

The panic of the situation faded; Mia needed to get to Flo. She saw the table behind her had a large glass vase sitting on it. Mia used the agent's distraction as an opportunity and picked up the glass object. As the agent turned around to see what she was doing she brought the vase crashing down over his head. He let out a groan as it shattered in her hands. He dropped to the floor and Mia ran over toward Flo. She knelt next to the woman and grabbed her hand. Andrew and Zack ran past her toward the incapacitated RAG agent.

"Please," Mia said. "Please tell me you're all right."

A bright red stain covered the woman's torso and her skin was almost gray. Mia already knew the answer to her question. She let out a small sob. Flo moved her head and Mia felt a small glimmer of hope. The woman's eyes fluttered open and closed, as if she were unable to choose a path.

"Flo?" Mia asked. "Can you hear me?"

"I miss the flowers," Flo said.

"You will be fine," Mia said. "You will see your flowers again."

"No," Flo said. "Mia?"

"I'm right here."

Flo's lips curved in a smile. "You're the important one," she said. "I know you will finish this without me."

"Don't say that," Mia said.

"It's all right," Flo said. "I know I did good in this world."

"And you will do much more," Mia said, fighting back the tears.

"This is the end to my story," Flo said.

Mia turned away and let the tears fall for a moment. Then she turned back to her mentor.

"I will make sure the world knows your role," Mia said. "Everyone will understand your actions."

Flo continued to smile. "I don't care about that," she said. "I know, and that is enough for me."

The woman started to convulse. Mia grabbed on to her face. She was dying and there was nothing Mia could do to help her. Flo stopped moving and blood started to drip out of the corner of her mouth.

"Open and honest communication," Flo said.

Her eyes tilted back inside her skull and her eyelids fell. She was gone. Mia let out a loud sob and picked the woman up in her arms. She wanted to hug her until her spirit came back, but Mia knew that wouldn't happen. She wasn't holding Flo anymore, only an empty vessel.

Chapter 28

The general held a meeting tonight with all the women in his settlement. He told us of women being attacked and promised us protection. I asked what happened to the attackers and he did not have an answer for me.

—The diary of Megan Jean

Time was standing still. Mia held Flo's body, but her arms felt empty. A hand touched her shoulder and she could feel its heat radiating through her. She turned her head and saw Zack leaning over her.

"We have to get out of here," he said.

Mia looked away and released Flo's body, setting her friend on the floor. She rocked back on her legs and stood upright again but still felt as if she were floating.

"How did this happen?"

"There was a misunderstanding," Zack said.

"Misunderstanding?" Mia asked. "People are dead. Lots of them. Some that I actually cared about, so I am going to need more than 'misunderstanding.'"

Zack glanced over his shoulder. Mia moved to his side to see what he was looking at. There was Andrew, gun drawn and pointed at the unconscious RAG agent.

"Finish him," Zack said. "We can't leave any loose ends."

"No," Mia said.

She pushed past Zack and went to Andrew. He kept his weapon pointed at the agent.

"Nobody else dies," Mia said. "We are here to save people, not kill them. He doesn't know any better."

Andrew lowered the weapon and turned to look at her. His face was still.

"Explain," Mia said. "Everything."

He looked away from Mia and walked toward Zack. Mia spun around to face them and did not hold back. She didn't care if her voice was loud enough to rupture their eardrums.

You will tell me everything.

"Grant," Andrew said. "The agent asked me why Grant Marsden was so interested in us."

"It wasn't your fault," Zack said.

"He mentions a name so I kill eight people?" Andrew asked. "We don't know what Grant knows, who he told."

Zack looked at Andrew but then shifted his attention back to Mia.

"They were trying to hit Andrew," Zack said. "But instead Flo was shot. Albin was next, then we fired back. Jesse and Bryan died, I was shot in the shoulder. Andrew is unharmed. You're bleeding from cuts in your hands. But we are alive. We need to keep moving."

Mia raised her arms and examined them. There was too much blood; she didn't know which was hers and which was Flo's. It didn't matter though.

"Why did you let Andrew go on the tour?" Mia asked. "You should have known it would be too hard for him."

"Agent Barker picked him," Zack said. "I didn't think this would happen."

"We should bury the bodies," Andrew said. "At least Flo and Albin."

"No," Mia said. "She's not in there anymore. They're just empty shells. It doesn't matter."

"Mia is right," Zack said. "The mission is blown. We're close enough to the border. We should focus all our energy on getting back to Affinity."

"We can't leave," Carter said.

He appeared out of nowhere, pulling the front door open. Mia had known he was alive since his body was missing, but she figured he was unaware of what had transpired here.

"Where did you go?" Andrew asked.

"It doesn't matter," Carter said. "We can't leave though. Mia is still alive so we push forward."

"With what plan?" Zack asked. "We lost; let's retreat and regroup. We have to assume Grant knows everything. We don't even know if Rex can get the paperwork for Mia to prove she was Grant's wife. Without it Mia's useless."

"And how will we cross the border?" Carter asked. "Do you have another helicopter we can steal?"

"We smuggle ourselves over," Zack said.

"Do you even know where we are?" Carter asked.

"Maybe twelve hours away from Mexico," Zack said.

"Leaving isn't an option," Carter said. "We head toward the capital."

"Zack is right," Andrew said.

"Mia is alive," Carter said. "She's fine. That's all we need."

"Mia could have been killed," Andrew said. "I won't risk her life anymore."

The three men continued to argue. Mia couldn't focus on their words. Too much had happened. She kept thinking about Flo and her final words. Open and honest communication. Mia wasn't about to leave any questions unanswered.

"Maybe that's my decision," Mia said.

All of them stared at her.

"We need to get out of here," Zack said. "I can find an Affinity contact and we can head across the border."

"Or we can push through," Carter said. "Get to the capital."

"Mia, you're in charge," Andrew said. "But Zack is right, this is too much for us to handle."

Andrew approached her. His lips were pressed shut. One look in his worried eyes made Mia feel selfish. She went to him and wrapped her arms around his waist. He leaned over her. Mia had just lost one of the people she admired most in the world, but he had taken a lot of lives, something he'd promised himself would never happen again. Mia couldn't lose Andrew too. If he needed the help only Affinity could offer him she would make sure he got it.

"We'll head back," Mia said.

There was a hand on her hip, pulling her out of Andrew's arms. She spun around to see Carter. His multicolored eyes were glaring into her.

"If we leave, my dad will die," Carter said.

"What are you talking about?" Mia asked.

She thought Andrew's memory had taken the worst beating from the militia, but now it seemed Carter couldn't even remember his father was dead.

"My dad, the one who risked his life to save yours, is alive," Carter said. "He is in the capital and unless we get there within the next fifteen days Grant will kill him."

Confusion filled Mia's head. She didn't know what Carter was saying.

"How do you know that?" Andrew asked. His voice was hard.

"We made contact," Carter said. "I've spoken to my dad. He is alive. Grant said I needed to get Mia to the capital and trade her for him."

"This whole time we've been trying to protect her when you're getting ready to sacrifice her?" Andrew asked, his voice growing louder, and he stepped in between Mia and Carter.

"No," Carter said. "Andrew, I told you back in France he was alive. I was going to tell everyone, but Grant told me not to and I couldn't risk him killing my father. Mia, please, we have to save my dad. If we go back to Affinity he'll die."

Mia was so overwhelmed by death. Flo was gone. Mia pictured Rod throwing himself out of the helicopter. He had done that for her. She couldn't let him die again.

"We're going to stay," Mia said.

"What?" Andrew asked. "No, you can't listen to Carter. He ran out of the room as soon as shots were fired here. He doesn't care about you or this mission. His motivation is selfish."

Mia looked into Andrew's eyes. He was serious. Mia didn't understand how he could take their friend's family for granted. Rod had done a lot for Andrew too. That relationship didn't matter to him at all.

"Carter, your father wouldn't want you to save him," Zack said. "Rod knew the risks. He would want the three of you safe."

"How could he know any of the risks?" Carter asked. "If Mia was some everyday girl none of this would have happened. We had helped other families sneak over the border before. There was no way he had any clue helping Mia and Andrew would lead to this. We have to save him."

"He knew the risks," Zack said with a stern voice.

"How?" Mia asked.

Zack turned his attention toward her; she watched as his features softened.

"Helping someone escape is dangerous," Zack said. "There are always risks."

"That's not what you said."

"I was only speaking in generalities," Zack said.

"No you weren't," Mia replied. She recognized the tone of Zack's voice. He was speaking like someone who had a personal relationship with Rod. "How did he know the risks?"

Zack rolled his eyes and let out a loud breath. "He knew your husband was Grant Marsden," he said.

How could Rod have known that? Something felt so wrong to Mia. She needed to ask a direct question.

"Is Rod part of Affinity?" Mia asked.

Zack went silent. He took a breath before answering.

"Yes," Zack said.

"So it wasn't by chance I contacted your group?"

"No," Zack said. "The computer was programmed for us to intercept any attempt at communication. Rod was going to take all of you to us."

"Why didn't he tell me?" Carter asked. "You're lying."

"We encourage our members living in America to keep quiet," Zack said. "Rod contacted Affinity five years ago. Mia, as soon as you arrived in Saint Louis you were on our radar. We contacted Rod to pick you up."

"Was all of this organized then?" Mia asked. "Our time in Mexico?"

"No," Zack said. "We thought you died in the crash. But we knew who all of you were the second you showed up at our base. We knew who you were the second Grant Marsden purchased you. He has been a person of interest for some time."

This couldn't be happening. Mia thought about her time at the Affinity base camp, her feelings of helplessness over planning the mission. None of it was in her control. She felt so used.

"It doesn't matter now," Zack said. "If you care about stopping the Registry we have to get out of here and regroup."

Mia felt so alone. Then she remembered she wasn't. Andrew felt the same way she did. She turned around to face him, but his face was blank and his eyes vacant. He didn't look down at her.

"Did you know about this?" Mia asked, certain the answer would be no.

His eyes closed; he didn't open them up before speaking.

"For a few days," he said. "I didn't want to upset you."

Mia didn't have a solid idea about love, but however Andrew was treating her it wasn't like someone who had true feelings for her. She felt all the emotions rush out of her body. She looked around at the three men. Carter wanted to trade her, Zack wanted to use her, and Andrew wanted to shield her. None of them cared about what she wanted. All of their motivations were unacceptable to Mia.

"We have to head back," Zack said. "All of this will be discussed further once we're at Affinity."

Mia took a page out of Andrew's book and didn't make eye contact with any of them.

"I need some time to think," Mia said. "Andrew was right. We can't leave the bodies. There are gallons of gasoline in the cars. You three stay in here and get the bodies ready. We're going to burn the place down."

Mia didn't make eye contact with any of them and nobody followed her out of the building. Dusk had settled in and Mia felt her own darkness taking over. She needed to take control, of her life and the mission. Her future lay in her own hands. The answers Mia had just received only created more questions. Mia realized she would never get them all answered unless she went to the start of all her problems.

Without thinking about Andrew, Carter, Zack, or Rod, Mia walked up to the first black SUV and climbed in the driver's seat. She saw the keys still in the ignition and turned the engine over. She put the car into drive and took off down the road. She wasn't certain how to get to her destination, but she could figure it out. She thought about Flo again. Mia wanted to emulate the woman and right now she was ready to take the lead.

Chapter 29

There is no money system here. At first it was refreshing, but now people are asserting their dominance by beating up the weak and taking what they want. I am grateful for my position close to the general, or else I would never survive this time.

—The journal of Isaac Ryland

Everything was fuzzy. Andrew followed Zack's lead and moved the body of a RAG agent to search his pockets, adding the identification and wallet to the already formed pile. Carter was tying up the unconscious agent in the back of the room. Once all the agents were searched Andrew went toward Flo and Albin. They were gray on the floor. Mia had called them shells, but they looked very much like people who had undertaken a noble deed for others.

Things became clearer. These good people were dead and it was Andrew's fault. As soon as the clarity came it vanished again; this time nausea returned with his foggy brain. The room felt like it was turning sideways and Andrew was unable to stand upright. He heard Zack and Carter call out, but Andrew couldn't make out their words. He hit the floor with a thump.

Someone flipped him onto his back and Andrew concentrated on Zack's face. He saw the man's lips moving but the noises made no sense. Zack's face started to distort and Andrew blinked his eyes but the picture didn't get any more focused. Andrew did not want to lose consciousness but could feel the blackness gripping him.

Zack looked away. He was talking to someone else now. Andrew wondered if it was Carter or Mia. Mia. Not only had Andrew caused so much death today, he had destroyed Mia's trust. He had promised her no more lies. Even if he had planned on telling her the truth about Affinity's knowledge the opportunity never presented itself. He regretted not lying to her with that explanation. Maybe he still could. The world started to settle back in place. Andrew could not make amends for his mistakes to the dead, but he could make it right with Mia.

"She's gone," Carter said.

"What?" Zack asked.

Carter's words made Andrew's world come back into focus. Andrew pushed himself up and ran past Carter and outside. He saw the two black SUVs waiting. The third was nowhere in sight. Andrew closed his eyes and tried to listen for the sound of an engine, but none could be heard. Instead the sound of the doors opening and two people walking out behind him came to his ears.

"Where did she go?" Carter asked.

Zack pulled out his cell phone. He was dialing Mia, but Andrew knew she wouldn't pick up. There was a reason she had taken off without them.

"Could someone have grabbed her?" Carter asked.

"There's nobody else here," Zack said.

"She wouldn't leave," Carter said. "She'll want to help my dad too."

"How long were we inside?" Andrew asked.

"She's not picking up," Zack said.

"Can't you use the GPS?" Carter asked.

"It was deactivated for finding her," Zack said. "In case one of us was captured and they got our phone."

"How long were we inside?" Andrew asked again.

"About thirty minutes," Zack said.

It felt like thirty seconds.

"You thought she was outside getting gasoline for a half hour?" Andrew asked.

"You were acting like a comatose man," Zack said. "I thought she needed some space to process all of this."

"Well you gave her enough space," Andrew said.

He started walking toward one of the SUVs.

"Where are you going?" Carter asked.

"I'm going to find Mia," Andrew said.

"She has a thirty-minute head start," Zack said. "She could be anywhere."

"There are only four places she knows in this whole country," Andrew said. "I'm willing to bet she's headed to one of them."

"Stop," Zack said. "How would she figure out where any of them are?"

"Her phone is filled with maps," Andrew said. "She can read them."

Andrew felt the man lay a hand on his shoulder. Andrew was quick to flip it off. He turned around and tried to punch Zack, but the man moved out of the way and Andrew almost fell over.

"This is your fault," Andrew said. "Why did you have to keep lying to her?"

"My fault?" Zack said. "You're the one who threw the first punch."

Andrew's breaths were heavy in his chest. He didn't know how to respond. His chest hurt, because Zack was right. This was all Andrew's fault.

"I didn't mean that," Zack said. "As soon as he mentioned Grant's name none of us were safe. I don't know how he found out."

"We have to find her," Andrew said. "She's not safe."

"We need her," Carter said.

Zack looked away.

"The mission is over," Zack said. "We head across the border back to Affinity. We have no cover."

Andrew started walking toward one of the SUVs again.

"She can find us," Zack said. "The GPS in her phone still works to locate others. Mia knows exactly where you are. If she wanted to stay with you she would have."

Andrew froze in his tracks. He felt a vibration in his pocket. He reached in and pulled out his phone. There was a text message from Mia.

> I am taking charge of this mission. I am getting the proof
> we need to prove my identity. I need some space. Head
> toward the capital. I will meet you there in three days.
> Please, give me my three days.

"Mia is familiar with the danger. She has firsthand knowledge from your first cross-country trip. Whatever the risks are she thought she could handle them. Are you betting against her?" Zack asked.

Andrew ignored him and reread the message before replying.

> Three days? Grant is out there, he knows you're here.
> How will you protect yourself? You need me.

> What I need is assurance. If anything happens to me,
> promise you will try to save Rod and stop the Registry?
> We have a better chance of not getting caught if we split
> up.

Andrew didn't have the time to reply before Mia sent another message.

Trust me. It is better this way. Even if Grant is as clever
as he thinks it will be harder for him to track us if we split
up. I need to keep driving. I will be safe. We will stop the
Registry. Trust me.

Andrew tuned out Zack and Carter and thought about what Mia
was saying. He didn't like it, but she was right. Andrew sent the only
words he could think to say.

I love you. Three days.

Mia replied right away.

I love you. Three days.

"We have three days to make it to the capital," Andrew said.

"I've been shot," Zack said. "First we need to take care of that."

Andrew spun around to face Zack. Carter was a few feet behind
him. His brow was furrowed. Andrew didn't know if he considered
Carter a deserter for running out of the room or smart for avoiding
bloodshed.

"What do you think?" Andrew asked.

"I think we need to find a new way to get my dad out," Carter said.
"I also think Mia can take care of herself better than you give her
credit for. She doesn't want rescuing at the moment."

How could Andrew be sure of anything if Mia wasn't near him?
Part of him wanted to drive after her and scream at her for taking
off like this. Then it clicked in Andrew's brain. Mia wasn't a child.
Andrew couldn't scream at her or keep her safe all the time.

"Zack, stay out here and search the SUVs for tracking chips,"
Andrew said. "Carter, come inside with me. Mia was right about one
thing: we're going to blow this place up."

"There won't be a chip," Zack said.

"How do you know?" Andrew asked.

"Your low-tech government wouldn't invest in one," Zack said. "That and who would be crazy enough to steal a vehicle belonging to a RAG agent?"

"Check anyway," Andrew said.

He started walking back toward the building. Carter followed him.

"What's the plan?" Carter asked.

"Mia needs time to herself and I am going to trust her," Andrew said. "We'll continue on toward the capital. Figure out a way to get your dad out. Mia is taking control. I have to trust she knows what she's doing."

"Thank you," Carter said.

Andrew stopped moving and grabbed Carter by the shirt collar. He clenched his fist around the material and brought the blond man's face closer to his.

"If you ever lie to me again I will leave you to die in the middle of a desert," Andrew said. "And don't think you can get through the rest of our time here without getting your hands dirty. No more running and hiding."

The look of shock on Carter's face did not fade away. Andrew released him from his grip and threw the man back a little. Andrew continued on his walk and Carter dutifully fell in line. Andrew hoped it would be for longer than tonight.

Chapter 30

The general held a meeting with his new board members. I am
the only one who thinks we should focus on what happened in
the past, to learn from our mistakes, and I kept my mouth shut.
I also found it odd there wasn't a single female present for the
board meeting.

—The journal of Isaac Ryland

Grant kept his fingers on the small revolver tucked in his pocket. He
climbed up the steps to the Hotel Austin, pleased that the foreign
dignitaries were receiving such poor accommodations. The group
should have arrived by now; all Grant had to do was figure out what
room Mia was staying in. He didn't want to kill her in the hotel. Instead he hoped to get her on his plane and kill her at his own home.
That way he could take his time and deliver the suffering she deserved.

There was nobody at the reception desk. Grant hit the bell several
times before an older man appeared from an office door.

"It's late," the man said. "Calm down."

The man's jaw dropped when he looked up and saw Grant standing there.

"Is it really you?" the man asked.

"I'm looking for a guest you have staying here," Grant said. "Could you tell me what rooms the RAG agents are staying in?"

The man continued to look at Grant in shock. "You're shorter in person," he said. "You look so tall on the TV."

Grant gave a pressed-lipped smile. "The RAG agents?"

"They're not here yet," the man said.

"Are you certain?"

"Called earlier to add some rooms to their block," the man said. "Seven more agents joined their party."

This did not bode well for Grant. That meant Agent Barker had not listened to him. Grant checked his watch. They should have beaten him here. Something had gone wrong.

"You can wait for them," the man said. "I could give you a room and call when they arrive."

"They're not coming," Grant said under his breath.

The man gave him a confused look. Grant turned away and pulled out his cell phone. He dialed Agent Barker's number and was not surprised when nobody picked up the phone. He put it back in his pocket and debated his next move.

Chapter 31

I tried to leave the area today. The guard protecting our section advised against it. I have been too scared to openly speak with the other women here about what is happening; that changes tonight.

—*The diary of Megan Jean*

The darkness helped Mia focus on the road in front of her. At first she appreciated the setting sun because it let her know she was heading north. Now the night was better because it made it easier to silence her inner monologue. *Flo is dead. You abandoned Andrew. You abandoned Rod. You abandoned your cause.* Flashes kept making their way through Mia's mind, but focusing on the headlights of the SUV quieted her thoughts.

Mia pulled over to the side of the road but did not turn the car off. She opened her phone and went to Andrew's contact information, held down seven, and a map appeared. He was standing still. Andrew had kept his word; they weren't chasing her down. She zoomed out of the map and saw her own red dot appear on the small screen. In a short time she had put almost forty-five miles between them, Mia realized she needed to slow down, she was traveling at almost 90 mph the whole time.

Not wanting to lose any advantage she had gained, Mia tried to think of any landmarks that could tell her where she was going. She zoomed out farther and saw that the map divided the areas. She was not far from the Midwest Area boundary line. Mia saw the city of Saint Louis on the map. She looked toward the west, remembering her trip into the big city, and saw the long highway. She scrolled north and saw the city of Schuyler, another spot from her previous travels. Then she saw the thick line between them. This was the highway that would lead her to her destination. Mia would have to check landmarks once she was close enough, but she didn't want to lose the cover of darkness.

Double-checking the initial directions that would lead her toward the highway, Mia took off again. She had twelve hours until the sun rose and another two before people were out on the road. Mia didn't have any idea if that was enough time, but she would take her chances. If she wanted to move on from her past life and figure out what type of person she was, she couldn't think of a better place to start than where she'd begun.

Chapter **32**

Repopulating America and protecting our borders are the top priorities of the grand commander (he decided on that moniker over "general"). There are six thousand men here and four hundred eighty-two women. I highly doubt I will be charged with fulfilling either of the grand commander's priorities.

—The journal of Isaac Ryland

The RAG agent was starting to come to. Andrew and Carter had just thrown him in the backseat of an SUV. The man was bound with his colleagues' ties, including one wrapped around his mouth, stopping him from speaking freely.

"I'm sorry," Andrew said.

The agent opened his eyes wide and Andrew brought his fist down hard. The agent fell back onto the seat, unconscious, and Andrew slammed the door, shaking his fist from the contact.

"Carter, I need you to drive this car," Andrew said. "Follow me and Zack. If he wakes up again honk your horn."

Carter nodded and climbed into the driver's seat. The engine hummed to life. Andrew stood in front of the building. It was now filled with gas from the kitchen stove; Andrew was surprised it actually worked and wondered what the main purpose of this building was. He pulled the bottle of oil he had taken from the kitchen, complete with the gasoline-soaked rag he'd placed inside of it, out from under his belt.

"Please forgive me for taking your lives," Andrew said.

He took one final look at the building. He closed his eyes as he took the lighter from his pocket. Andrew pictured his old orphanage, the pain and sickness the place was filled with. Andrew had survived that, along with his time in the fighting circuit, escaping from the U.S. with Mia, and what the militia had put him through. All of that was behind him now.

With a single stroke of his thumb the lighter came to life. He lit the rag and chucked the bottle as hard as he could. It broke through a window and Andrew ran into the driver's seat of the first car. It was already running. He slammed the door shut and took off down the road.

The rearview mirror held more interest to him than the road. He was speeding, but his eyes were behind him. He saw the flames go up before he heard the noise of the explosion. Even though his heart was racing he felt a sense of calmness come over him. The suffering was over.

"You did a good job," Zack said. His voice was weak.

Andrew's eyes moved to his passenger. Zack was clutching his shoulder.

"Now that the adrenaline's worn off I realize how much being shot hurts," Zack said.

Andrew handed him a water bottle, one of the many items the men had looted from the fake youth home. Zack released his injury and took a large gulp.

"I contacted Affinity," Zack said. "There's someone who will help me. We have to take this road until it ends, about eighty miles. Then head west another forty. There's a major highway that goes north to south across the middle of the country. You can't miss it."

"I know the road," Andrew said.

"Yeah," Zack said. "I forgot you're from here. Head south. Take the eleventh exit, about fifty miles. There's a hospital there. I have a number to call and someone will sneak me in, treat me, and release me."

"That's a few hours," Andrew said. "Can you make it?"

"I don't think it's that bad," Zack said. "It's not even bleeding much. It only hurts. I need someone to dig the bullet out and sew me up."

If Zack had a plan for the rest of their trip he wasn't volunteering his information. Andrew didn't want to ask either. He was busy making plans of his own.

The rest of the car trip was quiet. Andrew wasn't certain how much of it Zack was awake for, but whenever Andrew got nervous he reached out and made sure the other man was still breathing. As long as that was the case there was nothing to worry about.

Four hours had passed. It was close to midnight when Andrew pulled up to the hospital. Whoever Zack was speaking with, it was by text message, so Andrew had to rely on him for instructions.

"Pull around back," Zack said. "There's a delivery entrance."

The hospital was small and dark. Andrew thought it looked more like a clinic than a place where surgeries were performed. As he turned the corner a man came into view. He stood behind a wheelchair and Andrew stopped the car.

Zack opened the door and started to climb out. The man ran around the car to help him. Zack did not object as the doctor guided him to the rolling seat.

"Come back in five hours," the man said. "Right here."

Before Andrew could ask another question the door was slammed and the man was pushing Zack into the building, his legs kicking up behind him as he ran. Andrew wasn't sure where to head, but he didn't think he could stay here. He was about to put the car into drive again when a phone went off.

Mia; Andrew was sure it was her, calling to say she was done blowing off steam and on her way back to him. He stuck his hand in his jacket pocket, but his screen was still dark. The ringing continued and Andrew realized it was coming from one of the RAG agents' phones. Andrew reached into the bag of personal items in the backseat. He saw the lit-up screen and pulled the device out. The caller was listed as "Headquarters." Not willing to lose what little advantage they had, Andrew answered the phone.

"Barker?" An unfamiliar voice asked.

Andrew was silent.

"Agent Barker, are you there? It's Agent Mason."

"This is Barker," Andrew said in a muffled voice.

"Where have you been?" the voice asked. "You failed to check in with me. I gave you this assignment because you're one of my best agents. That does not give you the right to ignore your duties."

"Sorry, sir," Andrew said.

"How did it go?" he asked. "Did the lady buy it?"

"Yes," Andrew said.

"All women are morons," he said. "Are you at the hotel?"

"We decided to drive through the night," Andrew said.

"She was okay with it?" he asked. "Didn't require her beauty sleep?"

The man at the other end of the line let out a belly laugh.

"Ha ha ha ha," Andrew said.

"Are you keeping the extra men with you?"

"Yes," Andrew said. "All accounted for."

"So did you figure out what was bothering you?"

"What?"

"With that girl? You said something about the young one seeming off," he said. "Remember, that's why you asked for the extra detail. I told you it wasn't necessary. The bodyguards they brought are American."

Andrew didn't know how to respond.

"Well try to let the men sleep," he said. "And don't forget to check in tomorrow night. Let's keep it for ten P.M. Okay?"

"Yes, sir," Andrew said.

"Are you getting a cold?"

"Yes," Andrew said.

"Those filthy foreigners," Mason said. "Always dragging in their diseases."

The man let out another obnoxious laugh. Before Andrew could respond the car behind him started honking its horn. That could only mean one thing.

"Good night, sir," Andrew said.

He didn't wait for a response before hanging up the phone. He tossed it in the front seat and climbed out of the car. He couldn't see what was happening with Carter's headlights on, but Carter must have seen him since the horn stopped honking. Andrew drew his weapon from its holster. With his free hand he opened the back door. He got a clear view of the now-awake RAG agent with his arms around Carter; his hands were tied together and he was effectively choking his driver. Andrew cocked his gun and the man turned to look at him.

"I would stop that if I were you," Andrew said.

The man locked eyes with Andrew, then lifted his arms. Carter let out some gasps and coughs, but Andrew did not look away from the hostage. He had managed to work his way out of the makeshift gag.

"If you're going to kill me get it over with," the man said.

"What's your name again?" Andrew asked.

"Agent Quillian," the man said.

"I don't want to kill you," Andrew said. "But I will if I have to. Do you understand?"

The man nodded.

"What I need you to do is apologize to my friend," Andrew said.

"Are you serious?" the agent asked.

"Andrew, I'm fine," Carter said. His voice was hoarse.

"I assure you I am very serious," Andrew said. "Now apologize or I will shoot you dead."

The agent blinked several times; he was having a hard time processing Andrew's request. He turned his head toward the front seat.

"I'm sor—"

Before the man could finish his sentence Andrew brought the butt of his gun down on the agent's head. The man didn't have time to let out a moan before he fell back onto the seat.

"Can you drive?" Andrew asked.

"Yeah," Carter said.

"Well, follow me. We're ditching one of the cars," Andrew said. "And next time, tie his hands behind his back."

The door slammed shut and Andrew went back to his car. He hoped the honking hadn't brought any attention to the area. They needed to leave this place while the doctor treated Zack. Andrew climbed into his vehicle and drove out of the parking lot. He went out onto the road and headed west. He wanted to escape civilization. Once he drove far enough out he would drive the car off the road. Then Andrew, Carter, and Agent Quillian could have a nice long chat.

Chapter **33**

The grand commander gave a speech to the masses this eve-
ning. I did not agree with what he said, but even I found myself
swept up by his enthusiasm. He promised a better America and
stressed protection of our borders. Our settlement's numbers
will lower now as groups of men will be dispatched to guard
the major ports. I hope this results in less hostility.
—The journal of Isaac Ryland

The small plane Grant was flying landed close to the youth home. It
was easy to spot since the building was aflame. Grant walked toward
the fiery structure. There were no cars, so someone had survived. He
hoped it was not Amelia. He pulled out his phone and debated calling
the explosion in to the nearest RAG post, but that would mean questions. Such as, how did he know about the incident and why was he
interested in the French party?

Rage was working its way through Grant's body. If Amelia had
escaped this blaze she could be anywhere. He needed to locate the
survivors but felt trapped at the moment. If he made any move to trail
her it would create a problem for him.

A vibration went off in Grant's pocket. Grant pulled out his cell
phone and was surprised to see Rex calling at this hour. This was the

sort of trip Grant would have had Rex accompany him on, before the betrayal of course.

"Rex," Grant said. "What news do you have for me?"

"I'm coming home," Rex said. He was breathing heavily.

"Your undercover job not going well?"

"They figured out I was still working with you," Rex said. "I barely got out with my life."

"Where are you?" Grant asked.

"I stole a vehicle," Rex said. "I'm in Mexico."

"And Amelia?"

"She's still with them," Rex said. "I'm not sure what the plans are, but she is up to something."

"Do you need assistance?" Grant asked.

"Negative," Rex said. "I could use the travel to clear my head. I'm already on my way."

Grant paused before proceeding.

"I'm glad you're all right."

"Thank you, boss," Rex said.

"Take all the time you need," Grant said.

Grant didn't appreciate how all those around him doubted his intelligence. Rex was trying his hardest to convince Grant of his loyalty, while Carter had all but guaranteed Rex was working for the resistance.

"Did you run into some trouble?" Grant asked. "I expected you a week ago."

"We're back on schedule," Rex said. "I'm nearing America, but I'm driving."

"Why don't you fly back?" Grant asked.

"No money," Rex said.

"Yet you managed to keep your phone?" Grant asked.

There was silence. Grant didn't want his man to know he suspected him just yet.

"Can you drive all the way back?"

"I can't bring this car into America," Rex said. "It violates the technology ban."

Grant didn't want to lose his lead on Amelia's location, but he knew whatever happened would be brought to the attention of the RAG agents and the grand commander. Grant could not risk the grand commander guessing that he had any previous knowledge of the events. If Ian found out Mia was in the country it could mean the end of Grant's political career. There was not much he could do now.

"I can head to the Southwest Area," Grant said. "Cross the border near the coast. Call me with your location and I'll come pick you up. Can you make it there by morning?"

"I don't see why not."

"There's an airport about thirty miles north of the border. If you cross earlier head that direction."

"I'll figure it out," Rex said.

"I'm glad you're coming home," Grant said.

"Me too," Rex replied.

Grant hung up the phone and smiled to himself. He was happy Rex was on his way back. That would make it easier to monitor him and deal out the punishment that was necessary for Rex's betrayal. They would all pay, and then Grant could focus on the future. Absolute power was within his reach.

Chapter 34

Based on my writing skills I asked the grand commander if I could start writing our history. He informed me anything I write will be subject to his approval and review. Somehow I think this journal will provide more truth than what is to be written down and preserved for our descendants.

—The journal of Isaac Ryland

The terrain was more mountainous than Andrew had expected, but he hadn't seen a single house or sign of a person for miles. Even the pavement had given way to a gravel road. He turned off and started driving along the rocky landscape, Carter's headlights flashing in his rearview mirror. It didn't take long for Andrew to reach a destination he thought safe enough. He paused and turned the car off. There was a chill to the air, and a shiver ran down Andrew's spine. He hoped wherever Mia was, she was safe. He shook his head. He knew she was safe. That was the only way he could keep moving. A knock on his window startled him from his thoughts. Carter was waiting. Andrew pushed open his door and stepped outside.

"You left the agent alone?"

Carter lifted up his keys and jingled them in front of Andrew's face. "If he wakes up he's not going anywhere."

Andrew opened the back door and started handing Carter the bags they'd collected from the youth home. Andrew walked around to the passenger side and grabbed the rest of their belongings. He stopped in the back and lifted the trunk. There sat the two cans of gasoline.

"Are you going to blow up this car too?" Carter asked.

"No," Andrew said.

"How did Mia know that gas would destroy the building?"

"She grew up on a farm," Andrew said. "Gas is flammable."

"Oh," Carter said.

Andrew picked up the two gas cans and left the trunk open. He took solace in the fact that maybe an animal would call it home. He walked toward the other SUV, his arms full.

"What time is it?" Andrew asked.

"Two," Carter said.

"We have a few hours," Andrew said. "You should try to get some sleep."

"I'm not tired," Carter said.

Carter opened the back door and set his bags down. He walked around and opened the trunk. Andrew set the extra gas cans down and closed the hatch. The two men stood next to the car.

"You want to hit me," Carter said. "I can tell."

"I want you to tell me everything," Andrew said.

"I found out my dad was still alive when we made it to Affinity," Carter said. "Grant let me speak to him once a day. He gave me a time limit. Mia for Grant. That's all I know."

"What does *he* know?" Andrew asked.

"That we're coming back to America, that we are with a group of rebels," Carter said.

"Does he think we're coming to destroy the Registry?"

"I'm not sure," Carter said. "He may assume that, but he didn't hear it from me."

"How does he know we're here now?"

"Not from me," Carter said. "Before we left for France I told him I couldn't call any longer. It was too painful to hear my dad. All I said was I would be there with Mia by the deadline."

"You don't think a man that clever could figure out we were coming in with foreign aid?"

"How could he know that?"

"Because the whole reason Florence was here was for his wedding," Andrew said. "You don't think he's clever enough to put two and two together?"

"If he was wouldn't we have been greeted by him at the airport?"

Carter did have a point.

"You're going to call him," Andrew said, "and tell him that everything is going according to plan and you're still with Mia."

"Why?"

"Because as long as he thinks she's with us he won't go looking for her elsewhere."

"I can't," Carter said. "It was dangerous enough calling him internationally, when I didn't care if he knew where I was, but if I call him now, from inside America, he can trace me in a second. Then he'll kill all of us, including my dad, and then he'll know for certain Mia is inside the country. That creates more of a risk."

"Affinity had a medical contact; maybe there's some technology guy they know who could help us," Andrew said.

"In America?"

"Why don't you stop shooting down my ideas and start coming up with your own?"

"I've been trying to think of an alternative for weeks," Carter said. "I can't get my dad without Mia. I was hoping she would be willing to trade and then we could break in and save her."

"Why don't we break in and save Rod?"

Carter was silent for a moment.

"That might work now," Carter said. "Before I thought we were going to get too close to the deadline, but there's no more cross-country visiting trip. We can make it to the capital area and Grant's house in a few days, then scope it out and decide how to break in and save him."

Carter's mood elevated.

"Mia is meeting us in three days," Andrew said. "And I don't want her to think she has to sacrifice herself."

Carter frowned for a second, then his smile returned, but Andrew noticed the hesitation.

"By the time she returns my dad will be safe," Carter said.

"I can tell you don't believe me," Andrew said, "but she wouldn't abandon us. This mission is too important to her."

"What if she has?" Carter asked.

"Nothing has changed," Andrew said.

"What do you mean?"

"Mia is getting the information she needs to prove her identity," Andrew said. "Then we continue on with our plans."

"What about my dad?"

Rod had been nice to Andrew. He was one of the only men who ever was. He had given Andrew advice on how to handle his feelings toward Mia and taught him to act like a soldier. Andrew owed the man too much to ever walk away.

"I promise you," Andrew said, "I will do everything in my power to make sure we get him out of there, alive."

"Thank you," Carter said.

"Grab the bag with the identification," Andrew said.

Carter opened the back door. The RAG agent did not wake up. Carter walked back around and Andrew grabbed the bag from his hands.

"We need to find three agents who look similar enough to us," Andrew said.

Carter reached in and pulled out a stack.

"That's why I hid, you know," Carter said.

Andrew stopped and looked up at the other boy.

"If I died nobody would ever know that Grant had him," Carter said. "It wasn't because I was scared for my own life. I would die for Mia or you. But I'll never put anyone above my father. From here on out I won't run, as long as I have your word you will get him out, even if I die."

Coward. That was the word Andrew thought of for Carter, but with Mia missing Andrew appreciated what Carter had done. If their group had been under attack and Andrew was the only hope Mia had, he would have hidden too. Andrew nodded his head at Carter and the two went back to sorting through the identification.

Chapter 35

There are fewer than one hundred women living in my neigh-
borhood. I have a feeling that there are more of us, kept in
smaller sections around the city. My former friend believes it
is for convenience, but I can't shake the feeling a more sinister
purpose exists.

—The diary of Megan Jean

The sun was starting to rise and Mia was getting nervous. Everything looked familiar. The landscape was filled with cornfields and
random patches of trees in the background. For the past two hours
Mia had been getting off at every exit and heading west, trying to see
if anything sparked a memory of her former home. She remembered
from the night she left her father's farm that it was located on the
same road as the highway entrance, and that was all the information
she had. Mia had never known the name of her town, and she wasn't
certain she lived in one. There was nobody else nearby. Whenever
her father had taken her off the property they had always driven for
at least thirty minutes.

Mia glanced down at the gun on the floor that one of the Agents
had left. As soon as she arrived at her parents' home she would point
the weapon at her father, threaten him until he gave her the informa-

tion she needed. They had to have some proof of the sale of their daughter. Mia was certain her father wouldn't lose track of business records.

Mia came up to another exit and turned off the highway. She headed west and the sun was growing in her rearview mirror. The exhaustion was starting to overtake her. Mia didn't know what was worse, the mental or physical pain. She was starting to lose focus again. She needed something to distract her as she kept the car on the road while scanning the area looking for any semblance of home.

Andrew was always a good distraction, but the pleasant memories of his kiss, his touch, and the elusive smile he gave only her, the one where his brown eyes warmed and melted her insides, had been replaced. Andrew didn't trust her or believe in her. He still saw her as property, only now she was his property. His actions showed that. Andrew kept too many secrets from her and did so under the guise of protecting her. Mia did not need his protection.

The anger in her was rising again. All of them had used her. It started in Saint Louis. She thought about Lisa, the woman she didn't get a chance to speak with much. Lisa was Mia's first point of contact with Affinity and all of them kept it from her. If the world was a game of chess Mia felt like a pawn.

Mia was so distracted she didn't notice that the corn had faded away. Then she saw it. The long gravel drive. Mia turned her head and spotted the large farmhouse in the distance. Her heart started to ache in her chest and she headed down the drive. She thought about what she would say to her parents.

There were no words. Mia knew it would be difficult to keep her composure and not ask a million questions. But stopping the Registry was more important than hearing excuses about the society her parents were willing participants in. Mia hoped she could keep her nerves under control long enough to get the information she needed.

The farmhouse grew closer and before Mia knew it she was ready to stop the car. She switched off the engine. Mia picked up the gun and opened the door. She started marching toward the porch and up the steps. All of her rage bubbled in her chest. She would be in and out of there in ten minutes, not giving her parents the opportunity to call Grant and let him know his lost property had returned. Mia would tell her parents how she hated them and what awful people they were. But the second Mia's hand touched the doorknob she froze.

Mia did not hate her parents. They were victims of the system, just as she had been. If Corinna had been unable to open their eyes Mia was unlikely to change anything. This was a mistake. Mia felt the urge to run. She dropped the handle and twisted her body away. Before she could make it down the steps the front door swung open.

"Mia?"

She turned back around. It was her mother. It had been months since Mia had seen her. She was standing in the doorway, wearing her pajamas from the night before; her hair had started to gray but she was more beautiful than Mia remembered.

"Mia, is it really you?"

Mia stood on the edge of the steps. Open and honest communication. That was Flo's advice. Mia looked at her mother and was at a loss for words. She opened her mouth, but none came out. Instead a sob made its way toward Mia's lips. She felt her legs give out and was sure she would hit the porch, but instead her mother caught her. She wrapped her arms around Mia, who buried her head into her shoulder. Mia continued to cry. She cried for the loss of Flo, she cried for Affinity's betrayal, but most of all Mia cried because she was happy to see her mother.

Chapter 36

I met with the grand commander alone. I seem to have stumbled into a position of power and am unsure how I feel about my current circumstances. He has asked for my complete trust and confidence. I reluctantly accepted his offer, if only to discover what he has planned for his future America.

—The journal of Isaac Ryland

Andrew drove. He didn't know where he was heading and had nobody to guide him. Carter was asleep in the backseat with the agent, who was still passed out. Zack joined the other travelers in slumber, but Andrew didn't have that luxury. He wanted to ask Zack a million questions, but the doctor Affinity had located for Zack had deposited the man in the car already asleep and had said few words to Andrew when he loaded him in.

"He'll wake up in a few hours," the doctor said. "Tell him to take his medicine every four hours for five days."

"Where am I supposed to take him?"

The man gave a shrug. "Anywhere but here."

Those were his final words before slamming the car door.

That had put a damper on Andrew's plans. He knew they needed to dump the RAG SUV; however much time their group had before the higher-ups realized their French trip was a disaster was dwindling. Andrew was certain they would search for the missing vehicles right away. Zack's sleep was a medicated one though and Andrew couldn't steal a car with two unconscious men.

"Water," a voice said.

Andrew glanced in the rearview mirror. Agent Quillian was coming to. Andrew grabbed the bottle he had up front, unscrewed the cap, and passed it back.

"My hands are behind my back," he said.

"I know," Andrew said. "That's why there's no cap. Figure it out or I'll drop the bottle all over the floor."

Andrew glanced back as the man leaned forward and put his mouth on the opening. Andrew did his best to tilt the bottle backward. Some liquid made it into the agent's mouth and he gulped it down.

"Where are we?"

"Headed to the Southwest Area," Andrew said. "We might be there already."

"If you don't kill me you'll have to let me go," he said.

"Eventually."

"Why are you doing this?" Agent Quillian asked.

"Because I made a promise not to kill you," Andrew said.

"No," Agent Quillian said. "Why are you betraying your country?"

"Who said anything about betrayal?"

"You came home with a foreign dignitary, only to have them die along with good American men who didn't deserve it," Agent Quillian said. "I call that treason."

"I was protecting myself," Andrew said.

"The French are not our allies," Agent Quillian said. Andrew couldn't tell if it was a question or a statement, but he responded either way.

"Not your allies."

Andrew returned his eyes to the road. They were entering more mountainous terrain. It was stunning, but Andrew knew mountains meant fewer people, which meant the chances that they'd be able to switch cars were growing slimmer and slimmer. The road he was traveling on was not well cared for. He swerved to avoid a pothole.

"So what's your story?"

"It doesn't concern you," Andrew said.

"I've been knocked out three times," he said. "I think it concerns me quite a bit."

Andrew didn't respond.

"Are you mad about mandatory service?" Agent Quillian asked. "Avoided your duty and came back to exact revenge?"

Andrew still didn't give a reply.

"Maybe you got too comfortable living abroad, think you can change the future for the young men here?"

Another pothole appeared and Andrew couldn't avoid it completely. The car bumped over it.

"You don't have to tell me the details," Agent Quillian said. "Just your endgame."

"Why would I do that?"

"You're dead anyway," Agent Quillian said. "We're all going to die, so don't make me leave this world without answering some of my questions."

The young agent was probably right. Andrew had accepted that before they reentered America.

"Maybe it was about the girl? She was pretty. Is she really French? What did you guys call her, Mia?"

Hearing him say her name boiled Andrew's blood. He tried to block out the agent, but he kept on talking.

"I see I hit a nerve," he said. "Did you want to drag her back here so you could enroll her in the Registry? Then buy her? She would be way out of your price range."

Mia was not and never would be for sale. Andrew felt his skin crawl and didn't want the man to speak anymore.

"We want to stop everything," Andrew said. "Mandatory service and the Registry."

Quillian let out a laugh.

"It's not a joke," Andrew said.

"It's a pipe dream," Agent Quillian said. "Not a goal."

"What?"

"Who doesn't want to stop the Registry and mandatory service?"

Andrew hadn't, not until he met Mia at least.

"You think I liked giving up four years of my life? Being raised in a dump? Now I can't even touch a woman unless I save up enough money to buy a wife. That's the way my country repays me."

"You don't like the Registry?"

"Nobody does," Agent Quillian said.

Andrew was confused.

"It's the way things are," Quillian said. "Nobody can change that. By the time men are powerful enough to have a say they have a pretty little wife and a pretty little life and don't care anymore."

"You think women should have a say in who they marry?"

"I don't care about women," Quillian said. "I enjoyed my time overseas sampling some. Now I come home and there's nothing, not until I get married."

This man did not see the plight of the people. He only saw the inability to have his needs satisfied.

"Every man hates it, until he gets married," he said. "If you complain about it someone will hush you up. But it's a fact. You would know that if you ever served your time like a real man."

"What about throwing out sons?" Andrew said. "Does everyone hate that too?"

"Lots of guys in service pledge they'll keep theirs, but we all know we're lying," Agent Quillian said. "If you ever meet a boy raised by a father, you know that's all he'll ever be: a boy. They're given the worst assignments; I met one once and it was like talking to a dead man. The government places them in the worst countries on the front lines. If any of them survive their four years, they've seen way too much carnage to have any type of normal life. I hated my father every day of my life until the day I was discharged."

"Why don't you band together and do something about it?"

"What? Like you're doing? Look how far it's gotten you. Some of your team is dead, your girl is gone, and you're driving through the Rocky Mountains."

Andrew's head was so filled with worry for Mia and their future plans, he had forgotten his knowledge of America. He debated hitting the brakes and heading back, but then he remembered everything he'd heard about the Rockies might be a myth. Instead he pushed the accelerator down harder.

"So what?"

"The next major metropolitan area isn't for hundreds of miles," Agent Quillian said.

"Then we won't run into anyone," Andrew said. "You left us with plenty of gasoline."

"As a government employee I have to tell you that there is next to no law out here," he said. "If anyone gets their hands on you it will be personal justice."

The man was trying to get inside Andrew's head. He knew the statistics; the vast majority of the population lived within a hundred-mile radius of one of the major cities. People avoided this stretch of the country, even tourists. Andrew shook his head; Mr. Morrissey's farm wasn't close to a big city and it had been safe there. Then Andrew remembered leaving the farm and the man who gave them a ride. The truck driver had tried to attack Mia and Andrew had killed him. That was the type of person who settled in places like this.

There was still a road. Andrew focused on that fact. Even if it was greatly in need of repair, it existed. They would fly through this section of the country and continue on toward the capital. Mia would meet them there. Andrew was sure of that fact. Knowing he would see her again was enough motivation to risk any danger.

Chapter 37

The grand commander wants to build a perfect future genera-
tion. That includes arranged marriages between the women
who have been left alive and our best and brightest men. I ex-
plained no woman would accept an arranged marriage in this
day and age, but the grand commander has other ideas.

—The journal of Isaac Ryland

No one at the airport gave Grant trouble. He didn't need to show identification or clearance. Grant could tell the people there wanted his autograph more than to question his actions. He didn't offer his signature though. Becoming a celebrity was something he had done at the current grand commander's insistence. Grant didn't want the American people in awe of him; he wanted them to fear him.

Grant was still waiting for a phone call or for news to break about whatever had happened to the French visitors. He hated not diving right in, but it wasn't worth the risk of his involvement at this stage. Grant used the arrival of the Taiwanese guests as an excuse to land his plane at the airport, but he couldn't have cared less about them. He wanted to get Rex and make his way back to his home so he could plot his next move. The RAG agents in charge of the foreign visitors set to arrive waited on the tarmac near Grant.

"Copy that," a RAG agent said into his microphone. He started walking toward Grant. "Sir," he said. "I hate to bother you, but the airport says there's a man insisting he's here with you. He's becoming irate."

"Tell them to send him down."

Grant hadn't told the airport about Rex. He wanted his man flustered. Grant knew Rex was up to something and wanted him to witness the capture of his new employers. Grant wondered how much money Amelia and her organization had offered Rex; it must have been a lot because Grant kept the man well paid.

"Make sure they frisk him first," Grant said. "He can have no weapons on him or anything that could be used as a weapon."

The agent nodded his head and relayed his instructions into the microphone.

"Agent," Grant said, "I want you and your men on high alert."

"We were informed this was an easy assignment," the agent said.

"You were misinformed," Grant said. "Think of our visitors as hostile and be ready."

"Yes, sir," the man said.

The agent walked over toward his team and relayed their new instructions. Grant was pleased to see their demeanor change. All of them checked their weapons and then straightened up and stood shoulder to shoulder, forming a line behind the agent in charge. For a few moments Grant admired his power. The agent didn't question Grant's orders. If his initial interaction with RAG agents had been as successful, then Amelia would have never made it out of the country in the first place.

"Hey, boss," Rex said, breaking Grant's concentration.

It had been months since the two men had seen each other. Grant looked at the looming giant. His skin was darker and his hair longer, but Grant saw the same determination in the man's eyes. That determination used to work toward Grant's goals but was now focused on a more sinister purpose.

"You look like hell," Grant said.

The man's clothes were dirty and stood in contrast to Grant's khaki pants and lemon striped collared shirt. Grant breathed in and accidentally smelled the man next to him. He hoped Mia didn't have the same stink on her.

"And you need a shower," Grant said.

"I've been traveling across Mexico," Rex said. "I had to ditch my vehicle at the border and then walk for several miles before securing another to meet you here. What are we doing here?" Rex asked.

"I flew my personal plane down to get you," Grant said. "By luck a foreign dignitary is en route to land. I wanted to greet him."

"That doesn't sound like you," Rex said.

"Maybe I've changed since we last parted ways," Grant said.

He looked for a reaction from Rex, but none came. The man remained as stoic as ever. Grant was hoping to pick up on some sense of disloyalty.

"What country are they from?"

"Which would you expect?" Grant asked.

Rex was well trained; he raised his shoulders and didn't look fazed by Grant's question.

"It doesn't matter," Rex said. "They're all foreign scum to me."

Before Grant could ask another question a loud noise filled the air. Grant turned his head to watch the small plane land on the runway. He watched as the aircraft circled around. He started walking closer. He heard Rex's footsteps behind him. Grant stopped and turned to face the large man.

"I think it's best if you stay back," Grant said. "This is an official welcoming and you're in no shape to greet anyone."

Rex nodded his head and stepped backward. Grant glanced into his man's eyes. Grant couldn't tell if Rex was nervous or not. It was a pity he had been turned. Finding a replacement with the same skill set would take months, if not years. Grant turned his attention back to the plane. The first group started walking out. Two American soldiers, the escorts for the foreign visitors.

Next the supreme leader of Taiwan stepped out. He was older than Ian. The picture he had provided showed a man forty years younger. His wife followed, and she was close to his age. Next a woman more than a decade older than Grant stepped out. Two people of a similar age trailed behind her. Then the door closed.

The RAG agent in charge ordered these people patted down. Grant saw the look of confusion on their faces. He made it to the group and went straight toward the supreme leader.

"Is this your entire group?" Grant asked.

The man was trying to push the RAG agent away. He was yelling in another language.

"Answer me, you old fool," Grant said.

The man looked over at Grant. He wore a look of recognition on his face and started to speak to Grant in the same language. One of the American soldiers stepped forward.

"Sir, he does not speak English," the soldier said.

"Well, what is he saying?" Grant asked.

The soldier pointed down the row of people being patted down. The youngest woman, who was still close to thirty, hit the RAG agent patting her down with her purse. The agent backed away and drew his weapon. The woman let out a scream.

"She is his translator," the soldier said.

Their leader continued to yell in the strange language.

"Bring the woman over here," Grant said.

The RAG agent kept his gun drawn and walked her toward Grant.

"What is he babbling about?"

The woman was afraid. Her eyes glanced toward the leader and then back to Grant. " 'I am the king,' " she said. " ' I don't deserve this treatment. We are guests. Please tell them. I am here for your wedding.' "

The whole reason Grant wanted to meet these people was to ensure at least one country remained in fear of America.

"Tell him to shut up," Grant said.

The woman translated and the man did the opposite. His voice rose and his little face started turning red. Grant couldn't stand it any longer. He lifted his hand and gripped the man by the throat.

"*Shut your mouth,*" Grant said.

This did the trick. All the rage Grant was feeling came to a boil. Mia was roaming free around his country and Grant didn't have enough information to trace her yet. She had outsmarted him again. Grant couldn't wait to get his hands on Mia and wring her neck. The image of strangling her pretty little neck popped into Grant's mind and he began squeezing. One of the women let out a cry and brought Grant back to reality. He let go of the foreign leader. The man began coughing.

"Welcome to America," Grant said.

He turned around and stormed off. Grant glanced at Rex as he walked by. The large man's face remained still. Whatever victory Rex was feeling, Grant took pleasure in the fact that it would be short-lived. This was a misstep, but Grant was still certain all of his enemies would fall in the near future.

Chapter 38

I organized a meeting and found most of the women here share my fears. We are too isolated. Half of us want to leave and find another way to survive, or else flee the country until whatever is happening here settles itself. The other half don't want to admit what is going on in front of their eyes. These poor people lost more than most in the tragedy and even after all these months are still engulfed with mourning.

—The diary of Megan Jean

The sun was coming through the window and Mia fluttered her eyes open. The bed was so warm she didn't want to get up. She turned and nuzzled her favorite pillow. She couldn't remember the last time she'd slept so well.

As soon as the thought crossed her mind the memories came rushing to the fore. Escaping with Andrew, making their way across the country, avoiding the militia, finding a semblance of peace at Affinity, meeting Flo and losing her too soon. Mia shot out of bed. It was *her* bed. She was back at her parents' farmhouse. She looked down at herself: she was wearing a pair of pink sweatpants and a white tank top; her hair had been pulled back into a low ponytail and pinned away from her eyes. Mia did not remember changing.

Confusion turned to dread. When Corinna came home her parents had been quick to return their daughter to her husband. It was a stupid idea to come here and even more asinine to fall asleep. Grant was probably already on his way, courtesy of Mia's mother and father.

Mia looked around her room for the keys to her vehicle or the weapon she had brought. She debated jumping out of the window and making a break for it. Mia walked toward the blinds. The sun wasn't rising; it was starting to set. There was a knock on her door. Mia didn't have time to waste. She started lifting the heavy wooden window when the door creaked open.

"Mia?" Her mother's voice carried through the room. "Are you awake? We heard someone walking."

Mia flung the window open, but she froze. She had come here for a reason and if need be Mia could just overpower her mother and make it toward the front door. Mia wasn't the weak one any longer. She spun around to face her mother.

"How much time do I have?" Mia asked.

"What do you mean?"

Mia looked at her mother's face. The woman looked like she had aged decades in the time Mia had been gone. Instead of wearing a fine dress, she had on ripped jeans and a baggy white T-shirt that was covered with ash stains. Her beautiful hair was piled in a bun on the top of her head and she wore no makeup or jewelry. Mia wanted to ask questions, but she needed to keep her priorities straight. Showing concern for her mother's well-being might waste whatever precious time she had.

"Before Grant gets here to claim me. How much time do I have?" Mia's voice did not falter. Her mother looked shocked.

"Nobody is coming for you," she said. "At least nobody I'm aware of. Please sit down. I can tell you're scared."

"I'm strong," Mia said.

"I never said you weren't," her mother replied.

"How did I get up here?"

"You were so tired," she said. "I led you upstairs and helped you change."

She took a seat in the chair next to Mia's bed. Mia hadn't noticed the rocker was pulled up.

"I sat with you all day," she said. "It figures you'd wake up when I leave for five minutes to check on something."

Mia didn't say anything.

"You were like that as a baby too," her mother said. "You always slept better when someone else was in the room with you. But it was just as hard for anyone to leave you alone. You looked so peaceful sleeping. I could watch you sleep for hours and neglect my own rest."

"Why are you telling me this?"

"A lot has changed," her mother said. "If you don't want to sit here, why don't you come down to the kitchen? I can make something for you."

"The last time you made me food was years ago," Mia said. "Unless Father was eating too."

Mia's mother frowned and looked at the floor. "I thought I was preparing you," she said. "Getting you ready for the rest of your life. I wanted to cook for you every day. You are my baby and you've come home to me."

Mia's mother raised her head. Mia could see the tears glassing over her eyes. This was not the woman Mia remembered. Her mother was stern; she'd slapped Mia for suggesting she didn't want to get married.

"Would you rather talk first?" she asked. "I would love to hear how you've been. I was so sure you were dead."

The last part sent Mia's mother over the edge. She started sobbing into her hands. Seeing her mother like this caused Mia's own tears to well up; she couldn't help the reflex. She ran over to the chair and dropped to her knees. Her mother wrapped her arms around Mia and she returned the gesture.

"I'm so angry at you," Mia said.

"I know," she replied. "I'm sorry."

The words stung Mia. She felt guilt creep up into her heart. This reunion could not last long though. Even if Mia's family hadn't called Grant, she'd stolen a RAG vehicle and left a pile of dead bodies in her wake. Someone would be following her soon. The farm was filled with people. None of the young men her father employed could be alerted to her presence.

"I can't stay long," Mia said. She released her mother and stood up again.

"Why not?"

"Nobody else can know I'm here," Mia said. "I'm certain one of the workers saw the car. It's not safe for me."

"There aren't any workers," Mia's mother said.

"What do you mean?"

"There's nobody here who will let anyone know about your presence," she said. "I moved the SUV far down the driveway. So in the unlikely event that someone drives by, they won't see anything."

"I don't understand," Mia said.

"Why don't you take a few minutes?" her mother said. "Freshen up and come downstairs. I can get some food ready for you and we can have a nice long talk."

Mia's mother stood up. She reached out and grabbed Mia's hands.

"I love you," she said.

The words hurt Mia's heart. Her mother hadn't spoken them in years. Mia tried to remember the last time she'd heard that sentiment from her family, but she couldn't. Mia's mother released her hands and walked out of the room, leaving a stunned Mia to dry her tears.

Chapter **39**

Last night we made our break from confinement. It was not the most well-thought-out escape plan. I was one of the fortunate ones and now travel with four other women. We have yet to reach the edges of the city and are hiding out in an abandoned house. We hear sirens and search parties and hope they are not for us.

—The diary of Megan Jean

When Mia walked down the giant steps she noticed the house was in disarray. The dust on the pictures and the floor wouldn't have been noticeable to anyone else, but Mia knew her mother had been meticulous in her cleaning. Things really had changed. Mia walked down the hall to see her mother at the stove. She was cooking eggs.

"Breakfast for dinner?" Mia asked.

"Eggs are a good source of protein," her mother said. "And I'm making you an omelet. I remember how you loved them."

Mia took a seat at the counter while her mom started seasoning the pan. This was very overwhelming, but Mia needed to continue the conversation. It was the reason she had come back.

"Where is Father?" Mia asked. "I have things to say to both of you."

"Your father is not well," her mother said. "I'm afraid he isn't much for speaking these days. He doesn't leave the bed often."

Mia remembered her father being active. He was always running around giving orders and bragging about his latest sale.

"What happened?" Mia asked.

"After you ran away Grant paid us a visit," Mia's mother said. "He was unusually cruel. Your father slipped inside his own mind. At first it started with him waking up in the middle of the night and talking to himself. Then he started thinking everyone was trying to kill him. He fired Whitney's father, then sent all the boys away. He doesn't even speak much anymore. It's like he's living in a dream state."

"Did you call a doctor?" Mia asked.

"How could I? What if they took him away, where would I go?"

Into retirement, Mia thought. She cringed at the idea.

"It has been a bit of a blessing," Mia's mother said. "I run things around here now. The fields aren't quite what they used to be, but I grow enough food to survive."

"That's dangerous," Mia said. "Mother, what if someone came to check on you or came looking for Father? You would get shipped away."

"Trust me," she said. "Nobody is coming. We are the black sheep now. Our friends are nonexistent; all your father's vendors stopped placing orders. In the event anyone does come I have piles of cash lying around to pay them off, and if that doesn't work I have a shotgun too."

Mia's eyes went wide. This was not the uptight vision of womanly perfection Mia had idolized as a young adult.

"It's all because I ran away," Mia said.

"Don't apologize," she said.

"I didn't," Mia said.

She had known her parents would face repercussions for her actions, but she thought they deserved them for selling their daughters.

"I deserve that," her mother said. "And as far as the world is concerned you were kidnapped. Only a select few think you ran away."

"Then why do they avoid you?"

"It started right after you left," she said. "You father thought it was because they were all trying to kill him, but that made no sense. I think they were paid to leave us alone. I'm not sure if it was by Mr. Marsden or the government. Either way, people will do wicked things for the right price."

"Why would you think that?"

"I did," she said.

"Not the money issue," Mia said. "Why do you think they were paid?"

"A few days after you left, our house was stormed by RAG agents. They took every record of you. Searched through all the rooms, took all the pictures, anything with your name on it. I called your two older sisters and their husbands refused my calls. Someone wanted to make sure you never existed. I think they want us to die out here."

Mia cringed. That thought had never entered her mind. There was no record of her existence here. The trip was wasted.

"Why didn't they take you away then? You and Father?"

"I'm not sure," she said. "Once Grant started making television appearances I was sure they would, that your father's mumbling was right."

"Why didn't you leave?"

"Where would I go?"

"You could have run away like I did," Mia said. "Made it to Mexico."

"As much as I wish I was as brave as you, my darling girl, I am not," she said. "And for all your father's shortcomings he did take care of me and give me four beautiful girls. I couldn't leave him here. He needs someone to feed him and change his sheets. Sometimes the whole left side of his body goes numb, and his eyes roll back in his head. It's awful."

Mia's mother dropped the omelet on a plate and brought out two forks. She took a seat next to Mia and started picking at the food. Mia had a hard time mustering up an appetite.

"Please," her mother said. "Tell me about where you've been. How in the world are you still alive?"

Too many emotions were clouding Mia's head. She wasn't ready to share with her mother yet.

"Why did you do it?" Mia asked.

"What?"

"Put me in the Registry? Only teach me about being a wife? You slapped me when I tried to open up to you about my feelings."

Mia's mother took a bite. "I didn't know how else to act," she said. "I grew up hating my mother. She was cruel. She used to make me clean till my palms bled. Then when I would show her the sparkling job I did she would raise her nose at me and make me do it again."

"So that justifies your treatment of your own daughters?"

"Let me finish," her mother said. "When your father married me I was scared, but after I had lived with him for only a week he'd shown me so much more kindness than my parents ever had. I loved him for it. Whenever he asked me questions about myself or commented on the work I had done, it felt amazing to have the attention."

Her mother stopped and took a drink of water.

"When your eldest sister was born I was thrilled. I loved her so much and was going to treat her with the admiration she deserved, but then it hit me. My own mother loved me too. She treated me that way so it would be easier on me when I got married. What I mistook for cruelty was kindness. Her treatment made it easier for me to adjust to my new family.

"Still, I promised myself I wouldn't be like her," she said. "I was always loving to you girls. When your older sisters turned twelve they went off to finishing school. I didn't have to be stern. I wasn't so lucky with you; since you stayed here I had to try my hardest to act like I didn't care about you."

Mia understood what her mother was saying. Before Corinna made her late-night visit Mia couldn't wait to get married; she probably wouldn't have missed her parents at all. Leaving them was never a concern for her. Mia shook her head. That still didn't justify everything.

"Why not run away with us?"

"Your father would have thrown me out if I brought it up to him, and how was I supposed to leave with four little girls of all ages? I don't regret staying; if I hadn't you would never have been born."

Mia felt a twinge of guilt. Andrew was the only reason she had made it out of the country. On her own she wouldn't have made it to the highway. But she was not ready to let go of her anger.

"What about Corinna?" Mia asked. "She came to you as an adult for help and you threw her away."

"She made up for that," said a voice that came from behind Mia.

Mia recognized the fluttery, petite voice. She closed her eyes and froze. Mia knew she was shaking; she took a big breath and spun around, opening her eyes to see the familiar face. There was a woman with long blond hair in a side braid. She wore a pair of ratty jeans and an oversize sweatshirt. Mia was seeing a ghost.

Without realizing she was doing it, Mia stood from her chair. She raised her hands over her mouth and let out a gasp.

"Corinna?" Mia asked.

"Welcome home, little sister," Corinna said.

Mia bolted from the chair and latched on to her sister with both her arms. She felt the embrace returned and another arm drape across her back. Her mother kissed the top of her head.

"My girls, together again."

Chapter 40

As I predicted the women are aware they are more prisoners than anything else. A group made an escape. They were stopped and returned to their compound, but five are still missing. The grand commander has labeled the missing women his top priority and is taking measures to ensure the rest of the women under his leadership do not attempt the same feat.

—*The journal of Isaac Ryland*

"If you want to pull over I can drive," Carter said.

"Me too," Agent Quillian said.

"I'm fine," Andrew said.

The last few hours had gone smoothly. Carter had woken up and was chatting with the agent like they were long-lost pals, about nothing that mattered. Andrew knew Carter was doing him a favor by keeping the agent distracted and was starting to get annoyed with his duties. Andrew glanced at his phone. The sun was starting to set and Zack still wasn't awake. The GPS had stopped working a while ago, and Andrew hoped he was on the right road.

"You won't get service out here," Agent Quillian said. "If you're expecting a phone call it won't come through. Why do you think that bag of agents' phones has stayed so silent?"

"Maybe we should toss the bag," Carter said. "What if they have GPS?"

"If the car doesn't have a tracker the phone doesn't," Zack said. "Remember the technology ban? Those things are only good for texting and calling."

"You're awake," Andrew said to Zack. "How do you feel?"

"Like I slept for a week," Zack said.

"How's the shoulder?" Carter asked.

"The doctor had to dig a bullet out," Zack said. "That's how it feels."

"How did you find that doctor?" Carter asked. "Will he turn us in?"

"Affinity," Zack said. "I have an emergency contact. They located him for me."

Andrew was relieved that Zack had woken up. They needed to move their plans forward.

"That doctor is going to hang for helping you," Agent Quillian said.

"Hello, I'm Zack. I don't think I've had the pleasure of meeting you."

"You don't deserve to know my name," Agent Quillian said.

"Agent Trent Quillian," Andrew said. "He's twenty-five years old and likes to talk a lot."

"I never told you my first name," the agent said.

"I guessed," Andrew said, not wanting to explain that he had the man's ID badge.

"You've been awake for over twenty-four hours?" Zack asked.

"Try thirty-six," Carter said. "Do you ever sleep?" he asked Andrew.

"Where are we?" Zack asked.

"In the middle of no man's land," Agent Quillian said. "The Rocky Mountains. The most dangerous place in America."

"*If* we see anyone, they'll leave us alone," Carter said. "We don't have anything for them to steal."

"Keep telling yourself that," Agent Quillian said.

"Where are we headed?" Zack asked.

"Toward the capital," Andrew said. "Mia will meet us there."

"She made contact again?" Zack asked. "Did she find the documentation?"

"No," Agent Quillian said. "Lover boy is just sure his precious Mia won't let him down."

Andrew heard a gun cock.

"Andrew may have promised he wouldn't kill you, but I didn't," Carter said.

"Hey, man, I thought we were becoming friends," Agent Quillian said.

"Shut up or I will hit you over the head with this and knock you out again," Carter said.

Andrew was surprised by Carter but didn't object, especially when the agent went quiet. He returned his attention to Zack. Andrew was ready for the fight and had all his points preplanned.

"If you want to make it back home you're on your own," Andrew said. "I won't leave her."

"Negative," Zack said. "I used the good doctor's computer. I spoke with Affinity. They are aware of the situation. Our orders are to push forward."

"What about Mia?" Carter asked.

"Mia is now secondary," Zack said. "While she plays an integral part in riling up the people, we have some information we cannot sit on."

Andrew didn't ask what the information was and neither did Carter. There could only be one thing more important than Mia: the code to the room holding the master server. Carter stayed quiet on the Rod front too. Andrew felt new respect for his comrade. That was something the two of them would handle.

"How much time do we have?" Andrew asked.

"Grant Marsden's wedding is in two weeks," Zack said. "That is the night we act."

"Is the code changed every two weeks?" Carter asked.

"No," Zack said. "But at this event Grant will be formally named the next grand commander and based on what we know about him that will start Ian's death clock. Grant cannot become grand commander."

"Grant Marsden is a brave man," Agent Quillian said. "He is honorable and would do no such thing."

"Shut up," the three other occupants said in unison.

"See, if we could get Mia to go on TV at the exact same time we destroy the Registry, then people who like this guy would see Grant for the monster he really is," Carter said.

"Mia will be there," Andrew said.

"As long as we have the proof, everything will work out," Zack said. "Let's hope Rex does his part and we all meet together."

"Worst-case scenario, we destroy the Registry and service records," Carter said.

"Or die trying," Agent Quillian said.

"What?" Andrew asked.

"You don't think the entire organization knows Agent Barker hasn't checked in? That the French diplomats missed their tour? Every RAG agent in the country will look for you. They'll see the burned-down building and missing cars. You guys are sitting ducks."

Nobody responded to the RAG agent. The man was right. They needed to ditch the car before they rejoined civilization. Andrew glanced at the fuel guage. They were running low. Then he remembered the tanks in the trunk; when he pulled over Carter could take over for the night and Andrew could get some sleep. Zack rolled his window down.

"The air isn't too cold," he said. "We should pull over and sleep for the night."

"I don't want to stop if we don't have to," Andrew said.

"The agent is right," Zack said. "We can't show up on the other side of the mountains in this thing. We need a plan to ditch it, but we can figure out our next step in the morning. Nobody is going to come for us in the middle of nowhere. There's a dip in the road up ahead, pull over. We can find a place to start a fire and get some sleep."

"What about him?" Carter asked.

"I'll figure it out," Zack said.

Andrew was so tired, he did what he was told. The car pulled off to the side of the road and he killed the engine.

"This is a bad idea, gentlemen," Agent Quillian said. "We won't live through the night. The mountain people will find us."

"I've never heard of evil people living out here," Zack said. "Andrew? Carter?"

"Myths," Carter said. "Nobody lives out here."

"I know the truth," Agent Quillian said. "The government doesn't want people to know how dangerous this area is. Why have you never met a man who was from here?"

"Because nobody is from here," Andrew said. "It's fine. We can set up camp."

He took a big breath and opened the door. Zack climbed out and Carter followed. The agent stayed in the car. The group walked around to the back of the SUV. Carter popped the trunk and with his good arm Zack started lifting down the gasoline.

"What are you doing?"

"Hoping you boys kept the right SUV," Zack said.

Carter and Andrew helped unload the rest of the trunk. Agent Quillian turned around in his seat and was staring at them, not saying a word.

"I saw the RAG agents load these things earlier," Zack said. "They all have lower compartments. Two of them were filled with the luggage and one of them had emergency supplies."

Zack started feeling around on the felt floor.

"There's a button on the right," Agent Quillian said.

Everyone looked up at him.

"What? I could use some headache medicine," he said.

Andrew saw what he was talking about and hit the mechanism. The false floor popped up. Carter let out a sigh.

"Is it the emergency supplies?" Agent Quillian asked.

Carter leaned in and unzipped one of the black suitcases. Andrew saw the blast of colorful clothes and he started laughing.

"Women's clothing," Zack said. "I hope Mia won't mind if we burn some of these. Sorry about the headache."

Andrew and Carter lifted the luggage out of the car. There was a small path that led up from the road. The two men followed Zack as he climbed.

"I don't want to get too far from the car, but far enough, in case we need to hide. Lock the doors. Once we get settled we can come back for Agent Quillian."

"Already locked," Andrew said.

The agent was screaming. Andrew didn't turn around to look for him, but the man's cries told him one thing: he was more afraid of being left alone than traveling with strange men who had killed all his coworkers. Andrew shook away his doubts. He was way too tired to let his mind wander. Once he got some sleep his mind would recognize how foolishly the agent was acting.

Chapter 41

I helped with the search and by blind luck found the missing women. They are staying in an abandoned garage, no doubt waiting for the search to die down so they can make a break for the border. I saw them but did not draw attention to their location. These women are probably much more dangerous with a weapon than myself and a large part of me hopes they make it to freedom.

—The journal of Isaac Ryland

The sun was down, but Grant's spirits were lower. They made it back to Grant's mansion, and he still hadn't heard any news about the French. Agent Barker's phone was going straight to voice mail now; soon enough they would be reported missing and Grant could step in without drawing suspicion. He was now showered and changed into a set of maroon silk pajamas, complete with matching robe. He couldn't think of a more commanding outfit to wear while inflicting some pain.

He was unsure which of his two targets to deal with at the moment. Then the thought hit him. Grant could do both at the same time.

When he jogged down the stairs it was no surprise to see Rex waiting at the bottom. The man's awful stench was gone. He had showered and dressed in a tight black T-shirt and combat pants, the exact uniform Grant expected.

"Follow me," Grant said.

The man didn't question his orders when he followed Grant through the secret passage in the kitchen. They walked in silence among the dark hallways. Grant hoped Rex's fear was growing. Silence sometimes helped the mind envision what awful things lay ahead, and Grant did not want to disappoint.

Rex followed Grant out into the east wing. Grant did not slow his pace. They made it to the long corridor of rooms. Grant stopped and Rex almost ran into him. Grant took this as a good sign; the large man was off his game.

"I thought you might enjoy this as a welcome-home present," Grant said.

He pushed open the door to Rod's room. The man was unconscious. Grant forgot he had ordered the doctor to keep him under at all times. He glanced at the tray sitting next to the man's IV. There were three loaded syringes. One of them had to bring the man to life. Problem averted.

"I'd like to introduce you to Roderick Rowe," Grant said. "Also known as Carter's father and Amelia's assistant. Now, I like to think of him as my personal and most important guest."

Grant studied Rex's face. If the large man felt for the bedridden person he was showing no signs. Grant had expected some reaction, but he continued to smile, sure he could detect an involuntary indication Rex had switched sides.

"Have a seat," Grant said. "You're being quiet tonight."

"I'm tired," Rex said.

"Roderick has been my backup plan," Grant said. "I'm certain the young Mr. Rowe will trade his father's life for the life of my former bride."

Rex still gave no reaction.

"What do you say we wake him up?" Grant asked.

"Why?"

"I promised his son I wouldn't harm his father," Grant said, "if he delivered Amelia to me. It was simple at first, but Roderick has regained some of his memory and was asking too many questions, so I've kept him unconscious. We can't do any serious harm to the man. You know I keep my word. But if he awakes and is inconsolable we may have to use some force."

No reaction from Rex yet. Grant looked at the tray and picked up the middle syringe. He found the injection port in Rod's IV and steadied the needle.

"For all I know this might kill him," Grant said. "Should I inject him anyway?"

There was a slight hesitation, but Rex nodded. Grant pushed the fluid into the IV.

"Would it bother you if this man died?" Grant asked.

"No," Rex said. "He has nothing to offer."

Grant frowned. Even if Rex had switched sides, that would be the answer he'd give. Rod offered little to Mia's cause and Rex would never show concern for strangers. Grant opened his mouth to re-phrase the question but before he could get a word out Rod shot up in bed.

"Where am I?" Rod asked. "Where's Carter?"

Laughter escaped from Grant's lips. Of course he had chosen the right medication. Rex did his best to chuckle, but Grant could tell he wasn't as animated as he should have been. Grant stopped his laughter.

"Your son is helping return my wife to me," Grant said. "Then I shall kill her and the two of you will be on your way."

Rod was breathing heavily, unable to respond. Grant diverted his attention to Rex. The man's breathing had gotten heavier, but not enough for Grant to enjoy his affliction.

"Carter is not that dumb," Rod said. "You will never win."

"There are so many places on the human body that are capable of experiencing intense pain," Grant said. "Some so much even the mind can't mask what the person is feeling."

Grant spun his chair around and started to look for an instrument. He had to open a few drawers before he found a long needle that lay on a piece of blue cloth. It was designed to be inserted into a person's spine, but Grant wasn't about to paralyze his hostage. He turned his chair back around. Rex was still acting compliant.

"You've already lost," Rod said. "Just kill me."

The hostage started tugging at the cuffs on his wrists. *Perfect,* Grant thought. He grabbed the man's hand and held it down to the bed. Rod was too weak to overpower Grant. He looked at the vein and knew he had to avoid the main source of blood flow.

"I don't know which is more effective," Grant said. "Pain or fear. I'll go for both."

Grant slid the giant needle into Rod's wrist and down through his palm. Grant could see the tool under Rod's skin. The man started struggling and yelling. Grant kept going, watching as the large apparatus appeared under his skin. He pushed it all the way through his middle finger. Rod stopped screaming and was incapable of making noise.

"What do you think, Rex?"

Grant wanted a response, anything to signal Rex had switched sides, but the man was too well trained. He appeared as impassive as ever.

"Might as well do it all the way," he said.

Grant looked back down and pushed the needle in all the way. The tip burst out the end of Rod's finger. The hostage found his voice again and started screaming. Grant let go of the needle.

"Does this please you?" Grant asked.

"Are you trying to get information from him?" Rex asked.

Roderick was not the man Grant was after. Rex was doing his best to avoid Grant's questions, but his eyes were unwavering. There was no way to read the large man. Grant turned back to the tray and inserted another dose of medication into Rod's IV. It took seconds for the screaming man to become unconscious again. Rex continued to look straight ahead.

"I'm glad you're back," Grant said.

Rex nodded his head. He showed no hesitation. Their eyes would meet and Rex would stare right back. Grant looked down at Rod and noted the bleeding was minimal. Dr. Schaffer could clean this up in the morning.

Grant stood up from his chair and left the room. Rex followed. Grant hadn't lied. He was happy Rex was back. Now he had something to focus his attention on. Grant was certain Mia was in the country, but until he had a more accurate location for the girl Grant could plan the slow torture of Rex. He was exhilarated. The hunt was back on.

Chapter 42

We lasted three days, without water or food, before we were forced to make a move. It didn't take much for them to capture us, which the men guarding the city insisted was for our protection yet again. If anything about this incident gives me faith in the human spirit, it is the one person who showed us kindness by not turning us in even earlier. However, he was still in a position to help us and instead chose to ignore us, which might be just as bad as turning us in.

—The diary of Megan Jean

"Please," Mia said. "I have told you every detail from the past few months. Now tell me more about what happened to you."

She couldn't take her eyes off Corinna. It was like sitting with a ghost. Mia had been certain Corinna's husband, William, had killed her. Then she realized her mother and sister felt the same way being so close to her. Mia's relatives, like most of America, had thought she was dead.

"Before your father got really bad I made him drive me to William's house," Mia's mother said. "I wanted to speak with him about your father's medical condition."

"What could he have done?" Mia asked.

"He was a medic when he was in service," Corinna said. "But to answer your question, nothing. If David had been shot, then William might have been able to get the bullet out, but that was about it."

Mia didn't know why Corinna was referring to their father by his name but didn't think it was important enough to stop her story.

"William was not very happy to see us," Mia's mother said. "He refused to let us inside. I was left standing on his front porch and I looked up to see a familiar face staring back down at me from a window."

"I shouldn't have believed you were dead," Mia said. "I was wrong."

"No," Corinna said. "That night I left here William kept telling me nobody cared about me but him. I knew he was wrong. Laura did care about me. I could see it in her eyes."

Mia picked up on Corinna's calling their mother by her first name but again didn't ask why.

"But they sent you back?"

"What were they supposed to do? I was married and William's property."

The horror Mia felt at her parents' actions started to dissolve. She didn't know what else they could have done. If they lied and said Corinna wasn't here, William and the RAG agents would have searched the property and found her.

"To prove to me that my parents didn't love me, he told them I was dead and told me that they wouldn't bother to mourn. I thought he was right. I was defeated. Laura and David didn't ask any questions or request to attend a funeral service. I thought they didn't love me. Then I saw her at the window and I knew he was wrong. They did come for me."

"I lost it, started pounding on the door," Mia's mother said. "Screaming for Corinna. William came back with a gun."

"What did you do?" Mia asked.

"Begged," Mia's mother said. "I dropped to my knees and begged him to let me see my daughter. He kept insisting that she was dead and I had imagined seeing her."

"After my escape attempt William kept me locked in a room up-stairs," Corinna said. "It was a violent couple of months. I think he was planning to kill me if he couldn't break me into submission, but that meant he would have to spend more money on a new wife."

"Money was such a motivator for your father, I thought it might be for William too," Mia's mother said. "I had brought lots with me, to pay William for his medical services. I didn't know how much it would cost so I took a lot of money. That's when it hit me. I offered to buy back Corinna."

"And he accepted?" Mia asked.

"Not at first," Mia's mother said. "Then I went to the car and brought back all the cash I had. I gave him everything and he gave me back my daughter."

"Just like that?" Mia asked. "That's illegal; wasn't he scared you would tell someone?"

"What would happen if I told?" Mia's mother asked. "Your father was coming undone; William would get into some trouble, but Corinna and I would be sent away. William understood there was no risk. He had Corinna declared dead and I am certain he purchased a new, more compliant bride right away."

"We've been living here ever since," Corinna said. "It has been some of the hardest months of my life. Now you've come to join us."

Corinna reached out and took Mia's hand. Mia felt a warmth flow through her body. This felt right. Corinna was alive and her mother was a new person. The sun had almost set and Mia's mother stood up. She came back with some candles and matches.

"There's no electricity anymore," she said. "We make do though.

It will be a different story when winter comes; I'm sure the running water will stop by then, but we've been digging a well."

"Winter?" Mia asked.

She was jogged out of this fantasy and pulled her hand away from Corinna.

"It will pass," Corinna said. "Then in spring we can start the garden up again. We're so busy around here the time will fly."

"I can't stay here," Mia said.

Even in the candlelight she could see the look of hurt and confusion on Corinna's face.

"But we're together again," Mia's mother said. "It will be different this time."

"That would be hiding," Mia said. "It's not a life."

"I know you've spent time with rebel groups and international spies," Corinna said. "But that's not a life either. We can all be happy here. Together."

"You don't understand," Mia said. "If the government hasn't put it together yet I can assure you Grant has. We have about one more night at the most until the disaster at the orphanage is discovered. The first place he'll come looking for me is here."

"We'll be ready for him," Corinna said.

"With what? The one shotgun you have?" Mia asked. "He'll have an army. You two can't stay here either. I've put you in so much danger just by coming. If I had known I would have stayed away."

"Don't say that," Mia's mother said. "You coming home today is one of the happiest moments in my life."

"I mean it," Mia said. "We're leaving. All of us. I won't let anything bad happen to you because of me."

"What about your father?" Mia's mother asked.

"Him too," Mia said. "We're leaving tonight."

"Where will we go?" Corinna asked.

It didn't take long for Mia to come up with the answer.

"Someplace with people I trust," Mia said. "Corinna, I need you to find me a map of the Midwest Area. Mom, get one of the cars ready. Make sure there's extra gasoline in the back. Both of you pack supplies, food, water, and warm clothing."

Both women stared at her, neither moved.

"This is serious," Mia said. "Bad people will come here. They will take both of you away. Please, don't fight me on this."

"Think, honey," Mia's mother said. "What if someone sees us on the road? Three women and an incapacitated man traveling together? It's a bad idea."

Mia pushed her chair away from the table and went to the kitchen. She pulled open the first drawer and saw the pair of scissors. Without acknowledging either woman Mia walked behind Corinna and with a single cut chopped her braid off. Mia slammed the removed hair on the table. She walked over to her mother and chopped off the bun sitting on top of her head.

"I will find us some baseball hats," Mia said. "You're men now. Act like it."

Both women looked at her with wide eyes. Neither protested her missing locks and each stood up. Mia started leaving the kitchen.

"Where are you going?" Corinna asked, her voice shaking.

"I'm going to say hello to Father," Mia said. "And figure out the best way to move him."

Mia kept walking and she heard her family members start scrambling around to complete their tasks. Mia was appreciative of how compliant they were. Neither woman was stupid; they both were aware the chances of their surviving the winter were slim to none even if Grant wasn't after Mia. She knew most of their decision was based on fear. Mia was terrified too, but she wasn't about to let them know that. Her mother had helped prepare her for life and Corinna had started her on this strange journey. Now it was Mia's turn to play the role of leader.

Chapter 43

The escapees have been privately detained. The grand commander has yet to set up a prison or a set of basic laws for his men, but these women are jailed for only trying to get their freedom back. This is a cold, hard world we are entering.

—The journal of Isaac Ryland

It was colder than Andrew had expected. With the sun down there was nothing to counteract the wind. He was grateful that the mountains blocked some of the breeze, but he still scooted closer to the fire. They set up makeshift beds with the clothing and even brought the agent to join them.

"So what's the deal with the doctor?" Carter asked. "And you said earlier my dad was part of Affinity? Who are these inside people?"

"We shouldn't talk in front of the agent," Zack said.

"By the time this is all over it won't matter what he has to say," Andrew said.

Zack gave Andrew a half smile. Andrew recognized the gesture of approval. It seemed like Andrew and Zack were on the same page again. Their team would destroy the service list and the master Registry, putting an end to the American way of life. Andrew was sure of that.

"There are thousands of us," Zack said.

"But did you know him?" Carter asked.

"No," Zack said. "I checked in with headquarters and informed them of the situation. They contacted the nearest member with medical training."

"The population of America is close to four million people," Agent Quillian said. "The thousands who are behind your cause are nothing."

"What would you do?" Andrew asked. "If mandatory service and the Registry were no more?"

"That's impossible," Agent Quillian said.

"Pretend it's not," Andrew said. "You know about our plans."

The agent rolled his eyes and shook his head.

"I would get out of the country," Carter said. "Spend some time with my dad and come back after the dust settled."

Andrew watched Zack stare at Carter with narrowed eyes. "Rescuing Roderick is not part of the protocol," Zack said. "I'm sorry, Carter, but your father is as good as dead."

"Fine," Carter said. "Then I would stay and rebuild. I think I would like to open a school. Teach some of the abandoned youths what my dad taught me, or maybe dedicate my time to reuniting families."

Andrew was relieved Carter didn't react to Zack's comment. Zack didn't seem interested in the fact that Carter had moved ahead without protesting. Carter had Andrew's word and that meant something. He felt a sting at the way he'd betrayed Mia by failing to stick to it; that mistake would never happen again.

"I'd head home," Zack said. "Wait for my next assignment."

"What if you chose your own assignment then?" Carter asked.

"Fine," Zack said. "I would like to reorganize the armed services. America will still need an army, only a voluntary one. I'd help with the restructuring."

"Andrew?" Carter asked.

"I would marry Mia," Andrew said.

As soon as the words left his mouth he wished he could take them back. That was too personal of a thought to share; he was so tired his brain wasn't filtering right. He expected the other men to laugh at him, but instead they nodded their heads. Even Agent Quillian didn't laugh.

"As long as everyone else is sharing," the agent said, "if your half-brained plan were to come to fruition I would spend every waking minute of my time meeting every girl who came across my path."

Andrew raised his chin. Zack and Carter looked just as perturbed.

"What?" the agent asked. "When I was overseas I did quite well with the ladies. I don't know if you gentlemen noticed, but I'm quite the looker."

Carter burst out laughing first and soon they all joined in; even Agent Quillian laughed at himself. It was surreal; Andrew was in so much danger but felt safe for a moment, as if nothing huge was looming over them. It would have been perfect if Mia were there. He felt a pang in his gut and reached into his pocket to check his phone.

"I wouldn't bother," Agent Quillian said. "No service out here. That's the only reason you three are still free. Once you exit the mountains every RAG agent in the country will be looking for you."

"They don't have our pictures," Carter said. "We used fake ones."

"It's not RAG agents I'm worried about," Andrew said.

Even if they managed to fool the American government, there was no way Grant hadn't put two and two together by now.

"You should be worried about being out here," Agent Quillian said.

"We've heard you complain all night," Zack said. "We're alone and I think it's time we went to bed."

"Can you untie me?" Agent Quillian asked. He puffed out his chest and wiggled his hands, which were secured behind his back.

"Sleep on your stomach," Andrew said.

"That's not fair," Agent Quillian said. "At least move my hands to my front."

Andrew followed Zack's lead and lay down on the pile of clothes he was using as a pillow. He let his hands slip inside his suit coat and settled down for the night. His eyelids closed and Agent Quillian faded out. Andrew's sleep came quickly.

Chapter 44

There has not been an American child born in the past eight months. I am starting to see the grand commander's point regarding the necessity of continuing our race. The world is a much smaller place since the war and humans are a dying breed.

—*The journal of Isaac Ryland*

Today had been disappointing to say the least. Rex was asleep in his home on Grant's property and Grant still didn't have the proof of his disobedience. Inflicting pain on Roderick was entertaining but hadn't accomplished much. Grant expected a phone call from Ian about his abuse of the foreign dignitaries or the missing French group, but none came. Grant smiled at the thought of the RAG agents treating the people as hostiles. Their trip would be less than pleasant.

After parting ways with Rex, Grant sat in his office. He studied everything he could about the French group and kept waiting for an update. He looked at Roderick's phone. This was still his best link to Mia. If Carter was back in the country Grant was certain the young man would check up on his father.

"Sir," Brandon said.

Grant looked up from his desk to see his personal assistant in the doorway.

"Yes?" Grant asked.

"I've doubled the security as you requested," Brandon said. "The men are taking shifts and using one of the houses on your property as a base. In my opinion it feels more like you're preparing for a military invasion than a wedding."

"I did not ask your opinion, did I?" Grant asked.

"No, sir," Brandon said. "I'm heading home, unless you need my services for anything else?"

"Did you schedule the appointment with the technology outfitter?" Grant asked.

"That has proved difficult," Brandon said.

Grant let out a low groan.

"I am sorry, sir," Brandon said. "But the man you suggested did not want to speak with me. He said you already have all the available security."

Grant knew that was a lie. There was always something better available, being kept away from the public.

"I will handle it in the morning," Grant said. "Go home."

"Good night, sir," Brandon said.

Grant did not acknowledge his butler. Instead he went back to the screen, showing the faces of all the foreign visitors.

There was something Grant was missing. He hated sitting at home when he should have been hunting Amelia. He'd had enough of waiting. He picked up his phone and was about to call for an update on Agent Barker's whereabouts when he saw it was three in the morning. It would be difficult to get fresh observations or even the men on the line. He would have to wait until tomorrow.

A yawn escaped Grant's mouth. He could use a night of sleep too. He was about to shut off the screen when he noticed the icon for his security system flashing. Grant clicked on the image and saw that part of his security array was down. He scanned the details. There was a system reboot in progress for part of the home. Grant continued to look for more information. The cameras in the kitchen and dining hall were offline.

Grant was aware that his systems needed to refresh themselves. He did remember a refresh being scheduled, but he doubted it would happen in the middle of the night. He clicked on the camera for the kitchen. It would be offline for another fifteen minutes. He continued clicking away at the keyboard until one of his newly installed cameras came up. This one was planted inside Rex's home. Even though all of the lights were off Grant could see everything as if the sun were up. Things looked normal, undisturbed. Grant switched to Rex's bedroom.

There was the outline of a man sleeping in the bed. Grant zoomed in; sure enough, it was Rex, fast asleep. For a second Grant thought he was being paranoid, that maybe Brandon had scheduled the reboot of two unimportant rooms for early this morning. Right before Grant exited out his eyes caught a small light from under Rex's blanket. Grant zoomed in with the camera. It dimmed, but it looked like Rex's hand had reached down to cover the light.

A smile spread across Grant's face. Rex was doing this; there was some portable device in his bed. The man was far from asleep. Rex was working still. This was too early in the game. Besides, what could Rex want from the kitchen? This was obviously a test run. Grant wondered what the endgame was. The three most important rooms in the house were Grant's office, his laboratory in the basement, and Roderick Rowe's hospital room.

It occurred to Grant to head down to Rex's home and kill the man, but Grant wanted to find out his plans first and he was proving a fun distraction and an easy target. Besides, Grant was a patient man, and in order to deliver the necessary punishment he needed time to form a plan.

Chapter 45

I have been banished to a small cell, with no windows. I haven't seen or spoken to another person in weeks; at least that is how it feels. I write this knowing it will be taken from me and studied, but I would like to know what crime I am guilty of and how long I shall remain in solitude. I am not sure what the world has in store for me, but it must be better than this.

—The diary of Megan Jean

The stairs made more noise than Mia remembered. When she had walked down them earlier today her head was filled with too many distractions, but now she wanted to focus on anything except where she was heading. Once she reached the top Mia turned to the left. The candle she was carrying flickered its light across the walls. At the far end of the long hallway was the door to her parents' room. After hearing her mother describe her father's condition Mia did not know what to expect. She told herself not to worry about a reunion. The only reason she was up here was to figure out a way to transport him.

Mia relaxed her shoulders and continued her walk down the hallway. She made it to the door. There was nothing to fear. She put her hand on the doorknob and the creak echoed across the hall as she pushed it open. The candle didn't do much to light the dark room, but

Mia's sense of smell was overwhelmed. A putrid odor invaded her nostrils and she raised her free hand to cover her nose.

Mia's eyes went to the bed, but the sheets were pulled back and nobody was lying there. She stepped inside and examined the room further. It was destroyed. There were papers and piles of linens. Mia was looking at full plates of food lying on the floor along with half-drunk bottles of alcohol when a voice startled her.

"Did you bring me my dinner?"

Mia almost dropped the candle.

"No," Mia said.

Her father was at the window. He pulled back the drapes and moonlight came pouring in. Mr. Morrissey had always been on the heavy side, but now he looked like he had lost a third of his body weight. The excess skin hung off his face.

"Good," he said. "You're trying to poison me anyway."

Mia's father had yet to look away from the window; she didn't think he had noticed it was her, or if he had he didn't care.

"Why don't you get back in bed?" Mia asked.

"Because I am the man of the house," her father said. "Why are all these people arriving? Are you throwing another party? I told you no more guests."

The silence was burning Mia's ears. She knew there was nobody out there.

"I won't eat your food so you can't kill me," he said. "And now you keep inviting others inside, but they won't kill me either. I am far too smart for their tactics."

"Nobody is coming," Mia said. "We're alone here."

"What?" he asked. "I can see them, there are hundreds walking into our home. The home that I provided for you."

Mia noticed her father's arm starting to shake.

"I won't die," he said. "I will live forever."

"Dying is part of life," Mia said.

The words slipped off Mia's tongue when she pictured Flo lying on the floor. She stared down at the candle and mourned the loss of her mentor.

"Mia?" her father asked.

She looked up to see his eyes staring back into hers. He started to move toward her, dragging his left foot behind him. His eyes were wild and wide.

"But you're dead," he said.

"I'm alive," Mia said. She felt herself back away instinctively. "I'm here to help you."

Tears started to well in her father's eyes. Mia had never seen him cry. His jaw started to quiver and his face relaxed.

"I have missed you so much," he said. "My beautiful baby girl."

He held out his arms. Mia was overwhelmed with emotion for the third time that day. She felt guilty for fearing her father and started to walk toward the ill man. Mia held the candle in her right hand and opened her arms to embrace him. He held her tight.

"You're a ghost," he said. "You are here to take me to the other side? I'm not ready."

Mia pulled away from his hug. She held the candle to her face. "I am as real as you are," she said. "I am here to help you. We can't stay here any longer."

Relief crossed the man's face. Mia had never imagined this nice of a homecoming. She felt awful for what her father had been through and hoped she could help him.

"Don't think you can trick me for a second," he said.

His eyes dried up and a stern look crossed his face. Mia felt her smile fade away to confusion. She was about to ask what had gotten him upset when he spoke first.

"You will not take me to the other side," he said.

He lunged at Mia and she stepped out of the way, but not fast enough to avoid his knocking the candle out of her hands on his way to the floor. She watched it roll across the floor and went to grab it before the flame caught anything, but Mia felt a hand grip her ankle. She fell hard against the wood floor as the candle continued to roll out of her reach.

She looked at her father. He was pushing himself upward.

"I will destroy you before you can destroy me," he said.

"I want to help you," Mia said.

She had to look away at the candle. It stopped rolling at the foot of the bed and Mia watched as the flames quickly went up the sheet hanging to the floor.

Mia didn't want to hurt him, but she was out of options. She lifted her free leg and with every ounce of strength she could muster kicked him in the shoulder. He let out a groan and fell down, releasing Mia in the process. She scrambled upward toward the bed, looking for anything she could use to snuff the flames.

"That was a nasty trick," her father said.

Mia looked over and he was trying to stand back up again.

"I need your help," Mia said. "We have to stop the flames."

"You won't trick me again," he said.

He tried to tackle Mia, but she moved and he fell onto the fire that was engulfing the bed. Fire surrounded the man. He started screaming, trying to shake his clothes away. Mia reached out for his hand, hoping to pull him up. Black smoke started to fill the air. A pair of hands gripped Mia's waist and pulled her away.

"No," Mia said.

She squirmed to see who has behind her. It was Corinna. She was pulling Mia away from their father as he struggled against the flames. Another pile of papers caught fire and the smoke started burning Mia's eyes.

"I have to save him," Mia yelled.

"It's too late," Corinna said. "We have to get out of here."

She couldn't see her father, only hear his screams. Mia continued to struggle as Corinna pulled her down the hallway. The bedroom was glowing red. She felt Corinna's grip slip away and Mia broke free. She started to run toward the flames. Before she made it to the bedroom a ball of fire sprang from the doorway. Smoke made its way into the hall.

Corinna came back and grabbed Mia again.

"We have to get out of here," Corinna said.

Mia didn't fight this time. She was shocked at how terrible the situation had turned out. She ran with her sister down the hall and to the stairs without looking back.

Chapter 46

I was paid a visit by the self-proclaimed grand commander.
He had one question for me: Would I try to run away again?
My answer was yes and he closed the door and left. Next time
I will know better.

—*The diary of Megan Jean*

Mia and Corinna made it to the kitchen. Corinna grabbed the bag that was sitting on the counter.

"Where's Mother?" Mia asked.

"Outside," Corinna said, "getting the car ready."

Mia looked at the counter and picked up the map Corinna had set out.

Corinna went to the back door and slid it open. Mia followed her, shut the door, and started running toward the barn, which had been converted into a garage. Mia's mother was standing, looking at the three cars. Mia went to the closest one and opened the driver's door.

"We'll take this one," Mia said. "Throw the supplies in the trunk. Don't forget the gasoline. Do you have the keys?" Mia asked.

"Your father started to keep them inside after you stole the last car," her mother said. "I grabbed all of them. I don't know which one is for which. Girls, why are your faces so red?"

"Throw me the keys," Mia said.

Her mother tossed the ring at her and Mia grabbed them. She opened the driver's-side door and slid inside the vehicle. Mia fumbled a bit and grabbed the first key. It didn't work. She continued to try. The passenger-side door opened.

"Mia, what is going on?" her mother asked.

"Get in the car," Mia said. "Tell Corinna to get in the back."

"What about your father?" Mia's mother asked.

"Please just get in the car," Mia said.

She tried the fourth key and the engine sprang to life.

"I won't leave him," her mother said.

"He's dead," Corinna said. "If you don't get in the car you will be too, soon."

Mia heard Corinna slide into the backseat.

"What happened?" Her mother was frantic.

Mia opened the car door and stood up again. She needed to get her mother to focus.

"Please, Mom," Mia said. "I don't want to lose you too. We have to get out of here."

Whatever hesitation Mia's mother was feeling faded away and she slid into the front seat. Mia moved the car into reverse and started down the driveway.

"Both of you close your eyes," Mia said.

Mia turned around and flew down the long drive. She could see the second story was starting to become a full blaze. Mia was grateful for Riley's driving lessons, which would allow her to get away from this place as soon as possible. She hit the gas and sped down toward the highway. She glanced to her right and saw her mother's eyes pinched shut, tears creeping out of the corners.

After several minutes Mia spoke.

"We're safe."

"Safe from what?" Mia's mother asked. "What happened to your father?"

"He attacked me," Mia said. "The candle fell and the room went up in flames."

"Did you try to help him?" Mia's mother asked.

"Of course she did," Corinna said. "What sort of thing is that to ask your daughter?"

"Corinna saved me," Mia said. "I would have died too."

Mia's emotions were changing nonstop. She had wanted to help her father, to save him from whatever he had become, but she realized he was too far gone.

Her mother didn't respond and Mia welcomed the silence. Mia had never planned for tonight to happen this way. She knew where they were headed but wasn't sure of the directions. Mia knew she had to stop and examine the map but wanted to put as much distance between them and the house as possible.

"Can either of you drive?" Mia asked.

"A little," Corinna said.

"What about read a map?" Mia asked.

She was met with silence. Mia let out a sigh. Tonight was traumatic for her, but after everything she had been through Mia was growing used to loss. She felt her eyes start to well. Mia needed someone who understood her; Mia needed Andrew. She stuck her hand in the pocket of her sweatpants and pulled out the tiny phone. She couldn't call him yet, but as soon as they stopped it would be first on her list.

The gas light clicked on and Mia knew she had to pull over. This was the second time this had happened to Mia on this very road. If she had taken anything from that first experience it was that no other cars would drive by at this time of night.

"Why are you stopping?" Corinna asked.

"I need to refill the gas tank," Mia said.

The car came to a stop and Mia turned off the engine. The trip had been quiet so far. Mia glanced at her mother's tearstained face. Mia understood why she was upset. She reached out and grabbed on to her mother's shoulder.

"His pain is over now," Mia said.

"This doesn't feel right," her mother said. "I've never been this far from home without a man before."

Mia wondered if her mother had ever been away from home without a man.

"You'll get used to it," Corinna said.

It dawned on Mia that she had never gotten the story of Corinna's escape. She pictured her sister making her way across the country from the Northwest Area, very similar to Mia and Andrew moving closer to freedom.

"Tell me about that night," Mia said. "When you showed me the article. How did you get away from William?"

"It was easier than I thought," Corinna said. "He was so angry with me for having a boy that aside from hitting me once in a while he kept his distance. One night, after he was particularly nasty, I walked outside. I kept thinking someone would chase after me, but nobody came.

"William's home wasn't too far away from my finishing school," Corinna said. "The drive from home to school was engraved in my head, since we'd made it for holidays and summers. I stole a car and left."

"You could drive?" Mia asked.

"A little," Corinna said. "I'm lucky I didn't kill myself in an accident. I was driving so fast. My foot was glued to the pedal."

"That was brave," Mia said.

"And stupid," Corinna said. "Obviously they noticed I was missing very soon, since they were only ten minutes behind me. I was lucky I didn't run out of gas; I didn't even know what that meant."

"It was the same with me when I first drove," Mia said. "Except I was going really slow instead of fast."

Corinna gave a fake chuckle. This was hard for her to talk about.

"I owe you an apology," Mia said. "You could have run away to Mexico, been free, but instead you came back to warn me. I should have assumed William had lied, you were alive, and looked for you when I left."

"No," Corinna said. "You thought I was dead. Besides, I wouldn't have begun to think about traveling to Mexico. I'm the big sister. It was my job to make sure you knew. I should have shown you that article the first time I brought it home."

"Still, I'm sorry that—"

"I don't accept your apology because one isn't necessary," Corinna said. "And you're returning the favor now. That's all that matters."

Mia thought about Flo's lessons. She had stressed letting go of anger; maybe that extended to regret too. Mia tried to let her guilt over abandoning Corinna wash away. She had to make it up to her now.

"Stay in the car," Mia said.

She reached behind her and grabbed the gas can next to Corinna before stepping outside. Mia began filling up the tank and stuck her hand in her pocket. She didn't want to debate whether or not calling Andrew was appropriate, she just wanted to hear his voice and make sure he was all right. Mia found his name and sent the call. The line was quiet. Then a message sounded.

"The number you are dialing is not in service range. Please call again later."

Mia hung up the phone. She wanted to hear his voice but would settle for knowing where he was. Mia went to the GPS option for Andrew's phone and the screen flashed an error message. Horror filled Mia's mind at what might have become of him.

"Mia, is everything okay?" Corinna asked.

Mia saw her sister walking out of the car.

"Everything is fine," Mia said.

She repeated the phrase to herself. Mia knew she needed to believe that. Andrew was smart, and he had Carter and Zack. Mia
had her mother and sister and the two of them weren't capable of
taking care of themselves. That responsibility fell on Mia. Wherever
Andrew was, he was safe, and Mia would find him as soon as she got
these two settled.

The tank was filled now. Mia screwed the lid onto the can and
opened the back door. Corinna took the remaining fuel and Mia went
into the front seat. She turned on the light in the car and started looking at the map.

"What are you doing?" Corinna asked.

Mia traced her finger along the line signaling the highway. She
looked southwest for a familiar name. The city of Schuyler ran under
her finger and Mia studied the way.

"Looking for friends," Mia said.

Once she was satisfied with the directions Mia flipped off the light.
Her mother continued staring out the window when Mia brought the
car back to life. Nobody asked another question as Mia got back
on the highway. She focused on driving. It was necessary that they
reach their destination by the time the sun rose.

Chapter 47

I was a guest at the first wedding last night. I watched as two strangers pledged their lives to each other happily. The groom was another high-ranking official in the current regime. The bride seemed of little importance to anyone else in attendance.

—The journal of Isaac Ryland

The rising sun and noise from Andrew's companions made it impossible to sleep any longer. He remained on the ground and let out a long stretch, his back sore from the rocky floor.

"I have to relieve myself," Agent Quillian said. "You need to untie my hands."

"Carter just took you," Zack said. "What, you feel like you missed your opportunity to escape and now you've formed a better plan? It will have to wait until the next bathroom break."

"We survived the night without being attacked," Andrew said. "Zero points for Agent Quillian's theory."

"He's awake," Carter said. "So glad you could join the land of the living."

"How long have you been up?"

"Twenty minutes," Carter said.

Andrew pulled himself off the ground. Zack was using his good hand to reload the suitcases. Andrew started to join him. He left a pile of clothes on the ground and instead filled a canvas bag with the cell phones, water, and food they had taken from the car. He paused and opened one of the bottles, taking a long gulp.

"We have more in the car," Zack said. "Don't think you have to conserve."

"I need a shower," Agent Quillian said. "We all stink."

"I thought that about you the moment I met you," Carter said.

"Want to hear what I thought of you?"

Andrew ignored the two men arguing and used the opportunity to speak with Zack alone. He walked closer to the tall blond man and spoke in a whisper.

"The agent was right about some things," Andrew said. "We have to ditch the SUV. The moment someone spots it we're all dead. We should probably ditch the suits too."

"That is number one on my list today," Zack said. "The second we spot another car we're taking it."

"Then what?"

"We meet our contact outside the capital," Zack said. "Execute our mission and wait for extraction."

Andrew nodded and went back to packing.

"Wait," Zack said. "There is a timeline to this thing. I know Mia said three days, but if she doesn't show we're moving forward regardless. Do you understand?"

"She will be there," Andrew said. "I bet she's already called. No service out here though."

"You know, she is a female driving alone across America in a stolen government car; there is a chance she was picked up."

"Mia's smart," Andrew said. "She's safe. I know it."

"I want you prepared," Zack said. "This mission is bigger than all of us, including Mia. I don't want to leave you behind."

"You won't have to leave anyone behind," Andrew said.

Zack nodded and bent back down. Carter and Agent Quillian continued to speak and Andrew tuned back in to their conversation.

"I bet you would do good with the ladies," Agent Quillian said. "They would all go nuts for your crazy eyes. One blue, one green, right?"

"You think so?" Carter asked.

"Carter," Andrew said. "Stop making friends with our prisoner."

Carter straightened his shoulders and started to help pack up the camp. Some of the wood was smoldering from their fire last night. Andrew stopped and emptied his water bottle over it.

"Why are you bothering with that?" Agent Quillian asked. "It will go out on its own."

Andrew shrugged. It didn't seem right to leave the fire smoking. He took a small victory from hearing the embers burn out.

"Let's get going," Zack said.

Andrew checked his pockets. He had his newly acquired RAG identification and cell phone. He patted under his coat and felt his gun in its holster. Carter grabbed Agent Quillian by the elbow and started following Zack down the trail. Andrew brought up the rear. He couldn't wait to get back to a spot that afforded him phone calls. He would dial Mia immediately.

What would he say? Of course he would start with an apology and a promise to never keep anything from her again. He knew she was angry with him, but she still loved him, and that was enough to keep him going. Andrew focused on his thoughts too much and only stopped walking when he slammed into Carter.

"Ugh," Andrew said. He lifted his hands to cover his nose, which had slammed into the back of Carter's head.

"Why did you stop moving?" Andrew asked.

"I told you guys something bad would happen," Agent Quillian said. "Nobody listens to me."

Andrew ignored the pain in his nose and tried to see what the other men were looking at. The road was empty. Then it dawned on him. They weren't looking at anything. The SUV and the rest of their supplies were gone.

Chapter 48

I received another visit from the GC. This time I told him I would not run; he laughed and left the room. I wonder if this is my punishment for escaping, or if all woman are now subject to this mental breaking.

—The diary of Megan Jean

Schuyler, two miles. Mia repeated the phrase in her head and almost cried out when the sign appeared. She pushed the accelerator down and sped closer to her destination. Neither of her traveling companions seemed to notice. Mia glanced in the rearview mirror and saw Corinna's eyes were closed. Mia shifted her gaze to her mother; the woman was staring out the window, and tears stained her cheeks.

"You should try to get some sleep," Mia said. "I'm sorry about Father."

"My tears aren't for him," Mia's mother replied.

"I know you're scared," Mia said. "But things will work out."

"How is it you're so young and have so much bravery?" her mother asked.

"Brave" wasn't a word Mia would use to describe herself. A building appeared off to the side of the road. It was at least a mile away, but in the flat, dark landscape it stood out. She sighed with relief; another landmark she was familiar with. She remembered

Andrew's stories about being paid to kill other roaming youths for money. That was no doubt what was taking place at that establishment right now.

Mia debated telling her mother the real reason she had shown up at the house. Her original plan was to hold the woman at gunpoint until she received information verifying her sale to Grant. Mia thought it was pointless, and without that justification she had left Andrew for no reason.

"I ran away from my friends because I was angry with them," Mia said. "That's not bravery."

"You didn't run away, you came home," Mia's mother said. "Your father had been so sick for such a long time. I should have handled him; instead I let you walk into that room and I put you in danger."

"He thought I was a ghost," Mia said. "I don't think he was aware of what he was doing."

Mia felt her shoulders shake when the smell of the burning room came back. For all her father's faults, he did not deserve a death so violent. Mia let the tears well up.

"Don't you dare cry for him," Mia's mother said. "In all my years I never bothered wondering what happened after death, but I'd thought about taking that shotgun upstairs and ending his suffering for months. I wasn't strong enough. Whatever pain that man felt tonight, it was not your fault."

At her mother's urging Mia willed her eyes to dry before the tears touched her cheek. The two sat in silence again. Her mother's words echoed through her head. Mia had come home, but at what cost? She would have loved to hear Andrew's voice, but even that desire felt selfish. Her concern should have been with taking down the Registry and continuing Affinity's mission, but all Mia wanted was her friends back with her.

The sun was rising fast and Mia felt like she was driving in circles, but she knew it was the opposite. There was only one road she had taken to and from her destination and Mia hadn't detoured. Her hope was starting to falter; maybe her memory was playing tricks on her, maybe the house was the opposite way from the tavern. She didn't want her family to share in the tension she was feeling. She needed to keep things positive.

"You taught me about bravery," Mia said.

Her mother snorted. "All I taught you was how to cook and clean," she said.

"And read and write," Mia said.

"I only did those things to please your father and raise your worth," she said.

"That's not true," Mia said. "Maybe that's the rationale you gave yourself, but it was a lie. You taught me because you loved me. Grant Marsden is a horrible man, but if things had gone differently and I was his wife right now I would still be alive—and that is saying a lot—because of the things you taught me. Every little piece of advice and instruction you gave me over the years is part of the reason I'm still alive today."

Mia's mother didn't have a response. Mia continued.

"Do you remember when I was a little girl and I decided Bailey should sleep in my room?"

"How could I forget? That barnyard dog brought fleas into your bed. It took months to break the egg cycles."

"You were so mad at me," Mia said. "I remember getting yelled at and spanked."

"Looking back now I suppose you just loved that dog," Mia's mother said.

"You were right to punish me," Mia said. "But once it was all over and done, do you remember what you said to me?"

"No."

"You said thank you," Mia said.

"That doesn't sound like me."

" 'Thank you, Mia. I hate the way I found out, but if you hadn't brought that dog inside he would still have fleas.' "

"Well, that's the truth," Mia's mother said. "Your father didn't think it was a big deal since he was an outside dog, but I was so disgusted by the whole thing that I convinced him to start medicating the poor animal."

"That day you taught me that sometimes bad ideas can still have a positive outcome," Mia said. "And I'm grateful for that."

Mia's mother reached over to the steering wheel and squeezed her daughter's hand. Mia was about to let her mother know that they were on the road to nowhere, that Mia was unable to remember the way to her safe haven, when the sun started reflecting off a structure on the flat road. Mia's heart skipped a beat. They grew close and Mia recognized the dilapidated-looking small white house. She saw the giant barn looming behind it and Mia felt a sense of calm wash over her.

"Where are we?" Corinna asked.

Mia glanced in the mirror and saw her sister rubbing her eyes as she awoke.

"With friends," Mia said.

She turned the car down the driveway and was so excited she didn't think she could put it in park before she jumped out the door.

Chapter 49

Another visit tonight. This time I was shown the results of my escape attempt. Twenty-seven women fled the gates of our compound. Fourteen were returned immediately; my group of five remained unharmed, but eight are still unaccounted for.

—The diary of Megan Jean

Thump thump thump. Mia pounded on the door for the second time. The giant grin she wore was starting to vanish. She told herself maybe they weren't home, but then a memory came crashing back. Mia had spotted a wanted poster in Saint Louis, and the only way Grant Marsden could have known she was there was if the people who helped her had told him. That meant Grant had been here before.

Mia put her hand on the doorknob and tried to enter, but it was locked. Her need for safety was replaced by a need to make sure her friends were safe. Mia didn't think she could handle another death on her account. She turned to her side and started throwing her shoulder into the door. It still didn't budge.

Nothing would make Mia give up at this point. She backed away to the edge of the porch and lifted her leg. She would try to kick the door down to make sure the inhabitants were safe. Before her foot made contact the door swung open.

There stood Frank. He wore a bathrobe over his white T-shirt and flannel pants. His white hair was messed up and one of his eyes was closed. His hands held a shotgun pointed at Mia, but she wasn't fazed. She ran toward him and wrapped her arms around his waist. The gun dropped and he returned her embrace.

"Mia?" he asked. "What are you doing here?"

Frank didn't bother waiting for a response before yelling for his husband.

"*Alex,*" Frank yelled. "Wake up and get down here." To Mia he said, "We thought you were dead. How did you find us again? Where have you been?"

"I need your help," Mia said.

"It's yours," Frank said. "Get in here."

"I'm not alone," Mia said.

"Andrew and Whitney?"

Both names stung Mia for different reasons. She released Frank and backed up, shaking her head no.

"I am so sorry," Frank said. "They were good people."

Mia nodded, not ready to explain her whole story at the moment.

"But who are these lovely gems?" Frank asked.

"I know you said to stay in the car," Corinna said. "But we heard a lot of noise and wanted to make sure you were safe."

"Frank, this is my sister Corinna and my mother, Laura," Mia said.

"What is so important you had to get me out of bed . . . Mia?" Alex said.

He grabbed her by the shoulders and pulled her into a tight embrace. She didn't have a chance to pull away before he had lifted her off the ground and started swaying her back and forth in his bear grip.

"What are you doing here? Tell me everything," he said, letting her down.

Mia stood back and looked at him. He wore the same outfit as

Frank, only instead of cotton his robe was silk. His white T-shirt was a deep V-neck that showed off his developed chest. Blond hair that should have looked messy instead was the epitome of handsome. Andrew was Mia's love, but Alex was still the best-looking man she had ever laid eyes on.

"You haven't changed a bit," Mia said.

"That's not true," Alex said. "I've put on about twenty pounds! Pure muscle, you know. Frank loves it."

"Frank loves you just the way you are," Frank said.

Alex put a gentle hand on Frank's shoulder and the two exchanged a quick kiss. Mia glanced behind her, expecting to see her family's faces looking as shocked as Mia's had the first time she witnessed the exchange between the two, but neither Corinna or her mother appeared put off.

"I doubt anyone is about to drive by, but let's continue this reunion inside," Frank said.

He held open the door and Mia went inside first. She heard Alex introducing himself to Corinna and her mother and for a brief moment Mia felt at peace.

Chapter 50

The satellite station at the Florida coast was attacked. I thought the grand commander was overreacting when he sent men to guard the coasts. I was proved wrong. It seems my hopes for foreign diplomacy were in vain. Countries don't want to offer us aid, they want to take us over.

—The journal of Isaac Ryland

"This is an international nightmare," Ian said.

"Walk me through what happened again," Grant said.

"The prime minister of France is dead," Ian said. "Her whole group died in a fire at one of the youth homes. For the first time in years we open our borders and this is what happens. I should have listened to you."

"Was it really a fire?"

"Too early to tell," Ian said. "The bodies were burned beyond recognition."

"How do you know she was there then?"

"Some of her jewelry was flame resistant," Ian said.

He looked down at the pin of the American flag on his coat, as if that piece of information made him admire the pendant all the more.

"How many bodies were there?"

"Still digging through the wreckage," Ian said. "There were eighteen people in the building."

"Any word on what caused it?" Grant asked.

"How will any of these questions help you with the press conference?" Ian asked. "I don't want any cause for foreign concern."

"Do they know she is dead?"

"No," Ian said. "We forbade contact with the home countries while the leaders were under our care."

Grant let out a sigh and leaned back in his chair. He hated being on this side of Ian's desk. Grant belonged in the grand commander's seat. This was the break Grant had been waiting for. Now, if he was given permission, he could chase Mia without the grand commander's suspicion following him.

"If it were me, sir," Grant said, "I would start by talking to our highest-ranking officers stationed in France. Find out which politicians overseas are supportive of America and then finance those campaigns. Normally the candidate who spends the most money will win. Who is set to take over in the interim?"

"I've already taken those steps," Ian said. "Our best bet is the second-in-command anyway. Another female, but likely to follow in her predecessor's footsteps."

The wrinkles in his forehead increased as he glared at Grant. Then he relaxed.

"I suppose that's another reason I know you're a good fit as my successor. We think alike."

Grant smiled and nodded. "Since we think so much alike, I volunteer to visit the site of the explosion. Maybe then I can tell you what you need to hear and not what you want to."

"I take it you have reason to believe this was not a tragic accident?" Ian asked.

"National security is of utmost importance to you," Grant said. "When we first met you cautioned me against surrounding myself with yes-men. Do you really believe you're getting all the facts?"

"I have other confidants besides yourself," Ian said. "I am sending General Camp out this afternoon. As soon as he debriefs me on the situation we will inform the French government and give our press conference, where I want you at my side. Nobody inside the country is to know about this."

Grant frowned.

"Do you have another suggestion?" Ian asked.

"Pre-wedding jitters, I suppose," Grant said. "I was just looking forward to a distraction is all."

It was not difficult for Grant to press his lips with fake worry. He even forced his hand to twitch.

"Does this have anything to do with greeting the president of Taiwan yesterday?" Ian asked.

"I already told you I am baffled by his suggestions," Grant said. "I suppose foreign customs are a mystery to me."

"Well, his escorts do say he has been quite difficult," Ian said. "You can go in General Camp's place. It's a six-hour flight and you leave in an hour."

"If you allow me the courtesy of using my personal plane, it will only be a four-hour trip," Grant said.

"You are much too humble for a man of your means," Ian said. "I always forget. Whatever you are more comfortable with. Use my pilot though."

Grant tugged the wrinkles out of his khaki pants as he stood up. His pale yellow and white striped shirt did the job of sending the message he wanted. Grant knew he looked unassuming, but humble was not something he shot for. Either way he was pleased with Ian's decision. He knew there was something amiss about this so-called tragedy and planned on spending the entire plane ride studying his files on the French and their passengers.

Chapter 51

I inquired how the repopulation plans were going and regret asking. The response was that the remaining female population of our once-great country is being kept under lock and key as they are our national treasure now.

—The journal of Isaac Ryland

The wheels of the plane touched down near the site of the explosion. Grant had memorized the file, and while he appreciated some time, the four-hour trip wasn't necessary. Once he was grand commander RAG agents would be allowed some technological advances and Grant would be able to accomplish things like this without leaving the comfort of his own home.

Within minutes Grant was walking up to the site. He saw some agents standing around the smoldering building while other government workers were still spraying parts of the area. He counted thirteen body bags. That meant five were missing. In that moment he knew in his gut Amelia was one of them.

"Good morning, sir," a RAG agent said.

"Where are the other five bodies?" Grant asked.

"Excuse me?"

"There were eighteen people in this building," Grant said. "I count thirteen bags and I hope you understand the concept of basic math."

"These people were toward the door," the RAG agent said. "The generator and gas line were near the rear. That is where the building suffered the most damage. We assume they were back there."

"This was a tour of a fake building designed to give the French prime minister a positive opinion of our orphanages," Grant said.

"Youth homes," the agent said.

"Call them what you want," Grant said. "If the tour were still going on, wouldn't the prime minister have been in the back? Yet her body was toward the front."

"We're not certain," the agent said.

Grant turned around and looked at the landscape.

"And the cars?" Grant asked.

"What cars?"

"This group was traveling in a caravan of three SUVs," Grant said. "Where were the vehicles when you arrived?"

The agent was quiet.

"If you lie to me I will rip your spine out," Grant said. "Don't worry about whatever lie your boss told you to give."

"They were missing," the agent said. "No vehicles were on the scene."

"So that means at least three survivors?" Grant asked.

"Or they were stolen after the explosion," the agent said.

"Because that makes so much more sense?" Grant asked. "A phony building in the middle of nowhere bursts into flames and at least three random onlookers stole the cars instead of calling your offices?"

The agent struggled to speak.

"I don't suppose the cars have trackers?"

"No, sir," the agent said.

Grant knew that already, or else he would have chased after Amelia two nights ago. Another thing the technology ban made difficult for him.

"Please tell me your theory," Grant said. "Honestly."

"This does not look good for our organization," the agent said.

"I didn't ask for you to cover for your superiors' ineptitude," Grant said. "I asked for your honest opinion."

"It looks like five people survived the fire and ran off with the cars," the agent said.

"Do you believe the survivors were fellow RAG agents?" Grant asked.

"I think they were the soldiers escorting the French lady," the agent said. "Probably didn't want to return to their overseas duty and chose the coward's way out."

"That is a fine theory," Grant said. "What other information do you have to back this up?"

"None of the bodies have identification or phones," he said. "No RAG agent would leave these items behind. Also, there were shell casings. I believe the fire was set afterward to cover the bodies up. There were five soldiers escorting the French woman."

Grant was pleased. The agent's theory was sound. Of course the agent was not aware a woman matching Amelia's description was with the group.

"Do you have any other suggestions for how this played out?" Grant asked.

"Sir, in the spirit of honesty," the agent said, "there is reason to believe at least one of the survivors was the French woman's guest. It's just a theory, but the woman's body was identified because her jewelry withstood the flames. Then we sorted the remains by height and what other factors we could tell with the damage. It's too early to say for sure, but wouldn't a young female companion have the same amount of expensive jewelry? I think the rogue soldiers are holding her hostage."

The small hairs on the inside of Grant's ear rose. This man was clever. Now Grant had all the information he needed to hunt Mia down under the pretense of finding the deserters. Not even Ian would question his actions.

He turned to head toward the plane. As soon as he landed Grant would assemble his team. Then it hit him: Rex was a traitor and his team was defunct. Grant spun around. He looked the RAG agent up and down. The man wore the standard suit and tie. He was dark skinned with short hair, and sunglasses took up most of his face. Grant could tell the man was more than capable.

"You're coming with me," Grant said.

"I have orders to stay," he said.

"Are you married?" Grant asked.

"No," the agent said.

"What is your name?"

"Agent Gen Hansen."

"Well, Agent Hansen, you just got yourself a promotion," Grant said. "Your new orders are to follow me."

Grant spun around and started walking toward the plane. He was pleased to hear Hansen's footsteps behind him.

The missing woman was Amelia, and two of the soldiers were likely Carter and Andrew. Grant had underestimated her. She had executed thirteen people to get into the country. The game was back on, and this time he would win.

Chapter 52

My vision of the eight women living peacefully among the abandoned states disappeared today. I was shown pictures of their mutilated corpses, after they'd been "rescued" by less than desirable parties.

—*The diary of Megan Jean*

Laughter came from upstairs. Mia was not surprised her mother and sister were getting along with Alex. She wished she could join in their fun, but she and Frank were busy bringing each other up to speed.

"So Grant buried Alex alive," Frank said. "He gave him a straw to breathe through and I had to dig him up."

"I am so sorry," Mia said.

"It was not your fault," Frank said.

Mia was getting tired of hearing that.

"You're lucky you showed up here when you did," Frank said. "Grant promised he was a man of his word and would leave us be, but we've never felt safe. These are our final days here."

The small farmhouse with the beautifully decorated interior Mia remembered was bare now. Almost all the furniture and decorations were missing.

"We have a new place farther west," Frank said. "Alex doesn't want anyone to know where we're heading so we've been moving the furniture bit by bit the last few months."

"He thinks if someone helps you move Grant could find you easier?" Mia asked.

"It's more deserted than this place, if you can believe it. Making it harder for Grant to find us isn't the idea; Alex wants to make it impossible."

Mia understood and nodded her head. When she looked down she glanced at the phone in her hand. It still hadn't rung and every time she tried Andrew, Carter, or Zack it went straight to voice mail. The GPS wasn't working either.

"Andrew is in an out-of-service area," Frank said. "He's fine. I think it would take an army to stop that kid."

"I shouldn't have left him," Mia said. "I was angry and I ran away. I'm supposed to meet him near the capital tomorrow."

"You did what you had to," Frank said. "There is no way your family would have lived through the winter if you didn't show up at their door."

"So when is the big moving day?" Mia asked.

"The next trip is the last," Frank said. "I need to fill my van with the last of the furniture. Alex already left his car there. We're leaving this place to the elements."

"Do you have room for a few more passengers?"

"You know there is no need to ask," Frank said. "Alex and I were already talking about getting back in the smuggling game. Grant might think he's scared us into submission, but all he did was increase our desire to help the people of this country."

"Thank you," Mia said.

She stood up from her folding chair.

"Do you have any fuel I can borrow?"

"What for?" Frank asked.

"I need to leave," Mia said. "Make sure my mother and sister are safe."

"Why not you?"

"Andrew would come find me," Mia said. "I owe him the same."

"Andrew isn't stupid," Frank said.

"Neither am I," Mia said.

"If you leave by yourself to chase after a man, you are," Frank said. "Mia, you are in no condition to drive. When was the last time you slept? You're covered in bruises and you look like an eighteen-year-old girl. You won't make it one hundred miles.

"You told him one more day, right?" Frank asked. "Well, wait until tomorrow; if you still can't reach him then we'll talk again."

Mia nodded.

"He has people he can depend on," Frank said. "You have the same support system right here. Keep trying to call him and check his location. That is the best way to keep both of you safe."

"I feel so helpless," Mia said. "Abandoning him was my fault; don't you dare tell me it wasn't."

"Some bad decisions still have good outcomes," Corinna said.

Mia turned around to see her sister. Corinna's short blond hair was spiked up and she wore one of Alex's dress shirts with a belt tied around her waist. It was hard to take her seriously.

"Were you three playing dress-up?"

Corinna came closer and grabbed Mia's hands.

"I heard you say that to Laura," Corinna said. "Maybe leaving Andrew was one of those bad decisions."

"He needs me," Mia said.

"He will be fine," Corinna said. "You know that. What about stopping the Registry? Isn't that your main goal?"

Mia closed her eyes and let out a breath. She was being selfish again. Andrew had trusted her enough to give her space; maybe he needed some as well.

"I'm scared it won't be possible without him," Mia said. "I can't accomplish anything by myself."

"You don't have to," Corinna said. "We will find Andrew together. Once he is ready to be found. Until then, keep your focus on the big picture."

"Mia?" Mia's mother said as she rounded the stairs.

The dress shirt she was in was more ridiculous than Corinna's. It was a mix of neon orange and silver swirls that went below her knees. Mia burst out laughing.

"Don't laugh at my designs," Alex said. "You're next, by the way. Get in the shower and I'll see what I can do with you."

Corinna pulled Mia into a hug.

"You're the glue," Corinna said.

Mia closed her eyes and leaned into her sister's shoulder. Whether or not Mia was willing to admit it, a small part of her knew Frank and Corinna were right. Mia would do her best to wait until tomorrow. If Andrew still wasn't answering his phone then, she'd need to think about stopping the Registry more than finding him, however impossible that might be.

Chapter **53**

We are crossing the year mark of the new America and there are now close to one hundred children waiting to enter this world. I hope their generation does a better job of cleaning up this mess than we have.

—The journal of Isaac Ryland

Holding the black suit jacket was getting annoying, but Andrew didn't want to stop to put it in the luggage he dragged behind him. He debated tying it around his waist but even that small gesture would require a pause in their steps.

"I need more water," Agent Quillian said.

"We need to ration it now," Zack said.

"This is the mountains, not a desert," Agent Quillian said. "There are freshwater streams everywhere."

"And I don't want to stop to look for one until we have to," Andrew said.

He kept his eyes glued on the gravel road; the tire tracks from their SUV were visible. Whoever had taken it had to stop eventually and then the group would find their car.

"I warned you guys about the mountain people," Agent Quillian said. "But you thought I was bluffing and I'm the one being punished? Untie my hands, where am I going to run anyway?"

"We moved them to your front," Carter said. "That's good enough."

"Excuse me for not saying thank you," Agent Quillian said. "I'd rather not die of dehydration before the mountain people get me if that's all right. I look forward to living long enough to prove you fools wrong."

Andrew gazed ahead and the tire tracks still continued.

"We've been walking for hours," Agent Quillian said. "We're closer to sundown than sunup. We need to stop for the night."

"Relax, Agent," Andrew said. "If you keep talking you'll only exhaust yourself more."

The corner of Zack's mouth rose into a half smile.

"Maybe we should rest," Zack said. "I need to take my medication anyway."

The tall blond man went to a rock on the side of the road and took a seat. Andrew and Carter stood their suitcases up next to him. Carter went to his bag to pull out Zack's medication and Andrew went to the middle of the road and put his hands on his knees, trying to stretch out the pain in his back.

"I would kill for a pair of tennis shoes," Carter said.

Andrew turned around to see Carter pulling off his sock; a large blister had formed and opened on his big toe.

"That is nasty," Agent Quillian said.

"Your feet aren't hurting?" Carter asked.

"Not like that," he said. "I'm used to wearing the required RAG uniform though. These are broken in." He pointed to his own footwear.

"How far do you think we've walked?" Andrew asked Zack.

"On average, one mile every twenty minutes. Three miles an hour," Zack said. He looked at his phone. "Approximately twenty-five miles, give or take."

"This is the worst idea ever," Agent Quillian said. "You know that SUV can go about ninety miles an hour?"

"The road is too rocky," Andrew said. "They would crash if they went that fast. My guess is they're not going more than thirty."

"Plus the tire tracks are deep," Carter said. "So that means the car is going slow. I would even guess twenty."

"Great," Agent Quillian said. "We're only forty-five hours behind them, approximately."

The plan had been to walk until they could hitch a ride, but not a single other car had appeared on the road. Andrew knew the agent was right. The car was as good as lost.

"We were about two hundred miles away from crossing the region," Andrew said. "If we make it that far our phones will work again. We can call for help."

"Seven more days of this?" Agent Quillian asked.

Carter let out a wince as he poked his blister. Andrew was about to yell at him when a group of rocks slipped down the mountain about twenty feet in front of them. The whole group froze. They hadn't seen any movement all day. Andrew's first instinct was mountain people, but then he told himself it was probably an animal. There was a cliff, about forty feet up, and it was sloped. Andrew knew he could scale it.

"Hello?" Agent Quillian called. "Mountain men?"

"Shhh," Zack said.

The agent stood up. He shouted toward the cliff.

"I am Recovery of Abducted Girls agent Trent Quillian, of the Southeast Area. My badge number is one four one five six five three. These men are traitors and are holding me hostage."

"Shut up," Andrew said.

Carter had already stood up and was trying to cover Agent Quillian's mouth. The agent elbowed Carter in the gut and ran out toward the middle of the road. Andrew went after him.

"There will be a huge reward for my life and bringing these traitors to justice," Agent Quillian said.

Andrew grabbed the agent and tackled him to the ground. Andrew covered his mouth but the agent bit down hard on Andrew's fingers. He groaned in pain and pulled his hand away instinctively.

"Oh, thank you," the agent said.

He forced himself up to his feet and was staring at the ledge.

"Thank you," the agent said again.

Andrew looked up and saw five men standing on the cliff. All of them had rifles pointed down at the group. There was no way for Andrew's team to get the upper hand. Andrew looked to Zack and Carter; both men came to the same realization and raised their arms in the air. They backed up toward Andrew.

This wasn't the first time Andrew had been at the mercy of a group of renegades. He thought back to his time in the militia. Mia had rescued him then, but now there was no way she could know his location. He spent so much of the day worrying about her safety that his own had never crossed his mind.

The men on the ledge were speaking to each other, but not loud enough for Andrew to hear. He decided to use this chance to reach for his weapon. He was lying on the ground and some of the strangers' sight lines were blocked by the people standing.

"He's moving," one yelled.

"Fire," said another.

There was a whisk through the air and Andrew felt a piercing pain in his arm. He moved his head to the side and saw a small dart sticking out of his arm. Then he heard two bodies drop. Agent Quillian's fell last, and his eyes were filled with confusion. Andrew smiled at that fact before everything went black.

Chapter 54

People are starting to want to return to familiar ways, in-cluding using a monetary system. The grand commander has tasked me with creating our new bills and giving them worth. I am thankful he has put this trust in me and hope not to let him down.

—*The journal of Isaac Ryland*

The former RAG agent stayed close to Grant as he marched him through his mansion.

"There will be time for a full tour later," Grant said. "I find your background quite impressive. Eight years in service and three under your belt as a RAG agent. I must ask one last, personal, question though."

Grant neared the rear of his home. He stopped before one of the doors that led to the rear grounds.

"Have you ever taken a man's life?" Grant asked.

"Several," Agent Hansen replied.

Grant spun around and saw a small smile on Hansen's face. This man was a fine replacement.

"Then I would like to show you to your new home," Grant said. "It is occupied at the moment and I would like a demonstration of your expertise in removing the tenant."

Hansen reached for his firearm.

"I think an element of surprise is more in order," Grant said. "I trust you will know when the time is right."

After Grant opened the door he felt the sun beating down on him. Grant decided that once this was over with he'd change back into shorts. The summer season was ending but it wasn't over yet. Agent Hansen did not say a word as they made their way toward Rex's home.

"I am a fair employer," Grant said. "I require no uniform. You can dress yourself as you see fit."

They reached the spare house on the property and Grant did not knock before entering. He expected to see Rex seated in the main area. It should have been a living room, but aside from the two couches and coffee table it looked more like a tactical center. Agent Hansen seemed alarmed at the silence and started to unholster his weapon again. Grant raised his hand, signaling the agent to keep it down.

"Rex?" Grant called.

There was no answer.

"If nobody is home we'll have to wait for his return," Grant said. "Funny, he did not mention leaving the house today."

Grant made his way to the table. He started to bend down to go through the stack of paperwork Rex had left out, but his concentration was broken.

"Sir, get down," Agent Hansen said.

The sound of a bullet whizzing by gave Grant more motivation than the agent's words. Grant dropped to the floor behind the couch, certain the bullet had come from the other direction.

"Agent Hansen, are you alive?" Grant asked.

"Yes, sir," the agent said. "The shot came from the kitchen. About twenty feet behind you. I can't get a good look without exposing my location."

"So you were home, Rex?" Grant asked.

Grant stayed on the floor and went through his pockets. He had a small pistol on him and was grateful for the firearm.

"If I am going to die I am taking you with me," Rex said.

"Tell me," Grant said. "What did they do to make you betray me?"

Two shots were fired from the kitchen. Grant heard them hit the couch. The bullets or the gun wasn't high-enough grade to shoot through the stuffing and wood. Rex wasn't firing rapidly enough for it to be a high-powered weapon either. Grant assumed that whatever gun Rex had, it was capable of nine or twelve shots. Three had been fired already. Grant's weapon only had six. Grant turned himself around and fired over the couch three times, not trying to hit Rex, only aiming to elicit more of a response. Agent Hansen fired too and Rex returned with three more shots.

That meant Rex had between three and six bullets left, and that did not account for an extra clip.

"How did you know?" Rex asked.

"Your phone," Grant said. "One of the nice officers from the militia called and told me of your bravery in rescuing the girl and her friends. That roused my suspicions at first. Then your delay in returning, your lack of information, and the random power outage in my security system."

Agent Hansen fired another bullet and Rex returned the shot.

"I answered your question," Grant said. "Answer mine. I deserve that much."

"*They* didn't do anything," Rex said. "You did with your arrogance."

"This whole thing is because I punched you in the gut?" Grant asked.

"You still can't see the bigger picture," Rex said. "Your mission became too personal, your vision cloudy. You are no longer an effective leader."

"So you replace me with someone who drives a nobler cause?" Grant asked.

Grant fired two more shots. Agent Hansen fired another and Rex returned with three shots. Grant didn't know about Agent Hansen, but Grant was down to his last bullet and Rex likely had two left. Agent Hansen pulled the trigger again and Rex returned fire.

"We are down to our last shots," Grant said. "Agent Hansen, please go outside."

"Sir, I still have five more rounds," Agent Hansen said.

"I appreciate your diligence," Grant said. "But this is best handled between myself and my former confidant."

There was no sound of footsteps.

"Rex, you let him leave. If you fire on him I will rush over to you and blow this last bullet straight through your skull."

Rex did not respond.

"Besides," Grant said, "there is no honor in killing a retreating soldier, and I know how you value that sort of thing now."

"Agreed," Rex said.

"Hansen, leave," Grant said. "In the event this man walks out of this house alive I order you to let him go. He can take whatever he wants with him. Do you understand?"

"Yes, sir," Agent Hansen said.

Grant's ears rang from the sound of the bullets, but not intensely enough for him to miss hearing the sound of footsteps as the young agent walked out of the house.

"How do you want this to end?" Rex asked. "I'm a much better shot than you."

"First, I want to know what your plan was," Grant said. "If I'm about to die I have that right. I'm giving you free rein to leave if you're the victor here."

Rex was silent.

"I know Amelia and her men came in with the prime minister of France," Grant said. "That woman and the rest of her party perished in a fire. Amelia is inside this country, on the run. I know they're coming here for Roderick too."

"No," Rex said. "Saving him is not part of the plan."

This was news to Grant. Amelia and her motives had changed. She was leaving those who'd helped her to burn and not bothering to rescue others who had given her aid. She was turning quite ruthless in her pursuits.

"Then tell me the plan," Grant said as he reached behind his head and pulled one of the cushions off the couch.

"She is in the country," Rex said. "It was my job to come back here and find the file you kept on her. The next step is to blow up the capitol building, retreat, and broadcast to the rest of the world who she is and who you are."

A smile spread across Grant's face. Even if the Mission were destroyed the room housing the master Registry and service records would remain intact. Mia's group of rebels was full of idiots.

"I am not stupid," Grant said. "If that was your strategy it would have been too risky bringing her inside America's borders."

Rex let out a sigh. Grant wanted to keep him talking; that way he could be sure Rex wasn't trying to move closer to him.

"The broadcast will happen from inside the borders," Rex said.

"Interesting," Grant said. "And who knows how to take over our airwaves?"

"Outside computer hackers," Rex said.

"Should I have Rod killed then?" Grant asked.

He rolled up his pant leg and removed the dagger he had attached to his calf. He looked at the handle and saw the poison through the small window. It was Grant's newest invention and he knew it worked.

"They aren't coming for him," Rex said. "I didn't even know he was here until you introduced us."

The initial night of Rex's return he had not appeared surprised to make Rod's acquaintance, but Grant did warn Carter against sharing his knowledge. That was a possibility. Even if Rex was lying, Grant did not think he would get any more information from the man.

"How should we do this?" Grant asked.

Grant heard the sound of Rex's footsteps as he ran toward the couch. Grant dropped his gun and repositioned himself on his back. He saw Rex tower over the back of the couch and threw the couch cushion in the air. Rex fired his bullet and the cotton exploded. Before Rex could rethink his attack, Grant lifted the knife upward. Rex brought his arm forward to block the weapon and the dagger went straight into his forearm.

Rex went to pull out the knife, but it had worked. Grant could tell as the confusion set in on the man's face. Rex dropped to his knees on the opposite side of the couch and Grant stood up. He brushed the cotton off of his clothes and picked up his small gun before walking to Rex.

The large man was lying on his back. The site of the stab wound was inflamed and foam was starting to come out of the corners of Rex's mouth.

"I made this while you were gone," Grant said. "If I hold a small button down, the knife injects deadly poison, causing almost-immediate paralysis. Your nervous system is shutting down. I hear it's painful."

Grant gave Rex's gun a kick away from the man before bending down and wiping the loose cotton off of his face.

"If I leave you like this, with your stature it will take you about six hours to die. Your internal organs are starting to turn to mush as we speak."

Rex's eyes were starting to water. Grant had never thought he'd see this man so vulnerable.

"Lucky for you I still feel I owe you something for all your years of servitude," Grant said.

He pushed the tip of his gun in between Rex's eyes.

"And by the way," Grant said, "I am a much better shot."

Grant smiled before he pulled the trigger.

"Ugh," Grant said.

He stood back up and dropped the gun. Agent Hansen came rushing back inside. He stopped in his tracks once he saw Grant.

"I don't know what I was thinking," Grant said. "I should have stood much farther away."

Grant tried to brush off some of Rex's brain matter and skull fragments from his shirt.

"I wanted to change clothes, but I didn't want to have to burn this shirt."

Agent Hansen did not speak. Grant clapped his hands together.

"Welcome to your new home," Grant said. "Please take some time to get acquainted. I will send someone to collect the body and clean this mess up. We have some work tonight, so you might want to take inventory of what's upstairs in case you want anything. I can send someone to get your things later."

Grant nodded and Agent Hansen did the same, but his lips were still parted. Grant didn't know if it was in awe or shock.

"Please excuse me," Grant said. "I am much in need of a shower and some fresh clothes."

Grant squeezed Agent Hansen's shoulder as he walked past the man. He wouldn't be a perfect replacement for Rex, but if Hansen could stomach this mess he would do just fine.

Chapter 55

I received a new visitor, my old friend I came to this place with. She was glowing, explaining her new life to me, complete with husband and beautiful home in a gated part of the city. She is expecting a child. She did a good job showing her excitement, but I thought I saw some death behind her eyes.

—The diary of Megan Jean

Sleeping on the floor made the aches and pains Mia had been ignoring set in. She thought about the bed in Flo's house. It was so luxurious and comforting. The feeling of dread came. It was no longer Flo's house. Flo was dead. Mia pushed herself up; the sun was setting, flooding the room with a golden hue. Even though her brief sleep hadn't been comfortable, it had supplied Mia with a clear head. She grabbed her phone and opened the door before heading down the steps. Frank and Alex were busy in the kitchen. Mia was certain her mother and sister were still asleep.

"That wasn't much of a nap," Alex said. "Are you still set on looking for Andrew?"

Frank gave him a slight elbow. Alex wasn't supposed to mention Mia's initial plans.

"I'm selfish," Mia said.

"No," Alex said. "You're not selfish at all."

"It's okay," Mia said. "I'm aware of it. I'm part of something big, something good people lost their lives over, and my biggest concern is finding a boy."

Frank and Alex gave each other confused glances.

"I mean," Alex said, "he's more than some boy."

"But he is capable of taking care of himself, just like I am," Mia said. "I don't want to stop."

"Asking for help doesn't make you selfish," Frank said.

"I was putting finding Andrew over stopping the Registry," Mia said. "I'm sure he didn't falter. I want to stick with the plan. We have less than two weeks until Grant's wedding. I want to make sure that the Registry is stopped before then."

"You can't do that by yourself," Frank said.

"That's why I am asking for your help," Mia said. "We were supposed to make it to the capital by tomorrow, but I'm sure Andrew, Carter, and Zack will be there by the wedding date. If they're not we'll forge ahead anyway. Flo will not have died for nothing. I know it's a lot to ask. But will you help me?"

"With whatever we can," Frank said.

Mia saw Frank put his hand on Alex's.

"Thank you," Mia said.

"We want to help too," Corinna said.

Mia whipped her head to the side. In the former dining room her sister and mother were sitting cross-legged on the floor. Mia had been so determined to speak that she hadn't noticed them.

"It's too dangerous for you," Mia said. "Frank and Alex both did time in service. They're trained in something."

"You can train us," Corinna said.

She rose to her feet. "I wouldn't know where to begin," Mia said. "And we need a backup plan in place, just in case Andrew doesn't show up with the codes. I can't strategize and train you at the same time."

"We're not staying behind," Mia's mother said. "You have our help, whether you want it or not."

Mia wanted to fight with them, but she knew it would be a waste of time. She nodded her head, telling herself it was a false agreement.

"We should leave right away," Mia said. "You said your new home was closer to the capital?"

"We need a few hours to pack up the rest of our belongings," Frank said. "And then we should all get some real sleep before driving."

"As soon as possible," Mia said.

"I hate to break your momentum," Frank said, "but this is a big undertaking, the *biggest* undertaking. You want to head in with two men who have been out of service for years and untrained women?"

"First, stop thinking gender matters," Mia said. "Second, if at any point any of you decide this is too dangerous you can back out. I need the location of your new home."

"It doesn't have an address," Frank said. "Privacy and all."

"Is there any way I can pass on the location?"

"I mean," Frank said, "I can give you the longitude and latitude, but that won't help the average person."

"I don't want a barrage of people there," Alex said.

"Trust me," Mia said. "We only need one person to meet us there."

Alex gave Frank a nod and he opened a few drawers in the kitchen until he found a pen and paper. He wrote the coordinates down and handed them to Mia.

"Thank you," Mia said. "Remember, any of you can back out whenever you want."

Mia walked toward the door. She didn't want anyone near her when she made this call.

"Who is that girl and what did she do with my daughter?" Mia heard her mother ask. Mia was being the girl she wanted to be. One who cared about the bigger picture and the world around her more than herself or an individual.

There was a slight chill to the air and Mia wrapped Alex's shirt tighter around herself. The sweatpants Frank had lent her were double-knotted and still slipped down her waist. She made it to the fence and took a seat.

Mia typed in the number she'd spent weeks staring at, knowing it by heart at this point. The smartest, bravest, most experienced person Mia had ever met was on the receiving end. As expected it went to voice mail.

"It's Mia," she said. "I could use . . . I need your help. It's for a crazy plan, it might not work, but it has a better shot if I have you by my side. The coordinates are forty-seven degrees, thirty-two minutes, forty-eight point seven three eight seconds north, and one hundred thirteen degrees, forty-nine minutes, forty-five point six four five seconds west. I don't know what that means, but I'm assuming you do. I'll be there tomorrow and for the next week or so. Please come."

Mia hung up the phone, knowing if she continued the message she would ramble on with too much information. Riley had taught her better than that.

Chapter 56

I presented my monetary system to the grand commander. He was pleased with the new bills but cared little for my ideas about how to raise revenue for the government. He insisted he had a plan in place already.

—The journal of Isaac Ryland

A dull pain in Andrew's arm woke him up. It was pitch-black outside; he couldn't even see the stars. That was when Andrew realized he wasn't outside. He was in a room. His hands and feet were tied together, but he forced himself upright and took in his surroundings.

It was too dark to see much. The room he was in was the size of a closet and he saw light shine from a crack. He assumed that must be the door. He pushed himself up onto his knees and tried to feel for a handle.

"I heard a noise," someone said.

"He's awake already?" another voice asked. "That tranquilizer should have taken a few more hours. You better get Mikey."

Andrew heard footsteps. He saw the light under the door break. Someone was coming to the closet.

"Are you awake in there?"

Andrew didn't respond.

"Oh, come on," the voice said.

The door flew open and Andrew didn't wait to look at his newest captor before lunging forward and throwing his shoulder into the man's knee. The man let out a yelp and moved out of the way. Andrew tried to push himself up but felt a blow to his gut as the man kicked him.

"That really hurt!"

Andrew felt his legs curl up and he gasped for breath.

"The guy tried to take out my knee," the man yelled.

"So you kicked him in the gut?"

"He's a government agent, what does it matter?"

"That other guy said he wasn't," a voice said.

Andrew forced his eyes open. The two men arguing looked somewhere between forty and fifty, and they were covered in dirt and wore similar outfits: tight pants with boots and long-sleeved shirts. Andrew saw he had been in a closet, now he glanced around the rest of the room. It was small and led right outside; there was no door. Part of the ceiling was missing and Andrew could see the stars.

"What's your name?"

Andrew glared up at the man. He wasn't about to give any information to someone who'd just attacked him.

"I'm JR and the man who kicked you is Dustin."

JR bent down and hoisted Andrew up by the shoulders.

"I would like to cut off your ropes, but I need you to promise me you won't hurt us again. If you do that, or try to run, I will harm your friends. Do you understand?"

Andrew nodded. The man pulled out a hunting knife and sawed through the ropes around Andrew's hands; he bent down and did the same with his feet. Andrew had the perfect opportunity to kick the man in the head, but the size of the knife and the power behind his threat told Andrew not to.

"How come he's awake so soon?" JR asked.

"I've been drugged before," Andrew said. "Maybe I built up a tolerance."

JR scratched his head.

"Why did that other agent call you a traitor?" Dustin asked.

"I'm not sure," Andrew said.

"So are you a government agent?" JR asked.

Andrew glanced back and forth between the two men. He was about to lie when he took a good hard look at his situation. If these men stole a government vehicle they didn't have much respect for RAG agents.

"No," Andrew said.

"Then what are you?" JR asked.

"I am here to stop the Registry and mandatory service."

The two men looked at Andrew and then each other. Andrew thought about the absurdity of the statement he'd just made. After everything he had been through his whole life could be summed up in one outrageous statement. He started to shake his head and laugh. At first JR and Dustin looked at him like he was crazy, but soon they joined in with him.

The three laughed for quite a while. Andrew had to keel over at one point and wipe the tears from his eyes. Dustin started clapping and stamping his boot up and down. Soon it slowed and the silence was deafening.

"You might be the craziest person I have ever met," Dustin said. "And I mean that whether you're lying or telling the truth. Are you hungry?"

"Starving," Andrew said.

"JR is going to get us some food, maybe a drink or two, then I want you to tell me everything there is to know about you and your little traveling party," Dustin said.

"I look forward to it," Andrew said.

He meant it. Andrew wasn't certain these men would believe him, or let him live, but if he was about to die he looked forward to passing on his story before he left this world.

Chapter **57**

Our new monetary system is working well. I hate to admit how thrilled I was with the salary assigned to my position as a government employee, but I still worry about where the money will come from if we don't tax the people.

—*The journal of Isaac Ryland*

The phone rang. It was the grand commander. Grant had no desire to speak to Ian again, but he put on his best smile and picked up the phone.

"Good evening, sir," Grant said.

"I'm sure you're as sick of my phone calls as I am of making them," Ian said.

"Nonsense," Grant said.

If Ian was calling only to rehash their earlier conversation, Grant knew he would have a difficult time not lashing out at the man.

"Well, I was pleased to hear the explosion was only an accident," Ian said. "That is one less thing we have to worry about."

"Did you give any more thought to my request?" Grant asked.

"I think the RAG agents are capable enough," Ian said.

"Of course," Grant said. "But I could use the distraction of finding the survivors of the 'accident,'" Grant said.

"The press conference will be in three days," Ian said. "I need you here early; your speech will be prepared."

"What about notifying the French?" Grant asked.

"They're already informed," Ian said.

"Are they rioting in the streets for your head?" Grant asked.

"She wasn't well liked for her American sympathies," Ian said. "And her second is already making a play for backing."

"Will the people be shocked once she is elected and also shares her sympathies?"

"The illusion of democracy saves us every time."

Even Grant had to chuckle at the man's joke.

"The real reason I'm calling is about your request," Ian said. "With all of this happening I think it's best if you spend every day up until your wedding at the capital. This is a good time for you to get some hands-on learning."

This was unacceptable to Grant. He knew Mia was in the country and planned on spending every waking moment hunting her down.

"I'm getting nervous," Grant said. "Pre-wedding jitters."

"I'm surprised anything gets you nervous."

"Your daughter is quite beautiful," Grant said. "And there's another reason I want to take on this task."

"What for?"

"My last few days as a single man," Grant said. "I thought maybe I would do some last-minute traveling. Inside the country, of course. Reflect and prepare for my next stage in life. I might as well have a goal while I'm at it."

Ian was quiet.

"Sir, you are going to live a long, healthy life; I'll have plenty of time for hands-on learning over the years," Grant said.

"I already have you booked for *The Greg Finnegan Show* twice before the wedding," Ian said.

There was nothing Grant wanted less than another spot on Greg Finnegan's talk show. The country might have respected the man but Grant found him tedious and annoying.

"Don't you think my absence might increase the public's desire for me?" Grant asked. "Maybe make the wedding seem more grand?"

Ian paused again. "Be here for the press conference. If there is anything else I need you for I will give you advance notice."

"Thank you, sir," Grant said.

"Stop with the 'sir,'" Ian said. "You know I hate it."

"Good night, Ian," Grant said. "I'll see you in three days."

Grant did not wait for a reply before he hung up the phone. He had not anticipated Ian turning down his request to chase after the survivors of the French disaster but was happy to finally have the clearance. Tonight he would meet with Hansen; they would go over the possible places Mia could be and whether or not it was worth it to wait for her to come near the capital, since he now was certain of her final destination.

Grant went over to his walk-in closet and looked at the hanging mirror. The sun was down now and he had missed his chance to wear shorts. Instead Grant picked navy blue pants with a light pink and navy striped shirt. The stripes were vertical, which were supposed to slim Grant's figure, but he didn't need it. A knock on his door diverted his attention from his perfectly parted hair.

"Come in . . . Hello, Brandon," Grant said, greeting his head of staff.

"Sir," Brandon said, "we took care of the incident at the home on your property. I am about to retire for the evening, unless there is anything else you desire?"

"How was Hansen?" Grant asked. "The new occupant?"

"He was quite helpful in the cleanup," Brandon said.

"Good," Grant said. "I'm going to visit with him now."

Brandon bowed and started to walk out of the room.

"One more thing," Brandon said. "There was an alert on one of your items of interest."

There were multiple things across the country Grant wanted an eye on. If there was any news regarding these spots or people, Grant wanted the information. They were growing so numerous with his new undertakings that he'd passed most of them off to Brandon to monitor and personally tracked only the newest.

"Did someone else die?" Grant asked.

"No," Brandon said. "This was a report on a house. One in the Midwest Area. It went up in flames. I suppose there could have been people inside though. That wasn't in the news."

Grant stopped admiring himself in the mirror and turned to face Brandon. A second fire in as many days.

"Where in the Midwest Area?" Grant asked.

Brandon struggled to remember the details, but Grant knew what house he was talking about. The Morrissey farm. Amelia's father's home. She was turning into quite the firebug.

"It doesn't matter," Grant said. "Get one of my smaller planes ready. I will fly it myself, no pilot necessary."

"Yes, sir," Brandon said.

Grant pushed past him and out of the room. He started toward his massive staircase, eager to get Hansen and bring him along for the flight. Grant needed to know if Amelia had died in that fire. If she'd survived the fire and was stupid enough to return to her father's farm, that meant she would be easy enough to track. Amelia would be his by the time the sun rose.

Chapter 58

The grand commander suggested it is time that I take a wife. I was shocked he thought me worthy to carry on the population. Then he suggested I pay for the privilege with an advance on my salary. I now see how he plans to generate the funds to keep his new country afloat.

—The journal of Isaac Ryland

The candlelight flickered across the wooden room. Andrew was surprised something so small could give off so much light.

"I think you deserve one of these," Dustin said.

He reached into a small box behind him and handed Andrew a drink.

"I told you my story," Andrew said. "Who are all of you?"

"I think your RAG agent called us mountain men," JR said.

"That doesn't tell me much," Andrew said.

"We need to wait for your friends to wake up," Dustin said. "If their stories match yours then we know whether or not to tell you the truth."

Andrew took a gulp of his drink.

"Carter and Zack might lie," Andrew said. "I almost did."

"Why didn't you?" JR asked.

Andrew shrugged. He knew the reason: Mia. If he had just told her the whole truth he wouldn't have been in this situation right now. She would still be with him and they would have formed a better strategy together, but that was more personal than Andrew was willing to get.

"Don't worry about the blond men," Dustin said. "If your RAG agent backs you up—and he will if he thinks you're a traitor—you three have nothing to worry about."

"I take it you don't support the Registry?" Andrew asked.

"We don't support anything the American government has to offer," JR said.

Dustin gave him a smack on the side.

"What? Do you really think he's some spy sent by the grand commander to search for small pockets of people living in remote villages?"

"So this is a village?" Andrew asked.

Dustin gave JR another nasty look.

"We are a group of individuals who prefer solitude," Dustin said. "We self-govern and like our existence unknown."

"How long have you been living up here?" Andrew asked.

"A long time," Dustin said.

"And how many people are up here?"

"That's enough questions," Dustin said.

"I thought I knew everything about America," Andrew said. "Nobody mentions this area, except for in ghost stories."

"There is water," JR said. "That's all humans really need."

"Were either of you in service?" Andrew asked.

JR shook his head no and Dustin smacked him again.

"Stop that," JR said. "Either he's telling the truth and we can trust him or he's not and we have to kill him. What does it matter if we talk for now?"

"Mikey said keep him in the dark," Dustin said.

That made Andrew gulp.

"Did you steal our car?" Andrew asked.

"Yes," JR said. "Do not smack me for that. His question didn't make me divulge any of our secrets."

"Why?" Andrew asked.

"We don't see a lot of them parked on the side of the road," Dustin said. "Debated leaving it and letting you men go on your way, but we didn't know what you were up to."

"That and the car does us a lot of good," JR said.

"I think my friends and I will need it back," Andrew said. "That is, if you're okay with letting us continue our mission."

"Worry about that later," Dustin said.

There was a lull in the conversation.

"When will my friends be awake?" Andrew asked. "We really should be on our way soon."

"They're up now," JR said. "Being questioned the same as you, only you had about a two-hour head start on them."

"If you live alone up here how did you make the tranquilizer?" Andrew asked.

"Plants," Dustin said. "Nature is filled with wonders, if you know where to look."

"We live off the land," JR said.

"So a group of men living alone in the mountains?" Andrew asked. "Did you find each other after your time in the orphanage?"

JR and Dustin exchanged looks.

"Yes," JR said. He looked at Dustin for approval.

"We planned on reporting for service but forgot about our enlistment dates. Nobody ever came out here to get us, so we stayed," Dustin said.

"How did you steal our car and follow us?"

"That's simple," JR said. "A group of us stole the car, then five of us stayed behind and followed you. If those rocks hadn't fallen you would have never known we were there."

"What were you planning on doing?"

"Waiting until you died and then hiding your bodies," Dustin said. "Of course we assumed you were all RAG agents then. We thought about killing you but didn't know why that one was tied up. It made us . . . curious."

"Never kill someone unless you have to," JR said.

"Have you?" Andrew asked.

"Not me," JR said. "Dustin neither."

"But others here have?" Andrew asked.

"Not in a very long time," Dustin said. "Stop worrying about the other people here."

Footsteps came up to the door. Andrew could see the figures in the darkness approaching. He felt relief when an untied Carter and Zack walked into the room. Two men similar to JR and Dustin were behind them. Andrew rose from his chair and the two walked over. All three exchanged brief hugs complete with pats on the back.

"I'm not sure it was smart telling these men everything," Zack said. He gave Andrew a raised eyebrow.

"We're alive, aren't we?" Andrew asked.

"Dustin, JR," a man said. "Mikey wants to see us outside."

Andrew's two watchers rose and Zack and Carter took their seats.

"What is this place?" Carter asked.

"A group of men with no love for the Registry," Andrew said.

"I knew it," Zack said.

"Well they told me that," Andrew said. "It was obvious since they didn't kill us when I talked about stopping the American government."

"No," Zack said. "I've heard stories. There are pockets like this all over the country. That's why if we can delete the master server our plan will work. There are tons of men fed up with this way of life. They will rally behind us."

"I don't think we need to worry about the women not joining our cause," Carter said.

"We need to keep moving," Andrew said. "We're supposed to meet Mia near the capital tomorrow."

"Let's meet this Mikey and then get our car back," Zack said. "We can be on the road in an hour."

"Who's Mikey?" Carter asked.

"I think he's their leader," Andrew said. "My guess is his word is the law."

"You have part of that right," a voice said.

Andrew turned toward the doorway. The figure standing in the firelight wore the same tight pants and boots as JR and Dustin. There was a billowy blue shirt over them and a scarf loose around the neck. Over the shoulder a salt-and-pepper braid hung. The face was hard and had a few lines. The mouth showed a beautiful, toothy grin.

"My name is Mikey," she said. "It's a pleasure to meet you."

Chapter 59

The first child was born today. A baby girl. I can hear her screams echo through the capitol building and feel a sense that our nation will continue to prosper.

—The journal of Isaac Ryland

The Morrissey farmhouse was still smoldering when Grant landed. Workers stood around, waiting for the smoke to clear before they entered the property. Grant thought it a waste of time; there would be nothing in the house of use.

"Sir, you shouldn't be here," a worker said.

He lifted his hand to block Grant's access to the farm. Grant paused before running into the man's arm.

"Do not touch me," Grant said. "Do you know who I am?"

The worker wore a sneer and was about to yell at Grant. The man made eye contact and Grant watched the anger melt into astonishment.

"You're Grant Marsden," the man said.

He dropped his arm. Grant continued walking up to the house. Hansen remained close behind him.

"So this is where it all started?" Hansen asked.

"I suppose that's one way of putting it," Grant said.

He had spent the plane ride filling the agent in on Amelia's escape and where they stood now. They walked up the long drive, the gravel crunching underneath Grant's shoes. He looked down and saw the dust covering his navy loafers.

"I forgot how dirty it was here," Grant said. "I can't seem to keep clean today."

"What are you expecting to find?"

"Proof that she was here," Grant said. "I didn't expect this."

"Why not?"

"Amelia's parents sold her to me," Grant said. "I didn't think she would come to rescue them, but I didn't think she had it in her to come here and murder them either. I guess I was wrong."

They continued to walk past the house and Grant saw his proof sitting in the back of the driveway: the black RAG vehicle.

"Does this look like one of the cars taken from the earlier crime scene?" Grant asked.

"The plates are from that area," Hansen said. "Where are the other two cars though?"

"I'm not sure," Grant said. "Honestly I assumed two of them were left closer to the orphanage fire. But why would they drive all the way up here and switch to one of Mr. Morrissey's cars?"

"They didn't want to get caught," Hansen said.

"Four men dressed as RAG agents driving this wouldn't draw any attention," Grant said. "It would have been easier for them to switch the plates than ditch the SUV."

"Do you think they're still here somewhere?" Hansen asked, moving his fingers to grab his weapon.

"No," Grant said.

He walked farther toward the garage. The door was wide open and there were two cars inside.

"Last time I was here Mr. Morrissey had another vehicle," Grant said. "They left in his car."

"Maybe it performed better than the SUV?" Hansen said.

Grant ignored the man's stupid suggestion.

"Four men and a woman driving along in a government vehicle could be easily explained if anyone spotted them," Grant said. "What couldn't be?"

"I don't follow," Hansen said.

"They split up," Grant said. "Amelia came here alone."

"That would be suicide for her," Hansen said.

"She is still alive, so apparently not," Grant said. "If she were without a male escort it would be unexplainable if someone spotted her driving a government car."

"It would be unexplainable to see a woman driving any car," Hansen said, "regardless of the vehicle."

"True," Grant said. "Imagine you are an eighteen-year-old girl who knows how to drive. It would be dangerous if anyone saw you in the car."

"Not if she didn't look like a girl," Hansen said.

"Amelia is quite feminine," Grant said. "Even with a short haircut she still looks female."

"Then I would get off the road as quick as possible," Hansen said. "Find a person to smuggle me to my destination. Avoid the public eye."

"Exactly," Grant said.

"Does she have any other family in the area?"

"She has two sisters, but they're both married and neither of them is close," Grant said. "I don't believe they would give her aid."

"A friend?" Hansen asked.

"Amelia lived a sheltered life," Grant said. "Until she decided to run. There are very few people she knows at all in this country."

Grant turned around and started walking back down the driveway.

"Don't you want to look through the car?" Hansen asked.

"It won't tell us anything I don't already know," Grant said.

"I think you're wrong," Hansen said. "She's still with the men. It wouldn't make sense to separate."

Grant stopped and walked back to Hansen. He went straight for the SUV's driver's-side door and opened it.

"I am assuming the men Amelia is traveling with are somewhat tall," Grant said. "Do you think they would require the seat to be so close to the pedals?"

Grant did not break eye contact with Hansen. He didn't even bother to check if the seat was pushed forward, because Grant was certain Mia was alone when she switched cars. The agent's wide eyes told Grant he was right. Grant slammed the door and started walking down the driveway again. This time Hansen followed him.

"Don't doubt my methods again," Grant said.

"Where are we going now?"

"To visit one of the few people Amelia knows," Grant said.

After his last run-in with Frank Piozzi, Grant assumed the man knew better than to give Amelia aid, but he couldn't be certain unless he went to investigate for himself.

Chapter 60

Tonight is my wedding. I have yet to view my wife, but I hope that she is pleased with me. The honor of her hand in marriage has cost me a great deal.

—The journal of Isaac Ryland

A woman. There was a female leader in a hidden part of America. If someone had told Andrew that a few months ago he would have laughed in their face. Mikey strolled into the small room and up to the chairs in which Andrew, Carter, and Zack were seated.

"I have heard the most interesting story tonight," she said. "That you three, along with some others, are trying to stop the Registry. I also hear you have lots of outside help and your insane plan has a chance of success."

"More than a chance," Zack said.

"Well then the three of you have my blessing," Mikey said. "And you are free to leave."

None of them moved.

"Or stay if you like," she said. "You have a high regard for women and are welcome in our small community."

"Thank you," Zack said.

"I wouldn't thank me yet," she said. "We waited too long to bring you up here."

"What does that mean?" Carter asked.

"It means we used all the fuel from your car and already started ripping out the parts."

"We can walk," Zack said. "A few hundred miles to civilization, right?"

"If it was a straight plain," she said. "You're in the mountains. The road goes up and down here. It will be closer to five hundred."

"That's too long," Carter said.

"That's also if you don't die from the elements along the way."

Andrew was in shock. He was grateful they were allowed to go, but his gratitude was replaced by rage at the treatment of their equipment.

"You had no right," Andrew said.

"I had every right," she said. "You're the ones who abandoned your vehicle for a night." She looked into Andrew's eyes with matching fury. "Don't blame me for your foolishness," she said.

Andrew was at a loss for words. He struggled to pull together his thoughts but she continued.

"I do feel a bit bad though," she said. "We have one car here. Someone takes it into civilization, as you call it, once every other month and comes back with some much-needed supplies. They are on the road right now but won't be back for another ten days."

"Ten days?" Carter asked.

That was not good news to Andrew. He was set to meet Mia tomorrow; being trapped here for ten days would mean she would figure he was dead. He didn't even want to think about what could happen to her alone in that time. Andrew knew why Carter was getting worried too. That was too close to Grant's deadline for Rod. There were no other options though. Andrew didn't want to lose this chance.

"And we can take your car in ten days?" Andrew asked.

"Someone will drive you to the nearest town in ten days," she said. "From there you can find your own way."

Carter was about to protest, but Andrew cut him off. "Ten days then."

Mikey nodded her head. "Until then consider yourselves at home," she said. "One of my sons is setting up some beds for you."

Carter shot Andrew a dirty look and Andrew gave him a reassuring nod. That was pushing their deadline, but it was still doable.

"Dustin will take you on a small tour," she said.

"What about Agent Quillian?" Andrew asked.

"He is a threat to me and mine," she said, "and will be dealt with."

"Where is he?" Andrew asked.

"His execution is being scheduled," Mikey said. "If you would like to watch it can be arranged."

"You can't kill him," Andrew said.

"Just an hour ago he was begging us to kill you," Mikey said.

That didn't matter. Andrew had promised Mia he wouldn't kill the agent, and letting him die was the same as pulling the trigger.

"He is the exact type of person we are trying to save," Andrew said.

"JR," Mikey said. "Bring the RAG agent here."

"Andrew, don't push our luck," Zack said in a hushed voice.

It didn't take long for JR to drag Agent Quillian into the room. His ropes had not been cut; instead his face had. There was a gash next to his eye. He had sweated through his clothes and he hit the floor with a thud when JR released his arm.

"This young man seems to think you deserve to live," Mikey said.

"I do," Agent Quillian said.

"He knows of our plans," Andrew said. "He doesn't approve of the Registry either. He's too scared to stop it."

"If he escapes your custody he could set some of his brethren on us," Mikey said.

"I won't," Agent Quillian said. "I swear. Please don't kill me."

"Shut up," Andrew said.

"Plead his case again," Mikey said.

"Agent Quillian is the type of person who will rejoice once our mission is complete. He'll switch to our cause and your people will have nothing to fear."

"What if you lose or he escapes?"

"I won't escape," Agent Quillian said. "Please, I want to stay with these men. I hate the American government."

"Shut up," Andrew said.

He didn't break eye contact with Mikey. She wore a slight smile and held her hand out for Andrew to continue.

"You cannot kill him unless you're willing to kill me too," Andrew said.

"So you tie your life to his?" Mikey asked.

"Yes," Andrew said.

She paused and glanced down at the shaking agent.

"I'm feeling generous tonight," Mikey said. "The agent can live, but if over the next ten days I see him more than ten feet away from you the both of you are dead."

"Can we make it twenty feet?" Andrew asked. "He's a little annoying."

Mikey let out a laugh and clapped her hands.

"Thank you," Agent Quillian said. "Thank you . . . thank you . . . thank you."

"JR, cut off Trent's ropes," she said. "Agent Quillian is dead, but he lives."

Mikey stood up from her chair and started walking out of the building. She turned and gave Andrew a nod and a wink, cementing what Andrew already knew. Mikey had had no desire to kill Agent Quillian; instead she'd made sure Andrew had a loyal follower for life.

Chapter 61

I have agreed to a match. I can no longer stand the solitude and fear my desire to have a family outweighs my moral issues with what has taken place.

—*The diary of Megan Jean*

The group sat in a circle on the kitchen floor, eating the meal Alex had put together.

"I can't take the silence," Alex said. "We have to talk about what you're planning."

"I already told you," Mia said. "I'm planning on stopping the Registry and mandatory service."

"I'm more thinking how," Alex said.

Mia shrugged.

"Let's make a list," Alex said. "That will at least give me a better idea."

"I don't see how it will help," Mia said. She didn't want to talk about this in front of her mother or sister. They were already scared and Mia did not want to push their limits. Alex ignored her protests and came back with a pen and paper. In big letters he scribbled "Stop the Government" at the top of the page.

"We have thirteen days until Grant's deadline to save Rod," Mia said. "That's when I'm planning on regrouping with Andrew, Carter, and Zack."

"What if you don't hear from them by then?"

"We need to have a backup plan for Rod's rescue," Mia said. "I won't leave him to die."

"Okay," Alex said. "Let's stick with one mission at a time. Pretend that Andrew and company don't exist. What is your plan?"

Mia paused for a moment. She knew she should reconnect with Affinity. They had the best resources, but she also knew their virtual attack was scheduled for the night of Grant's wedding.

"We have to take out the master server," Mia said. "When is Grant's wedding?"

"Two weeks."

"That's the night," Mia said. "We need to sneak into the capital and destroy the server."

"Then what?"

Mia let out a sigh. "We have to find someone to get me out in the public eye," Mia said. "Prove who I am, what Grant has done, what the system has done, and let them know the Registry has been destroyed."

"Do you have a media connection who can pull that off?" Corinna asked.

Mia shook her head.

"What about that group you were working with?" Mia's mother asked. "Can you contact them? Maybe they can send in another team."

"Zack was the one who had a direct way of contacting them," Mia said.

"They haven't tried to contact you?" Frank asked.

Mia pulled out her phone and set it in the center of their circle. "Not at all," she said. "But my phone was special. It's harder to trace. I don't know who had access to this number except for the people I was traveling with."

"Can you figure out a way to track them down?" Frank asked. "Maybe over the Internet?"

"That would take too much time," Mia said. "Even if I do, they'll take control of whatever we're trying to accomplish, and for all I know they would tell me to step down and abort our quest."

"Okay," Alex said. "But closer to the date?"

"If we don't come up with another solution by then," Mia said.

"And how are we planning on breaking into the capitol building and destroying the master server?" Frank asked.

"Affinity was working on obtaining the passcode to the room," Mia said.

"But you don't want to contact them?" Frank asked.

"Then we'll blow up the capitol building; fire has done a decent job so far," Mia said.

She heard her mother gasp. Mia turned and gave her an apologetic face.

"This is a pretty vague strategy," Frank said.

"Is the van all packed up?" Mia asked, eager to change the topic.

"We can leave at dawn," Frank said.

"What did you do with my car?" Mia asked.

"Drove it into the cornfields," Frank said.

"We should get some sleep," Mia said.

"This isn't much of a list," Alex said.

"We won't need your list," Mia said. "I'll hear from Andrew soon and our initial strategy will be back on."

Mia's frustration had reached a breaking point. She stood up from the floor and turned for the front door. She didn't stop and bolted out into the cold night air. Andrew still wasn't traceable and Riley hadn't returned her call. Mia felt the world resting on her shoulders and wasn't sure she could handle the pressure. There was a hand on Mia's shoulder and she jumped from the touch.

"Are you all right?" Corinna asked.

"You scared me," Mia said.

"Sorry," Corinna said.

"I know this is a bad idea," Mia said. "It isn't an idea at all. I'm depending too much on other people."

"You'll think of something," Corinna said. "We have some time. Alex shouldn't have pressured you."

"No," Mia said. "He has a right to know what I'm asking of him."

"I wish I was as strong as you," Corinna said.

"You are," Mia said. "I'm sorry I didn't come for you when I first left."

"I'm glad you didn't," Corinna said. "You thought I was dead and it's dangerous out here."

Mia didn't have a response.

"Don't be so hard on yourself, you—" Corinna was cut off by a loud noise.

Mia and her sister turned their heads upward and saw a small plane fly by. It looked like it was making a landing on the road.

"That was strange," Corinna said.

A knot formed in Mia's gut.

"Do planes fly this late at night?"

"Go back inside," Mia said. "Get everyone out here. We need to leave now."

Mia didn't wait for Corinna to respond. She ran out toward the street and stuck her head out to see the small plane had come to a stop about a few hundred feet from the house. A weapon, Mia needed a weapon. She ran back and saw her party huddled on the front steps.

"Mia, what's going on?" her mother asked.

"Frank, where is your shotgun?" Mia asked.

"In the van," Frank said.

"Get to the van now," Mia yelled.

She turned and ran for the van. She pulled open the back doors and climbed inside, moving her hands over all the packed items searching for the barrel of the gun. She found the weapon and grabbed it before jumping back outside.

The group was heading to the van. Mia helped her sister and mother into the back while Frank and Alex were going to the front doors. Mia heard the footsteps approaching and knew it was too late. She slammed the back doors and jumped into the grass, lying on her stomach as she watched the man approach. The van had roared to life and Mia hoped they would take off without her.

The pink stripes from Grant Marsden's shirt glowed in the moonlight as he came into view. *Please reverse and run him down,* Mia tried to mentally plead with Frank. Grant signaled to the man following him to point his gun at the back of the van. Grant walked out of Mia's sight and up to the driver's-side window.

"Mr. Piozzi," Grant said. "Are you going somewhere?"

Mia watched as the reverse lights came on and the man with Grant fired his gun through the back of the van. Mia had to hold a hand over her mouth in order to stop herself from joining her mother and Corinna in screaming.

"I wouldn't do that if I were you," Grant said. "Why don't you turn off the engine and we can all have a nice chat?"

The sound of his voice made Mia shudder. Mia held the shotgun up as best she could without giving away her position. She closed one eye and tried her hardest to aim at Grant's henchman. If she could take him out then Frank and Alex could overpower Grant. Mia didn't hesitate and pulled the trigger; nothing happened but a loud click. The man turned to look at the grass.

"Open the back doors," Grant said. "Let's meet the Piozzis' guests."

"I think I heard something," he said.

"And I think I cannot wait to see my loving wife," Grant said.

He pulled open the back door to the van. Mia left the empty gun in the grass and tried her best to slink farther into the field. She watched her mother and sister step down.

"Mrs. Morrissey," Grant said. "I never expected to see you here. And who is this lovely charm?"

Grant did not close the back of the van as he walked them toward the far side. His worker went around and pulled Alex out of the passenger side. Mia heard Frank slam the door as he exited. The van was still running.

"Where is she?" Grant asked.

"Not here," Frank said. "Probably on the other side of the world."

"Frank, we've been through this before; don't treat me like I'm stupid," Grant said.

Grant raised his voice.

"Mia, I know you're out there," he said. "Come and say hello or I will start executing your friends."

Mia was shielded by the van. It was her only salvation. Then a thought clicked in her head and she had an idea.

"I think I will start with the young girl," Grant said. "After all, she's the only one I've never met before."

Mia moved while Grant spoke, using his voice to conceal the sound of her steps. She made it to the back of the van and climbed in the open door, then slid along the floor. Her sister started to scream and it only made Mia move faster. She wiggled forward and entered the front seat.

"I am losing my patience," Grant said.

Mia slid up the driver's seat enough to look out the window. Grant was standing with Corinna to his left. Frank, Alex, and her mother were holding each other while Grant's man pointed a gun at them. There was enough space between the two groups for Mia to take out the henchman. Grant, who was standing with Corinna, might be a problem.

"Don't," Mia's mother yelled.

She broke free of the group and ran toward Corinna. Mia knew this was her chance. She gripped the steering wheel and jerked the van to the left. She pushed her foot down on the accelerator as hard as possible and tried to shield her head as the bullets started flying through the windshield.

"No!" Grant yelled. "I want to kill her."

It didn't matter though. Mia had overtaken Grant's man and she felt the van bump up and down as she ran him over. Mia swung the car around and heard Frank and Alex climb into the back. Her mother and Corinna were holding each other on the grass. Mia wished they would run for her car instead of sitting there.

Grant was close to them, but his attention was on Mia. He was trying to look at her through the glass. A smile crossed his face and he started to turn his attention back to the women on the ground, but Mia hit the accelerator again, this time charging at Grant. He dove out of the way, and Mia had separated him from her family.

"Get in here," Frank yelled.

Mia looked around; she didn't see Grant.

"Drive," Frank yelled. "We're all here."

A bullet came through the driver's-side window and glass exploded everywhere. Mia slammed her foot down again and the van screeched off the front lawn and onto the road. Mia ignored the screams and the sound of shots being fired as she sped away.

"Can he follow us?" Corinna asked.

Mia was approaching the small airplane. Instead of avoiding it she made sure to ram into part of the wing, destroying Grant's method of travel. She looked in her mirror and saw the machine, along with the silhouette of Grant standing behind her.

"Is everyone all right?" Mia asked.

Her mother and sister were crying.

"We're okay," Frank said. "We're all okay."

"I don't know where I'm going," Mia said.

"Just drive," Frank said.

Mia didn't care how fast she was going, it wasn't quick enough. The cold wind from the shattered window filled the car and Mia was aware of the cuts on her face.

"Hey, Mia," Alex said.

She glanced at him in the mirror.

"I will never question one of your decisions again."

Chapter 62

My wife is lovely and quiet. There is no sense of love between us, only duty. I hope that if we are blessed with a child this will change.

—The journal of Isaac Ryland

All of the cameras were on Ian. Grant stood behind him with a solemn look on his face.

"America offers its deepest sympathies to the people of France and hopes both nations can move forward from this tragic accident. Thank you."

With the final words the cameras were shut off, and Ian walked away from the microphone. Grant went for his crimson tie and started loosening the knot.

"Are you enjoying your last weeks of bachelorhood?" Ian asked.

"I've been making some changes with my staff," Grant said. "Doing a little traveling."

"For the record," Ian said, "nothing changes for you after marriage. You can continue on with life as you see fit. It is my daughter who should be the nervous one."

Grant didn't want to justify his cover again. He had spent the last three days trying to figure out where Frank and Amelia could have gone and was coming up with nothing. By the time he had secured transportation from that middle-of-nowhere farm the group was hours ahead of him. He felt his fingernails dig into his palms, he was clenching his fists so hard.

"Eleven days until the wedding," Grant said. "How are the rest of the foreign travelers doing?"

"I sent them home," Ian said. "They understood after the accident with the French woman."

Grant smirked.

"I know you're thinking I should have listened to you in the first place," Ian said.

"I did not say that, Ian," Grant said.

"But you were thinking it," Ian said. "There is still so much for you to learn about this position. I wish you would continue shadowing me."

"We have years ahead of us," Grant said. "I can't learn everything at once."

"I suppose," Ian said. "But you are going on *The Greg Finnegan Show* at least once before the wedding. He did not like your building-anticipation idea."

"If you still want to use the wedding as a grand display of political power I need to devote my time to making sure it is lavish and perfect."

"The wedding is the husband's day," Ian said.

"Then I should be on my way," Grant said. "Staffing for the event, of course."

Grant bowed and left the pressroom. He didn't want to hear any more of the old fool's ideas or suggestions. As soon as Grant obtained the code to the Registry Ian would be dead.

When Grant arrived at home he went straight to Hansen's place. He did not knock when he entered the room. His man was sitting on the new couch going through his computer.

"Did you find anything yet?" Grant asked.

"Nothing," he said. "We should have killed them all that night."

"I thought you were dead," Grant said.

Mia had hit Hansen with the van but failed to run him over with the wheels. Grant was a little grateful for that; he didn't want to search for a second all over again.

"Roderick Rowe is still our best bet," Grant said.

"I thought you said she wouldn't come for him," Hansen said.

"The clock is ticking on Carter's deadline," Grant said. "If she went to save her mother and sister that means Rod is on her radar."

"There's been no sighting of the men," Hansen said. "They could be dead."

"That would please me," Grant said.

"Why not alert someone?" Hansen asked. "The RAG agents could be a huge help."

"They failed me last time," Grant said. "And I need the utmost discretion here. If the grand commander finds out she is back in the country he will most likely have me killed to avoid any unpleasantness she may cause."

"If I were him, I would have killed you months ago," Hansen said.

"Me too," Grant said.

"She can still ruin everything," Hansen said.

"She needs proof she is who she says she is to cause any real damage," Grant said. "As far as the idea that she came to destroy the Registry, I don't think it plausible. She came back for her family and friends, then she'll flee again."

"There is no activity from Frank or Alex Piozzi in the last several months," Hansen said.

"You haven't been able to find a bank account?" Grant asked.

"They closed them out over the summer," Hansen said.

"Keep at it," Grant said.

He started to walk out of the house.

"Where are you going?" Hansen asked.

"If we can't find her first I need to prepare for her arrival," Grant said.

Grant kept moving until he was outside. Amelia would come for Roderick and Grant would make sure that her presence would not go unnoticed.

Chapter 63

My new partner is distant and cold. We live in a large house, not far from my former friend, but I am afforded no guests since the streets are deemed too dangerous for a female to travel alone. I find this hard to believe since we are in a gated community but comply nonetheless.

—The diary of Megan Jean

The ranch was beautiful, but given Alex's taste that did not surprise Mia. He was trying his best to make the place his own, and Mia's mother and sister were eager to help.

"I want sky-blue ceilings in every room," Alex said.

"Won't that distract from other colors?" Corinna asked.

"It will be subtle," Alex said. "At first glance you will think they're white."

"Why?" Corinna asked.

"Because if I need to feel like I'm outside I can, just by looking up," Alex said.

Mia knew he needed that feeling after having been buried alive but hoped he'd spared Corinna that detail.

"The nearest store is fifty miles away," Frank said. "And I'm only making one trip this month, so you better make sure your list is as detailed as possible."

"Let's move on to the other rooms, ladies. You can help me decide on the color schemes there too," Alex said.

The group of three walked off; Mia didn't follow.

"I can't stay with you," Mia said. "Alex is trying to make this place a home, but with me here you risk losing everything."

"We've been over this," Frank said. "If Grant finds us—and that is a big if—it won't matter whether you're here or not. He will want his revenge on us for helping you. That damage is done and we're safe here."

The group had been here for three days now, and Andrew was still unreachable. Frank was the only person Mia could speak to about the events that had happened before they left. She knew Alex could handle it but he was too good at keeping the other women distracted.

"How did you find this place?" Mia asked.

The house was one floor and spread out. There were five bedrooms, three bathrooms, and a giant kitchen, along with three rooms for gathering and a giant unfinished basement. It was designed to look rustic but Mia could tell it couldn't have been more than ten years old. She walked to the back of the kitchen and looked out at the scenery. A mountain range decorated the sky and lush greens were everywhere. A cow let out a long moo from the group in the distance.

"I built it," Frank said. "Before I met Alex I thought I would move up here. I came to visit a few times over the years but knew this wasn't his speed."

"You lived in the middle of nowhere at your last house," Mia said.

"There's a big difference between neighbors five miles away and fifty," Frank said.

"How do you know Grant can't find it?"

"It was nothing when I first bought the land," Frank said. "Paid for it with the money I earned from service; I knew I didn't need to save for a wife."

They laughed a little.

"But I took a job elsewhere," Frank said. "The years went by and I saved up enough money to build the house. It's self-sufficient. I was about a year out from moving up here when I met Alex. Living alone in solitude didn't seem like such a good idea after that."

"Still," Mia said. "There must be some paper trail."

"There's not," Frank said. "Besides, before I took Alex's last name I was Frank Smith. My guess is there are at least one hundred of him across the country. By the time Grant can narrow it down your plan will be in full swing."

"My plan is nothing at the moment," Mia said. "Keep my mom and sister distracted until Andrew comes back into reach."

"If that's what you think is right, we'll all back your play," Frank said.

"It's the only option I have at the moment," Mia said.

"Glad to hear you've learned some patience," said a voice that carried through the room.

Frank spun around and Mia felt his hand grip her shoulder. Mia did not share his tension over the new arrival. Standing in the entrance to the kitchen was Riley. Her red hair was pulled up in a ponytail; she wore her tight black pants and matching jacket, with a giant pack swung over her shoulders. Mia ran to her and wrapped her arms around her onetime trainer and friend.

"You came," Mia said.

"You called," Riley said, her Irish accent flowing off her tongue.

Mia released Riley and took a step back. The redhead dropped her bag to the floor.

"New haircut?" Riley asked.

Mia pushed her hair behind her ears.

"Interesting outfit . . ."

Mia looked down. She wore one of Alex's shirts; this one was bright blue with yellow swirls. A belt was tied around her waist and Frank's sweatpants hung off her figure.

"How did you get here?" Mia asked.

"You're not far from the Canadian border," Riley said.

"About twenty miles," Frank said.

"So you walked into the most guarded country in the world?" Mia asked.

"It took a little more than that," Riley said. "I got your message three days ago. I had to monitor the border and then I stowed away on the bottom of a truck; if they hit one speed bump I would have been flattened. Then I waited until they stopped and followed the coordinates."

"So you were in Canada when I called?"

"No," Riley said. "Getting to Canada was easy. I hopped on a plane."

"Did you find Nathan?" Mia asked.

She raised her hands to cover her mouth as soon as the words slipped out. Mia regretted bringing up Riley's missing husband. Riley gave her a sharp look. She turned her attention to Frank and held out her hand to him.

"Riley," she said.

"Frank," he said back. "You didn't tell anyone about this place, did you?"

"I am a strategist for the Irish government. They pretty much let me have free rein," Riley said. "But even they would have a problem with me crossing into America. My location is known only to you. I take it you're the owner?"

"I am," Frank said.

"I'm not one for small talk," Riley said. "Mia, explain the situation and let's move on from there."

"I need to rescue Roderick Rowe, Carter's father who is very much alive, from Grant Marsden's house, then take out the master server holding the Registry and service list," Mia said. "And we have less than two weeks."

Riley gave Mia a smirk. "And here I thought you would have a challenge for me," she said.

"This is serious," Mia said. "Grant's wedding is in eleven days, and Rod's deadline is in ten."

"I know," Riley said. "Let's take a few minutes and sit down. Then you can tell me everything and we will go from there."

Mia was elated. Sitting around waiting went out the window. Riley was the smartest person Mia had ever met, and with her help Mia felt she could accomplish anything.

Chapter 64

My wife is expecting, and I should be thrilled, but I am not. Being a government official has opened my eyes to the goings-on of our new world, which includes children being raised by our government.

—*The journal of Isaac Ryland*

"I feel like a girl in these pants," Carter said.

Andrew thought he had a point. They were wearing the same tight clothes as the rest of the mountain people, complete with homemade shirts. Carter's was dark yellow and Andrew's green; outside of that they were dressed the same.

"Just say thank you," Andrew said. He was happy to change out of the suit.

"We're lucky they're giving us clothes," Trent said.

Agent Quillian was no more; now he was just Trent. Andrew noticed Trent was much more agreeable, though still annoying.

Andrew walked outside the wooden structure that was housing them. He looked down the tiny street at the other six buildings, all of which were connected. They were in disarray, much like the place Andrew was staying. He'd offered to fix the roof on their first day here, hoping Mikey would give him a task to distract his thoughts.

"No, thank you," Mikey said.

"I know what I'm doing," Andrew said. "Don't you want to protect your people from the elements?"

"I want to protect my people from your people," Mikey said. "We found this place like this and intend to leave it that way. I don't know who left this here, but I'm grateful. We must be ready to move into hiding at any moment. Fixing these buildings up would let someone know people lived here."

Though the only people Andrew had seen were Mikey, Dustin, JR, and the two who escorted Carter and Zack. He didn't think five people needed so much space.

"We have a week left here," Andrew said. "Let's keep under the radar and then be on our way."

"What are we doing today?" Trent asked.

Andrew hoped it would be something more exciting than what they'd done the last three days. They hadn't been allowed to leave their building. Then last night Mikey had dropped off the new clothes. She said it was a trade for the luggage they'd brought with them. Andrew knew that meant their few belongings now were Mikey's property.

"No clue," Andrew said.

"Good morning, boys," Mikey said.

She walked out from one of the other buildings.

"Are we going to see Zack?" Carter asked.

Their blond leader was being housed somewhere else. Mikey explained it was due to his gunshot wound. Zack didn't object to his relocation so Andrew hadn't either.

"Didn't your mother teach you any manners?" Mikey asked.

Carter stared at her blankly.

"Oh," Mikey said. "Sorry, I forget about the outside world sometimes. Here's a lesson: wait for your elders to speak first.

"There's a week until the car comes back," Mikey said. "We have agreed it is too long to keep you cooped up. My people are getting tired of having to avoid your building and I don't want to move you out of my sight, so today you're going to meet everyone."

Mikey eyed the three men. Andrew opened his mouth to ask a question.

"I'm not finished," Mikey said. "Close your mouth."

Andrew did as he was told. Being instructed that way would normally have raised his ire, but for some reason he felt guilty for not following Mikey's instructions.

"There are forty-two people under my care," Mikey said. "I don't expect you to remember all their names, but I do require you to act gracious and show them the respect they deserve. Not everyone will want to talk with you and not everyone is aware of what life is like in the rest of this country. I will not tolerate you spoiling their minds."

She gave the three a stern look. Trent looked confused and Carter acted like he was about to burst with questions. Andrew had a few of his own he wanted to ask.

"If you have a question raise your hand," Mikey said.

Carter and Trent both shot their arms up. Mikey picked Carter.

"What do you mean?"

"We don't tell the little kids about the Registry or service," Mikey said. "They don't know about RAG agents, wars, or life outside this settlement until they hit their teenage years. Then we break it to them slowly."

"Why?" Trent asked.

Mikey reached out and smacked him. It wasn't hard enough to hurt, just to shock him. Andrew snickered and Mikey looked at him with a sharp glare. He stopped laughing.

"Raise your hand," Mikey said.

Carter shot his up again before Trent got the chance and Mikey pointed to him.

"How did you end up here?"

"I fell in love with a boy when I was sixteen," Mikey said. "We ran away together. Over the course of our cross-country expedition we met a few others who wanted to join us and we kept running. There were eight of us when we stumbled upon this place. We decided to stay for a night, which turned into a week, then a year. Relationships developed and we had children. As our children grew up some of them fell in love and had more children. That does not mean we're inbred; get that idea out of your minds."

Andrew didn't know what that meant but didn't bother to ask.

"Any more questions?" Mikey asked, staring at Trent.

He raised his hand and lowered his head at the same time.

"Who do they think we are?" Trent asked. "The children. Should we have a cover?"

"Don't talk to them," Mikey said. "They've been told you're from a neighboring community. We couldn't have you walking around in suits. The older ones know who you are though. Try to keep to yourself."

Mikey turned and started walking. Andrew followed, curious what he was about to see.

"One more thing," Mikey said. "Stay away from the girls. If they'll let you."

She didn't turn around, but Andrew could tell from her voice that she was smiling.

Chapter 65

I gave birth to my first child. I could not tell you if it was a girl or a boy because it was taken from me. My husband informed me the baby did not survive, but I heard a cry. Whatever plans are in motion regarding the children in this country they do not involve a family unit.

—The diary of Megan Jean

Mia waited for Riley in the kitchen. The rest of the group had met their newest member and were waiting outside, per her instructions, but Mia needed to talk with her first. She heard Riley's footsteps coming down the hall and stood up.

"I knew you would still be in here," Riley said.

"You didn't say anything when I explained my situation," Mia said.

"Well," Riley said, "you have two problems. Number one, you cannot bank on reconnecting with Andrew and Zack, which makes stopping the Registry nearly impossible."

This was not the news Mia wanted to hear.

"Number two, it is too risky to pull off two operations so close together," Riley said. "If you don't want to involve Affinity you need to pick one or the other and we can focus. Would you rather attempt to save Rod or attempt to stop the government?"

"I want both," Mia said.

"The way I see it," Riley said, "Rod has a deadline. I know that you're scared about Grant taking over the grand commander position, but the deadline to stop the Registry is arbitrary. You don't have the code that Affinity was supposed to supply, so there is no rush. Rescuing Rod I can help you with. After that we regroup and put our minds on the next mission."

"How long?" Mia asked.

"Until what?"

"Once we rescue Rod, how long do we wait to take out the Registry?"

"A year," Riley said. "At least."

"Well what if Andrew comes back and they have the code?" Mia asked.

"You can't worry about what-ifs," Riley said. "Do you even have a way out of the country?"

"Zack was the only one with a way to contact Affinity," Mia said. "Rod might know how though."

Mia cringed at the thought of his affiliation with Affinity, a fact he had kept hidden from her.

"That's another reason it's important to get Rod out," Riley said. "Affinity is more capable of smuggling people out of the country than I am. If you want to save your mom and sister you're going to need Rod."

Mia sighed but nodded. Riley was right. It made perfect sense and had been staring her in the face the whole time. Mia tried to push stopping the Registry to the back of her mind. Getting Rod out should be her focus, but Mia knew it would eat at her still.

"Let's regroup," Riley said. "I want to see what I'm working with."

Riley led the way out to the yard.

"Line up," Riley said.

The group looked confused for a moment.

"Come on, shoulder to shoulder," Riley said.

Frank went first, then Alex stood next to him. Both men had on jeans. Frank wore a white shirt while Alex was in a skintight ribbed muscle shirt. His arms did look larger. Mia's mother had on a blue T-shirt that hung on her thin frame like a dress, with a pair of long underwear as her pants. Corinna had put back on the outfit she'd fled the house in, a pair of fitted jeans and a baggy flannel shirt. None of them looked intimidating.

"Frank and Alex," Riley said. "You both served? Do you remember how to fight?"

"I think my fighting days have passed," Frank said. He ran his hands through his silver hair.

"I didn't ask if you wanted to fight," Riley said. "I asked if you remembered how."

Frank nodded.

"I want to see you and Alex," Riley said.

"I am not fighting him," Alex said.

"Would you rather fight me?" Riley said.

"You're a woman," Alex said.

Riley raised her fists.

"If you want to help Mia I need to know what task to assign you," Riley said. "I need to know you can defend yourself."

"Trust me," Alex said. "I can. Worry about the ladies."

Riley dropped her fists and marched toward Alex. She brought her leg up and kicked him in the side. He wasn't expecting the blow and fell over. Frank started to drop to the ground but Riley put a hand on his chest.

"He's fine," she said. "Now you."

Mia watched as Frank glanced down at Alex, who gave Frank a thumbs-up. Riley threw a punch and Frank got out of the way. She circled around him, avoiding his attack. Riley went to bring her leg up, but Frank blocked the kick. Mia was familiar with Riley's training and knew she was going easy on him.

"You're not bad," Riley said.

She relaxed her stance. Alex had stood back up and she signaled for him to come forward. He did much better this time and almost avoided her hits altogether. This back-and-forth went on for several minutes until Riley backed away.

"That's it?" Alex asked.

"I know your skill level and what it takes to beat you," Riley said. "That's all I'm looking for at the moment. Now you, Mrs. Morrissey, step forward."

"Please call me Laura," she said.

Mia saw the fear on her mother's face. There was no way she had ever seen anything close to combat, but Mia trusted Riley to know her limits.

"Handsome," Riley said. "Since you don't fear women, step forward."

Alex walked over.

"Laura, I want you to hit him as hard as you can," Riley said. "Alex, you stay still and take whatever she throws at you. It might be best if you closed your eyes."

Riley backed away and Alex shut his eyelids. Mia's mother looked nervous.

"It's okay," Riley said. "You won't hurt him. Give it all you got."

Mia's mother nodded her head. She brought her hand back and flung it at Alex's face with full strength. The slap echoed off the mountains in the background. Alex grabbed his stinging cheek and Mia's mother looked shocked. Frank burst into a fit of laughter. Riley joined him.

"Sorry," Riley said. "I should have been more clear. I meant punch him."

"That really hurt," Alex said. "Stay away from the face."

"I'm so sorry," Mia's mother said. "She told me to."

Mia knew Alex was exaggerating; she had been on the receiving end of a slap once before. It wasn't pretty, but the pain would fade.

"I think we have our work cut out for us," Riley said.

Mia crossed her hands over her chest and watched the rest of Riley's assessment. She felt a calmness wash over her. Mia had trained with Riley once before, and their efforts had resulted in the rescue of Andrew and Carter. Mia had no doubt Rod would be out of Grant's home safely in the upcoming days.

Chapter 66

It was difficult for me to accept my daughter is now property of the American government. I confronted the grand commander about this and his words did comfort me. She is part of the next generation and must be raised to accept that fact. I agree it would be hard for her mother or myself to ready her for the life she must lead under these dire circumstances.

—The journal of Isaac Ryland

"Let's go over the plan one more time," Zack said.

"We've been over it one hundred times," Carter said.

"The car comes back here for us in three days," Trent said. "We should be overprepared by then."

Andrew, Carter, and Zack all turned to the corner of the wooden room. Trent sat in a chair with his arms crossed.

"What?" Trent said. "I'm as much a part of this now as you three. I want to help."

"You're only in this room so Mikey doesn't have you killed," Zack said. "As soon as we're out of here you're back to prisoner status."

"You think I would betray you?" Trent said.

"The first chance you get," Zack said.

"Andrew, tell him how I've changed, how I've helped you since we've been here," Trent said.

The group spent their days helping out around the camp. Trent was always at Andrew's side. Earlier in the day Andrew had been chopping wood and Trent was right next to him, slamming the ax down on the logs. Andrew found the activity relaxing; he didn't need to focus on stopping the government or worry about Mia's whereabouts. Instead he focused on the wood. He got too lost in his activity and forgot to drink. Trent was paying more attention to Andrew than himself and made sure he stayed hydrated. Andrew admitted he enjoyed the assistance, and the fact that Trent never tried to attack him with the ax. Andrew shook his head.

"Stay quiet," Andrew said.

"Back to the plan," Zack said.

"We should arrive at the capital the day before Grant's wedding," Andrew said. "We meet up with your contact and lay low until the following night. There will be less security at the Mission that night since every important person will be at Grant's estate."

Andrew didn't think it was the right time to mention his and Carter's plans to go after Rod. He glanced at Carter who seemed to agree and continued on with the explanation.

"That night we start a small explosion at the office building across the street," Carter said. "The guards out front will go check on the flames and we'll sneak inside."

"Dressed as guards ourselves," Zack said.

"Right," Carter said.

"Then I stay behind and watch the door," Andrew said. "To monitor if anyone has noticed our presence."

"I escort Zack to the hidden room with the server," Carter said.

"I punch in all the codes Affinity has obtained," Zack said. "And then we get out of there."

"Someone will know right away," Trent said. "It's a bad plan."

"What would you do differently?" Andrew asked.

"There are security cameras everywhere," Trent said. "Don't you think they'll notice someone entering the grand commander's secret room?"

"Affinity has guaranteed us someone will remotely control all the video feeds between 7:41 P.M. and 7:57 P.M.," Zack said.

"So you have sixteen minutes to pull this off?" Trent said. "It will take you that amount of time just to walk inside."

"Why is it only sixteen minutes?" Carter asked.

"That's the longest a hacker has been able to stay in the system undetected," Zack said. "Any longer and they'll get bounced out."

"What if that night they get bounced after two minutes?" Trent said. "Then you're all dead and the Registry lives on."

"Pointing out problems without giving a solution doesn't help," Andrew said.

"I have a solution," Trent said. "Take me with you. I'm a legitimate RAG agent. They'll let me in, especially if I say I have information for Grant Marsden about his ex-wife."

"You want to draw Grant there?" Andrew asked.

"He won't come," Trent said. "It's his wedding night. The men will trust me though."

"Even if that was an option how would that help us?" Zack asked.

"Because the guards will be more distracted by me than a fire," Trent said. "And once you're in the building I'll take them out. Then I can monitor the security cameras and make sure nobody is coming in or out."

"That's Andrew's job," Zack said.

"He's just watching the doorway," Trent said. "I can get into the security room."

"You don't even know where that is," Carter said.

"Of course I do," Trent said. "First floor to the left of the main entrance. There are an additional two guards posted there at all times."

"How do you know that?" Andrew asked.

"I'm a RAG agent," Trent said. "Former, of course. Even if all three guards run to check out your little fire you still have the two inside, and that doesn't include the fifty-plus roaming the halls."

"There won't be fifty," Zack said.

"Say there are twenty," Trent said. "Three men still can't take them all."

"But four can?" Carter asked.

"Makes for better odds," Trent said.

"Once the virus is planted, what's the rest of the plan?" Zack asked.

"Try to get out of there," Andrew said. "Don't wait for anyone. Make it back to our hideout."

"So you'll all abandon each other?" Trent said. "So much for team-work."

"There's a good chance all of us will die," Zack said. "But it would be worth it if we succeed in destroying the Registry."

"We give our contact the go-ahead to appear on television. They present the file Rex has taken from Grant's house about Mia's escape," Carter said. "Affinity starts destroying all the online copies of the Registry and service list. We tell the people it's over."

"What about Mia?" Andrew asked.

"If we regroup with her she's the one who goes live," Zack said.

"What if the people still want to follow Grant? Have him rebuild the Registry and service list? Without Mia they might still have faith in him."

"That is a chance we have to take," Zack said. "There might never be an opportunity like this again."

"She'll be there," Andrew said.

"Has anyone heard from Rex?" Carter asked. "Did he get the file?"

"Not the last time I made contact," Zack said. "But I wouldn't worry about Rex. He can take care of himself and if Mia doesn't show up the file is worthless."

"We should kill Grant then," Trent said. "To make sure people don't stay loyal to him."

"If he dies before we can make our move it would turn him into a hero," Zack said. "And then someone else would take his place."

A knock sounded on the door. Andrew turned to see three girls in the doorway. All of them wore the same tight pants and long-sleeved T-shirts.

"We thought you guys might be hungry," Dawn said.

She was the leader of the group; Andrew guessed she was in her early twenties. Her brown hair was kept short and tucked behind her ears. She walked over with a dish and set it down in front of Zack.

"We don't make much dessert up here," she said. The plate held three brown lumps.

"We tried to make brownies," Karen said.

Andrew looked to the door. Karen had lighter and longer hair. She didn't follow the tray in and instead leaned against the wall, her eyes glued to Trent.

"Carter, you have to try one," Kristin said.

She was already at the table, picking a brownie off of the plate and holding it to Carter's mouth. Her blue eyes were magnified by large glasses and stood in stark contrast to her long black hair.

"I would try one of your brownies," Trent said. "But I'm not allowed at the table."

"We only had enough to make three," Karen said. She walked over and picked one off the plate.

"Sorry, Andrew," Dawn said. "But we didn't think you'd want one."

"No apology necessary," Andrew said.

Of the forty-two people in the camp, six were unattached females in the age range of Andrew and his team. Over the past week they'd made it a point to speak to the men whenever possible. Kristin had approached Andrew the first night and all he did was talk about Mia. Since then none of them had seemed interested in him and for that he was grateful.

Carter was turning his head, trying to avoid eating the brownie Kristin was waving in front of his face.

"There's a few people sitting around a fire tonight," Dawn said. "We hoped you guys would join us."

Dawn reached down and put her hand over Zack's, then pulled away before he had the chance to.

"We have a lot of work to catch up on," Zack said.

"Please say you'll come," Kristin said.

"The last time we joined you for socializing you beat us up," Carter said.

Two nights ago the group of girls had played like they were lovesick puppies, then asked Carter if he would teach them how to defend themselves. It did not end well for Carter.

"I'm just a little girl," Karen said. "How could I beat anyone up?"

Andrew looked behind him and saw Trent chewing his brownie.

"Trent, I wouldn't eat that," Andrew said.

Reality seemed to come back to Trent and he spat the food on the floor before scraping the rest off his tongue. All three girls broke into fits of laughter.

Mikey had warned the group about the girls in the camp, but Trent seemed too enchanted to remember. These women were not like the average American girl and seemed to enjoy finding ways to torture the visiting men.

"We'll come to the fire," Zack said. "If you promise to treat us like normal human beings."

Kristin leaned away from Carter. Her voice dropped the seductive drawl. "We're just having fun," she said. "We don't meet a lot of new people, especially ones who think women are for sale."

"None of us think you're for sale," Andrew said.

"How come the first night we met three of you were drooling all over us?" Dawn asked.

"Because you're pretty," Carter said.

"I bet you think I would make a great cook and cleaning lady too," Kristin said.

Andrew let out a laugh. These women had power and knew how to wield it.

"I will scrub every inch of your room if you let me spend time with you," Trent said.

The guys turned and looked at Trent. He stared at Karen. She had a small smile on her face.

"The brownies were the prank tonight," Dawn said. "We promise, just some people sitting around."

Carter looked at the brown lump.

"What are these?" Carter asked.

The women laughed again.

"Look for the campfire," Kristin said. "If you decide to join us."

Dawn signaled to the other girls and they left the building.

"These people are nuts," Carter said.

"Mikey told us to keep our plans to ourselves," Andrew said.

"It would be easier to avoid them if they were hostile," Zack said. "But they're messing with my head."

"I think they're wonderful," Trent said.

Zack rolled his eyes.

"Can we go to the fire?" Trent asked.

"Let's review our strategy again," Zack said.

"It might be fun," Carter said. "They promised no more pranks."

Zack gave Andrew a look; he was the deciding vote.

"Review one more time," Andrew said. "Then we can go visit for a little while."

Andrew looked behind him at Trent. The man was staring out the door, trying to watch the women walk away. Andrew thought about his first interactions with Mia; he'd had a hard time treating her like an equal. But Trent was not above treating himself like less of a person for women, even though they were trying to cause him harm. Maybe if there were more people out there with his attitude, stopping the Registry wouldn't be so hard.

Chapter 67

I have had my third child ripped from my arms now. My husband no longer wastes his time with lies. I am certain all baby girls are being groomed as wives, but whatever is happening to the baby boys troubles me more. I have thought about denying the opportunity to have another child but fear whatever outcome would await that decision.

—The diary of Megan Jean

Sweat was pouring down Mia's forehead. Her body ached from the abuse she'd subjected it to. Riley charged at Mia from across the open room and Mia ducked, avoiding her right arm. She did not turn around fast enough and felt Riley's foot hit her back, and Mia fell to the ground.

"I think that's enough for this morning," Riley said.

She walked over to a chair and grabbed a towel, tossing it at Mia.

"I'll never beat you," Mia said.

"No," Riley said. "You won't, but you're getting much better. You could beat an untrained person with ease."

Mia forced herself up and wiped the sweat from her forehead. She looked out the window and saw Corinna and her mother working with Alex and Frank outside. They looked much less spent.

"What is the point in training my family?" Mia asked. "You know I don't want them anywhere near danger."

"It keeps them busy," Riley said. "Makes them feel like they're part of the team."

"We have four days to get Rod out," Mia said.

"And we leave tomorrow night," Riley said. "Are you ready?"

"Still no word from Andrew," Mia said.

"We don't need him for the rescue," Riley said. "Focus on one thing at a time."

"Once this is over," Mia asked, "where are you headed?"

"After we rescue Rod?" Riley asked.

Mia nodded.

"Right back here," Riley said.

"What?" Mia was surprised.

"You're my friend," Riley said. "Pretty much the only one I have. This place is secure. I'll stay with you until you no longer need my services."

"That makes you sound more like an employee than a friend."

"Nonsense," Riley said. "Friends help each other. You need what I have to offer and I will supply you with it."

"What do I help you with?"

"Not thinking about my husband every second of the day," Riley said.

Mia was quiet for a moment.

"Tell me where you've been," Mia said. "Maybe I can share some insight."

"Not much to tell," Riley said. "After the lead in Mexico turned out to be wrong I went back to Ireland. I wanted a new mission; they told me no, that I was still incapable of thinking straight. But I know they think I'll lose another agent if I have an operation again."

"That's not true," Mia said.

"Maybe it is," Riley said. "I'm lucky in a way. They didn't force me to quit; I have the Irish government backing my trips across the world chasing a ghost."

"He's not dead," Mia said.

"He is dead," Riley said.

"You don't know that," Mia said.

"Yes," Riley said. "I do."

"How?"

"I followed a lead to another militant group," Riley said. "They had him there for less than a day before he was executed."

"I'm so sorry," Mia said.

"I destroyed their base," Riley said. "Killed hundreds of people in the process. It didn't make me feel any better."

"Then why are you still looking for him?" Mia asked.

"Because if I tell my government he's dead then I'm all out of missions," Riley said. "They'll give me a desk job or let me go off peacefully to spend the rest of my days doing as I please, when rescuing people and working on dangerous strategies is all I want."

"I didn't realize," Mia said. "I shouldn't have been going on about Andrew."

Mia felt a lump in her throat. If Riley's husband was dead maybe Andrew was too.

"I know how your brain works," Riley said. "Stop it. Andrew was not captured by a dangerous military presence—well, technically he was, but you already saved him from them. Focus on things you can help. Like rescuing Rod. It's the only way to stay sane."

Mia went back to the window. She watched as her mother and Frank fought with sticks.

"Are you teaching them how to sword-fight?" Mia asked.

"I think it's one of the more fun ways to defend yourself," Riley said.

"Thank you," Mia said. "For all your help."

"Get cleaned up," Riley said. "You need more relevant skills. We're working on shooting this afternoon."

Mia hated guns, but over the week her aim had been improving.

"Do you think I'll have to kill anyone?" Mia asked.

"Not if everything runs smoothly," Riley said. "But that doesn't mean you shouldn't be ready."

Mia nodded, but the thought of ending a life sent a shiver down her spine. There was no way she would ever be ready for that.

Chapter 68

A revolution sprouted up. In only a few short years the lesser-paid men realized they were never going to be married and staged an attack. Rather than fight our own a compromise was reached. Every man will start out the same and serve his country before he is eligible for a bride, meaning when the first generation of young females comes of age their husbands will be well into their forties and fifties. My conscience is clouded, but I see few other options.

—The journal of Isaac Ryland

The gray-haired man lay in bed, sound asleep. Grant had ordered Dr. Schaffer to keep Roderick Rowe sedated at all times. The man was a nuisance and Grant couldn't wait to get rid of him. Whether that meant handing the man off to his son in exchange for Mia or using him to test weapons on made little difference at this point.

"So when is the deadline?" Hansen asked.

"Four days," Grant said.

"How are you going to proceed?"

"I haven't decided," Grant said. "I would love to post guards outside his room in case he tries to escape, but then I risk bringing more people in on the fact that he's here."

"Who knows?"

"Me, you, and the doctor," Grant said. "My harboring a dead man to exchange for my dead wife might not go over too well with the grand commander."

"I see," Hansen said.

"If they come it will be with the intent of sneaking him out," Grant said. "So he must be monitored."

"Why not kill him now?" Hansen said. "You're not really going to let him leave."

"I toyed with the idea at first," Grant said. "I am a man of my word."

"And now?"

"Now I'm getting angry," Grant said. "I'm sure Carter will want proof of his father's life, so for the moment he must live. Which leads me to another problem. I am going to have to wake Mr. Rowe and he will likely be screaming and yelling, making all sorts of noise, so any guard will be within earshot."

"And with all the people showing up at the house to get the place ready for the wedding . . ."

"I won't be able to move him to another wing," Grant said.

"What about your work space?" Hansen asked. "It's secure, it's soundproof, and you have easy access."

"It's filled with weapons," Grant said. "I need to keep my inventions more secure than my prisoner."

"So he stays here?" Hansen asked.

"If we were able to find out where Frank Piozzi went none of this would be an issue," Grant said.

"The man is a ghost," Hansen said.

"He shouldn't be," Grant said. "I hate it when the technology ban works against us. If he had more of an online presence it would be impossible for him to stay hidden."

Grant was giving serious thought to lifting the whole ban once he was grand commander. He had his whole house monitored with the best technology. He didn't think it would be too much of a stretch to use similar devices on a national scale. That way he could monitor his entire country.

"Good evening, gentlemen," Dr. Schaffer said as he walked into the room.

"What's the diagnosis?" Grant asked.

"The leg casts will come off today," Dr. Schaffer said. "He won't be able to walk very well, but I expect a full recovery with physical therapy."

"When you wake him will he be able to stand?"

"Most likely," Dr. Schaffer said. "But he will need support to move. His legs have been inactive for some time."

"Make sure he is restrained," Grant said. "Wake him up in three days. If I need him roused earlier make sure I have the necessary equipment."

"Of course, sir," Dr. Schaffer said.

Grant stood up to leave. Hansen rose as well.

"You're staying here," Grant said.

"Why?" Hansen asked.

Grant pointed to the rifle he'd brought with him for the trip down.

"They may come early for him," Grant said. "I want you to shoot anyone who walks through that door unless they knock three times before entering. Without hearing the three knocks, fire at will; don't wait and see who it is."

"What if it's you?" Hansen asked.

"Then I deserve to die for failing to follow my own directions," Grant said.

"What if it's me?" Dr. Schaffer asked.

Grant grabbed the door and gave it three taps.

"I recommend you get used to knocking," Grant said.

He left the two men and started down the abandoned halls of the east wing. He made a detour down one of the secret passageways since the public entrance went out into the ballroom, and that place was crawling with workers preparing for the wedding. Grant had built this place with the intent of staffing it to its greatest capacity, but he had grown accustomed to having few people around and found the invasion of his home quite annoying.

Grant knew she would come for the man. He hoped it wouldn't be her who pushed open the door first, since Grant would prefer to kill Amelia Morrissey himself, but time was running out and he would take what he could get at this point.

Chapter 69

I spend as much of my time on government planning as possible. I can no longer stand the look of helplessness and lost hope that covers my wife's face. If there is any positive to take away from our situation it is that my daughters will be too ignorant to feel the same unhappiness as their mother.

—The journal of Isaac Ryland

The sun was rising and Andrew leaned against the door frame to take it all in. He was back in his suit, which had been cleaned but still looked pretty beat-up. It was the best cover he had though, since today they were leaving the camp and returning to the real world.

"Up already?"

Andrew turned to the left to see Mikey walking over. He hadn't noticed her.

"I can't sleep," Andrew said.

"I never sleep," Mikey said. "We won't start the walk back for another two hours, and the trip is about four hours. Which you have to take blindfolded. You should have gotten some rest."

"That's the closest road to this place?" Andrew asked.

Mikey nodded. "You can stay here," she said. "I think I already know your answer, but I still had to make the offer."

"Well, you have your answer then," Andrew said.

"I'm serious," Mikey said. "You've been good at helping out. Your whole team—even Trent has fit in all right."

"Thank you," Andrew said. "For not killing us or anything."

"You're welcome," Mikey said. "I don't suppose it mattered though; you're walking into certain death."

"What if we win?" Andrew asked. "Will you come down from the mountains?"

"If you win we won't know for a few months, until we need to send someone into town again," Mikey said. "And even then America will be in disarray. Who's to say the next leader won't try something worse?"

Andrew hadn't given much thought to what would happen after the Registry and service list were destroyed.

"That's impossible," Andrew said. "It can't be any worse than it is now."

Mikey shrugged. "I'm sure that's what the people fighting the Great War thought," she said.

"Once we make it to the car how long until our phones work again?" Andrew asked.

"It would be faster if you wanted to go the way you came from," Mikey said. "Since you're heading west I would guess another eight hours."

"We'll make civilization by nightfall," Andrew said.

"I wouldn't call it civilization," Mikey said. "We're more civilized than they are."

"If we're successful I'll come back and let you know," Andrew said.

"I hope that's not possible," Mikey said. "If you find your way back here that means we shouldn't have let you leave."

Andrew heard rustling behind him. He looked over his shoulder to see Carter sitting up in his sleeping bag.

"This is good-bye," Mikey said. "Dustin and his brothers are going to walk you down."

"Until next time," Andrew said.

Mikey rolled her eyes and nodded her head before turning around. Andrew knew he should be scared of heading back into mainstream America, but there was too much at stake to let fear crowd his mind.

Chapter 70

I am pregnant again. I don't feel happiness or sorrow. There are too many conflicting feelings inside me. I try my hardest to focus on the positives. I am helping to repopulate my once-great country, which I risked my life for.

—The diary of Megan Jean

Two days until Rod would meet his demise. Mia felt knots growing in her stomach. Everyone went about their day as usual, but Mia knew this was not an ordinary day. As soon as the sun set she and Riley were leaving for Grant's mansion.

"What are you doing alone in here?" Alex asked.

He came into the kitchen and went to the fridge. He wiped sweat off his brow and took out some purified water.

"Riley is making more bullets," Mia said.

"Maybe soon we can all train with the guns," Alex said. "I know you said she has a system, but I can't think of a time when having a sword is going to beat a firearm."

"You and Frank already know how to shoot," Mia said.

"I was talking about Corinna and Laura," Alex said. "Why don't you come outside with us?"

"I need to strategize."

"Did you and the queen bee figure out our method of attack?" Alex asked.

"We're working on it," Mia said. "We have time now."

"Grant gets married in three days," Alex said. "I take it that deadline is out the window?"

Mia nodded her head. She wasn't lying about that part.

"As soon as you figure out our part, let us know," Alex said. "Until then I must return to my swordplay."

Alex did a fancy bow and Mia waved good-bye.

"That's it?" Alex asked. "No laugh? No funny comment? What is going on with you?"

"Nothing," Mia said. "I'm sorry, your bow was funny."

"Don't say that," Alex said. "Saying something is funny without laughing is worse than not laughing at all."

"I have a lot on my mind," Mia said.

"We all do," Alex said. "Any word from Andrew?"

"None," Mia said. "If I call him it still goes straight to voice mail."

"You sound more annoyed than concerned," Alex said.

"What is that supposed to mean?" Mia asked.

"It means something is weighing on you," Alex said. "I can tell by your responses it's not taking down the Registry, Grant's wedding, or Andrew. So what is it?"

"Everything you just mentioned," Mia said.

"When you feel like talking about it there are four people outside who would love to let you lean on them," Alex said.

"I'm fine," Mia said.

"Sure," Alex said.

He turned and started walking out. Mia wanted to stop him and let him know about saving Rod, but that would risk involving Corinna and her mother. Mia wouldn't let them get hurt, so instead she kept her mouth shut and let him walk out. The knot in her stomach felt like it was tightening.

Chapter 71

I said good-bye to another child this evening. This makes number six in ten years. I feel like an awful person admitting it, but it does get easier.

—*The journal of Isaac Ryland*

Andrew had no idea what direction they were walking in. The blindfold was making it impossible to keep his wits.

"Be careful," JR said. "It gets steep here."

Andrew reached out and grabbed the man's shoulders as they made the chain again and walked down the trail.

"How did you get all of us up here?" Trent asked.

"You were unconscious," Dustin said. "And we had two donkeys with us. Two of you were loaded on them and two were dragged for the most part."

"We all took turns dragging you," JR said. "It took a while."

"Longer than this?" Zack asked.

They had to have been walking for close to four hours.

"No donkeys today," Dustin said. "They're ahead of us unloading whatever goods Tim brought back."

"Who's Tim?" Carter asked.

"The driver," JR said. "He'll be mad when he sees you three."

"Why?"

"Because he just got home," Dustin said. "And now he has to drive back out."

"Can't one of you take us?"

"Tim is the only one who knows how to drive," JR said.

"Stop," Dustin said.

The group froze.

"You can take off your blindfold," JR said.

Andrew let go of the man's shoulder and pulled down the black cloth. They were standing on a cliff. Andrew rubbed his eyes for a moment, then walked to the edge; about thirty feet down was the road. The rest of the group started walking to the right. Next to the road was a rock formation, and behind it stood a large black pickup truck. It would be impossible to see the vehicle from the road.

As they neared the truck Andrew got a better look at the area. Behind the black vehicle was their SUV.

"I thought our car was destroyed," Carter said.

"We stayed here for ten days when the car was here the whole time?" Zack asked.

Andrew expected to see red, but his breathing was even. He was more interested in hearing the explanation than in pouring his anger out, but he could feel it growing inside him.

"The day we took your car we took all the gasoline and put it into this guy," the man who must have been Tim said. "The group who came down to unload said to fill it back up and change the oil. You're good to go."

"So you stole our car and took the gasoline from it to fill your car?" Andrew asked.

"We can't go to the same city every time we need supplies," Dustin said. "It will draw attention. With the fuel we stole from you Tim was able to drive farther than normal."

"I would consider this a gift," JR said. "Mikey was planning on keeping your SUV and dropping you off. She just changed her mind this morning."

"You guys are a piece of work," Zack said. "Gifting us our own car back."

"Changed the plates for you too," Tim said. "We keep a spare set of phony ones to switch out every time I head out of here."

"Thank you," Andrew said.

Dustin walked up to Andrew and put the keys in his hand.

"I'm not much for good-byes," Dustin said. "I've never had to say one before."

Andrew nodded his head at Dustin and JR. He wasn't big on this stuff either.

"Can you do me a favor?" Trent asked. "Tell Karen I look forward to the day I get to clean her house."

Dustin and JR gave Trent a raised eyebrow. Carter walked over with a pair of handcuffs. Trent turned around and put his arms behind his back.

"Don't," Andrew said.

Carter paused.

"I don't think those are necessary anymore," Andrew said.

Carter nodded.

"How do we get out of here?" Andrew asked.

"They want to make it to the capital," JR said.

"That's a far drive from here," Tim said.

"We'd like to avoid areas like this one," Andrew said.

"Drive the car down the hill," Tim said. "Make a left. Travel for about a mile, then make another left. It's all gravel roads so you need to pay attention. Once you're on that one stick on it for about eight hundred miles."

"Mikey said we were eight hours away," Andrew said. "Not eight hundred miles."

"In about eight hours you'll hit some small towns," Tim said. "But the next major city is closer to fourteen."

"But our phones will work in eight hours?" Andrew said.

"I don't have a clue," Tim said. "I've never used a phone."

"You'll be tempted to drive fast," Tim said. "I wouldn't push it over fifty. These roads are dangerous. One sharp turn and you can spin out."

"Do we need to worry about more mountain people?" Trent asked.

"What?" Tim asked.

"You know," Trent said. "The people who live in the mountains and want to rob and kill us?"

"It was a fluke we found you," Dustin said. "If there are other groups of people living out here they want to be left alone. Don't stop and sleep for the night and you'll be fine."

"Was there anything else Mikey wanted to give us?" Andrew asked.

"A jug of water is in the car," JR said.

Andrew was hoping for a gun but knew it was unlikely.

"Good-bye," Andrew said.

The three men nodded at them and Andrew turned to walk toward the car. Zack was seated in the passenger seat already.

"I was about to honk," Zack said. "Let's get out of here."

His phone was sitting on his leg.

"What's that for?"

"As soon as we get a signal I'm calling Affinity," Zack said. "I want to tell them we're safe and find out our next instructions."

Trent and Carter climbed in the backseat.

"Why isn't he handcuffed?" Zack asked.

"He's fine," Andrew said.

"These people have made you soft," Zack said. "He's still not helping us."

"I know," Andrew said.

He turned over the engine and the SUV roared to life. Andrew had liked it here, more than he enjoyed his time with Affinity or the French. He wondered if once this was all over his life could be more like this.

Chapter 72

I haven't gotten out of bed in weeks. My husband got angry with me and it felt nice to get some emotion out of him. I have survived too much to give up now and must find some motivation to continue on.

—*The diary of Megan Jean*

"Today I knocked Frank down," Corinna said.

"I don't know if I should congratulate you or reprimand Frank," Riley said.

"Congratulate Corinna," Frank said. "She executed that behind-the-back spin-around move you taught us yesterday."

"It was a more formal name than that," Alex said.

"Names aren't important," Riley said. "Thinking on your feet is. Rarely are fights choreographed."

"And how is shooting going, Mia?" her mother asked.

Mia looked up from her plate. She hadn't been paying attention.

"What?" Mia asked.

"Are you hitting all your targets?"

"I'm getting a lot better," Mia said.

"I never thought I would be discussing fighting and guns with my daughters," she said. "Or encouraging them in these activities." Mia's mother frowned.

"The idea is that you never have to use these skills," Riley said. "They're there in case of an emergency."

"When you first met in Mexico did you teach Mia how to use a sword first?" Corinna asked.

"We played a lot of chess," Mia said.

"I've never heard of the game," Corinna said. "Mia, will you teach me?"

Riley had taught Mia chess to sharpen her mind and increase her patience. Mia never wanted Corinna to have to make the types of decisions she had.

"Of course," Mia lied.

"Mia didn't have as much to learn as you do, we had more time," Riley said. "And it was only the two of us. Once I'm satisfied with her skill level you'll have two teachers."

Alex let out a yawn.

"We should get some sleep," Mia said.

She stood up from the table, avoiding eye contact with any of them. Mia knew she might not make it back from rescuing Rod. If she saw any of their faces she feared she would burst into tears.

"I am tired," Riley said.

"Training like this takes it out of me," Frank said.

The rest of the table took turns agreeing.

"Good night," Mia said.

She walked down the hallway into the room she shared with Riley. Mia peeled off her oversize sweatshirt and sweatpants and stepped into the tight black leggings Riley had given her. She pulled on a fitted black T-shirt and was reaching for a black jacket when the door opened.

"What was that?" Riley asked. "Are you trying to make them suspicious?"

"I might never see them again," Mia said.

"That was how you were acting," Riley said.

"I'm scared," Mia said.

"Don't be," Riley said. "At least not tonight. We need to survey the grounds."

Riley went for her small backpack and took a quick inventory.

"Do you have everything packed?" Mia asked.

"Yes," Riley said. "Did you get the car keys?"

"I swiped them from the kitchen this afternoon," Mia said. "Do you realize if we don't make it back then all they have is the van filled with bullet holes?"

"At least we're leaving them that," Riley said. "And Frank did a good job patching up the holes; you can hardly tell what the van went through."

Mia knew she was right. If Frank hadn't brought the second car up earlier then Mia and Riley would be taking their only means of transportation tonight.

"We wait one hour," Riley said. "Make sure everyone is asleep then we leave."

Mia nodded her head. The next hour felt like days.

Chapter **73**

A group of young women was declared old enough to marry today. The grand commander made me responsible for finding a way to distribute their photos and wedding costs. I am happy for the new job and distraction.

—*The journal of Isaac Ryland*

The road was pitch-black. Andrew had already had to pull over twice to refill the gas tank and the group still wasn't getting any phone service. Zack kept raising the small device in the air, as if that would help him get a signal.

Andrew glanced in the rearview mirror. Trent was fast asleep and Carter was staring out the window. His face was covered with worry. Andrew knew why; after tonight they had two days to rescue his father. The two hadn't had much time to discuss their options, but rescuing Rod was still Andrew's top priority.

"Are we close to your old home?" Andrew asked.

"I don't have a clue where we are," Carter said.

"The mountains are starting to change to red," Andrew said. "That's how they looked from your backyard."

"How can you tell in the dark?" Carter asked. "They all look the same to me."

"Not the color," Andrew said. "But the red mountains went flat on the top. The large peaks are disappearing; they're starting to turn flat."

"I hadn't noticed," Carter said.

Andrew glanced in the mirror again. Carter smiled a little. Their attention shifted when Zack's phone made a noise. Andrew felt a vibration in his pocket. They were in a service area. Before Andrew could pull out his phone Zack was already dialing out.

"Don't pull over," Zack said. "We don't have time."

Andrew kept driving.

"Yes," Zack said. "It's me."

Andrew knew it was going to get annoying only hearing one side of the conversation.

"How should I proceed? . . . Five days? . . . Shouldn't be a problem . . . Can you locate my position? . . . Twelve hours? . . . It's a relief to hear your voice too . . . Thank you. Good-bye."

Zack hung up the phone. Andrew and Carter waited for him to speak.

"We are to head straight for the capital," Zack said. "The operation is still going ahead as planned. We're twelve hours away. Once we get closer I need to call for a rendezvous with Affinity's local contact. We move ahead from there."

Andrew pulled the car over.

"What are you doing?" Zack asked.

"Making my phone call," Andrew said.

He unbuckled his seat belt and climbed out of the car.

"We can't stop," Zack said.

Andrew slammed the door, not caring about Zack's rationale. His hand was shaking as he pulled out his phone, but he was too focused to notice. His fingers started punching in the number he'd obsessed over so many times the past week. The phone started to ring and Andrew felt his breath tighten. He was so hopeful she would answer his call.

Chapter 74

My husband hit me today. We have been together for well over a decade now and he has never touched me that way before. It only cemented the idea in my mind that I am no longer a person, only a piece of property.

—The diary of Megan Jean

Mia tried her best to tread lightly on the gravel leading up to the car. She went for the driver's seat while Riley walked around to the other side. The click of the door opening echoed across the sleepy ranch. Mia slid into the front seat and closed the door. Riley climbed in and did the same.

"So where are we going?" a voice asked from the backseat.

Mia let out a shriek. Her heart was thumping in her chest. She turned to defend herself, only to see a smiling Alex sitting in the backseat. Her sister was next to him.

"We weren't sure which car you would try to take," Alex said. "So Frank and Laura are guarding the van. We got a little cold and decided to sit inside."

"What are you guys doing here?"

"You've been acting so secretive; today was the worst," Corinna said. "Then you felt the need to sleep at seven thirty at night? We're not as stupid as you think."

"I don't think you're stupid," Mia said.

The back door opened. Frank and Laura slid in. The four were crammed together in the backseat.

"Mia, I know you've changed in the past few months, but I've known you since the day you were born and can read you," her mother said. "Now, will you tell us what is going on?"

"We're going to rescue someone," Riley said.

"Stop," Mia said.

"We want to help," Corinna said.

"I can't focus on saving Rod if I'm worrying about all of you," Mia said. "You and Mom especially."

"So we're supposed to stay back and worry about you?" Mia's mother asked.

"We have limited time," Mia said. "You're not ready to assist."

"Mia's right," Riley said. "You'll slow us down."

"How will I slow you down?" Alex asked.

"Not you so much as them," Riley said. "I'm sorry, ladies, but you can't defend yourselves. I was having you learn with the sticks as a distraction."

"We figured that out the first day," Mia's mother said. "Frank and Alex have been teaching us how to fight. We only use the stick in front of the window or when we think you're watching."

"I've lost too many people already," Mia said. "If I'm too worried about you I can't save Rod."

"Where is Rod?" Alex asked. "Where are you stealing our car and running off to?"

"He's at Grant's house," Mia said.

Everyone started responding at once. It was clear they were not on board with Mia's plan. Riley whistled and they all got quiet.

"Mia and I know what we're doing, or at least I do, and Mia is necessary for my strategy."

"You're not taking my daughter to a madman alone."

The group started talking all at once again. This wasn't part of the plan. Mia felt a vibration coming from her jacket pocket. At first she thought it was a reaction to all the voices speaking at once, but then she remembered her phone. Mia reached in and pulled out the small device to see the number she'd been dialing over and over appear.

"Hello," Mia said.

She opened the car door and walked away as fast as possible.

"Andrew, are you there?"

"Yes," Andrew said. "I'm here."

Mia felt like a weight had been lifted off her chest. He was alive.

"Where have you been?" Mia asked. "Where are you? I shouldn't have run off like that."

"I'm safe, for now. It's so good to hear your voice."

"I was scared something happened to you."

"No you weren't," Andrew said. "Deep down you knew I was safe, just like I knew you were."

Mia smiled at his comment. "Where are you?"

"I'm not sure," Andrew said. "The GPS should work again. You can track me. Where are you?"

"About two hundred miles east of the capital," Mia said.

"We're supposed to meet there in twelve hours," Andrew said.

"Meet where?"

"I won't know until we get closer," Andrew said. "I want to come to you."

"I was about to head that way," Mia said. "I'm going after Rod."

"That's a bad idea," Andrew said.

"Grant's house is on a gigantic piece of property an hour south of the capital," Mia said. "I am going to the area to scope it out and plan our attack."

"I wish you wouldn't," Andrew said. "But I didn't expect to hear anything else."

"Will you meet me there?"

"I'm at least eleven hours away," Andrew said.

"Well then I'll arrive first," Mia said.

"I have to hang up," Andrew said. "We're on a bit of a time crunch."

"Please don't hang up yet," Mia said.

"We'll discuss everything in person," Andrew said.

"All right."

"Mia," Andrew said.

"Yes?"

"If you ever leave me for this long again I don't think I can survive it."

A bigger smile spread across her face. "I suppose eleven more hours won't kill you?"

Andrew let out a laugh. "I hope not," he said. "Protect yourself."

"I'll see you soon."

"Bye."

With the final word came a click and the line went dead. Mia lowered her phone and went to the map. She highlighted his name and held down seven, prompting the GPS feature. The map zoomed out, covering the entire country. A green dot started flashing. Mia zoomed in on the blinking icon. Andrew was in the Southwest Area, near the borders of the Midwest Area and the Northwest Area.

"Mia?" Corinna asked.

Mia looked up; all of them were out of the car.

"I don't have time to argue," Mia said. "I don't think any of you are stupid. I just wanted to protect you. I feel a bit awkward because the way I treated you was how Andrew treated me, so I understand your anger and hurt. This is a dangerous mission; I don't want any of you to come, but I won't stop you from joining."

Mia looked at the group. They all wore their everyday clothing. Frank's white T-shirt looked electric in the moonlight.

"You have five minutes to change into dark, fitted clothing," Mia said. "Whoever is coming, be outside by then. Frank, does the van work?"

"Except for some cosmetic issues," he said.

"Five minutes," Mia said.

All four of them went for the house.

"That was a distraction, right?" Riley asked. "We're leaving while they change?"

"No," Mia said. "I can't keep them here. I shouldn't have tried."

"I can't guarantee their safety."

"Could you have guaranteed mine?" Mia asked.

"No," Riley said.

"We have to give them the benefit of the doubt," Mia said. "Besides, we're not going it alone anymore. Andrew is meeting us there."

"Now, he's probably someone I can work with," Riley said. "Congratulations."

Mia's smile faded. Andrew was alive and he was safe, but for how long?

Chapter **75**

I look back at the woman I once was and realize she is still here. I may not have the strength or physical ability I once possessed, but I have promised myself I will change my situation and run free once again.

—*The diary of Megan Jean*

The group moved to the van with Frank and Alex in the front seats and the women in the back.

"It's already better that we're with you," Mia's mother said. "There was a chance the two of you could have been stopped. How would you have explained driving alone?"

"Trust me when I say both of us are capable drivers," Riley said.

"I didn't say you weren't," Mia's mother said. "But this isn't Ireland. Two women driving alone will draw a lot of attention."

"Mia drove from the site of the explosion to your house undetected," Riley said.

"In a government vehicle with tinted windows," Corinna said. "Who would stop that thing?"

"Can we stop the arguing?" Mia asked. "We're together and nothing is going to change that."

"We should arrive at Grant's establishment in four hours," Riley said. "From there we scope out the place, try to determine where Roderick may be stashed."

"Do we know Grant is there?" Corinna asked.

"It's likely but not certain," Riley said. "He might be searching for Mia still."

"There is no way Grant got approval from the government to track me," Mia said. "They want me dead and forgotten."

"I know that for a fact," Mia's mother said.

"What do you mean?" Mia asked.

"The day you were declared dead, men showed up at our house," Mia's mother said. "They tore through everything. Took every picture, every document, wiped your father's computer. They told us it was standard procedure in a situation like yours."

"Did they tell you I ran away?"

"No," Mia's mother said. "They reaffirmed that you were kidnapped, and that any attempt to say otherwise would be regarded as treason. I'm surprised they didn't shoot us on the spot."

"That would have drawn more questions," Riley said. "If anyone out there thought Mia ran away and survived, then came looking for her parents, only to find they had disappeared too, it would have created a conspiracy theory."

"Why not say they died from mourning my death?" Mia asked.

"Because in America parents aren't supposed to love their children," Riley said.

"I fooled them though," Mia's mother said.

"What do you mean?" Mia asked.

Mia's mother reached for her bag. She opened it up and stuck her hand inside, feeling around for something before pulling out a small album. She tossed it to Mia.

"I was making it as a wedding gift," she said. "To show how you've grown over the years."

Mia went to the first page. It was her baby picture, complete with a copy of her documentation on the opposing page. She flipped through the next few photos. They were always only of her. The last one was a copy of her Registry photo and on the opposite page was a copy of her and Grant's marriage certificate, complete with a picture of the two of them together. Mia had on a long black dress and Grant had on a suit; it was from their meet-and-greet.

"How did you get this?" Mia asked. "I don't remember posing for a picture."

"I couldn't help myself," Mia's mother said. "I snapped one of the two of you when you weren't looking. You can only see your profiles, but you look so happy."

Mia did. She remembered that meeting and nothing about it had been happy. Then Mia realized she wasn't looking at Grant; she was gazing behind him. Andrew had been their server that evening.

"I wasn't even making it for you," Mia's mother said. "I thought it would be a nice gift for Grant. I made one for all your sisters' husbands too."

"Why did you keep this?" Mia asked.

Mia's mother reached out and took her hand. "Because I didn't want to forget you."

"Are you insane?" Riley asked, breaking the tender moment.

"What?" Mia's mother asked.

Riley was looking in the rest of the opened bag. She started pulling out stacks of cash.

"I don't have a clue how much this is," Riley said. "Tens of thousands of dollars; why would you travel with this?"

"You said grab what we need," Mia's mother said. "When I showed up at Corinna's money seemed to help, so I grabbed some."

"This is too much," Riley said. "What were you planning on buying? An airplane?"

"Mia's father handled the finances," Mia's mother said. "This was what I got out of the house before we left. I think even more burned up after."

Mia's mother turned back to look at Mia with a face of regret. A shiver went down Mia's back as she remembered the house fire. Mia didn't have time to focus on what had passed. She needed to look toward the future and gave her mother a reassuring smile.

"I wish I had pictures of you," Mia said.

"There's no need for us to have pictures of each other," Mia's mother said. She lifted her hand and pointed it at Mia's heart. "Because we'll always live in here."

Mia's mother smiled and settled back down. Riley diverted her attention to Frank and Alex, making sure they were on the correct route.

"Tonight, surveillance only," Riley said. "Then we make our plans."

"Where are we sleeping?" Corinna asked.

"We hoped to head back to the ranch," Riley said. "But with Andrew coming in the morning, probably wherever we can find a safe place. I would try to nap now if I were you."

The group tried to settle in among some of the blankets and pillows Frank had thrown in the back.

"Good job on bringing the money," Riley said. "If there's one thing America loves more than its virtues, it's cash. It might come in handy."

Mia could tell Laura was smiling and Riley was softening. She clutched the phone in her hand and tried to will herself to sleep.

Chapter 76

I have finished my system for distributing the information on the females. The grand commander was pleased with my methods and I am proud to serve him.

—*The journal of Isaac Ryland*

"Only three more nights and you're no longer a bachelor," Ian said. "Did those nerves fade away?"

"Now it's only excitement," Grant said. "I can't wait to marry Nina."

"Tamara?" Ian asked.

Ugh. Grant had taken a guess on his bride's name. Ian let out a laugh.

"You can call her whatever you like," Ian said. "In three days she'll be your responsibility."

"I was surprised to hear you had dropped by," Grant said.

"I wanted to check out the preparations," Ian said.

They walked through Grant's home and into the ballroom. It was decorated in gold and red and set for three hundred guests, none of whom Grant had invited.

"Tomorrow you'll go on *The Greg Finnegan Show*," Ian said.

"I don't think I can spare the time," Grant said. "I'll be busy with the last-minute preparations."

"Nonsense," Ian said. "Besides, he's coming here to film."

"Here?" Grant asked.

"Yes," Ian said. "He can show America what your home and your wedding decorations look like. Every girl will imagine her wedding as being this grand and hope for a husband as accommodating as you."

"I don't like having this sprung on me," Grant said.

"It won't be live," Ian said. "He'll be here in the early afternoon, ready to film with his crew. Walk him through the ceremony space, the kitchen where the meal will be prepared, and end in here. It shouldn't take more than a few hours."

"I'll be staying here the night before the wedding," Ian said. "I want to give you an early wedding present then."

"I don't need any presents," Grant said.

"I can see that," Ian said. "But trust me when I say you'll need this one."

Grant wanted Ian gone. With only two nights left for Rod, Grant was certain Mia would be near. He would keep watch in the room with Hansen for as long as he could, making sure her arrival didn't go unnoticed. Grant let out an exaggerated yawn.

"I suppose it's time I let you get some sleep," Ian said. "I know I took up most of your day going over paperwork."

"Paperwork" was Ian's code word for out-of-date policies Grant had to pretend he would continue after he took over as grand commander. It was exhausting and unnecessary.

"I'll see you to the door," Grant said.

He led the man back the way they'd come in, through the long hall and into the foyer. There two of Ian's guards waited.

"I hope you realize the importance of your training," Ian said. "Running the country is not as easy as it seems."

"I know the responsibility," Grant said. "You make it appear so simple; I can only hope to follow in your exact footsteps."

Ian smiled at Grant and nodded. He placed his hand on Grant's shoulder. It felt like the man's fingertips were made of fire. How dare he act so familiar. Grant wanted to grab the man's hand and break his wrist. Instead he stood with a perfect smile.

"You are a good choice for my replacement," Ian said. "The best there is."

"Thank you for saying so," Grant said.

Ian patted Grant's shoulder twice before removing his hand. Grant looked at his white knit sweater and decided to burn the thing as soon as Ian left the house.

"Good night," Ian said. "Greg will be here by noon tomorrow."

"I'll be waiting," Grant said. "Drive safe."

Ian nodded and walked out of the house. Grant was glad the man was gone. He went to the stairs, determined to change before he sat vigil with Hansen for the night. If Mia did show up at least that would require some of Grant's expertise, and for that he was grateful.

Chapter 77

I have started walking. I am alone most of the day and there is no one to notice my absences. Our neighborhood is surrounded by a fence twenty feet high topped with barbed wire. I thought about cutting the fence but am sure it is electrified or monitored. Whatever it is my husband does, it must be very important for him to be able to afford this much security.

—The diary of Megan Jean

By the time they exited the van it was almost two in the morning. The way Mia saw it, that meant six hours until Andrew's arrival. Time was moving slowly.

"I don't see a house," Corinna said. She tried her hardest to keep her voice low, but it still echoed along the trees.

"We're leaving the van here and walking," Riley said. "Two people need to stay behind."

"Why?" Alex asked. "Were you and Mia planning on watching the car?"

"Stop with the comparisons," Mia said. "More people, new plan."

"If someone spots the car we need a cover," Riley said. "We no longer have to take the risk of our vehicle being towed and I'd like to take advantage of that."

"Why two people?" Corinna asked.

"To keep each other company," Riley said.

"Oh," Corinna replied.

"I was kidding," Riley said. "In case there's a problem one person can warn us. So any volunteers?"

"I'll stay," Mia's mother said.

"Frank, that means you volunteered yourself," Riley said.

"Why me?" Frank asked.

"You two can pose as a married couple easier than her and Alex," Mia said.

Riley grabbed a pack and handed it to Mia. She swung the heavy bag over her shoulders while Riley grabbed the second pack. She took out a meter.

"Follow me," Riley said.

She crossed the empty road into the trees on the opposite side. Mia signaled for Alex and Corinna to follow first. Mia gave her mother a quick hug and Frank a nod.

"You'll be fine," Mia said. "Take care of him."

Mia gave her mother a wink and started after the rest of the group. They were making more noise than Mia would have liked, stepping on twigs and leaves. They were too wet to make a crunching sound; Mia was thankful for that bit of luck. Corinna slowed down until she was closer to Mia.

"What is that box she's carrying?" Corinna asked.

"An electronics detector," Mia replied.

"Why?"

"Grant's not the average American," Mia said. "We don't know how far back his security system spreads. This will make sure we don't cross over into his area of coverage. When we're close enough it will tell us where his defenses are."

"How far away are we?" Corinna asked.

"About five miles from his actual house and about four and a quarter from where his land starts," Mia said.

"How did you find this out?" Corinna asked.

"Riley," Mia said. "She said his house has been on television a few times and that made it easier to trace the information she needed."

"Where will the security system start?"

"That depends on how paranoid he is," Mia said. "But my guess is it won't spread that far."

"Why?"

"Because Grant is rich, powerful, and capable," Mia said. "He isn't paranoid. He's cocky."

"You knew him well?" Corinna asked.

"I learned a lot about him when I was running away from him," Mia said.

"Keep quiet," Riley said. "Grant could have the woods crawling with guards."

"I doubt that too," Mia said.

"Why?" Corinna asked.

"Because if someone finds me lurking around America before he does it could mean trouble for him," Mia said. "Notice when he showed up at Frank and Alex's house he didn't have a team with him. He's not a very trusting person. He would be too scared a guard would ask questions or recognize me somehow."

"Either way, I don't want to take any risks we don't have to," Riley said. "So stop talking."

Mia didn't answer that time.

The group walked for another hour before they took a rest.

"How long have we traveled?" Corinna asked.

"Almost five kilometers," Riley said.

"So we should be at his house?" Corinna asked.

"Kilometers are different from miles," Mia said. "We have another mile or so before we reach the edge of his property."

"Why did we park so far back?" Alex asked. "We crossed at least three roads."

"Because if we get caught then the others won't," Mia said.

"And vice versa," Riley said.

"Huh?" Corinna asked.

"It means we'll be safe if Mom and Frank are caught," Mia said.

Riley passed around a bottle of water and everyone took a sip.

"Why do you call Mom by her name?" Mia asked.

"Anger," Corinna said.

"I thought you'd forgiven her," Mia said.

"I have," Corinna said. "But that doesn't mean I forgot that she sold me off and then threw me away when I came running home."

"What else could she have done?"

"I miss my baby boy every day," Corinna said. "I think about him nonstop, wondering where he is, how he's doing. I would give my life to see him one last time. Laura did not feel that way about us. I won't call her 'Mother.'"

Throughout all of this Mia had forgotten Corinna had birthed a son.

"Have you tried to find him?" Mia asked.

"How?" Corinna asked. "I'm a single woman who's dead to the world. How could I look for a little baby with no records?"

"Maybe that's how Mom felt," Mia said. "About sending you back and selling us. There was no option for her."

"I was more of a mother to my child in the five hours I had him than she was in the eighteen years she had me," Corinna said. "Whatever bond I have with my son she never had with us."

Mia knew her sister was being irrational, but the argument would continue in circles at this point.

"If the Registry and service list are destroyed I will dedicate every breath I have to finding him," Corinna said.

"Does he have a name?" Alex asked.

Mia had forgotten about Alex and Riley, but both were looking at Corinna with sorrow in their eyes. Mia was shocked to see this display from Riley.

"I called him David, after my own father," Corinna said. "At the time I didn't realize his marrying me off was bad. It wasn't until my baby was taken that I understood the horrible situation I was living in."

"David is a good name," Alex said. "I'm sure somewhere out there he's dreaming about his mother."

"That's a lie," Corinna said. She wiped away a tear. "He couldn't remember me, but thank you for saying so anyway."

"We should keep moving," Riley said.

Everyone stood up again. There was nothing Mia could say to comfort her sister. Corinna's words only fueled Mia's hatred for the world they lived in.

Chapter 78

*Our subdivision dead-ends at the ocean. The fence stops here
as well, but it is a giant cliff and it is impossible to round the
edges without slipping to my death into the waters below.*

—The diary of Megan Jean

Ninety minutes later the group stood on the edge of Grant's property.
There would have been no way to tell if Riley hadn't had her machine
out. The group stood in a line among the trees.

"We have to move slowly from here on out," Riley said. "If this
device picks up an electronic pulse we need to stop; if it doesn't
we push forward until we have a clear view of his home. Keep in a
straight line, we don't want to set anything off."

Riley didn't wait for a response. Even though none of the terrain
had changed Mia felt like the air had thickened. Almost as if Grant's
evil touched everything around him.

As Mia had predicted no electronic pulse came. They walked
another half hour until the trees started to clear. Riley walked even
slower, not wanting to blow their cover to a naked eye. The edge of
the tree line was coming even closer and Riley dropped to her stomach. The rest of the group followed her lead and they wiggled through
the forest. Mia could feel the wet leaves sliding down her shirt and
mud squishing against her clothes. Soon they were on the edge of their

cover and Riley stopped moving; with one hand she signaled for them to come up next to her. All four lay on their stomachs. Mia looked up and in the distance stood Grant's monstrosity of a home.

"It's a shame he's so awful," Riley said. "You would have had a lot of resources."

"I'll take freedom over money," Mia said.

Riley took off her pack and Mia did the same. Riley pulled out a pair of binoculars and handed them over to Mia. She looked through the lenses and it was as if she were standing right outside.

"We're at the west side of the house," Mia said. "I can see his driveway on the north side. In the back there are five smaller homes."

"I think there are more than that," Riley said.

"Do you think Rod will be in one of those?" Corinna asked.

"No," Mia said. "Grant will be close to him."

Riley reached over and hit a button on the binoculars. The house and surroundings went away and all Mia could see were faint red marks. She pulled her eyes away from the glasses and Riley grabbed them.

"What was that?" Mia asked.

"Thermal imaging," Riley said. "We're looking for body heat now."

"What do you see?" Corinna asked.

"We're not in the best spot," Riley said. "From the looks of it all of the bodies are on the east side of his estate."

"Maybe the west wing is closed off?" Mia asked.

"No," Alex said. "The east wing is the one that's not open."

"How would you know that?" Mia asked.

"Grant's been a regular guest on *The Greg Finnegan Show*," Alex said. "I might hate Grant but Greg is the most beautiful man in the world . . . next to Frank of course."

"Grant gets on the show and talks about his house?" Mia asked.

"One episode was a tour," Alex said. "Don't give me that look.

I like interior decorating and Grant wasn't really featured in that episode."

"You didn't think to mention Grant has a closed-off wing to his home?" Mia asked. "That might be perfect for hiding someone?"

"They never said what side it was," Alex said. "Just that his house was so big some of it wasn't in use."

"How do you know it's the east side then?" Riley asked.

"Give me the binoculars," Alex said. "On regular mode please."

Riley flipped the switch and handed them across Mia. Alex looked through the lenses.

"The cameramen went up the driveway, then went to the right up the stairs leading to the second floor. Which would make that the west side. I didn't know what way his driveway would face."

"It doesn't matter," Riley said. "We would have made the same expedition anyway, only maybe have come from the other side."

Riley pulled out her electronic map.

"Which would have been much more difficult since his property dead-ends at the ocean, twenty miles away," Riley said.

"So Rod is in the east wing?" Mia asked.

Riley took the binoculars back and switched the mode again.

"I can count four people in the house," Riley said. "I expected more."

"Can you zoom in any farther?" Mia asked. "Look for clusters of people together."

"This thing can zoom in so far it will be like we're standing in the room with them," Riley said. "There are three bodies together on the lower level of the east side of the home. One is lying in a bed and two are seated."

"Rod would be restrained or tied down."

"It doesn't look like any of them are moving," Riley said. "But I don't see any other options. Every other body is alone in a room lying down."

"Rod would require guards," Mia said. "I'm assuming that's Grant and Rex."

"Isn't Rex on your side now?" Alex asked.

"Yes," Mia said. "At least I think so; it's hard to tell where the man's loyalties are, or if Grant hasn't figured it out and killed him."

"Did he tell you Rod was there?"

"I don't think he knew," Mia said. "He warned us Grant had a plan but didn't know what it was. There's no way for me to make contact with Rex. Zack might be able to if he shows up. We all had our own roles. But Grant wouldn't trust just anyone to sit in there with Rod."

"What about that guy who showed up at my house?" Alex asked.

"I ran him over," Mia said. "Remember?"

A pit in her stomach formed over the idea of killing another person. She wanted to forget all about that man.

"What is the plan now?" Alex asked.

"Call your husband," Riley said. "Tell him to move the car to just outside Grant's property on the north side."

Riley stood up and walked back into the trees.

"Stay here," Mia said.

She went after Riley.

"What are you doing?" Mia asked. "I thought this was a survey trip."

"Our target only has two guards," Riley said. "I'm going after him now."

Chapter 79

"That is insane," Mia said.

Riley was going through her backpack. She pulled out a holster and handed it to Mia before putting one around her own waist.

"We'll never have another opportunity like this," Riley said. "It's stupid to waste it."

"How are you planning on getting inside," Mia asked, "then taking out whoever is in that room?"

"The way you spoke about this guy and his reputation I expected a fortress," Riley said. "Even if he knows we're coming his defenses are minuscule."

"That's what he wants you to think," Mia said. "He is very smart and very dangerous."

"He can't fake body heat," Riley said. "There are ten people in that giant house. Even if they know we're coming I can take them. Are you in?"

Riley pulled out another gun and attached a silencer to the end. Mia held out her hand and Riley handed her the weapon.

"We shouldn't kill him," Mia said. "It might screw up the bigger plan that's back in play."

"I know," Riley said. "But we can knock him out and rough him up a little. If that other man in the room is on your side it will be a piece of cake."

"So what's your strategy?"

"Figure out where his security system starts," Riley said. "As soon as we trigger it he'll know it's us, but he can't call for any agents or backup as long as you're with me."

"So we let him know we're coming?"

"Maybe your man in the room will knock him out for us," Riley said. "Then we grab Rod and make a break for it."

"If that is Rex and if he is really on our side, don't you think he would have done that by now?" Mia asked.

"Still," Riley said. "Two on two? How hard can it be?"

"This isn't like you," Mia said. "You're acting reckless."

"Alex," Riley called.

He came over to them. Riley threw him a gun.

"You're not scared to shoot anyone are you?"

"No," Alex said.

"Three on two," Riley said. "Does that make you feel better?"

"I want to help," Corinna said.

"You can help by meeting Frank and Laura," Riley said. "Follow the tree line north to the street. Tell them to wait for us outside the gate. Leave now."

Corinna took off along the tree line. Mia was grateful she was out of harm's way.

"Now, he is going to want to kill you," Riley said. "But if you don't accompany us we have no guarantee he won't call in extra security. So when we get near the room you need to stay out of sight. I don't want you anywhere near him. Do you understand?"

Mia nodded her head.

"Alex, we are expendable," Riley said. "He knows who you are and your relationship with Mia. He has no clue who I am or what I'm capable of. I have an electronic scrambler. I'm going to take it with me and go in separately. I want him to spot the two of you. Mia, take this."

Riley put the electronic sensor in her hand.

"Stay out of the way of any electronics," Riley said. "I'm going to circle the house to come in through the east side. I want you to wait here twenty minutes and then enter the view of his cameras from this end. He should come after you."

"But Rod is on the opposite side," Alex said.

"I'm coming in from that direction," Riley said. "I think Grant will be too distracted by you to notice his security system failing on the east side. I'll enter the house and come up through the opposite way. I will get Rod. You two meet me by the front door."

"What if he doesn't come after us?" Mia asked.

"Then break into the house and head toward the east wing," Riley said. "But don't lose your way. That house is huge. Remember where the door is. Alex should know the layout."

"I remember the episode," Alex said.

"Try to keep his eyes on you," Riley said. "And kill anyone who isn't Grant."

Mia gulped. She wasn't ready for this.

"Wait twenty minutes," Riley said.

She left her bag on the ground and secured what must have been the scrambler to her wrist. The binoculars hung around her neck.

"This is crazy," Mia said.

"It will work," Riley said. "Twenty minutes."

With that Riley took off along the trees toward the back of the house.

"She should have taken the sensor with her," Alex said. "For all she knows she's setting off Grant's security right now."

"I'd never underestimate Riley," Mia said. "She knows exactly what she's doing."

Alex nodded and watched her jog away.

"We might die tonight," Alex said.

Mia looked up at him.

"That thought has crossed my mind a lot, and I'm still here," Mia said.

"I'll take luck over skill anytime," Alex said.

Mia gave a short fake laugh. The sky was starting to lighten. Mia pulled out her phone and checked the time. It was almost five A.M. In two hours she would see Andrew again. Mia repeated that in her head, assuring herself that she would survive the next couple hours.

Chapter **80**

The launch of the Registry was a success. Every female gener-
ated more of a profit than her listing price. It is not required
that this next generation of females live in the capital with their
husbands. I do not know how the grand commander will moni-
tor their offspring.

—*The journal of Isaac Ryland*

The laptop wasn't showing any sign of movement, but Grant's eyes
never tired. He had the outside of his house on the screen. A projection of the interior was displayed on the wall.

"How are you still awake?" Hansen asked.

"Patience," Grant said. "This is the most exciting night I've had
in several months."

"Your former employee told you she wouldn't be coming," Hansen
said. "There is a chance all of this is pointless."

"You joined the game late, my friend," Grant said. "I have gotten
to know Amelia quite well. A few things have surprised me, but I can
read her now. She is coming. If not tonight then tomorrow night, but
she will be here."

"Do you think she's going to just appear at your front door?"

"I've learned not to underestimate her," Grant said. "She was
clever enough to escape the country with little help, and now she has

a terrorist organization behind her. She ran you over. It is in your best interests not to underestimate her either."

"What will you do if she shows up?" Hansen asked.

"Try my hardest not to kill her on sight," Grant said. "But that scale keeps tipping."

"I'd shoot her straight through the eye," Hansen said.

"I went through that phase," Grant said. "But now I see a slow death in her future. It's a shame. She is the closest I will ever come to my equal."

"For a woman?"

"For a person," Grant said. "She thinks she's noble, but she is ruthless like I am. She's killed several people who stood in her way, has a natural ability to pick up on concepts. She's a survivor and won't let anything stop her."

"How do you figure?"

"She killed her father for one," Grant said. "Abandoned those who helped her. She only cares about herself."

"If that were true why wouldn't she stay hidden? She was already free."

"Mia has fooled herself long enough," Grant said. "But she thinks the same way I do. She's not back here to take down some government conspiracy. She is here to right the wrongs done to her. Mia started with Andrew, then her father, and I'm next."

"Who is Andrew?"

"He's a problem," Grant said. "One of the men I think burned up in that fire at the fake orphanage."

"I thought you said he got away."

"If he had don't you think he would be with her?" Grant asked. "But he was nowhere near our last encounter. I think he's dead."

"Then why come for this man?"

"Because," Grant said, "she doesn't want him. She wants to come for me. It's another way for her to justify her actions."

"I'd hate to prove you wrong," Hansen said, "but I don't think she's coming."

"I accept your apology," Grant said.

"I never said I was sor . . ."

Hansen's voice trailed off when Grant changed the projection on the wall. One of his security cameras had a hit. Running across his land was none other than his wife.

Grant stood up and went toward her projection. He ran his hand down the image of her face.

"You were right," Hansen said.

"I always am," Grant said.

"What now?"

"Now we wait and watch," Grant said.

The cameras switched and Grant got a view of Mia and Alex. He laughed as they tried to pick up a rock and throw it through a window. The glass was unbreakable.

Chapter **81**

I thought I was growing too old to carry a child, but I was proved wrong. This only adds to my resolve to start a new life somewhere far away.

—The diary of Megan Jean

Mia could feel Grant's eyes on her. She didn't know where he was, but he had to know her exact location.

"I thought this would be easier," Alex said.

"We have to get inside," Mia said.

"The glass won't break."

With few other options Mia went up to the window and pushed it inward. It fell open with ease.

"So they don't shatter, but they open wide?" Alex asked.

"It's a way inside," Mia said.

She pushed herself up and climbed in through the window. Alex followed her into the dark room. The lights flipped on. They were in a library. If Mia weren't scared out of her mind she would have been overwhelmed by the number of books.

"How did that happen?" Alex asked.

"He's letting us know he can see us," Mia said.

"Is that a good thing?"

"I'm not sure," Mia said.

A light clicked on in the hall and the library light went off.

"I think we should head that way," Mia said.

"This is a bad idea," Alex said.

"We're still alive, aren't we?" Mia said.

Mia went out into the hall. That light went off and another lit up.

"He's leading you right to him," Alex said.

"I guess we can rule out his wanting to kill me on sight," Mia said.

They rounded a few more corners and crossed the front foyer. Mia looked to Alex, who nodded.

"We should stop here," Alex said. "Draw him out."

Alex's idea was sound. Mia didn't know whether to proceed or not, but then she remembered Riley coming in the opposite way. If they gave Grant a second to look away from them he might notice her.

"You know he can hear us," Mia said.

"I didn't think about that," Alex said.

"Grant, stop this," Mia said. "It's me you want, and I want Rod. I'll make a trade."

Mia dropped her gun on the floor. The light leading the way started flashing on and off.

"If that's the way you want it, I'm coming armed," Mia said.

She picked up her weapon again and the lights went dark.

"Fine," Mia said. "I'll find you without your trail."

"This is a bad idea," Alex said.

"There could be men all around us," Mia lied. "Don't be stupid."

The light came back on and Alex held his gun in front of him. They'd won that battle and continued following the trail of lights. Mia tried her hardest to remember the way to the door. They followed the lights to a giant ballroom. The space of the room was overwhelming. Mia felt too vulnerable. All the lights went out except for one above a single door. Mia half expected the door to open by itself, but it stood closed.

"Are you sure?" Alex asked.

"What option do we have?" Mia asked.

Chapter 82

The grand commander intends to let the next generation of females be raised by their parents. He has developed an ingenious system requiring their placement in the Registry when they come of age. I am still in awe.

—The journal of Isaac Ryland

It didn't take long for Grant to spot the van parked outside his gates. It wasn't visible from his personal security camera, but he had installed some extra ones on the front gates and he recognized the vehicle immediately.

"They're in the house," Hansen said. "Send someone to grab them."

"I don't know what her plan is," Grant said. "But she wants to draw us away from him, and I won't have that."

Grant stood up and went to the bed. He pulled a gun out and pointed it down at the unconscious man.

"She won't try anything while he's still a hostage," Grant said. "Look at the screen. Can you see any movement on any of the other cameras?"

"One of the screens is dark," Hansen said. "Never mind. It was a fluke, it's just dark outside."

"What camera?" Grant asked.

"The one on the east side of the house."

"Turn on the hall lights," Grant said.

"I don't know how to work your system," Hansen said. "Technology is not my strong suit."

"Fine," Grant said. "Then switch with me. No matter what, don't take your eyes or weapon off of this man."

Hansen stood up and went toward Rod. He looked silly pointing an assault rifle at the sleeping man, but Hansen hadn't had enough sense to pull out his pistol.

Grant went to the computer and checked out the screen. Everything looked normal. He watched Mia and Alex walk down the hallway. They were almost outside the door. Grant stood up and pointed his gun toward the door. He looked at his security system monitors. They were right outside.

"I have a gun pointed at Roderick," Grant shouted. "If Alex steps in my line of sight I will shoot him dead, and if you try anything funny all of you are gone."

There was silence. Grant heard a hand reach for the doorknob and it creaked open. Standing in the middle of the door frame was Amelia. She held her gun straight in front of her, a look of pure hatred across her face.

Chapter 83

Every day I walk to the ocean and envision my escape. I have been testing the fence at that area. If I can break through, then make my way down the coast until I find a boat docked, maybe I will have a chance at freedom.

—*The diary of Megan Jean*

"What are you doing?" Alex asked.

He was crouched down next to the room housing Rod. Mia was going against Riley's instructions, but their ploy was over with. She saw the redheaded woman pressed against the wall, twenty feet away from her. Not close enough to show up in whatever camera angle Grant had. This was Mia's only chance and she was taking it.

Grant was staring right at her. His gun was pointed at her head. Mia glanced to her left. Rod was lying in the bed. A man who wasn't Rex had a giant weapon next to his head.

"I want Carter's deal," Mia said.

"What deal is that?" Grant asked.

"Me for Rod," Mia said. "Alex will take him now."

"That wasn't transferable," Grant said.

"Then we can all kill each other," Mia said.

"Step inside the room," Grant said. "Then Hansen can push the bed out to Alex. I wouldn't take your time. Ever since you ran over Hansen he has been eager to get his revenge."

Mia knew not to trust Grant; she was unsure how to proceed.

"I think revenge is your game," Grant said.

Mia stepped inside the room. She blocked the door from slamming shut and trapping her.

"Hansen, wheel the bed out," Grant said. "But don't take your weapon off of him."

"Where should I push the bed?" Hansen asked.

"To the hallway of course," Grant said.

A smile spread across his face. Mia knew he had no intention of letting any of them leave alive. The only reason Grant hadn't pulled the trigger yet was because of his arrogance. Mia had a feeling whatever death he was imagining for her was one thousand times worse than being shot in the head.

"What if they try to take me hostage?" Hansen asked.

"Tell them I don't care for you one bit and will spill your blood as quick as I spilled Rex's," Grant said.

Mia breathed in hard. She kept her gun aimed at Grant and slid along the wall of the room, giving Hansen the space to wheel Rod's bed into the hallway.

"Oh," Grant said. "You didn't think I would notice you turned my man against me?"

"I was never certain he switched sides," Mia said.

"I was," Grant said. "Tell me, do you regret his death? Or your father's? Or that of the agent you beat to death with a rock?"

"You mean the night I beat you?" Mia asked.

"If you beat me then why are you in my house?" Grant asked.

"I wanted to rub it in," Mia said.

"I should shoot you right now," Grant said.

"I'll pull the trigger first," Mia said.

Grant did something so unexpected Mia didn't know how to respond. He lowered his gun.

"I'm all yours," Grant said.

Every ounce of Mia's being told her to pull the trigger, but she knew that would mean Rod was dead, since Grant's newest henchman still had the weapon on him. She tried to focus on the future. If Grant's wedding didn't happen, then her chance at destroying the Registry would evaporate too. He had to survive tonight. Grant broke eye contact with Mia. She kept her focus on him as he made his way to the door. Mia was scared he was going to head into the hallway, but instead he lifted his arm and flung the door shut.

"Alone at last," Grant said. "You haven't killed me yet."

"Back away from me," Mia said.

"Maybe I underestimated you," Grant said.

Mia tried not to show any fear as he positioned himself in front of her, ignoring her request. He crept closer to Mia and she responded by pulling the gun into herself, making sure it was still pointed at him. Grant reached up and put his hand on her shoulder. Mia tried hard to fight off the chill that came with his touch. He ran his hand down her arm and pulled the weapon from her hand before flinging it across the room.

Chapter 84

The grand commander has decided it is time we expand across the country. I have been chosen to head up one of the new areas. We are no longer fifty states but five sections that are part of something bigger. I am eager to take my new post.

—The journal of Isaac Ryland

Her fear was intoxicating. After he'd waited all this time, she was his. Grant had won. He took a few moments to rejoice in this moment. Grant moved behind Mia. He placed his hand on her shoulder and forced her to her knees.

"I really did want a long, drawn-out death for you," Grant said. "But I have too much on the line."

Grant pulled the small revolver he had tucked away out of his pants. He cocked his weapon and pressed it to the back of Mia's head.

"You were more trouble than you were worth," he said.

Grant looked down at her and felt his finger flinch. Before he could pull the trigger the door flew open, almost knocking him down. Grant raised his weapon and fired, hoping to kill anyone who would disrupt this moment. He shot at nothing and then felt intense pain between his legs. He instinctively tried to protect himself, only to see Mia rise and bring her hand up under his chin. The impact made him bite his tongue and fall back. A foot came down on his wrist and he reflexively released the gun. A redheaded woman stood over him.

"This was not part of the strategy," she said.

"I had to improvise," Mia said.

He looked up to see Mia pointing his own gun at him. Her arms were shaking.

"Kill him," the strange woman said.

"I'm thinking about the bigger picture here," Mia said.

There was a sharp pain in Grant's side. He curled over and tried to grab Mia's foot as she kicked him over and over in the side. He felt her kick upward and his head flew back. Grant stared at the floor. There was a trickle of blood. He wanted to bring his hands up to check if it was his. He shut his eyes, knowing when to bide his time.

"Where are Rod and Alex?" Mia asked.

"Alex is wheeling Rod out," the stranger said. "I took care of the other guy as soon as they left the room."

There was a third person? How did Grant miss that? Someone clever enough to break into his home undetected too, and a woman at that. He kept his eyes closed, faking unconsciousness.

"Let's get out of here," Mia said. "Before I do kill him."

The two women left with Grant's weapon. He heard their double footsteps down the hall before forcing himself up. Grant cracked his jaw and spat. His saliva was bright red. He went out of the room. Lying on the floor was Hansen's body. They'd forgotten to take his weapon. Grant picked up the rifle and ran toward the main entrance.

He pushed open the door to the ballroom to see Mia and her red-headed friend sprinting toward the other side. Grant lifted the rifle and pulled the trigger. The redhead let out a yelp and Mia bent down to wrap her new friend's arm around her shoulder, leading her out of the ballroom. Grant ran across the room into the hallway. He spotted the trail of blood and was glad he'd made contact. He kept moving through the halls, hearing their movements but unable to catch up.

The front door was wide open and the moonlight poured inside. Grant knew they'd made it outside. He saw their figures making their way down his driveway. Grant stopped and took aim. It was dark, but he had a shot at Mia and fired. He didn't wait this time and took aim again. Grant could tell by their movements that he hadn't made contact.

Instead of chasing them, Grant decided to try a more accurate method. He walked back into his home and ran up the stairs and into his bedroom. He went for his closet and pulled out one of his favorite weapons before going to his window. Grant looked through the scope on his favorite rifle. He spotted the white van. Alex was loading Rod into the back. Mia was helping the redhead inside.

"It's not as personal as I would have liked," Grant said. "But good-bye, Mia."

He had a perfect shot at her back and Grant didn't hesitate as he pulled the trigger. A loud scream cut through the air. Grant turned around and sat down. This weapon was one of his first inventions. A sniper rifle that was incapable of missing. There was no way she'd survived that shot. Grant smiled to himself and ran his tongue over his bloody teeth. At least she was dead. Of that he was certain.

Chapter 85

Something is happening. My husband hasn't told me, but people are moving our things. I must act quickly or else my chances of escape will disappear.

—The diary of Megan Jean

The driveway was so long, Mia didn't think they would ever reach the street. She was trying to help Riley run while Alex was flying down the driveway with Rod in his bed. Grant was right on their tail. Mia could feel him. They never stopped moving. Alex and Rod were too far ahead to be in danger and Mia was grateful.

"Drop me," Riley said. "I'm too much weight."

"Where did he get you?" Mia asked.

"My calf," Riley said. "Save yourself."

"Stop being so dramatic," Mia said. "We're almost there."

She knew that was a lie. Grant's driveway was too long. Mia tried to move toward the side, hoping the darkness would protect them. Riley kept throwing her good leg farther ahead, but she was getting heavier. Frank came into view. He was running up to them. He stopped and grabbed Riley, flipping her over his shoulder. Mia took the time to look behind her. Grant wasn't chasing them. She didn't think that was a good sign.

"Hurry," Frank yelled.

Mia started running, trying to stay behind Frank and Riley. She kept looking behind her; nothing was coming. Then the van was close enough to touch and Mia felt relief. Maybe Grant had passed out from his injuries, or maybe he had just given up. But Mia knew that rang false. He had another plan. She worried the grounds were lined with bombs.

They made it to the van. Alex was getting Rod into the back. Frank dropped Riley on the bumper and Mia tried to help her inside. Riley scooted herself back and Mia took a moment to pause. She remembered the feeling of the gun at the back of her head and a tremor went through her body. Then there were arms around her. Mia looked up to see her mother embracing her.

"You did it," she said. "I am so proud of—"

Her mother suddenly went limp. Instead of Laura holding on to Mia, Mia found herself gripping her mother. Mia let out a scream. She could feel her clothing getting wet with her mother's blood.

Chapter 86

I have never felt more betrayed in my life. The security team surrounding my home informed me of my wife's daytime activities. While I have never been a fan of punishing her, she has left me little choice in this matter.

—The journal of Isaac Ryland

Andrew's nerves were getting the best of him. Carter was driving; Zack and Trent were fast asleep in the backseat. Andrew knew he should be sleeping too. He had a long night in front of him.

"Where is Grant's house in relation to our final destination?" Carter asked.

"I'm not sure," Andrew said. "It can't be too far though. An hour or two at most."

"Tomorrow is the deadline," Carter said.

"And we will get Rod back," Andrew said. "Mia was headed there last night to check the place out."

"So are we going to turn her over to Grant, get my dad, and then bust her out?" Carter asked.

"No," Andrew said. "We're going to see what Mia thinks is best first, but I think Grant would kill her before we got Rod out of the house."

"I can't think of another way," Carter said.

"Don't talk about it," Andrew said.

He heard Zack rustling in the backseat. The blond man did a long stretch and let out a yawn.

"What time is it?" Zack asked.

"Almost six," Carter said.

Zack reached for his phone and flipped the screen open.

"I have directions to our destination," Zack said. "I wish my arm wasn't in this cast."

"I have to call Mia," Andrew said, "and tell her where to meet us."

"Can't she just track our cell phones?" Carter asked.

"I don't want her to sit around and wait for us to arrive," Andrew said. "Besides, we have to pull over soon anyway and refuel."

"Barely made it," Zack said. "We have one can of gas left."

"One is enough," Andrew said.

Carter pulled over to the side of the road.

"We're heading to sixteen sixty-five Evans Avenue," Zack said. "From the looks of it on my screen we're a little under an hour away."

"Thanks," Andrew said.

He jumped out of the car and opened the back door, pulling out the gas can. Trent climbed out of the backseat.

"I need to relieve myself," he said. He wiped the sleep away from his eyes and stumbled to the side of the road.

Andrew started filling up the tank before he pulled out his phone. He dialed Mia. The ringing made his heart thump; a part of him was scared she wouldn't answer. He told himself it was an irrational fear, that she was still safe, but what he heard on the other end proved him wrong.

"Hello?" Andrew yelled.

He could hear screaming and crying, a mix of voices.

"Andrew?" an unfamiliar voice asked.

"Where's Mia?" Andrew asked.

"She can't talk right now," the voice said. "Where should we come meet you?"

It was a trap; Andrew was sure of it.

"My name is Riley," the voice said. "I helped Mia rescue you from the militia."

"Is Mia safe?"

"She is inconsolable," Riley said. "But she's uninjured."

"I want to speak with her," Andrew said.

"I wish you could," Riley said. "But I don't think that's going to happen. Please, we're driving around in a white van that can easily be spotted. We need help or you will never speak to her again."

Trust. That was something Andrew tried so hard to work on. He had little reason to trust the voice on the other end of the phone.

"If you don't tell me where to head we'll all be caught," Riley said. "Please."

"Sixteen sixty-five Evans Avenue," Andrew said. "Inside the capital. Can you find it?"

"Yes," Riley said. "Thank you."

"What happened to—?"

The line went dead before Andrew could finish his question. Andrew tried to tilt the gas can and fill the tank faster. A new wave of adrenaline drove his movements. He was too lost in his thoughts to notice the black SUV that had pulled up behind him. The car door slamming shook him from his thoughts.

"Having some car troubles, brother?" a man asked.

Andrew looked him up and down. He wore the black suit of a RAG agent.

"Needed to fill up the tank," Andrew said.

"There are stations all around here," the man said. "Why carry your own fuel?"

"We already had it," Andrew said. "Might as well use it."

"Your suit is dirty," the man said. "Hardly up to code, and you don't look familiar; what territory are you with?"

"We're in town for Grant Marsden's wedding," Andrew said. "We're personal friends of his."

The man seemed taken aback by Andrew's lie, but that faded and his cockiness returned.

"I am sure you've heard three of our vehicles disappeared," the man said. "We've all been encouraged to follow procedure and verify identities. Do you mind if my partner runs your plates, and can I see you and your men's badges?"

Andrew was not about to lose now. "Only if we do the same for you," he said.

"Of course," the man said.

He reached into his pocket at the same time Andrew moved for his belt. Neither man brought his hands up with identification. Instead each held a pointed weapon.

"You're done for, deserter," the agent said. "My partner is calling in your vehicle as we speak. You have five minutes before this place is filled with RAG agents. Put the weapon down and come in without a fight."

Andrew couldn't see through the tinted windows, but he hoped Carter and Zack were aware of the situation. Andrew didn't break eye contact with the agent, but he was sure Trent had full knowledge of the happenings.

There wasn't a viable option at the moment. Andrew needed Carter or Zack to act. Andrew heard a car door open, but he could tell it was from the other vehicle. Another man walked out, with his gun drawn.

"Did you call it in?" the agent asked.

"They're on their way," he replied.

Andrew would not be taken prisoner again. He looked at the two men and hoped he could shoot both of them before one returned fire on him. That way Carter and Zack could still make it to Mia and their safe haven. He was getting ready to pull the trigger when he saw

Trent walk up, a huge rock in hand. He smashed it over the second agent's head. The man let out a groan and his partner lost concentration for a second. Andrew heard the first agent gasp before a red stain started to appear on his shirt. He dropped to his knees and Andrew saw Trent, holding the second agent's weapon, the smoke still billowing from the barrel.

"I bet you're glad you took off the handcuffs," Trent said.

"We have to get out of here," Andrew said.

He lowered his weapon and went for the driver's seat. Carter moved to the passenger side while Trent climbed in the back next to Zack. Andrew didn't look back as he sped away from the bodies on the road, hoping whatever time they had was enough to get a head start on whoever else was about to storm the scene.

Chapter 87

I leave for my new post today and am reluctantly taking my wife with me. I asked for a divorce, however the grand commander admitted he has not made accommodations for unwanted women yet and I must wait until these are available.
—The journal of Isaac Ryland

There was a small pool of blood at the end of the driveway. It wasn't as much as Grant would have liked to see but was enough to convince him of the owner's death. Grant was happy they had taken the body with them; it meant less cleanup for him. It was morning; the red spot looked brown in the golden rays of the sun. He heard thunder in the distance and was satisfied rain would wash away the stain before anyone important showed up.

Grant went back inside and patrolled the rest of his home. The west wing was in perfect shape. Almost as if his visitors had never arrived. The east wing was a different story. Grant opened the door to the hallway and the scent of death was fresh in the air. He walked toward Hansen's body and bent down as he approached. Two gunshot wounds, one to the back of the head and another to the chest. Whoever that woman was, she had some military-level training. Grant didn't remember hearing a weapon go off.

He left the body for now and went back into Roderick's former room. Grant lifted up the computer and reviewed the security tapes from the east side. The woman didn't show up on any of them. Whenever she walked into view the camera went black. Grant followed the roaming blackouts. They continued every time she would have stepped into frame. Her face was never captured. If there was a silver lining, it was that Grant's beating wasn't recorded either. The woman had an electronic scrambler, and he knew none of the cameras would have recorded any scene she was present for.

Grant had assumed Mia's plan was to draw him out of the room and have one of her untrained friends rescue Roderick. He didn't think another person would have been able to enter the premises. Grant followed the trail of blackouts in reverse and saw that the woman had entered through an abandoned room at the end of the hall. Grant stood up and went to investigate.

This wing of the house was impenetrable. He couldn't understand how she would have gained access. A cool breeze came through the open window. Grant walked over and examined the scene. A circle, big enough for someone to crawl through, was cut out of the inch-thick glass. He stuck his head outside and saw the removed glass leaning against the house.

Only three types of blades could cut through the windows on Grant's home: one made of diamonds, which would be impossible to find; one that had been heated up to over a thousand degrees Celsius, which the women couldn't have done without a portable scientific-grade oven, which also didn't exist; and a blade Grant had created himself, which he had sold to the American government a long time ago. He wasn't sure what connection the mystery women had, but if she owned a knife like that she was no layman. For the second time one of Grant's own inventions had been used against him. He made a fist and punched what was left of the window. His knuckles exploded in pain.

"Sir?" Dr. Schaffer asked.

Grant turned to see the man standing in the door frame.

"Good morning," Grant said.

"What happened here?" Dr. Schaffer asked.

"Your patient is gone," Grant said. "Your services are no longer required."

The doctor stepped into the room. "You look like you could use a checkup," he said.

He grabbed Grant's hand and forced his fingers outward.

"Have you looked in a mirror?" Dr. Schaffer asked. "Your face is all bruised and your lip is bleeding."

"It's dried blood now," Grant said.

He took his hand back and started to work his fingers back to life.

"Do you have any need for a cadaver?" Grant asked.

"Anything to help further medical advances is appreciated," the doctor said.

"Take Hansen from the hallway," Grant said. "He's all yours."

Grant headed out of the east wing. He needed to shower and rest. Last night had not gone as planned, but if there was a positive outcome it was that Amelia Morrissey was finally dead.

Chapter 88

I am in a new place, with stricter rules. I have lost my baby because of my husband's actions and for the first time feel truly defeated.

—The diary of Megan Jean

The van came to a halt. Mia had stopped crying, but she couldn't look away from her mother's body. Corinna leaned her head against Mia's shoulder. She still held their mother's lifeless hand. Someone touched Mia's back, but she didn't look away.

"We're here," Alex said.

The back of the van opened. The two front doors opened too. Frank and Riley exited. Mia heard Rod's bed being wheeled out.

"It's time to get out of the van," Riley said.

"I'm staying here," Mia said.

"Me too," Corinna said.

"That's not a good idea," Riley said. "I am so sorry about your mother, girls."

"*I am not leaving her!*" Mia yelled.

Corinna lifted her head off of Mia's shoulder and went to speak with Riley. In a few seconds Corinna was back. She sat on the other side of their mother.

"This is my fault," Mia said. "I should have made her stay at the ranch."

"You didn't have a say in that," Corinna said. "She would have held on to the bumper and made you drag her here."

"I'm toxic," Mia said.

"That couldn't be more false," Corinna said.

"She is the third person I love who I have gotten killed," Mia said.

"It isn't your fault," Corinna said. "If she hadn't jumped out of the van you would be dead."

"She didn't even know," Mia said. "All Mom wanted was to hug me."

"No," Corinna said. "She wanted to protect you. The danger wasn't gone yet; Laur—Mom knew that."

Mia looked away from their mother and up at Corinna. Her sister had a soft smile on her face and tears pooling in her eyes.

"That is what a true mother does," Corinna said. "She is more than willing to sacrifice herself for her child."

Corinna reached out and wiped a tear from Mia's eye.

"You're not toxic," Corinna said. "You are involved in a dangerous line of work."

"What about Father?" Mia asked.

"Like Mom told you," Corinna said. "Don't shed a tear over him. What died in that fire was a shell of the man he once was. Father left us a long time ago."

"And Flo?" Mia asked. "Whitney? Rex? They all died helping me."

"It could have as easily been you," Corinna said.

Mia had thought she was near death several times, but someone always managed to save her. If she gave up now, all those lost lives would have been for nothing.

"This isn't over," Mia said. "I have to finish the fight."

"You will," Corinna said. "And I will stand right beside you to the very end. But for now let's try to get some sleep."

Mia looked down at her mother's body. She choked back another round of tears.

"I am so sorry," Mia said. "It's not fair we didn't get to say good-bye. But I want you to know something. I am thankful, now and every day for the rest of my life, that I have you as a mother."

Corinna picked up Mia's hand and slowly turned her away from their mother's body. They stepped outside of the van into a large garage. Mia didn't care where they were at the moment. She wanted a bed where she could cry herself to sleep.

Chapter 89

I have intimate details on the new families living in my area. They are happy and, as the grand commander predicted, do not object much to turning over their sons. I believe it is because they are so thrilled to keep their daughters.

—*The journal of Isaac Ryland*

Andrew drove as fast as he could down from the hills and the deceased RAG agents they'd left in the road.

"How much time do we have?" Andrew asked.

"An area like this?" Trent said. "Twenty-minute head start, easy. Cross your fingers we don't run into any other official vehicles."

"Can we stop and steal another pair of plates?"

"We are half an hour away from our contact," Zack said. "He lives on the outskirts of the capital. We might get lucky and not pass a single other car. I don't want to waste time going into a city. Did you send Mia there?"

"Yes," Andrew said.

"You don't sound thrilled," Carter said.

"Something went wrong," Andrew said.

"What?"

"I don't know," Andrew said.

"Mia is a strong person," Zack said. "You'll see her soon."

Nobody moved. Andrew pressed the accelerator down harder.

"Let's not forget the important thing. I'm part of the team now," Trent said.

"No," all three men said in unison.

The house was large. It stood on top of a hill. Andrew did not slow down when he drove toward the attached garage. As Zack had been notified it would, the door to the structure started to rise. Andrew saw a beat-up white van parked on one side. He slowed down and parked his SUV next to it. He recognized the vehicle as belonging to Frank and Alex.

"Let me do the talking," Zack said.

Andrew didn't wait for anyone. He unbuckled his seat belt and climbed out of the SUV. He made his way toward the van. The back door was open. He saw a giant red stain on the carpeting.

"I didn't realize you would be coming in two groups," a voice said.

Andrew looked toward the sound. Standing at what must have been the entrance to the home was a man. He wore a white bathrobe tied over red pajamas. His dark hair was cut short on the sides and left long on the top. He was about Andrew's height but had an extra twenty pounds to him. Andrew ran toward him.

"Where's Mia?" Andrew asked. "Is she all right?"

"The pretty one with the bob?" he asked.

Andrew did not know what that meant.

"All of your friends are inside," he said.

"You're Greg Finnegan," Carter said.

"The one and only," he said.

"The most trusted man in America is working for the rebels," Trent said. "I never would have guessed."

"What happened to letting me do the talking?" Zack asked. "My name is Zack."

"I know all about you," Greg said. "But my contact did not mention you would be so . . . attractive."

Andrew didn't have time for the small talk. He started toward Greg, ready to push him to the side and search every inch of his home for Mia.

"They beat you here by almost an hour," Greg said. "Two of the girls are sleeping. I didn't expect a comatose man but did my best to make him comfortable."

"Comatose man?" Zack asked.

"I need to see Mia," Andrew said.

Greg moved to the side and motioned for the four of them to enter his home. Andrew walked inside first. There was a small hallway with several closed doors. It ended at a larger hallway.

"Go left," Greg said.

Andrew walked several feet until they were in a kitchen. The guests at the table rose. Andrew recognized Frank and Alex. A redheaded woman was with them. All three looked dirty. Alex had puffy red eyes while Frank's looked glassed over.

"Andrew," Frank said.

"Where is Mia?" Andrew asked.

"She's asleep," Alex said. "Greg was kind enough to give her some medication."

"Trust me when I say an earthquake won't wake that girl up," Greg said.

"What happened?" Andrew asked.

"We rescued Rod," the redhead said. "Her mother died in the process."

"My dad is here?" Carter asked.

"Did you two know about this?" Zack asked. His voice was fueled with anger. "This is irresponsible. You risked our entire operation. Who are you people anyway?"

The redhead turned toward Zack. She was shorter than him, but her build and demeanor were intimidating. She took a step toward him and dragged her other leg behind her. Andrew saw a white bandage wrapped around her calf.

"My name is Riley," she said. "I am a strategist for the Irish government. These are Frank and Alex; they risked their lives to save one of your group members. Before throwing a temper tantrum, why not take the time to say thank you?"

"Where's my dad?" Carter asked. "He's in a coma?"

"It looks like an induced coma," Riley said. "Depending on how long the medication takes to get out of his system he'll wake up sometime in the next twelve hours."

"Where is Mia?" Andrew asked.

"Upstairs," Greg said. "Second bedroom on the right."

Andrew spun around toward the hallway they had come down. He saw the stairs near the front door and started toward them.

"She's asleep," Riley said. "You can't do much for her now."

The words went right past Andrew's ears and he ignored them. He rounded the stairs and took them two at a time until he reached the top. He spotted the second door and swung it open. There was a bed in the middle of the room and Andrew saw a figure under the blankets.

"It really is you," a female voice said.

Andrew felt like he was seeing a ghost. Sitting in a chair with her legs curled underneath her was Corinna, Mia's older sister. He hadn't seen her in two years, and even then they had not been familiar with each other.

"She kept trying to explain which farmhand Andrew was," Corinna said. "But you all blended together for me."

"I thought you were dead," Andrew said.

"I know it's not me you're here to see," Corinna said. She uncurled her legs and stood up from the chair. "I was sitting with her, but I'm guessing you can relieve me now."

She walked past Andrew and put a hand on his shoulder in the process.

"You look like you could use some sleep now too," Corinna said.

Her hand fell off his shoulder and he heard the door close behind her. Andrew walked over to the bed and sat down. There was Mia. He brushed the hair away from her face and she didn't stir. Andrew had never felt such relief in his life. He didn't even bother to take off his shoes before lying down next to her and wrapping his arms around her waist.

Chapter 90

I have found an occupation to keep my wife busy and out of my hair. She is assisting with the male offspring of our area and I am surprised by her natural maternal instincts.

—The journal of Isaac Ryland

The makeup smelled like flour as the young man patted another layer on Grant's face.

"Normally you don't need so much," he said. "Your skin tone is so even."

Grant felt like a woman, sitting in the chair having his bruised face hidden under the pancake. Greg Finnegan's crew had arrived and they'd made one of Grant's studies a prep room. They were not wasting time getting Grant prepped for his final interview as a single man. Even though Grant was running on next to no sleep, he smirked. Now that his wife was really dead this was actually his first interview with Mr. Finnegan as a single man.

"Was it nerves?" the man asked.

"Excuse me?"

"That made you fall?" he asked. "I've been married for two years now and I was a little nervous before the wedding."

"It wasn't nerves," Grant said. He would never take marriage advice from someone who had a minor job on a television program.

"Greg pays us nicely," the man said. It was like he could read Grant's thoughts. "I only had to work for two years before I had enough money saved to buy a decent wife. Of course she wasn't the daughter of our supreme leader."

"What happened to you?" Ian asked.

Grant looked away from the makeup artist to see Ian walking into the room.

"I want to look good on camera," Grant said.

"You've always turned down the makeup," Ian said. "I'm glad to see you're starting to take these things more seriously."

"All finished," the makeup man said.

Grant stood up from his chair. He held out his hand and met Ian's grip. The old man was wearing a pair of white pants and a navy blue polo with navy shoes. The outfit looked like it could have come from Grant's closet.

Grant reexamined his own attire. He wore a pair of gray pants with a pink cashmere sweater. Ian's outfit was a bit too summery and Grant was pleased he was the better-dressed man.

"I didn't expect you so early," Grant said.

"My morning plans canceled so I thought I would show up early and watch the taping," Ian said.

He took a seat in the makeup chair and the other man started to pat his face.

"Planning on making an on-air appearance?" Grant asked.

"I'm not ready to rule it out," Ian said.

The door to the study opened again and Greg Finnegan himself walked inside. Grant tried his best not to roll his eyes at the man. He noticed Greg's wardrobe. He was in a pair of light blue pants and a lime green striped button-up. His outfit was also something Grant expected to find in his own closet. This was not the usual attire of the television host.

"Ian, Grant, a pleasure as always," Greg said.

"I hope you don't mind that I'm using your man here," Ian said.

"Not at all," Greg said. "Take your time and then he can do me."

"Are you two mocking me?" Grant asked.

All three men stared at him.

"With the clothes?" Grant asked.

Greg Finnegan started to laugh. Grant felt his ire rise.

"Not at all," Greg said. "Look around."

The makeup artist was in jeans, something Grant would never consider wearing, but his shirt was a light purple and white checkered print. The material was cheap, but the design was something Grant found appealing.

"You've started a fashion trend," Greg said. "All men across the country are starting to dress like you, or at least try."

Grant gave a pressed-lipped smile. He was an original and wanted to keep it that way.

"Just another demonstration of how much the people love you," Ian said.

Love and adoration were not things Grant was concerned with. He couldn't wait until today was over with. In fact, he couldn't wait until Ian's life was over with and Grant no longer had to deal with these tedious appointments. Once Grant was grand commander he would never make another television appearance on *The Greg Finnegan Show*.

Chapter 91

I informed the grand commander of my wife's help with these babies. He seemed interested in her skills but ordered that she only stay with those under the age of two. I wouldn't want her poisoning the minds of the older children either.

—The journal of Isaac Ryland

"So can you give us a hint as to your wedding-night attire?" Greg asked.

Grant let out a rehearsed chuckle. "Some things are best kept as surprises," he said.

"Thank you to Grant Marsden for letting us tour his home again, and don't forget to tune in two nights from now, when the wedding is broadcast live."

"I wish everyone across the country could attend," Grant said. "But my home is not that accommodating."

Greg let out a loud laugh and Grant forced the pasted smile to remain on his face. He would never let such lowlifes into his home.

"We do have one final announcement before our program finishes," Greg said.

He stood up from his chair and Grant rose from the love seat. They were in his home; he hated that Greg sat on the single seat chair. It made it look like he was the homeowner, the one in control.

As Grant had predicted, Ian walked on camera. He shook Greg and Grant's hands before sitting down on the couch.

"Grand Commander," Greg said.

"Hello, Greg," Ian said. "Thank you for inviting me on your program."

"The honor is mine," Greg said. "There is an announcement you wanted to make?"

Ian turned to look straight into the camera.

"There are rumors flying around that I am stepping down," Ian said. "I wanted to reassure the American people that those are entirely false. I will be your grand commander until my heart ceases to beat."

Of course he will, Grant thought.

"But even I am not immortal," Ian said. "I was planning on waiting until the big day to make this public, but I don't want to overshadow this exemplary young man's wedding. When I do pass it is my intention that Grant Marsden continue in my footsteps as the next grand commander of this fine country."

Surprises were not one of Grant's fortes. He had thought this announcement would be made in a formal press conference, not on a cheap nightly talk show.

"That is fantastic news," Greg said. "It appears Grant is at a loss for words."

"I hope that day does not come for several years," Grant said. "But when it does I will try my best to continue on in your place."

Grant kept his eyes on Ian and not the camera.

"I am certain the rest of the country is as happy with this development as I am," Greg said. "Good night, America. I will see you tomorrow."

The camera cut out.

"That went well," Greg said. "I'll make sure your awkward pause is edited out, but in two days the ceremony will be live, so you better be on your best behavior."

Greg stood up and started directing his crew to pack up their equipment.

"Why didn't you tell me you were doing that?" Grant asked.

"We had discussed it before," Ian said. "I thought you would be pleased."

"I am," Grant said. "Was that my early wedding gift?"

"You're welcome," Ian said. He leaned in to Grant's ear and whispered, "Six, eleven, thirteen, two, four, fourteen, ten, eight, fourteen."

Grant's eyes went wide.

"Now let me tell you how you change the code," Ian said. "But I won't allow that until I'm on my deathbed."

"Thank you," Grant said.

He meant it. Ian had given Grant everything he needed to kill the man and take over the country. Amelia was no longer a threat and everything required for Grant to take power was in place. It was the best day of his life.

Chapter 92

My husband thinks I have given up any attempt at escape, but he could not be more wrong. I am more than a woman, or a mother; I am a person and will strive to be treated as such.

—The diary of Megan Jean

Mia's eyes popped open from her dreamless sleep. The room was dark, but she could feel the body in bed next to hers. She turned over and saw Andrew; a piece of his brown hair had fallen over his forehead. He was alive and next to her, safe. One thing had gone according to plan. She thought about the last time they'd slept so close to each other. Mia had tried to kiss him; he'd woken up and yelled at her. Back then she'd thought they would never be together, but so many things had changed since that day. Mia moved her head forward and placed her lips against his.

She felt his arm pull her tighter against him. Their kiss grew deeper, but soon he was pulling away.

"I've missed you," he said.

Mia did not want to speak. She didn't want to hear an apology or make one of her own. They were past that. She didn't want to talk about her parents' deaths or her run-in with Grant. Right now she only wanted Andrew, and she had him. She rolled him over onto his back and climbed on top of him.

"I don't want to separate again," Andrew said.

Mia bent down and kissed his lips. His hands gripped her cheeks and he tried to lift his head to meet her. Then his lips closed off again.

"Will you marry me?" Andrew asked.

A small breath escaped Mia's lips.

"Never," she said.

His arms went up behind her head and pulled her back down toward his. She never stopped kissing him. He returned her passion and they fell into each other.

Chapter 93

My years in the new area have gone by smoothly. I am supplied more than enough money to take care of the young boys and pay my employees. I could not have hoped for such a wonderful life.

—The journal of Isaac Ryland

"We should find out where everyone else is," Mia said.

Andrew kept his arms around Mia. He didn't want to get out of the bed, but he knew she was right. He gave her a kiss on the top of her head before she rolled away from him. He pulled on his clothes while she did the same. Andrew could not remember a time in his life when he had been this happy. He felt a hand grip his wrist and turned to face Mia. She didn't say anything and instead gave him another deep, passionate kiss. When she pulled away the gray light from the window was pouring in and her blue eyes looked electric.

"If I died today I would die a happy man," Andrew said.

"You shouldn't say that around me," Mia said. "It might actually happen, and I'd like to do that again at some point."

"Married or not, I am yours forever," Andrew said.

"I've known that since before you did," Mia said.

She slid her hand down his arm and stood up from the bed.

"I thought Greg Finnegan would have a larger house," Andrew said.

"There's no way this is his home," Mia said. "My guess is this is one of his many houses."

"I didn't realize Affinity's members were so famous," Andrew said.

"Are you ready to head downstairs?" Mia asked.

No, Andrew thought to himself. He wanted to stay in this room and hear what had happened to Mia the past couple weeks. He wanted to hold her while she talked about Flo and her mother. He wanted to hear anything she had to say, but he knew where she wanted to go right now, so he said the only word he could.

"Yes."

She stood up from the bed and he followed her to the door. They walked down the stairs. Something smelled amazing; Andrew felt his mouth watering. They made it into the kitchen and there stood Greg Finnegan, working away over the stove.

"Good, some of my visitors are awake," Greg said. "By the looks of it that sleep did you good. The two of you are glowing."

Andrew felt his eyes widen and he looked away.

"Everyone else is asleep," Greg said. "I expect them to start tumbling downstairs soon. I thought you could all use some food and then we could start our plans for the next two days."

"Plans?" Andrew asked.

"Of course," Greg said. "In two nights we take out the Registry and mandatory service, and Mrs. Marsden makes her television debut."

Andrew looked at Mia. He wasn't sure she was ready for more action after losing her mother and rescuing Rod. Instead of fear or apprehension, a large smile crossed her face. Andrew felt like everything was right in the world again.

Chapter 94

I finally did it. I am stowed away in the back of a truck. I have no clue where it is heading, but it is better than where I have been.

—The diary of Megan Jean

Riley hobbled into the kitchen with Alex. She was smiling and laughing. They stopped when they spotted Mia.

"How are you doing, sweetheart?" Alex asked.

"I would be better if the two of you would stop looking at me like that," Mia said.

"You were so upset this morning," Riley said. "With good reason. Maybe you should take some time to yourself."

"Time is something we don't have," Zack said.

He walked into the kitchen as well; another man followed behind him. Mia recognized him but couldn't place him at first. He walked up to her and held his hand out.

"Trent Quillian," he said. "We met a few weeks ago. Sorry about holding a gun to your head and all that stuff."

"It's been an interesting couple of weeks," Andrew said.

Mia did not return his handshake. He gave a nervous laugh and put it down.

"I told you not to kill him," Mia said, "not to start trusting him."

"I'll explain later," Andrew said. "But he has proved himself."

"Why do you say we don't have any time?" Riley asked Zack.

"Grant's wedding is less than forty-eight hours away," Greg said. "That is when we strike."

"No," Riley said.

"Absolutely not," Alex finished.

"You two don't have to help," Mia said. "But we're moving forward."

Both of them looked at her with shock.

"You just lost your mother this morning," Riley said. "I was shot in the leg, your big Affinity leader has his arm in a cast, one of our members is in a coma—we need more time."

"I'm ready to finish this," Mia said. "You don't understand how dangerous Grant is; if he spends one day as grand commander I can't imagine the horrors that await this country."

"Andrew," Alex said, "talk some sense into her. We need to regroup."

"I trust you, Mia, but Rex is dead," Andrew said. "There is no way to prove you're Grant's wife. They'll make you out as a liar."

"That does make things a bit difficult," Greg said.

"Did you grab all the bags from the van?" Mia asked.

"They're by the garage," Greg said.

Mia walked over toward the entrance. There she saw her mother's satchel. Mia flipped it open and pulled out the book before she returned to the group. She handed it to Greg. He started flipping through the pages before slamming it shut.

"So it is settled then," Greg said. "More than enough to prove Mia's identity."

Mia silently thanked her mother.

"I've prepared a delicious meal for all of you, so please have a seat."

Mia could feel Alex and Riley staring at her in disapproval, but

Mia knew once this was over her mother's death wouldn't have been for nothing, and that was more important than focusing on her grief.

The table was long and had a bench on each side where four people could fit, with a chair at each end. Everyone took a seat.

"What about Corinna, Carter, Frank, and Rod?" Andrew asked.

"Frank is in the shower," Alex said. "He'll be down soon."

"I made enough for everyone," Greg said. "But we should let them sleep as long as they like. I can only hang out here another hour before I head home."

Mia gave Andrew a look; her initial guess was correct.

"I was wondering why the most trusted man in America lived in such an average house," Trent said.

"This is not in my name and not traceable back to me," Greg said. "I use it to house runaways."

"I never would have guessed you were sympathetic to women," Mia said.

"Why?"

"You seem so loyal to the grand commander," Mia said.

"Keep your enemies close," Greg said.

They all sat down around the table. Footsteps came from down the hallway. Mia tried to see who was coming. When Carter stepped into the light Rod's arm was draped around his shoulder. Andrew stood up to help them and Mia walked over with him.

The portly man had lost a great deal of weight. He looked like flesh and bones. His gray hair was greasy and stuck to his head.

"I would give you a hug," he said, "but if I take my arm off of Carter's shoulders I think I'll fall."

Mia wrapped her arms around his waist. She felt her eyes sting with tears of joy, knowing they wouldn't fall.

"I am so sorry to hear about your mother," Rod said. "I owe her my life."

"I'm sorry we didn't come for you sooner," Mia said.

"I didn't tell you about my relationship with Affinity to protect the cause," Roderick said. "I thought by keeping Carter in the dark I was giving him more of a childhood. I should have known better than to keep something like that from you."

"It's done with," Mia said. "No more apologies."

She released Rod's waist. Carter and Andrew helped him sit at the table. Mia caught sight of his bandaged wrist and wondered what atrocities Grant had put the man through. Her desire to stop him only strengthened.

"It appears I'm the newbie," Rod said. "I don't know most of you."

The group went around and gave introductions.

"I'm Zack," Zack said. "Also a member of Affinity."

"Have we ever had personal contact?"

"No," Zack said. "But I was aware of your existence."

Soon Frank and Corinna came down and squeezed in on one of the benches.

"So, Riley," Rod said. "Irish government? How did you get in contact with this group?"

"I helped Mia pose as a prostitute in order to rescue your son and Andrew from a well-organized and unstable militant group that was brainwashing them," Riley said.

Rod's cheeks puffed up as he formed a smile. "I suppose in another situation that would sound abnormal," he said. "But not here."

Andrew passed Mia a salad bowl and she put a scoop on her plate. Mia took a look around the table. All of the people she loved most in the world were present. If they hadn't been gathered together to bring down an unfair government it would have looked like they were here to celebrate a holiday. Some of them were family, some cherished friends, and others newcomers who shared Mia's outlook. It shocked her that even in this time of sorrow and struggle she felt a sense of happiness.

Chapter 95

My wife has left me, as if she could make that choice. The grand commander is furious. He fears that if she escapes the country foreigners will not understand our new way of life and send whatever armies they have inside to stop us. I have put all my efforts into finding her.

—The journal of Isaac Ryland

Everything was in place for the wedding. Grant sat at his desk and twirled a pen in his hand. Things were looking up. His ascension to supreme leader was secure, he had the code to the Registry, and Amelia Morrissey was dead. But Grant knew those who supported her were still in the country. He pulled out his file on Amelia, the one Rex had wanted to steal. He flopped out the photographs. One of Andrew, one of Carter, one of Roderick, one of Alex, and one of Frank. Photos of Amelia's mother and sister were not necessary; they would be useless in any attempt to overthrow him. Grant was still missing the image of the redhead and the two agents who'd fled the burning orphanage.

He assumed the two unknown agents were part of Mia's secret society and trained fighters. The redhead was some sort of assassin and could not be underestimated. It made Grant uneasy that they were in his country and nobody was searching for them.

Still, there was nothing they could want directly from Grant except revenge. Grant had already requested the security at tomorrow night's event be tripled and didn't think he had a thing to worry about. As far as stopping the Registry, the only two people who knew the code were himself and Ian. If everything went according to plan soon only one person would know the code. A knock on his office door startled Grant. Before Grant could invite the person in, the door swung open. Ian walked into the room with a bottle of liquor and two glasses.

"I was delighted to accept your invitation," Ian said. "I thought we could celebrate tonight. This is a reserve scotch from my private collection."

He poured two glasses and handed one to Grant. This was the way it should be: Grant on the powerful side of the desk and Ian on the other. Grant asked Ian if he still wanted a guest room at his house for the evening. With the running around going on tonight and in the morning, Grant insisted.

"I have some concerns," Grant said. "About security. Will the Mission be guarded tomorrow night?"

"Of course," Ian said. "Not everyone is invited to your wedding. Do you have reason to believe we need extra security?"

"A hunch," Grant said. "There are those who wish us ill."

"If that were the case they would be better off attacking your home," Ian said. "The most important people in the country will be here. If anything happened to us it would be pandemonium out there."

Grant smiled. Ian did have a point and calmed Grant's nerves. Taking out the master Registry was an impossibility. They were much more vulnerable here. Besides, as soon as Grant got Ian out of the way he would not have to explain the rationale behind his decisions.

"Let me show you to your room," Grant said.

He picked up a file from the desk and led Ian out into the hallway. Two guards were at the door waiting to follow them.

"Gentlemen, please trust that I am as safe here as in my own home," Ian said. "I do not need you to escort me."

A smile crossed Grant's lips. The old man was making this easier for him.

Chapter 96

It has been three days and I still have not located my wife. I asked for satellite surveillance or any technology available. The grand commander refused my requests. He claims technological advances are what led to America's downfall. I must respect his wisdom.

—*The journal of Isaac Ryland*

Ian's room was one of Grant's least favorite. The color scheme was yellow and gold. It was hard not to feel warm in the large suite, but it did not fit in with the rest of his home. Grant walked in first and went straight toward the bathroom door, dropping the file he was carrying on the bed. He flipped on the lights and went under the sink.

"I don't think I've ever seen this room before," Ian said.

"I'm not as proud of it as the others," Grant said from the bathroom.

He pulled out the bag he had hidden under there earlier and took out a syringe, an array of knives, and a yellow rain jacket. Grant put the jacket on first, then took the needle out, tucked the black canvas bag under his arm, and went back into the main room. Ian had picked up the file and started looking through it.

"What is all of this?" Ian asked.

Grant tried hard to hide his giddiness. If he laughed his ribs ached from the beating he had received yesterday morning. Ian looked over at Grant; his mouth hung open and his brow crunched down. Grant brought up his free hand and stuck the man in the neck with the solution Dr. Schaffer had prepared earlier. Ian started to fall and Grant made sure to push him onto the bed.

"I know you can still hear me," Grant said. "Now, what question should I answer first?"

Grant turned Ian's face so he was staring at him. Even though the paralytic had made it impossible for Ian to move his facial features, Grant recognized the terror in his eyes and it sent a shiver of pleasure down his spine.

"I learned my lesson recently about getting clothing dirty," Grant said. "Hence the raincoat."

Ian's eyes strained to move, but Grant knew it wasn't possible.

"This file is your medical history," Grant said. "I had my personal physician prepare it himself."

Grant reached down and grabbed the file. He started to pull out the pieces of paper and hold them in front of Ian's face.

"As you can read, it says you have been suffering from severe depression," Grant said. "An archaic disease that struck the mind. The doctor has prescribed you a variety of medications and urges you to step down from your position."

Grant flipped through the pages.

"It describes how you confessed your desire to step down but feared the humiliation that would come along with doing so," Grant said. "I won't bore you with the details."

A single piece of paper was left. A small note. Grant waved it in front of the man's face.

"I'm not sure if you remember handing this to me," Grant said. "But let me read it out loud for you: 'Grant, Best of luck. Ian.' I know you meant that as encouragement when I was heading to check out the French disaster, but I think it makes a decent suicide note."

Grant took the file and placed it in Ian's hand. Then he watched as it tumbled out onto the floor. Next Grant unrolled his knives. He made sure to take his time, picking up each of them and examining its sharpness.

"I have wanted to kill you since the third time we met," Grant said.

He tapped the knife on his chin, as if he were struggling to remember some important detail.

"Or maybe it was the second," Grant said. "I can't be sure."

Grant put the knife down and picked up a plain kitchen knife.

"Ah," Grant said. "This one will do the trick."

He moved behind Ian and placed the knife into the man's right hand. Grant kept his fingers tight around Ian's hand, forcing the man to grip the instrument of death. He brought the blade to Ian's neck and pressed it down hard enough so blood started to pool.

"I suppose some last words are in order," Grant said. "Since you can't speak I'll have to think of what you might say. I'll go with: 'I am an outdated fool.'"

As Grant pronounced the last L, he dragged the knife across Ian's throat in a slow motion. Ian's flesh splitting made an almost crunching sound. Once Grant had made it the entire way across he got up from the bed and moved in front of Ian. The man was still alive; Grant wasn't sure which would kill him first, exsanguination or drowning from choking on his own blood. Either way suited Grant's needs. He reached down to Ian's shirt and plucked off the pin the old man admired so much.

After picking up his knife set, Grant carefully removed the rain slicker. He turned off all of the lights and went into the hallway. He stopped in his room, hid the evidence of his crime to destroy later, and made sure no blood was on his clothing before heading down the steps. The grand commander's guards were posted at his front door.

"Ian was feeling a bit emotional," Grant said. "He asked that we leave him for the evening and that someone wake him up by seven A.M."

The two guards nodded and did not seem to take an interest in Grant's jovial mood. He made his way toward the banquet hall, thrilled that tomorrow would be not only his wedding, but the ceremony cementing his absolute power.

Chapter 97

The truck stopped for the fifth time and I had to get out. I needed to find water and food, but I couldn't risk it. So I laid my weak head down and continued on to my unknown destination.
                                                                    —*The diary of Megan Jean*

Mia did her best to untangle herself from Andrew's legs. She went to the closet and grabbed the first thing she got ahold of before heading into the hall. She was relieved nobody had made it to the shower before she did.

After Mia was done washing up she pulled on the blue-and-purple-print dress she had grabbed in the dark. It had a square neckline and princess sleeves. Mia wished she had grabbed sweatpants but was happy to have clean clothes.

When Mia made it down the stairs Greg was serving breakfast. Riley was seated at the table. She was wearing the same black outfit Mia always saw her in.

"Do you have an unlimited number of tight black pants?" Mia asked.

"Black is my color," Riley said. "Sit."

"Are we going over everything again?" Mia asked.

"You know that's how I work," Riley said.

Greg dropped a plate of pancakes off at the table.

"Grant's wedding starts at eight o'clock tonight," Mia said. "Nothing will happen until close to then. We split up in our groups, and I explain my story on television once we get the go-ahead that the Registry has been destroyed."

"Corinna, Frank, Trent, and Alex will be with you the whole time," Riley said.

"I'm not nervous," Mia said. "Your group has the harder mission."

"You should be nervous," Zack said.

Mia hadn't even noticed he was downstairs. He held his phone in his hand; his body was stiff and Mia thought there was some sweat forming on his forehead.

"What is it?"

"Last night Grant murdered the grand commander," Zack said. "He was wearing his American flag pin and Affinity has the whole thing recorded. They want you to introduce the video along with your speech."

"Do you think showing a brutal murder on television will help our cause?" Mia asked. "We don't need it."

"Some Americans may be sympathetic toward Grant if his only concern is with a runaway wife, but nobody will able to look the other way over killing the supreme leader," Zack said. "Even if we fail at destroying the master server you are going on television to present this."

"Will Affinity's hackers take out the online copies?" Riley asked.

"We need them to," Zack said. "Or else someone will download it and another master list will be created, but if we take out the master at the same time the copies are destroyed, there is no backup. It would take years to gather all the information again and who knows how many people would defect in the meantime? It will start a rebellion."

"How long will it take to destroy the copies?" Mia asked.

"Not as long as you think," Zack said. "Affinity has destroyed them before. But it will be useless without the destruction of the master list. Mia, your story and this video can start a revolution regardless."

Mia knew Zack was passionate about stopping the Registry. His whole life revolved around bringing an end to the suffering in America.

"What if during this revolution you predict, another leader rises who wants to continue with the information they already have accessible, the Registry? It will just create a contest to see who gets there first," Riley said.

"She's right," Mia said. "Destroying the master needs to stay the top priority."

"No," Zack said. "Your speech is now more important. Affinity sent me a copy of what you're supposed to say."

"Then stay with me," Mia said. "Send someone in your place to plant the virus."

"That might work better," Riley said. "With your injured shoulder you're a liability."

"You have an injured leg," Zack said.

"A bullet grazed me," Riley said. "I'm fine." She stood up from her chair and started doing jumping jacks to drive her point home.

"Who will go in my place?" Zack asked.

As if on cue footsteps came down the hall. Mia turned to see a sleepy Trent Quillian walk into the room. He seemed oblivious to all the eyes on him.

"Do you have any coffee?" he asked.

"Andrew assures me we can trust him," Mia said.

"Trust who?" Trent asked.

He took a cup of coffee from Greg and sat down next to where Riley was standing.

"What's your story, red, you got a husband?" Trent asked.

Riley brought her fist down into Trent's stomach. He dropped his cup of coffee and raised his hands to defend himself as he sprang up from the table.

"He'll do just fine," Riley said.

"What was that all about?" Trent asked.

"We leave here at noon," Greg said. "Someone better clean up that spilled coffee and broken mug before then."

Chapter 98

I sent word to every person who traveled through my home and workplace the day my wife vanished. I am eagerly waiting for a response from the parties.

—The journal of Isaac Ryland

It was the morning of Grant's wedding. He woke extra early and reviewed the security detail for that night.

"Sir," a guard said.

Grant turned to look toward him. It was 7:03 A.M. He'd expected this person two minutes ago.

"There has been a problem," he said. "We need your assistance."

Faking concern, Grant followed the man up to the room housing Ian's body. Grant held a hand over his mouth and looked away.

"It appears he took his own life," a guard said.

"We have notified the heads of the service branches," the other guard said. "They are on their way here."

Anger flared in Grant's mind. He should have been consulted before that decision was made.

"Cover him up," Grant said. "I don't want anyone to see him like this. Was there a note?"

One of the guards handed Grant the papers he had planted while the other pulled the blanket over him.

"He did seem sullen," Grant said. "But I did not see this coming."

The knife fell as the guard covered up Ian's body. Grant bent down and picked it up, examining it as if he had never seen it before.

"And in such a gruesome manner," Grant said.

The heads of the navy, army, marines, and air force sat in Grant's office. He had never felt such power.

"This is a terrible development," one said.

"And on the day of your wedding."

"It makes sense," another said. "If he thought you were ready to take over."

"He did speak highly of you."

"Perhaps you're right," Grant said. He pulled his shirt forward. "He did gift me this last night; maybe it was his way of saying good-bye."

The small American flag pin Ian had loved so much was prominent on Grant's attire.

"I think it is best we keep this quiet now," Grant said. "There is no need to mix sorrow with celebration."

"How would you like to proceed?"

"We explain his absence with word that he fell ill," Grant said. "Tomorrow a press conference will be held stating that he died during the night. Nobody will know of his suicide."

"That is kind of you, to keep his memory intact."

Grant nodded his head at the men. One of them stood up from his chair and got down on a knee. The other three followed and bowed their heads. Grant could not contain his grin. Today he was in total control.

Chapter 99

The truck stopped again. It was too soon. I listened to the man walk to the back of the truck and open the doors. I hoped we were long out of America's borders.

—The diary of Megan Jean

Everyone spent the morning on edge. Greg left after breakfast and the rest of them couldn't do much but worry or think. Mia felt like time was standing still, but once the clock struck noon she couldn't believe the morning was already over with.

"Are you ready?" Frank asked.

He rose from the kitchen table. The two groups started saying their good-byes. Mia went to Riley first.

"Are you going to wish me luck?" Mia asked.

"No," Riley said. "You don't need it."

The two shared a quick hug before Mia moved on to Rod.

"I'll see you later tonight," Rod said.

"I'm sorry you can't come with," Mia said.

"Someone needs to stay here and guard the house," Rod said.

He squeezed Mia's shoulder before she went to Carter.

"Good luck, princess," Carter said.

"I'm no princess," Mia said.

He brushed a piece of hair behind her ear. "I never said thank you," Carter said. "For saving my dad."

"Because you didn't have to," Mia said.

She leaned in and embraced Carter. He squeezed her tight. "You will always be my princess," he whispered.

He let go of Mia and she turned to see Andrew, who stood by her side.

"I don't like separating from you again," he said.

"After tonight you won't have to," Mia said.

Andrew leaned down and kissed her. Mia tried her best to ignore the ooohs and ahhhs coming from her friends. She broke away from him and started walking toward the door, not wanting to make this harder than it already was. He didn't let go of her hand and pulled her back in.

"If something goes wrong . . . ," Andrew said.

"I won't let you say good-bye," Mia said. "I will see you tonight."

She leaned in and gave him a quick kiss on the cheek before turning down the hallway. Every ounce of her being wanted to turn around, but she was scared that if she caught a look at Andrew's face she would crumble with fear.

Mia went into the garage with the rest of her group. Greg had managed to procure a car for them. Mia had never asked what he did with her mother's body, but she told herself it didn't matter. Mia carried a piece of her mother's soul with her, and after tonight so would the rest of the world.

Chapter 100

*He closed the back of the truck. I feared the driver had seen me.
My suspicions were confirmed when I heard a bolt go down. I
listened to his phone call. I was certain my husband was on the
receiving end.*

—The diary of Megan Jean

Zack offered Mia his good arm when she exited the car. They were
in front of Greg Finnegan's television studio. Mia felt wrong being
out in public like this, but nobody knew who they were or would
pay them any attention. It looked like Mia was Zack's wife, while
Corinna was fortunate enough to have married Alex and Frank was
a friend along for the ride. They entered the building. A single man
sat at the desk.

"How can I help you?" he asked.

"We're friends of Greg," Zack said.

The man pulled out a list. "Greg has a lot of friends," he said. "I
need more than that."

"Zack, Alex, their wives, and Frank."

The man looked at the list and then looked back up at them. "I'm
sorry," he said. "Please follow me."

He went into the back room. It opened up to a huge studio space.
Mia saw Greg's couches in the back corner. She remembered her par-

ents watching the show every night. Her father had even once taken her mother to a taping. Her mother used to brag about it all the time.

"Usually this place is crawling with people," he said. "But most of them are set up at the Marsden house for the wedding. I don't get to head over there until later."

The man clearly expected the group to react with jealousy, but everyone remained quiet. He stopped at a door that opened up to a small room. There were two couches and a vanity, complete with every makeup and hair care product Mia could imagine.

"Have a seat," he said. "I'll let Greg know you're here."

Everyone picked a couch and sat down.

"Shouldn't this have been more covert?" Alex asked.

"Who's here to hide from?" Mia asked.

It didn't take long for Greg to come inside.

"Mia, sit down in the chair," Greg said. "We have two hours to make you look perfect."

There was a knock at the door and two workers came inside. They didn't introduce themselves before one went for Mia's makeup and the other for her hair. Greg had warned them about this. It would be too difficult to hide them inside the studio. It was easier to tell his crew Mia was his date for the wedding since his partner wasn't feeling well.

Mia did not object. They didn't need this cover to last forever, only a few hours. She didn't mind when the men started pampering her.

"We have to get this finished quick," the makeup man said. "But it shouldn't take long. You are one lucky man. So nice of you to lend your wife to Greg."

He was speaking to Zack, Mia's fake husband. These men were used to treating women like property. Mia hoped that would change soon.

"If you don't have enough time, stop talking so much," Greg said.

That seemed to make an impression on the makeup artist. He didn't open his mouth again.

An hour later and Mia's hair was pinned up, giving the illusion that it was much longer. Her eye makeup was a smoky maroon, making the blue in her irises pop. The two crew members left the room, neither bothering to comment on her new look. As soon as the door closed Zack spoke up.

"Was that necessary?" Zack asked. "She doesn't need to look so done up to speak the truth."

"The American people think they're watching a wedding," Greg said. "If she doesn't look perfect they will change the channel before she opens her mouth."

Greg did have a point and Mia knew Zack wouldn't understand. Frank, Alex, and Corinna gave no argument.

"It's three o'clock," Greg said. "I have to leave. You're all alone in the studio. Stay in this room. I'll be back by seven; we'll go on the air at eight."

Greg left the room like the tornado he was. Mia sat in the chair. She looked at her reflection in the mirror. She ignored the makeup and new hairstyle. The girl looking back at her wasn't beautiful because of her features or makeup. She was beautiful because tonight she would start something that could not be undone.

Chapter 101

She never left the country. I laughed when I heard how close she was to the capital. I could complete some business while I went to pick her up.

—*The journal of Isaac Ryland*

The sun was starting to set. Andrew glanced nervously at the wall clock. They had five minutes until it was time to leave. Riley, Carter, Trent, and Rod sat around the table with him. Andrew was dressed in all black, courtesy of Greg Finnegan. Andrew thought the shirt material was too thin to provide as much protection as it should have. He nervously fingered one of the guns that was around his waist. Riley and Carter had on similar outfits. Trent was wearing a clean RAG agent suit and Rod sat in a sweat suit.

"I should be coming with you," Rod said.

"You would hold us back," Riley said.

Andrew shot her an annoyed look. Her eyes went wide and she shrugged her shoulders.

"She's telling the truth," Rod said. "It just seems wrong that I have my family back and you're all leaving without me."

Andrew watched as Rod beamed at Carter.

"You have become more of a man than I ever thought possible,"

Rod said. "I want to force you to stay here with me and keep you safe, but it wouldn't be right or fair. The rest of the world needs you more than I do."

Trent looked uncomfortable at the relationship between Carter and Rod. Andrew had been at first too. He'd given up wondering what his own father had been like long ago, and no doubt Trent had too. Being faced with Carter and Rod's affection resurrected those dormant thoughts.

"You, Andrew," Rod said, "have learned to let people in. You're not a one-man show anymore; instead you are a true leader."

"We have an hour's drive to the Mission," Riley said. "We should get going."

Everyone stood up from the table. Andrew followed Riley toward the garage but was stopped by Rod's grip on his arm. He pulled Andrew's ear down to his mouth.

"Take care of him," Rod said. "Take care of all of them."

Andrew put a reassuring hand on Rod's shoulder and nodded his head. He continued his trek toward the car. There were no false good-byes for Andrew. Instead he accepted that there was a good chance the group would fail and he would die tonight. If that was the case, he was glad to go out the hero Mia had always thought he was.

They were in a nondescript car, unlikely to cause any notice. Andrew kept his hand in his pocket while Trent drove through the streets of the capital. He turned the small device that sat in his pocket over and over again. He went over Zack's instructions in his head. Make his way toward the hall of paintings, hit the panel leading to the hidden room, punch in the code, and stick the small device into the master server. It sounded so easy, but Andrew expected much more of a battle.

"Remember," Riley said. "Wait for nobody; once we have confirmation run toward the television station. We regroup there. If the confirmation does not come leave exactly at eight P.M. Does everyone remember where it is in relation to the Mission?"

There was no possibility any of them would get lost if the other three were obsessing over directions as much as Andrew was. He nodded his head. The group drove past the Rook, a tall building shaped like a piece from an old game, meant to remind the country of a time long forgotten. Andrew saw the Mission come into view. Trent pulled down a side street and found a place to park the car.

"This place looks deserted," Carter said.

"What?" Andrew asked.

"The whole city," Carter said. "We passed next to no cars and I haven't seen anyone walking around."

"A lot of important people live here," Trent said. "They're at the wedding."

"Or sitting in front of their television sets waiting for the broadcast," Riley said.

"Don't forget these," Trent said.

He held up three pairs of handcuffs. Andrew snatched his and put them around his wrists. He heard the clink of the metal as Riley and Carter did the same. Trent let out a loud burst of laughter.

"My, how things have changed," he said.

"We're just playing prisoners," Riley said.

Trent handed each of them a key to their own cuffs. Andrew climbed through the divider into the backseat and sat next to Riley and Carter.

"We have thirty minutes," Riley said. "Let's try to finish in twenty."

Trent put the car back into drive and continued toward the Mission. Andrew couldn't decide if he was headed toward certain death or the start of a new world order.

Chapter 102

I begged the grand commander to let me leave her there. She deserved to be someone else's problem now. He promised me all in good time.

—*The journal of Isaac Ryland*

Nobody cared about Ian's absence, not even his daughter or public wife. Grant wondered if any of the wives he kept in private would mourn his loss. Not that it mattered. Grant was alone in his room. He examined himself in his closet mirror. He wore black pants and a black dress shirt. He straightened his gold tie and vest before putting on a crimson velvet jacket. Grant admired himself. His wedding attire was worth more than most people's homes.

Grant moved his arms and the small flecks of gold stitching showed off subtly in the mirror. He was the all-American male and looked the part. But one thing was off. He reached into his pocket and pulled out the American flag pin Ian had worn. He stuck it on his lapel and had to admit it gave him a certain look of glamour.

Grant leaned into the mirror and examined the bruise on the side of his face. It was starting to show through the makeup. He couldn't have that.

Even though he found the process degrading, Grant had little option but to summon Greg Finnegan's makeup artist again. When a knock on the door came, Grant went to greet the helper. It was the same man from yesterday. He carried a kit and a light-up mirror.

"You might be the most distinguished-looking groom I have ever seen," the man said.

Grant didn't need another person to tell him that. He was aware of that fact himself. Grant held his arm out and motioned for the man to enter. He went for Grant's desk and started setting up his supplies. Grant took a seat and the man started rubbing the makeup on his skin.

"Less than an hour left," the man said. "How are those butter-flies?"

"Excuse me?" Grant asked.

"Stomach nerves? I mean, you're getting married on national tele-vision, that has to increase the adrenaline."

Grant didn't bother with a response.

"On my wedding day I was throwing up in a bucket," he said. "It was out of happiness though."

Grant wished the man would shut up.

"My outfit wasn't nearly as grand as yours," he said. "I wore my old service uniform . . . not even the fancy one because I didn't move up in rank that much."

"You got here fast," Grant said.

He wasn't in a mood to bloody his knuckles and thought if the man continued with his story Grant would be forced to deck him in the jaw out of annoyance.

"I was sitting downstairs waiting," he said.

"I assumed Greg would be having his makeup done."

"Greg went to pick up his date."

"His partner?" Grant asked.

"No," the man said. "Poor Nicholas isn't feeling well. A friend is letting him take his wife as an escort. Strange if you ask me, but boy, was she beautiful. One of the most beautiful girls I've ever seen. I did her makeup earlier today. She had big blue eyes, shorter hair but long enough for me to give the illusion of length."

This struck Grant as wrong. No man would lend his wife out for the evening. If she was beautiful that meant her husband had a lot of money, and that rule went double for wealthy men.

"The rumor is Nicholas and Greg are splitting up anyway," the makeup man said. "We don't like to gossip too much but the last time I saw Nicholas was at your old wife's funeral. Funny, I almost forgot you were married before. Sorry if I'm opening up old wounds, I sometimes—"

"This conversation is very boring," Grant said. "Why don't we play a game where you don't open your mouth?"

No, Grant thought to himself. Amelia was dead; that description could have fit a number of women. For all of Greg Finnegan's faults, he was a proud American. Grant wasn't about to let paranoia overtake him. Another knock came on the door. Grant was happy for the distraction. The man in charge of audio walked into the room.

"Are you ready for your microphone?"

"Yes," Grant said.

He stood up from his chair and the man walked over with the small black box he would hide under Grant's clothing.

"Are you planning on taking the jacket off tonight?"

"Possibly," Grant said.

"Lift your arms and untuck your shirt. I'll hide the box in the back of your waistband and run the mic up to the front of your shirt. Hide it under your tie."

Grant did as instructed, happy that this would be his last microphone fitting. Once the man was done he went to the controller he carried and put headphones over his ears.

"I'm going to turn this on," he said. "Give me a few test words."

"Let me know when you're ready," Grant said.

The man flipped the switch and then winced in pain. He flung the headphones off his ears and they hit the ground. Grant wasn't expecting that response.

"Ahh," the man said, wincing.

"Are you all right?" the makeup artist asked.

"That is the second time this has happened to me this month," he said. "There's something giving feedback close to the microphone."

"What do you mean?" Grant asked.

"Another electronic device," the man said. "It happened with the grand commander a few weeks ago. He insisted he didn't have anything on him. We scanned the whole place for additional electronics and couldn't find anything. It took me thirty minutes to get the mic set to a frequency that didn't cause that noise."

"Maybe your equipment is faulty?" the makeup artist suggested.

Of all the foolish things Grant had done, this was the one he was the most embarrassed about. The one thing he had in common with Ian was sitting on the lapel of his jacket. Grant ripped off the pin.

"Try again," Grant said.

"You don't know how bad that hurts," the man said. "Let me get a scan set up first."

"No," Grant said. "Right now."

The tone of Grant's voice was threatening enough. The man picked up his headphones and nervously switched them back on.

"Oh," he said. "Must have been a fluke. You're fine now."

The pin. It wasn't a pin at all, but a bug sent to record the grand commander. Grant didn't know if it was a camera or only an audio recorder, but either way whoever had access to its information now had the key to the master Registry. Amelia's existence didn't seem so important anymore.

Grant rushed out of the room, dropping the pin in the process. He ran down the stairs, ignoring the glares of the guests who had just entered his home.

"You look fabulous," one said.

Grant kept moving toward the back. He made it to the head of security for the event.

"Has anyone noticed anything suspicious?" Grant asked.

"Everything is running smooth," the guard answered. "Why, did you hear something?"

"Shhh," Grant said.

He needed the quiet to think. Most of the important people in America were heading to his house. That left the Mission very vulnerable. If he brought in an entire team to help him it might create too many questions. Whoever the people who bugged the pin were, they were armed with the knowledge that Grant had killed Ian. This information would give any American the right to kill him and strip him of the grand commander title he deserved. He pictured the redheaded assassin, the bumbling Alex, and whoever else had been helping Amelia. It could be them trying to destroy his country. Tonight would be the perfect night to attack.

He went back through the hall, pushing past the guests who were heading toward the site of his ceremony until he was out the front door.

Grant ran down the length of his driveway, blocking out the greetings people were giving him. He made it toward the valet who was parking people's cars. Grant grabbed the set of keys a new guest was handing over and ran toward the driver's side of their sporty red car.

As soon as he started the car he hit the gas pedal.

Chapter 103

I spent most of the drive fantasizing ways to punish my wife. I decided it was best to leave her locked alone in a room for several weeks.

— *The journal of Isaac Ryland*

The car came to a stop at the gate of the Mission. Like Affinity had predicted it did not appear to be guarded well. There was a single guard blocking the iron gates that surrounded the building. He got up from his post and walked around toward Trent's lowered window. Trent held his RAG badge out the window.

"Business here, sir?"

"I have some prisoners to escort," Trent said.

The guard looked back at the three in the backseat. "This is not the jail," he said.

"These are special cases," Trent said. "Grant Marsden requested I bring them here."

"I haven't received any notice," the guard said.

"Well, it is his wedding night," Trent said. "Maybe he called it in late? I can help you check."

"Stay in your vehicle," the man said.

The first bump, Andrew thought. The guard started walking back toward the booth. Trent waited until he was in front of the car before opening his door.

"Sir, I instructed you to stay in your vehicle," the guard said.

Trent met him at the front of the car.

"I really wanted to stretch my legs," he said.

The guard reached for his gun. Trent held his hands in the air.

"I am a close personal friend of Grant Marsden's and I know he would hate for this to get screwed up. I would really appreciate it if you let me take a look at your logs."

Trent went toward the guard, his hands still in the air, and draped one around the man's shoulders. Andrew couldn't hear what they said but recognized the movement Trent was trying to hide from the security cameras. Trent held the man up but had already shot him with the silenced gun in his pocket. Trent walked the man's body into the booth and set him down in the chair. Andrew hoped whoever was watching thought this looked like a friendly exchange. Trent hit the button and the gate rose. He turned around and waved at the dead body for good measure before climbing into the front seat.

"Piece of cake," Trent said.

Trent drove the rest of the way up to the front. He left the car parked outside and stepped out. The two guards at the front door came down to meet him. It appeared they hadn't drawn any unwanted attention yet. Trent opened the back door. He grabbed Carter and pulled him out.

"I'd appreciate your help with the other two," Trent said.

A guard came over and pulled Andrew out of the car. The third came and grabbed Riley.

"This one is a woman," the guard said.

"She's an Irish spy," Trent said. "I wouldn't get too close to her. Now, Mr. Marsden instructed me to take these three to the most secure room here. He didn't trust the jail, explained it to your man down there."

"Normally Charlie calls us when a car is driving up," a guard said.

"You do have special holding cells, right?" Trent asked.

"Of course," the other guard said.

They led the three prisoners through the front door; the crimson and gold interior was more lavish than Andrew had expected. He waited for Riley to take her shot. As soon as Andrew heard the moan from the other guard he pushed away from his guard and pulled his gun, angling it up and firing twice. Riley took off running. She had to make it to the security room before any other people were notified of their presence.

Trent started dragging the guards' bodies back to their posts. Andrew took off running, with Carter right behind him. Both men undid their cuffs as they ran. No alarm had sounded yet and Andrew took that as a good sign. He ran the memorized path and soon they were in the hall of paintings. Carter went flat against the wall. He had to keep watch and provide cover and nodded at Andrew to keep going.

Everything went according to plan. Andrew found the false panel and the door swung open. He ran down the steps toward the keypad. He typed in the memorized code Zack had given him. The door did not open. It blinked at him in error. Dread covered Andrew's face. They had lost.

Chapter **104**

I started destroying the cargo the driver was delivering until he opened up the back door. He put a knife to my neck and in an instant I remembered my combat training and took it away from him. He looked helpless at the receiving end of my blade. I couldn't bring myself to kill him though; instead I took off running.

—The diary of Megan Jean

Mia kept pacing back and forth. She'd spent the afternoon thinking of what to say and took solace in the fact that Greg would lead her.

"He should have been here fifty minutes ago," Zack said.

"Greg wouldn't let us down," Alex said.

"You're saying that about a man who has been lying to his own country for years," Zack said.

"Maybe something happened to him," Corinna said.

Mia feared that was the case. They heard a noise and Mia froze in place. She heard footsteps heading toward the waiting room. Zack drew his weapon.

"Where did you get that?" Frank asked.

"Greg said not to bring a weapon in here," Alex said.

The door swung open and Greg Finnegan stood there in his full formal attire.

"Apologies for my tardiness," Greg said. "But I had to pick up this."

He was carrying a garment bag over his shoulder. He stepped into the room and hung the bag. He brought the zipper down and a long, flowing dress spilled out. It had wide crimson straps that met at a gold belt. A shimmering piece of gold material went up the center. The skirt was cut asymmetrically and seemed to move on its own.

"You were late because you had to pick up a dress?" Zack asked.

"I don't have time to argue with you," Greg said.

He went toward Mia and put his hands on her shoulders.

"Change and meet me on the studio floor," Greg said. "Men, come with me."

Greg stormed out of the room and Mia was left alone with Corinna.

"Are you nervous?" Corinna asked.

She went toward the garment bag and took the dress off its hanger. Mia stripped out of her clothes and Corinna helped slide the gown over her head.

"I don't know what to say," Mia said. "This seems like such a mess. This obsession with beauty is part of the ideals I want to end. Greg thought getting this dress was more important than prepping me."

"I saw the dress back at the house," Corinna said. "Greg wasn't late for that reason."

Mia gave Corinna an accusatory glance.

"I have always been a bit of a snoop," Corinna said. "He was late because he didn't want to prep you."

Corinna gripped Mia by the shoulders.

"You know what to say," Corinna said. "Whatever your heart tells you. I have never admired a single person as much as I admire you."

"I'm not special," Mia said.

Corinna spun Mia around so she was looking in the mirror.

"Do you know what I see?"

Mia didn't respond.

"I see someone with a kind soul. You had everything you ever wanted, first with Grant's proposal, then finding love with Andrew. The two of you could have gone off and lived a safe, quiet life, but instead you came back to help people you don't even know and will probably never meet. I don't know if I would have had the courage to accomplish that."

"This all started because of you," Mia said. "When you told me about that magazine article it changed my whole outlook."

"No," Corinna said. "This started years ago when the Registry was put in place. We are the ones who are going to stop it and you will lead us in that endeavor."

Mia turned around and gave her sister a hug. She was at a loss for words. This felt too real.

"What if I made a mistake?" Mia asked. "What if Andrew dies tonight?"

"You wouldn't love him if he wasn't willing to take that risk," Corinna said. "Now get out there, sit on that couch, and wait for your signal to begin your story."

Mia gave a half smile. She forced her fears away. She wasn't doing this for herself or for those she loved. Mia was doing this for the whole world.

Chapter 105

The truck driver told me she went on foot down toward the ocean. The last thing I wanted to do was run after her, but I had few other options.

—The journal of Isaac Ryland

Andrew needed to calm his mind. His fingers were shaking; this was the most important moment of his life. He breathed in and exhaled slowly. Once he calmed down he began to type. He hit each number on the keypad with a sense of certainty. Six, eleven, thirteen, two, four, fourteen, ten, eight, fourteen.

A beeping sound came, different from the last. The door began to open and Andrew felt his heart jump into his chest. He didn't waste any time and ran into the small room.

The master server was a giant piece of electrical equipment. Andrew thought it looked a little outdated compared to Affinity's equipment. He reached into his pocket and pulled out the small device that held the virus, found the opening, and slammed it into the port. He watched a green light flash on the device. Soon all the lights on the server started flashing different colors. It had worked. Andrew pulled out his phone and hit "send." He heard Zack pick up on the other end.

"It's finished," Andrew said.

There was a click on the other line. The first part was done, but now Andrew had to make sure the servers were destroyed beyond salvation. He pulled out the small pieces of putty Zack had given him and slammed one against the base of each of the two towers. Next he pulled out two vials of liquid. He unscrewed each cap carefully. Once he slammed them into the putty mixture he'd have fewer than thirty seconds before they combined to physically destroy the room. Andrew closed his eyes and with each hand pressed the vials into the putty. He turned to run and at the worst possible moment fell over his shoes. He hit the ground hard but didn't take much time to recover before he sprinted back into the hall. The sound of the explosion was louder than Andrew expected. He wasn't far enough away and felt a rush of air push him forward. He hit the ground again; his back felt warm, but he forced himself up and continued down the hall.

The sound of the explosion had passed, but an alarm was sounding through the entire building. Andrew felt like he was running for his life as he made it through the maze of the Mission, certain a guard would be upon him any second. Carter was gone. Trent was gone. Andrew hoped they were on the way to the studio.

No guard came into view; they were probably too distracted by the fire the small bombs had caused. Andrew raced past the front doors and down the steps. His lungs felt like they were about to explode, but his mind was too preoccupied by happiness to notice. It was done. They were successful.

His thoughts were distracting him too much though. Andrew didn't see the outstretched arm come out of nowhere, and because of the speed he was traveling he fell flat on his back. He opened his eyes to see Grant Marsden staring down at him.

"You're too late," Andrew said.

Those were the last words he spoke before his world went black.

Chapter 106

The driver had informed me my husband was moments behind. I could smell the salty ocean air. I was so close to freedom I could taste it.

—The diary of Megan Jean

Mia sat on the couch next to Greg. He kept picking up her dress and spreading it out. They both froze when Zack answered a phone call. He hung up right away and dialed out.

"The master is destroyed," Zack said. "It's up to you to finish the rest."

He hung up the phone again. That was enough information for Affinity to start attacking the online databases. Corinna let out a scream and started jumping up and down with Frank and Alex. Mia watched as Zack tried to keep a straight face, but a smile kept appearing on his lips. Greg leaned over and wrapped Mia in a large hug, moving her back and forth. She let out a small laugh and did the same.

"Remember," Greg said. "You need to hit that button on my signal."

Corinna went to her station and kept a finger pointed over a red circle. Once she put her finger down everything would start.

"Don't be nervous," Greg said. "I want you to give your speech, then I'll start in with questions about anything you missed. We'll end with the video of Grant."

Greg pulled out his watch. He was waiting for the clock to strike 8:01 P.M.; by that point people would have tuned in already. Mia sat up straight and smoothed the rest of her dress down.

"Here we go," Greg said. "Aaaaannnnnnndddd push it.

"Good evening, America," Greg said. "I promised you a special show tonight and I am going to deliver on that promise. I want to start the program out with this young lady, who has a few words for you."

Mia turned to face the camera. She swallowed hard, not knowing where to begin. She glanced around the room. Everyone was staring at her. Then she saw Corinna's face. Her sister was glowing and Mia maintained eye contact with her.

"My name is Mia Morrissey. I am Grant Marsden's wife. I want to take this opportunity to tell you a little about my world. I live in a place where families are kept intact, not just those created by blood, but ones made through the bonds of friendship as well. People agree to spend their lives together not because of money or appearances, but because they love one another. In this place individuals have rights. You can watch your sons grow old, you can be a part of your daughter's life past her wedding, you can have relationships with the generations that follow in your bloodline.

"There is open access in my world too, where not only are you aware of what your leaders are doing, but you can have a say in who they are and how they behave. Some of the leaders are actually women, who are bright and educated, who care just as much about the people of their home countries as they do their loved ones. I am here to tell you that my world is happening all around you, and now it can happen in America."

Mia stopped. She turned toward Greg. He had tears forming in his eyes.

"Why don't we start from the beginning?" Greg asked.

Mia felt herself relax. She was ready to tell her story and not leave anything out.

Greg finished up his closing and Corinna pushed the red button again. The room was silent.

"What now?" Mia asked.

"We wait for their reaction," Greg said.

"Affinity is sending a pickup for us," Zack said. "We have to get back to Greg's safe house."

A loud noise came from the back of the studio. Mia watched as Riley rolled through the door. Mia ran to meet her. She was out of breath. Carter and Trent came in next. Mia smiled, waiting for Andrew to come through. The three caught their breath and Mia kept still.

"Where is he?" Mia asked.

Her body started to shake with concern.

"Where is Andrew?"

"I thought he was right behind me," Carter said.

"I didn't see him," Trent said.

The studio went quiet. Mia heard a vibration coming from the dressing room. She ran over to her phone and saw Andrew's name appear. She picked it up right away.

"Are you all right?" Mia asked. "Where are you?"

"Hello, Amelia."

A chill and a shiver of terror ran down Mia's spine.

Chapter 107

My wife was more clever than I gave her credit for. She was smart enough to try to make it to the ocean, the only possible method of international travel left open.

—The journal of Isaac Ryland

Grant dug through Andrew's pockets. He tossed the young man's weapons and took his phone. He would use this to hunt down the rest of them.

Dragging the unconscious man proved more difficult than Grant had anticipated. He pulled out his knife by the flagpole in front of the Mission and cut the rope. The flag came tumbling down and Grant worked fast to tie up Andrew. He did his hands first, securing them behind his back before attaching them to his feet and leaving enough length between them so Grant could pull his captive across the grass.

Once Grant had made it to his car and thrown Andrew in the backseat, he started off. He wasn't sure where to head at first; his home was off-limits since a large number of guests were still there. The radio in Grant's car cut out.

"We are now delivering a special report broadcast earlier on The Greg Finnegan Show: *'My name is Mia Morrissey. I am Grant Marsden's wife. I want to take this opportunity to tell you a little about my world. I live in a place where families are kept intact, not just those*

created by blood, but ones made through the bonds of friendship as well.' "

Grant switched the radio off. He let out a scream and slammed the steering wheel. She was alive. Grant hadn't made it a mile away when a looming structure came into view. The Rook. A structure that represented the past but was also a symbol of moving forward. This would do fine. Grant pulled up on the front lawn and opened the door to his car. A guard came out to meet him. Killing Amelia was now priority number one.

"It's fine," Grant said. "I am your new grand commander. I have permission to use whatever building I desire."

The guard looked twitchy; no doubt he had heard or seen Amelia's speech. Grant dropped his arms to his sides in an exaggerated motion. He felt for his gun while trying to keep the guard preoccupied.

"Please tell me you're not believing what that silly little girl said on television," Grant said.

Before the guard could respond Grant raised his weapon and shot the man twice. He fell dead. Grant went toward him and pulled out his keys. He looked inside the building and it appeared deserted. Grant went back for Andrew and dragged him out of the car and inside the cement structure. He made sure to leave the door unlocked behind him and took Andrew into the elevator. The doors opened on the top floor. It was a tourist attraction. The floor was made of glass, letting the viewer feel like they were walking on air sixty feet in the sky. It was easier to drag Andrew on this surface and Grant was grateful.

He made his way toward the door on the far side of the room. It didn't take long to find the right key and Grant stepped through to a small set of wooden stairs. He climbed them and pushed open the hatch at the top. The temperature had dropped and the wind blew across Grant's hair. He pushed Andrew up the steps and into the cold air before slamming the hatch behind him.

Grant leaned against the wall and caught his breath. Then he pulled out Andrew's phone. He went to Mia's number and hit "send." The ring sounded twice before he heard her voice.

"I am on the roof of the Rook," Grant said. "Come alone or I will kill him."

There was some heavy breathing on the other end.

"How do I know he's not already dead?" Mia asked.

"You don't," Grant said.

"What do you want?"

"To see your brains bashed in," Grant said.

"So you'll kill me and then kill Andrew?" Mia asked.

"You must not love him that much with all these questions," Grant said.

Mia was silent.

"I would like to have a little chat with you before you meet your demise," Grant said. "And if you perform every act I request of you Andrew will be set free."

"I have your word?" Mia asked.

"Yes," Grant said. "Your first instruction is to come alone."

Grant hung up the phone. He wanted to scream in frustration, but even if Mia and her crew had been successful in destroying the Registry, there was nothing Grant couldn't fix. He would get his revenge since he was in possession of the thing Mia valued above all else: Andrew.

Chapter 108

My wife was only an hour ahead of me and her tracks were easy to follow. I couldn't wait to bring her home and give her the punishment she deserved.

—The journal of Isaac Ryland

The blood on Andrew's face had dried, but his head was ringing with pain. He felt a cool breeze run over his body and started to lift his head.

"Oh good, you're awake," Grant said.

Andrew started to force himself up, but he found his arms were tied to his feet, making it impossible to get up. Andrew started to struggle against his bonds.

"I didn't want you to escape," Grant said. "Don't worry, as soon as our little trade-off happens I'll cut you loose. I think it would be a worse punishment to let you live with Amelia dead."

"What trade-off?" Andrew asked.

"I used your phone," Grant said. "I hope you don't mind. I was hoping I could use it to locate Amelia, but that failed. So instead I told her to come here, alone. We're on the top of the Rook, by the way."

"We won," Andrew said. "You lost. Give it up."

He forced his body sideways so he was up on his knees. His arms were still behind him, attached to his feet. He continued to try to work his way out of the rope. Grant laughed at Andrew's comment.

"Amelia and I are both still breathing," Grant said. "That means the game isn't over."

"It isn't a game," Andrew said.

"All of life is a game," Grant said.

Grant was at the edge of the building. Andrew wanted to charge him and throw himself over.

"I have a gun," Grant said. "Come at me and I will shoot you dead. Then I will shoot Mia as soon as she walks through that door."

"You're planning on doing that anyway," Andrew said.

"Not quite," Grant replied.

He was looking off into the distance.

"You won't have to wait much longer," Grant said. "She's here."

Andrew looked at the man in front of him. With his grin and his red velvet jacket he looked like pure evil. Andrew pulled against his bindings. They were loosening, but not enough to break free. His will stayed strong. Mia had survived too much; there was no way Grant would take her life.

Chapter 109

I won't go back. I can't live another moment as someone's property. I will make my way to the ocean tonight and find freedom one way or another.

—*The diary of Megan Jean*

As Grant had said it would be, the door at the bottom of the Rook was unlocked. Mia took a breath as she walked inside. There were no lights, but the elevator door was open at the bottom. Mia stepped inside and the small closet doors closed. She thought back to Saint Louis. That was the first time she had ridden in an elevator. Back then she had never heard of such a contraption and was momentarily mesmerized when they moved up and down. Now Mia was prepared. She knew what to expect and the ride took less time than she anticipated.

The door opened and Mia stepped outside onto the small glass platform. She looked down and regretted her decision. But now was not the time for fear. She walked forward toward the open door. There was a set of six wooden steps that led upward. Mia started the climb. She took a breath before using her arms and popping the hatch open. The night air sent a chill down her spine and Mia wished she had taken the time to change out of her formal dress.

"Come up and join us," Grant said.

"Mia," Andrew said. "Run. Get away from—"

She heard a smack and was sure Grant had hurt Andrew again. She ran up the steps. The two were on the roof. Mia made it all the way outside and let the metal opening fall with a loud clang.

There was Andrew on his knees; his hands were behind his back and Grant stood behind him with a gun pointed at his head. This was not the first time she and Grant had faced off against each other in odd attire. His red velvet suit matched her flowing red and gold gown. They looked like a bride and groom.

"Did you bring a weapon?" Grant asked.

"You said not to," Mia said.

"I've informed Andrew that if he opens his mouth I will put a bullet through yours," Grant said. "So I recommend not asking him any questions."

"I don't care if I die," Mia said. "You promised if I came you would let him go. Kill me and get it over with."

"No," Grant said. "I promised if you followed my every instruction I would let him go. If I have to shoot you that means you failed at listening and that means I get to shoot him too. Do you understand?"

"Yes," Mia said.

"There is that submissive attitude I was hoping to bring out of you," Grant said. "I would have made you a wonderful wife."

"The Registry is destroyed," Mia said. "Women are no longer for sale."

"So I've heard," Grant said. "But we were legally married, and the rest of the laws are still in place, so that means you are and will be mine until the day I die."

"I've heard enough of your speeches," Mia said. "You said I have to follow your instructions, so instruct."

"You've proved too difficult to kill," Grant said. "So I want to see you take your own life. It's simple. Jump."

Mia looked at Andrew. His eyes were about to bulge out of his head. Even with Grant's gun pointed at his head he continued to struggle. Mia looked away. She walked toward the edge. The higher points of the building came to her chest, while the lower parts were at her waist. She glanced down as she circled the outer edge.

"If I refuse?" Mia asked.

"Then I will shoot Andrew and you next," Grant said. "Take your pick. Jump or I will kill both of you."

Mia stopped walking. She turned around to face Grant, trying her hardest not to make eye contact with Andrew.

"I do this and he lives?" Mia asked.

"Yes," Grant said.

Mia turned away and climbed onto one of the lower ledges.

"No, Mia!" Andrew yelled.

"If you say another word I will shoot her," Grant said. He cocked his weapon.

"It's okay, Andrew," Mia said. "I promise."

She spun back around to face Grant and Andrew again. The wind blew across her and Mia felt her dress rise up again.

"Any last words?" Grant asked.

Mia kept her hands at her sides. She smiled at Andrew before she bent her knees and jumped up in the air, forcing herself back right beyond the ledge.

"*Mia!*" Andrew screamed, his voice echoing in her ears.

Chapter 110

Tonight I watched my wife fling her body over a cliff into the ocean. I didn't cry. I didn't even bother to look at her body. I wanted to, but I couldn't. This way of living has left me heart-less and for that I am thankful. Otherwise I would have to face the atrocities I have been party to.

—The journal of Isaac Ryland

The adrenaline from seeing Mia jump off the edge was enough for Andrew to rip free of his ropes. His body fell forward and he caught himself on the stone before pushing his legs up and running toward the edge. The only noise Andrew could hear was the sound of his own heartbeat. He leaned over and thought he might faint. Hanging only a foot down was Riley. She was holding on to the side of the building somehow and grabbing on to her back was Mia, her red dress hanging in the wind. Andrew wanted to reach out a hand for her, but Mia shook her head no.

Andrew's hearing returned and the sound of Grant's laughter flowed through the air. Mia had promised him everything would be okay. Andrew had not known her plan, but he had to trust her, and that seemed to mean playing the part.

"I didn't think she had it in her," Grant said.

Andrew started moving toward Grant. The other man's laughter stopped and he raised his weapon at Andrew.

"I promised to let you live and I will," Grant said. "If you attack me and I shoot you in self-defense, that does not mean I did not keep my word."

Andrew stopped moving and held his hands up. He had to get that weapon away from Grant. Andrew started to act like he would if Mia were actually dead and there was nobody to attack. He dropped to his knees and brought his hands to his eyes, faking tears.

"I hope that you live a long life," Grant said. "And think about her every day for the rest of your life."

"It was over," Andrew said. "You didn't have to kill her."

"But I wanted to," Grant said.

"You're a dead man anyway," Andrew said.

"I don't think so," Grant said. "The Registry is destroyed, but my reputation is only tarnished. With Mia dead I can explain my side of the story. How I was desperately in love with her and never wished any harm on her. How the grand commander was forcing me to wed his daughter, so I had to kill him to stop the wedding. How I ran out of my wedding to find her and tell her we could lead the new order together. I am the grand commander, after all."

"Liar," Andrew said.

"Who cares?" Grant asked.

"You can't lead the people," Andrew said.

"Why not? Mia did tonight, and she was just a stupid little girl."

The other man walked closer to Andrew. He was going to check out Mia's body. Andrew had to act now. He waited until Grant was right at the edge.

"Mia has something you will never have," Andrew said.

"What's that?" Grant asked.

Andrew watched as Grant looked over the edge. There was no way he didn't notice Mia hanging there.

Within a second Andrew leapt onto Grant, not giving the man a chance to react. He reached for Grant's wrist and forced him downward.

"Friends," Mia said.

Andrew watched as she let go of Riley with one hand and used it to grip Grant's shirt, pulling him over. Andrew pushed Grant's legs and looked down as the man let out a scream, plummeting toward the ground.

Without waiting another second, Andrew grabbed on to Mia's free arm. She let go of Riley and Andrew pulled her back up and over the side. They landed on the top of the roof and Mia put her arms around Andrew's neck.

"It's over."

He wasn't sure if he was asking or telling.

Chapter 111

I am free. I was ready to end my life rather than turn back to Isaac, but it appeared fate was on my side. I tossed my body over the ocean cliff. The water felt invigorating and I shortly lost consciousness after impact. Someone didn't think it was my time to go. A fishing boat, of all the luck. We are en route to Guatemala, and the Canadian fishermen share my affinity for freedom. I plan to dedicate the rest of my life to stopping the travesties happening in America.

—*The diary of Megan Jean*

When Andrew released Mia she realized the rest of her friends had made it onto the roof.

"What happened?" Andrew asked.

"Alex, Carter, and I were at points on the wall," Riley said. "The rest were waiting with weapons to storm the roof and take Grant out."

"He told Mia not to come alone," Carter said. "And naturally she didn't listen."

"I tried to give you hints," Mia said.

"Those were the worst five seconds of my life," Andrew said.

Standing at the top of the Rook, Mia looked around at their faces. Frank and Alex were holding each other, with huge smiles across their faces. Riley, Carter, Trent, and Corinna were laughing and hugging. They had done it. The Registry was destroyed. Corinna held her arms out and Mia went away from Andrew and hugged her sister. In the distance an explosion sounded and Mia broke the embrace.

"What was that?" Mia asked.

"The people are rioting," Frank said. "Some of them in happiness, some in anger."

Mia could see fires in the distance and hear groups chanting; they were too far away to make out any words. A loud pop came and everyone turned toward the entrance. It was Zack opening the hatch. He used his good arm to climb to the top and join everyone on the roof. He walked over toward Andrew and shook his hand. The two men patted each other on the back.

"What happens now?" Mia asked.

"A new world," Alex said.

"Who will lead them?" Mia asked.

Over her entire experience she had never thought of that question. Destroying the Registry was her goal; she hadn't considered the aftermath. Hearing Grant's final words to Andrew made her think of the future. She could not let someone like him step up.

"It will take a few weeks for the people to calm down," Zack said. "I know Affinity would like to set up a new government."

"The Irish will likely be interested in offering help," Riley said.

"What about the Americans?" Mia asked. "What will they want?"

"Who knows?" Trent said.

"Our time is done," Zack said. "Affinity is sending someone to pick us up from Greg's place. We have to get back there."

Zack started walking back toward the door and the group started to follow.

"I'm staying," Mia said.

"What for?" Riley asked. "You did your job."

"When I went on the air tonight I told the people the truth," Mia said. "Something nobody has done in a long time. This is my home; I can't abandon it any longer."

"You want to lead them?" Zack asked.

"I want to help them," Mia said. "And I can do that more easily if I stay here."

"This country is dangerous and volatile," Riley said. "Not everyone will be happy with what happened tonight."

"I know," Mia said. "But that's not enough to make me leave."

"That's your decision," Zack said. "But if we're going to make our pickup we need to leave now. Mia, I wish you the best of luck and I hope to see you again soon."

He started walking toward the door. Riley came up to Mia next.

"You have my number," Riley said. "Call and I will be here in a heartbeat."

She gave Mia a hug before following Zack. Frank and Alex walked by next. Mia could see the tears in Alex's eyes. They didn't need another good-bye. Mia leaned in and gave both of them a hug.

"Thank you," Mia said. "For everything."

"Trent, are you coming?" Zack asked. "Affinity could use a man of your caliber."

The former RAG agent nodded to Mia. He stuck out his hand to Andrew and the two shook.

"What about the rest of you?" Mia asked. "You don't need to stay here."

"I want to find my son," Corinna said. "And then I want to help you."

"Carter, what about your father?" Mia asked. "He's waiting at Greg's house."

"We'll see each other again," Carter said. "But I think you're going to need me more than he does."

Carter walked up to Mia. He wrapped his arms around her and gave her a kiss on the top of the head. There was no romance in his touch. Mia imagined this was what having a brother would feel like.

"We can't stay up here all night," Carter said. "Corinna and I will see the other group off and wait for you at the bottom."

Corinna nodded her head at Mia as she walked away with Carter. The door slammed shut and everyone was gone. Everyone but Andrew. Mia turned to face him.

"You can leave too . . ."

"Stop," Andrew said. "You know my place is wherever you are."

He put his arm around Mia's shoulders and pulled her next to him. Mia turned her head up to face him. He lifted his free hand and brushed her hair away from her face. Their lips met and Mia was certain she didn't need anything else to tell her this was love. Mia broke away first. Andrew kissed her forehead before they turned around to look out across the landscape again. In a matter of minutes the fires had doubled.

Mia wasn't sure what the future would hold. In the recent past she had been a naïve brat, anxiously awaiting her wedding day, and now she was the figurehead of a revolution. Wherever her life led her, Mia knew it wouldn't be easy, but she thought about the man next to her and the people at the bottom of the stairs. Mia was surrounded by love and friendship, and that was enough to keep her going.

"Do you think those people out there want to kill me?" Mia asked.

"I'm sure some of them do," Andrew said. "But you wouldn't be Mia Morrissey if there wasn't someone who wanted you dead."

Death was a part of life. Mia thought of her fallen friends. Whitney, who taught Mia basic life skills. Flo, who taught Mia to look inside of herself for a power she never knew existed. Her mother, who forced Mia to realize everyone's actions had a motivation and there could be love inside cruelty. The three would be remembered forever. Mia would make sure of that.

Mia had imagined she would feel peace once the Registry fell and

Grant was stopped. Instead she felt like there was more to accomplish. Mia had grown so much, but she wasn't finished. The people would need a leader, and if they would have her Mia wanted to continue her fight for her home country. After all, the Registry had risen to power from the ashes of a once-great country. Mia didn't see a reason why that greatness couldn't rise again.